Chain-Smoking Vegetarians and Other Annoyances in L.A.

Chain-Smoking Vegetarians and Other Annoyances in L.A.

a novel by
Sandra Ann Miller

SAME Ink

Published by SAME ink

SAME ink
2554 Lincoln Blvd.
Suite 239
Venice, CA 90291
www.sameink.net

ISBN: 978-0-9997625-3-0

Cover design by Susan Black/rubudesign

Also by Sandra Ann Miller

Temporary

*A Sassy Little Guide to Getting Over Him —
10 Steps to Heal Your Heart After an Unhappy Ending*

*A Sassy Little Guide to Getting Over Him —
the Young Adult edition*

Chapter One

I'm having one of those surreal, out-of-body experiences as I watch him go down on one knee. It's happening in slow motion, like a special effects team has taken over the scene. But, I'm not on a set. This isn't happening in a studio. We aren't in post-production. This is real. It's happening. To me.

And this is what I get for trying to be nice.

It takes me a moment to fully understand—or, at least, accept—what he's doing. I want to shout, *No! Stop! Not here. Not like this. Not in front of them!* But I'm too stunned to say anything. This is just unbelievable. And rather annoying.

Why now? Why here? I mean, we are in the Valley, of all places. At a barbecue, of all things. Not exactly where one would expect a proposal to occur. After all, this isn't Texas. We are in L.A. Home of many picturesque locations, fabulous restaurants, noted hotels and a multitude of grand venues…none of which are located in the stucco-encrusted hellhole that is the 818. We just dined on paper plates, for crying out loud. Did he really think that now would be a good time to take the ultimate lunge? After five years and two days of dating, when all we've talked about for the past two months is ending it, he picks this moment to pop that question. Like that would actually change things.

I wish I could stop him before he goes any further. For some reason, I've lost the ability to speak. This must be what it's like when someone wakes up in the middle of surgery due to insufficient anesthesia. I can't move or scream, but I am hyper-aware of what's going on. And, let me tell you, it's mortifying.

I find myself growing irritated. Bordering on angry. As I listen more intently, it becomes clear that this is one shitty proposal. A proposal—even one that's unwanted—should be a private moment, and candlelit. It certainly should not be done in the presence of my frenemies. His friends are the last I would want to share this with. Yet, there they stand with smiles perfectly perched, faking fondness. And…hold on a sec. Does she really have a tear in her eye? You've got to be kidding me. She really does have to make everything about her. Even this. Unbelievable. And I can smell the Marlboro of that Birkenstock-wearing nuisance. At least she skipped the patchouli today. Thank God for small favors, right? But, it's a big one I need. Something like a bolt of lightning, the jolt of an earthquake, even a friendly swarm of killer bees; anything that would take the focus off of us would be greatly appreciated.

As he reaches into his pocket, I feel the world tilt. My hands have gone clammy and my stomach churns. I'm not sure if it's what he's about to ask or what I've ingested. I taste chicken. And potato salad. Perfect. Food poisoning. Exactly what I need right now. No, wait. He just opened the ring box. They still make marquise-cut? Nope. It's pear, to match the teardrop-shaped birthmark on my thigh. Now, that is truly the last thing I need.

"One way or another, I'm gonna find you. I'm gonna gitcha, gitcha, gitcha, gitcha," Deborah Harry sings out from my bag. Reminding me of the night with Jilli when we thought it would be funny to set Blondie ringtones. Retro upon retro. An idea that only seemed brilliantly kitschy clever after our third margaritas. Baja Cantina can be dangerous in that way. Jilli chose the more obvious "Call Me", citing her love of *American Gigolo* and Richard Gere. Somehow, I got the stalker tone.

"One way or another I'm gonna gitcha! I'll gitcha!"

The music only adds to the tension. I wonder who might be calling. Whoever it is, he or she has about the same crap timing Tim does. I have to fight the urge to answer it, though. That would probably come off as rude.

It's doubtful that anyone witnessing a proposal expects to hear a "No," let alone one followed with, "Jesus Christ, Tim. What the fuck were you thinking?" I suppose there are better ways to turn down such an offer. But, in all fairness, I was ambushed here. I am as surprised by my reaction as anyone else, literally taking a step back when I said it. I didn't intend to be cold. I didn't mean to seem cruel. And the pale shock on Tim's face brings home the finality of what I have done. Our relationship has been severed by the fatal blow of a *No*. There won't be a way to mend this. A get-back-together situation cannot exist. It's over. Done. Finito.

Thank God.

I turn and go before the smile I feel coming on would be noticed by anyone. The kerfuffle of gasps and tittering is still audible as I flee the backyard and run through the house to the street and my car. What I do not hear, gratefully, are Tim's footsteps following me. Even so, I can't stop myself from bounding into a run. High heels do not slow my pace. It's the exhilaration of liberation. It's over. I can breathe. I inhale and take in the scent of jasmine from the night, now smoke-free. The cobalt sky is darkening and a shiver runs down my spine. It's only May. An evening chill is to be expected, even in the Hell that is the Valley.

I pull away, leaving a hint of rubber on the road. I do my best to keep from speeding back to Venice and a place that will no longer be my home. I don't want a moving violation to delay me. I want to get there so I can get out for good. No traffic. For once, the freeway is clear. Blondie keeps playing, but I hit the button to silence the song without checking to see who might be ringing. The curiosity is gone. I need a moment alone. I turn up the radio, open the moonroof and put down the windows, letting the fresh air wash over me. A random song by some random group is playing on the college station. A song I hear played on Indie1031.com, too, that I know maybe three words of, but I sing along with what I know and scat the rest. Belt out some la-la-las. There was never a happier, single, homeless girl than I. The future looks so bright on this night in L.A.

It's funny to think that three months ago I would have said yes to Tim's proposal. Three months ago, I would've burst into tears of stunned excitement. Convinced myself that I was jubilant; that marriage was the right thing for us, and this was the day I had waited thirty-two years for. I would have fallen to my knees with him, hugged and kissed him and said, *Yes, yes, yes, yes!* I wouldn't have minded that he did it in a backyard at a barbecue for the seventh anniversary of a couple perpetually teetering on the fence between elation and divorce. It wouldn't have bothered me that we were surrounded by people I was, at best, apathetic toward, and a few I outright loathed. Three months ago, I would have been speeding home to our shared townhouse—the one he bought with his father instead of me, though

I make half the mortgage payments and still am not on the title—to make the appropriate plans. By the end of the weekend, a date would have been set, guest list completed, location reserved and invitations designed because, like any assistant worth her salt, I work swiftly with the details and can hammer out an event for five hundred in half a day. I've never understood how women could labor over a wedding for a year or more. I simply don't have the attention span or patience. But none of that matters now. That's what would have happened three months ago. Three months ago, everything changed.

• • •

I was standing in Karen's kitchen on that Friday in February when my life turned inside out. Something like that, something completely life-altering, can only happen when you least expect it. As if the script was crafted by McQuarrie, there was no way I could've been ready for what was about to unfold. Keyser Söze stopping by would have been less of a shock.

I work for Karen Ellis, the legendary, acclaimed actress. As I'm sure you know, Karen Ellis was huge in the Eighties and Nineties. She more or less paved the way for the actresses of today, setting box office records and getting paid more than most of her male co-stars. She's a groundbreaking, two-time-Oscar-winning beauty. The first gold man was for Best Actress in 1993 for her gut-wrenching role in *It Better Be*. Sadly, she's been suffering the Supporting Actress curse since winning in 2005 for *Jonah*. Tall, thin and stunning still with her emerald green eyes and flowing blonde hair, Karen doesn't look her age, but she's been around long enough for people to remember it. That's one of the downsides of starting your career at nineteen; at fifty-three, you seem one hundred.

There's hardly any drama to speak of working with Karen. I say 'hardly' because this is Hollywood, and there's always some drama brewing. It's our booming industry. A botched lunch reservation can cause hysterics resembling the loss of a limb or a loved one—or disgusted rage like you just pissed on their lawn, and for no good reason. Fortunately, that's not how it is with

Ms. Ellis. She's sane without the assistance of mood-stabilizers, is neither a lush nor a pill-popper, and does not 'powder' her nose. Anymore. You know, the Eighties. Karen's smart, witty and kind, and we have a good time working together.

Karen and I share the same colorful vernacular and favored use of four-letter wording. Shit happens. So does the occasional cocksucking-motherfucker. And that's ladylike language in this town. If you've ever been on a film set, you will know that it's always rated NC-17 for foul language, strong sexual content, inappropriate relationships and slanderous rumoring. Thick skin is a requirement. It's the only way to survive, move on and move up. Especially if you are toiling in the studio system.

I've stepped outside of that and into the realm of personal assistanting. That wasn't planned, let me assure you. But it's where I've been for the last four years, which, for a personal assistant—a position more likely to last six minutes or six months—means I'm due for a gold watch. But, I've grown comfortable in my gig. Four years in and I've misplaced some of my ambition and goals. And, the fact that I'm about to turn thirty-two and am still an assistant, whether or not the word *executive* sits in front of it, I feel like I should start to be concerned. Concern would take effort. The last time I watched *Mommie Dearest* I thought Carol Ann didn't have it so bad. Even though my job isn't exactly the *career* I thought it would be, I certainly can't say that it's boring.

My typical workday is anything but. When we're not on location for a film, I start at ten and generally leave by five or six. Yes, working for an actress has really difficult hours. This enables me to have something of a life. I even have the luxury of hitting the gym in the morning without having to wake at the ass-crack of dawn, which is both nice and necessary. If you think the camera adds ten pounds, try standing next to an icon. That's why I suck up the expense of a personal trainer.

"Do you feel that?" he breathed into my neck.

"Yes," I gasped.

"Again. Again. Again. Perfect. Squeeze. Again. Almost there. Almost. Yes! Yes!" he cheered.

I let out a moan and he handed me the towel.

If you saw Marco, you'd understand why I don't mind waking at six on a Friday morning to sweat and ache, or choke when I write him the check. Marco is from Milan. In spite of living in L.A. for more than ten years, his accent is tiramisu thick and just as delicious. Part Adonis, part gigolo, Marco is the clichéd tall, dark and handsome. His body is carved to perfection like a Greco-Roman statue with every muscle noted, perfectly toned, strong and painfully sexy.

"You are looking fantastic, El," Marco said, patting my ass for emphasis.

"Thanks," I panted, out of breath from the squats.

Let me tell you, there's no need to completely give up carbs when you can hire a hot trainer. His tawny eyes are piercing and, I had to admit, he makes my heart beat a little faster—usually because he was yelling at me to do more, faster, harder or deeper. It is as kinky as it sounds. If we both weren't in serious relationships, I would seriously consider taking the flirtation we shared one step further.

"Like that should stop you," Jilli chided after we bumped into him at The Rose one Sunday brunch.

Jillian Raines is my best friend. She and I have differing views on relationships and monogamy. Meaning I believe in them and she doesn't.

"Come on, Jilli. You know I don't cheat. Besides, I pay him. That would be a little sleazy, and maybe even illegal."

"By the look of him, El, not only would you get great sex but he'd probably train you for free. Think of all the money you'd save," she said with a knowing nod.

I sipped the remainder of my mimosa and Marco sent me a smile from across the restaurant. Those eyes. Those lips. That body. That backside. It was like an apple you just wanted to bite into. Jilli's logic was starting to make sense. When the waitress came around again, I opted for coffee instead of another cocktail.

I leaned over and rubbed by butt at a red light. Staying is shape does mean the occasional pain in the ass. I turned up the seat heater of my Jetta, hoping that might help. It was going to be a long weekend if I was already sore from Marco's workout by the time I drove into work.

My office is in Karen's Bel Air home, which is either a twenty- or forty-minute drive, depending on the time of day and route chosen from where I live in Venice. I say 'I', even though there is a 'we', because Tim is often away on location shooting a film. He's a camera operator. We've lived together for the last three of the five years we have been together. In spite of being in a relationship, I have a lot of alone-time because, even when Tim is home, I might be on location or travelling with Karen. It's all part of the job.

Bel Air is rather self-explanatory, while Venice was famous for its 'colorful', if not tacky, boardwalk, The Doors, its faux canals, Muscle Beach, aging hippies, gang warfare, cheap socks and overpriced real estate before it became known as *Silicon Beach*, making the overpriced real estate absolutely obscene. I love my 'hood. I adore its kookiness, its diversity. It is what it is in Venice, but that is changing quickly. I fear Dogtown will soon be as bland as Santa Monica or Brentwood, with a hipster effort to make it another posh enclave. But, the duckshit along the canal paths should pretty much stop that in its tracks. No one wants bird turds on their Tod's.

In order to avoid the annoyance of traffic, I make it to Karen's on side streets. I've no need to trouble myself with the freeway and the constant irritation of L.A. gridlock peppered with doses of road rage. Near-death experiences exhilarate me not. I've even sussed out a route that has minimal red-light cameras. Paparazzi are bad enough, but those annoying photogs have a way of sneaking up on you, too.

To be efficient, I run errands on my way in. Quick stop at Starbucks for a venti-quad-coconut-no-foam-latte so I'll be alert and functional, then to the postal center—conveniently located on the same block as the 'bucks (don't think that was an accident)—where the mail's delivered at a safe and private distance from Karen's home. If necessary, I'll swing by her manager's office or the accountant's if there's something pressing. Yes, we can always hire a messenger but, since I pretty much work alone, it's nice to see the faces that belong to the voices I know so well over the phone. There were no extra stops needed that day, so I took Beverly Glen into the East Gate of Bel Air and to Karen's home.

Each day, as I walk into the manse, I'm greeted by Ruth, the house manager, and Sally, the golden retriever, whom I adore but am tragically allergic to. After giving Sally some morning love, I wash my hands and keep a healthy distance for the rest of the day in my allergy-proofed office, antihistamines at the ready. Snotty is more than just an attitude for me at times.

My office has a view that most executives would backstab for. From my roost, I can almost see Arizona on a clear day. The room is simply decorated with custom-made furniture. In addition to the standard desk-chair-MacBook Pro, printer/fax/scanner/copier, files set up, I have a sitting area with a sofa to lie on for script reading that was done in rich leather, making the area free of feminine fabric so as to keep the dust and dog hair down to a minimum. Several of Karen's movie posters are framed in black to serve for art and hang on the custard-y walls. An almost-too-large TV is mounted in between with every channel known to man and a TiVo to capture the important shows, like *RHONY* and *Game of Thrones*, because there are deep philosophical discussions on both with Karen. I also have a phone—a real, live landline—that I believe is broken because it never stops ringing.

It was ringing that morning, before I could take my seat, check messages or start my computer. It continued to ring as I flicked on the lighter to ignite the large Diptyque votive that sat on the coffee table. I liked my day to be scented in lilac. When I touched flame to wick, I said in my head, *This is going to be a great day.* I don't know why that popped into my brain; it was kind of an odd thought. In all honesty, I merely aspired to get everything on my to-do list done. Which in and of itself would be impressive since it was two pages long. With the candle now alight and the wish for a wonderful day burning, I grabbed the call that was disturbing my peace before it went to voicemail.

"Hey, El. TGIF, right? So, Bev wanted me to call you and get Alex Robinson's phone number. Do you have it?"

It was Anise, my least favorite spice and the most annoying assistant in town. Anise works for Bev Watson, the producer of

Karen's last film. Anise rings me almost daily asking for yet another phone number. Just to be clear, the digits 411 are not in mine.

Alex Robinson is a VP at Quick Studios. I know this because I read the trades, not because he and Karen have a relationship. And, no, I don't have his number. I did have access to it, as did anyone with a subscription to Baseline, which is what I opened to get Anise half the numbers she asked for.

It's a strange phenomenon in this town, the imaginary hierarchy of assistants. Everyone wants to network and have as many connections as possible, but always with the under-current of one-upmanship. Anise calls me with the pretense of camaraderie, but letting me know all the while she was above me on the town's totem pole. She works for the producer of five number one films; I work for an actress with declining box office. Unfortunately, I had little interest in this ranking, or which rung on the success ladder I fell, which possibly explains my career's meteoric rise to mediocrity. But I finally had it with pain-in-the-Anise. I was no longer going to be her information operator.

"Sorry, Anise, I don't have it. Why don't you call the studio's main number?"

I could tell by her silence she was confused by this reply.

"Oh," she finally said. "You don't have his direct? Bev wants his direct."

I explained to Anise that we don't work with Alex. We don't need his direct number. And, if we did, I'd call the main number, talk to his assistant and ask for the direct for when I rolled calls with Karen. I further explained that, if she were doing this on the sly for Bev, she should call someone who is working with Alex and ask them for the number or call the studio, get connected to his office and fake like she was updating her contacts. I finished with, "And, when all else fails go IMDB Pro. Gotta go. Karen's waiting for me. Bye!"

I heard Anise, "But…but…," before the receiver hit the cradle. And I didn't give a fuck…fuck.

There are three kinds of assistants in Hollywood: Those who think you're automatic best friends because you're both assistants to celebs, execs or other VIPs; those who think they are "Vice" whatever their boss is (Vice Studio Chairman, Vice Hot Hollywood Agent, Vice Superstar), and lord over you; and those who just do their jobs. I'd like to think I fall into the third category. Anise lives somewhere between one and two but has to kiss my ass a bit because Bev wants Karen to do her next movie. I find this sort of politicking to be tedious and exhausting, which is why there is always something from Starbucks in my hand.

I made my way to the kitchen and started the kettle for Karen. This, too, was part of my routine—get the messages, go through the emails, sort the post, grab the calendar and my notepad, then make Karen some green tea. I didn't have to do that; it wasn't in the job description or even something she requested. But there is something very relaxing about making tea, even if you're not the one to drink it. Ruth waved goodbye as she left to go to the market. I pulled Karen's favorite mug from the cupboard, one from Tiffany, in its iconic blue, bowed with a white, ceramic ribbon.

I was thinking about all that I had to get done so I could have a quiet, peaceful, long, President's Day weekend. My last quiet weekend before Hell broke loose. All I wanted to do was sleep. Hibernate in that little, two-story, too-white cave I called home before the whirlwind of Awards Season struck its final blow. I even turned down Palm Springs with Emily and her boyfriend. Being a third wheel isn't exactly my idea of fun.

I had been single, for all intents and purposes, for the past six weeks, and I felt the need to prepare for myself for coupledom again, and that was better done alone. Tim was due back two weeks after the awards storm. Of course, if I wasn't able to talk my way out of it, I would be on my way to Vancouver with Karen for her next film. If this kept up, Tim and I might never see each other. Not exactly the upside of two people working in the same industry. And it was kind of sad how accustomed to the apartness we had become.

"Stop playing with your hair, El," Karen warned from her *New York Times*. "You'll get split ends."

When I'm stressed, I play with my hair. It rests in the center of my back; a natural soft brown accented with overpriced, honey-colored highlights. I had been twisting it up into a knot at the top of my head and letting it drop, then tying it into a chignon at the nape of my neck as I went through my thought process. Karen and the kettle's whistle finally broke me from my hair-twisting trance.

Karen had come in moments after the kettle hit the stove—her timing, always perfect. I poured the water over the organic bag, handed Karen the hot cup, and our typical morning ritual continued. She sipped green tea, I sucked down my latte and, over our varied forms of caffeine, we'd talk about the night before and go over the day ahead at the huge island in the middle of her kitchen. Then, after indulging in gossip and finishing our beverages, we'd retreat into our respective offices, at opposite ends of the house, to tend to actual business.

"So, do you think I should go with Dior again this year?" Karen asked, closing her newspaper and opening a few lookbooks from the stack that arrived the week before. "Or maybe something from Armani? I have to make a decision by, like, yesterday. I can't believe I've left this to the last minute. Again. Then again, I do love Prada. And Chanel. So many to decide from."

She wasn't really asking me. Just her train of thought blowing steam. I opened the calendar. Aside from the dress selection, we needed to go over her schedule for the next three weeks. I'm old school when it comes to scheduling. One glitch in a sync last year sent us into a calendar clusterfuck, so now it is strictly pen to paper, leather-bound by Tiffany and stamped with the initials EL. It's a bit more luggage to drag about, but less of a chance for a fuck up.

We had meetings, wardrobe fittings, interviews, the Spirit Awards (she was scheduled to present), the Oscars (also to present), and Fred Leonardo's famed pre-Oscar bash coming up in the next two weeks—and I say 'we' because I'm usually there for all of it, excluding Fred's party. Even his assistants don't go to those, not since the invention of TMZ and omnipresence of in-phone cameras.

After all that, Karen would go up to Vancouver for two weeks for a supporting role in an indie film. Notice I didn't say 'we' there. That's the film I'm trying to wriggle out of. She can survive without me for that short bit of time, and Canada holds little allure. Please. It's not like we are talking Paris or London. I longed for some quiet time in L.A., with several stops at some of our finer spas. I needed a facial, a wrap, scrub and a rub, not to mention a wax. But, first things first.

There was only one meeting on the day's agenda, and it was of utmost importance. Karen was in the process of a deal to host her own talk show. Yes, I know they are dime-a-dozen, the hallmark of hasbeenism, but Karen was a natural for this. Beloved by the public, trusted by Hollywood, she was sure to be a success. Even I had to admit that. I also had to admit that television was the last thing I wanted to be involved in. After all, I studied film, and we film folk can be a bit snobby about it. You can go on and on and tell me how TV has changed, and, yes, there isn't the stigma to it there once was to it. You can point out how many film stars are on the boob tube today and list the progressive shows on cable. I'll even tip my hat and program my TiVo to them. But, we weren't talking that kind of TV; we were talking a talk show, and that was tough to chew let alone swallow.

I'm sure you must be having a chuckle over the fact that I went to film school and work as an assistant. Go ahead and guffaw. I get it. I'm still not able to fully accept it myself. See, when you go to film school, you have aspirations of being a great director, a prolific producer, an acclaimed writer, not a personal assistant. Especially not one to an actress. Assisting a director, producer or hot writer gives one more cred than working for a movie star. And, no, Karen has never called me in the middle of the night to come over and check out how her ass looks in a pair of jeans. Obviously, my career was far from where I thought it would be. The idea of being involved in a talk show made it seem that much farther.

I thought by now, now that I've crossed the threshold of thirty, I would have an office (in a building) and assistant of my own—that I would be a producer, since I'm one of the few who never caught the directing and/or writing bug. It was a long and winding road that brought me here—one day I'll tell you about it—and I'm slightly embarrassed to admit that I like my job. Actually, I love my job. Granted, it wasn't producing movies, it wasn't curing cancer—it wasn't even producing a fundraiser for curing cancer—but it's been a great four years in which we've made five films, and attended many premieres, parties and festivals for them. Travelling on someone else's nickel is never a bad thing. And, because Karen is still A-List, I get A-List treatment, too.

I travel in chauffeured sedans and fly first class. I stay at the best hotels with carte blanche to charge what I need to the room (though, I'm not the type to go overboard on that). I've worn designer gowns to galas, been adorned with loaned Harry Winston jewels and given outfits for premieres. I get gifts from companies who want to be sure that Karen gets her gifts. I am offered VIP discounts at the finest stores and from the best designers (I have yet to use them because, even with it, I'm nowhere near able to afford it). I can get a reservation anywhere, tickets for anything, but I get these perks not because of who I am, obviously, but because of whom I work for. And Karen gets these perks not because she is a legend—after all, even legends are quickly forgotten in this town—but because she is a genuinely nice person and people genuinely adore her. Especially the right people. It's almost a dream job. Almost. My aspirations of being a producer are hidden away for the time being. Right now, I have to coordinate her calendar.

"So, the meeting today is at twelve-thirty at their offices. They'll order in lunch. I asked them to send over the menu so you could put your order in now. Here it is. Let me know what you want and I'll call it over. The meeting will probably go long so I'll program directions there and to the Pilates studio from there, in case you want to go after. They have openings and will hold a slot for you. I guessed you'd be done by two-thirty, so there's a three o'clock reserved now and Ruth put your gym bag in the car." I rattled this off in a single breath.

"Cancel Pilates. I have yoga tomorrow. And I won't need directions because you're going with me, so you can drive, right?" Karen asked, looking up from the look-books.

I hated going to meetings with Karen. I was either

completely ignored or my ass was so grossly kissed I left with a diaper rash. I could usually get out of them easily, but she had been forcing this one on me all week.

"Karen, I am so overloaded today. Do you have any idea how far behind we are?"

"I'm sure it can all wait until Monday," she said like someone who has an assistant.

"Monday's a holiday," I reminded.

"Tuesday should be fine, too. You have to go to this meeting, El. I need you there." With those green eyes batting at me, I couldn't say no, as much as I wanted to.

"But you don't need me there, Karen. Howie won't even be there. This is just a simple meet-and-greet with the whole team to see if you like each other. If you like each other, you'll take the next step and outline ideas while the lawyers work out the deal. You know the drill. I'll just be in the way."

"This is different, El. This is huge for me. I'm basically saying that I'll walk away from movies and become a…God, I don't even know if I can say this…a…*tee vee* personality."

"I think the term you're looking for is 'talk show host.' They want you for a talk show, Karen, not an infomercial."

"But isn't that what they really are? An infomercial for a book, a movie, a cause, an emotional weakness?"

"No, but that's one way to pitch it to them," I returned.

"I don't know what I'm thinking, El," she whined. But we both knew she was thinking about the money, and the epic sums of it they were offering. "I can't go up against Ellen. She is a talk goddess. And I heard that Oprah might be making a return. She broke the mold. She killed Phil Donohue, you know."

"Phil Donohue is alive and well, Karen. And you wouldn't be taking on *Ellen*. You'd be taking on Kelly Ripa, Hoda, Kathy Lee and *The Price is Right*. They want you for mornings, not afternoons. They have the network and slot all set for you. It will be perfect."

Karen's manager, Howie Saunders, had given me all the details, contacts and vast amounts of information; all the stuff he knows Karen wouldn't look at until she absolutely had to. As an assistant, you must know all without anyone realizing you do, and only share what you know when you truly have to and only to those who truly have to know it. It can be a minefield. Navigating takes years to master and, even then, there are times when you set one off without meaning to.

"The mornings? Well, who the fuck will be watching me in the mornings? Senior citizens and stay-at-home moms? You can't really talk about drug addictions and sexual peccadilloes with them."

"Karen, take the meeting and just listen. Let them woo you. Pretend it's a first date and play by *The Rules*."

Karen's eyes lit up with curiosity. She had been married three times and was a fierce player of those *Rules*. The woman was never without a date...or five.

"I can do that," she said, straightening her posture. "But I need you there."

"Karen, I still have to coordinate the travel to Vancouver and make sure the deal memo is set. Sitting in a meeting with you would take me away from that. And you know we can't trust production to get the travel done right. You'll end up with an aisle seat in business and a white stretch limo. How fucked would that be?" I deadpanned.

Karen plopped down her empty mug on the island, making a hollow noise. "Oh, Ellen, sometimes you take all the fucking fun out of everything." This behavior was new. Karen wasn't a tantrum thrower. "You have to come to the meeting because there will be a surprise there for you, okay?" She crossed her arms, let out a huff, and I think even a tiny pout.

"Karen, I hate surprises. And a Mrs. Beasley's muffin basket in my honor would not be so much a surprise or kind gesture as an undermining of my diet and expansion of my ass. Of course, if Jon Hamm will be there, then that is the greatest surprise ever and you can skip my birthday present this year."

Karen was not amused. "I want you to be a producer on my talk show," she blurted.

"What?" I couldn't believe what I had heard.

"We were going to announce it at the meeting and make the offer there, but you blew that with your goddamn stubborn streak and obsession with work."

"What?"

"Will you stop with the whats already and tell me you'll go?" Karen asked looking disappointed. "Now you've got me all in a twist and I won't be able to drive, dammit. Now you'll have to go. So there."

"What? Wait. When did you work all this out?" I was stunned that she was able to manage something like this behind my back. I couldn't even be excited; I was too damned confused trying to reckon how she did this without me even getting a hint.

"You know, I do find you indispensable, El, but I have been doing this longer than you've been alive. I know my way around a calendar and a conference call. I have a cell phone and my ways," Karen said with a smirk.

"Karen, what else aren't you telling me? Anything else I should know?"

"Nothing, you little twerp. I wanted you to move up with me. Move on with me. I want you to have a career and a future with me. Not just spend your days making my appointments and coordinating my wardrobe."

I was both deeply touched and hurt by that statement. And she knew it.

"You know what I mean," she covered, then stood there waiting for my reaction with a lovingly maternal, patient smile.

"Fuck it. Fine. I'll go. Just pick out what you want to wear for the Oscars so I can check that off my list, please." I started twisting my hair again.

Karen walked over and gave me a hug. "Call Miuccia," she said and walked away.

And that's how it happened. At ten-forty-two on a February Friday morning. That's when my life changed. It wasn't a lightning bolt from the sky that altered my world, but a simple declaration in a kitchen.

I felt a cold, tingling rush come over me; euphoria mixed with uncertainty. It was just starting to register. I'd be a producer. Granted, one on a talk show, but a producer nonetheless. Very apropos to the theme of my life: Getting what I wanted, just not how I wanted it.

I steadied myself at the sink just in case I'd throw up. Not that I'm a puker *per se*, but one never knows. This was a new sensation for me: Validation. That very rare occurrence when your boss recognizes your talent and your worth. You hear about that happening in this town…once every ten years or so. I could very well toss my cookies, piss my pants or, more likely, faint, crack my head on the tile and die, right there in the kitchen, of happiness and a brain hemorrhage. I certainly felt something strange coming on. But, instead of a lurch into the basin, I leaned over and burst out into a fit of laughter. Hysterical laughter. The laughter that comes so hard that your ribs hurt and your eyes water. Like when you see someone falls ass over teakettle. And this was ass over teakettle. My life was turning upside down. In the best possible way.

I tried to regain my composure. Should I call Tim or Jilli to share the news? Chances are I'd be sharing it with their voicemails. Tim was on set and Jilli was likely in a meeting. Development executives always are, even if they are really getting their superfluous fuzz ripped away. Texting or emailing something like this seemed impersonal, if not desperate for attention. I decided to keep it to myself for the time being. I was having lunch with Jilli tomorrow. I would tell her then. I had other calls to make, anyway. The dress. The travel. The deal memo. A manicure, pedicure, bikini wax and faux tan were also required.

An assistant's work is pathetic, and never, ever done.

Chapter Two

You can only hold your breath for so long. At a certain point, you have to inhale or die. I realized that when I felt a little lightheaded riding up in the elevator to the office where the meeting would be. I had fucking forgotten to breathe. What kind of dope does that?

"Don't be nervous, El," Karen gently said.

Too late. But I smiled at her assuredly. Stood up straighter, adjusted my top and brushed the creases from my pants. At least today I didn't take 'casual Friday' too literally. I was wearing an attempt at an Audrey Hepburn gamine look in quotidien black. The end of the week was typically saved for inconvenient errands and filing, for which I have a unique technique involving sorting papers on the floor first while watching Bravo and eating popcorn with M&Ms. I normally wear yoga capris or something even more tragic for such tasks, not wanting to waste good dry-cleaning clomping around downtown or trying to find some obscure shop along Ventura Boulevard. Happily, I made an effort with my makeup as well instead of merely camouflaging my spots and dark circles—another Friday 'look' of mine. I can be pretty lazy on the last day of the workweek, tired from the non-stop pace of the four days before it. Somehow, today was different from the get-go.

"Karen Ellis and Ellen Patterson for Wyatt Knight," I said to the receptionist as we walked into the posh offices of Group Force Entertainment.

GFE had originally been a sports management firm. They partnered a few years ago with a few former Hollywood bigwigs to enter into television and film production. Their film division folded last year—football players, as it turns out, are terrible actors. But, their TV side was kicking ass. They currently had the top-rated shows on the major networks, were infiltrating cable and won a slew of Emmys, many of which adorned the entryway.

The office was clean, angular and modern, favoring a

clinical white and gray. A massive Pollock served as the backdrop to the lobby. I'm not a fan. His work reminds me of sneezes, so I sat with my back to it as we waited, watching the tall, thin, well-dressed staff pass by. I tried to remain calm, or appear to be, while flipping through *Vanity Fair* as Karen scanned the latest gossip in *Us Weekly*.

"Cocaine, herpes, ODs; it's like the Eighties all over again," Karen reported as she flipped though the pages.

I had yet to meet with anyone at GFE. It was early days, or so I thought. Usually, Howie would bring me in by the third meeting or, at the very least, a conference call if things were looking serious. Even Howie had been devious in this situation. Conspirators. I shook my head and grinned at the thought. I'd have to send him some scotch.

I was trailing off in a new job daydream when my iPhone vibrated. Email. There were fourteen new messages from the time I left Karen's. The latest was from my sister, Gwen:

> I have left you three voicemails. Hello? Manners! I thought part of your job was returning calls. Like I said on my messages, Mom isn't well again. You should come up and see her and pretend to be a caring daughter. Call me or call Mom. And don't ignore this email. I know you will get it. You live on that phone.
>
> Your sister (in case you forgot),
> Gwennie
>
> ________________________
> Gwendolyn Patterson
> Realtor - Specializing in Your Next Home!

I let out sigh of disdain that must have been louder than intended because Karen asked, "Everything okay?"

"Yeah. Sure," I smiled and deleted the message.

I'm not what you would call 'close' with my family, or what's left of it. I didn't exactly have a fairytale childhood, but who did? Unless, of course, you would call *The Wizard of Oz* a fairytale. My mother, Kitty, is pretty much the Wicked Witch of the West and my sister is her flying monkey.

Kitty and I haven't gotten along since I was fifteen, which is probably typical. But, even before that, we lacked the innate bond mothers and daughters are supposed to share. It was more like we tolerated each other, taking cues from sitcoms and family dramas as to how we should relate. Sad, but true. It kind of helped to have a script and stage direction.

```
INTERIOR  -  FAMILY  HOME,  KITCHEN  -
AFTERNOON

DAUGHTER  brings  home  her  report  card.
All  A's.  MOTHER,  who's  preparing  a
wholesome    family    meal,    sees    the
report  card  and  breaks  into  a  broad
smile.  Mother  warmly  embraces  Daugh-
ter,  tells  her  how  proud  she  is  of
her   and   her   hard   work.   Daughter
smiles  as  Mother  places  the  report
card  on  the  refrigerator,  securing  it
in  place  with  a  magnet.

FADE  TO  BLACK
```

A standard scene, right? Well, Kitty did a rewrite. Her response was, "You're supposed to get all A's. Anything less means you didn't try hard enough."

Kitty was a C student. Gwen was a B.

During my teenage rebellion, I took to calling Kitty my *momster* and Gwen my *sinister*. It stuck. For good reasons. Later, I found out Jilli has a *smother* and two step-*bothers*.

My father, who was more of a sperm-donor than a dad, was written out ages ago. My parents divorced when I was seven and Gwen was four. Bitter would be an understatement as far as the dissolution of their marriage was concerned. He refused to pay child support and my mother refused to let him see us. Somehow, I don't think that was exactly a punishment for ol' Mick Patterson. I never saw him again. Not even when Kitty took him to court for back support payments.

"The only good thing to come out of that marriage was your sister," Kitty has told me more than once.

You might think that's a horrible thing for a mother to say to her eldest, but I prefer to see it as a *Get Out of Jail Free* card. I know Gwen's her favorite, and that's fine by me. When Kitty grows old and feeble, her favorite can take care of her, leaving me well off the hook.

When I was nine, my father died of a heart attack while jogging or something. I say 'my father' because I've always had my doubts that Gwen and I actually share the same paternal DNA. I'm fairly certain he's mine since I inherited his asthma and allergies, something my mother cursed him for every time my sister begged for a puppy, or Kitty had to pay my doctor bills. And Gwen is a blonde. Neither of my parents is blonde, although Kitty later adopted the peroxide hue as her own. I keenly remember the slap I got when I was ten and reminded everyone at a family dinner about that nice neighbor man who was so attentive with the garbage cans when my father was away on "business"—he had shining blonde hair and fondness for my mother's coffee. I was accused of being dramatic and difficult. My deductive skills were never complimented.

Because I was young and hadn't seen him in so long, my father's death wasn't such a great loss. Kitty had remarried shortly after the divorce, so I had a new dad to deal with. Mick was just going to stay gone forever, which is what I had always expected. I didn't blame him. Kitty made nothing easy for anyone. Upon dad's death, I was informed there was money set aside for my sister and me from a life insurance policy required by the divorce settlement. I wouldn't see it until I turned thirty.

Thirty came and went, and the money never arrived. That's when I found out it wasn't set up in a trust account but a CD and my mother miscalculating the end date. To be honest, I was surprised the money was even still there. Under Kitty's reign, anything could've happened. Gwen will be getting her money when I do. She's now twenty-eight. Come to find out, there was no limitation on when I could get the money. Nothing was stated in the will or divorce decree. It was just my mother's need to control, withhold, wield power. When I think of how broke I was in film school and how that money (any money) would have helped—not to mention the interest rate I'm paying on my student loans—my eye begins to twitch from the repressed rage. What's done is done. According to Kitty, I should have the money in three months, shortly after I turn thirty-two. She won't say how much, just that it's "enough." I asked for the paperwork and bank statements along with the check. I don't trust her and she knows it.

I'll deal with my mother, Gwen and her email later. Right now, I have to get into meeting mode. I'm about to meet my new colleagues.

Craig, Wyatt Knight's assistant, came out and escorted us to the conference room. I had spoken to Craig to co-ordinate the meeting. He's not the brightest Crayola in the box. Watching him swagger through the halls and interact with his co-workers, it was evident young Craig thought himself to be a player. He was one of the more annoying assistants this town is plagued with—the type living off his father's money and his uncle's connections, fully expecting to be a headline on Deadline within a year. I suspect it will be for something criminal.

As Karen and I took our seats, Craig asked if we wanted any beverages.

"Water, mineral water, Coke, Diet Coke, iced tea, coffee, hot tea, herbal tea, cappuccino, frappuccino, latte…" The list of liquids droned on and on.

Karen interrupted with, "Still waters, two, room temp. Thank you."

The room was actually a giant fishbowl situated in the center of the GFE floor where every staffer could walk by and look in, and they did. I stared out of the glass walls, feeling very exposed. Karen was unaware, continuing to browse another rag. I regretted not bringing reading material, and I didn't want to bother with my iPhone. I sipped my Voss instead.

It was a full twenty minutes before the meeting convened; which, by Hollywood standards, was still on time. I was gnawing on my thumb by then. If I don't twist my hair, I bite my thumb when the stress hits. I had also started turning my chair like a bored child. I caught myself as I was about to swing around in a full three-sixty, remembering my age and to act it. Before the boredom grew any worse, someone finally burst into the glass cage. I looked up.

"Not a great way to start things off, Wyatt," Karen chided, checking her watch.

Only a woman that gorgeous could get away with saying something that direct. Only a man that stunning would be worth the wait. Wyatt gave me a warm smile. I felt air in my mouth and realized it was hanging open. I shut it immediately.

"Very sorry, Karen," he said, finally looking away from me and going to her for the professional hug and single-cheek kiss of lazy Americans. "New York kept us on a conference call. If it wasn't related to your show, I would've hopped off but I thought you'd want to hear the latest."

His voice was deep and resonant. It stirred in the pit of my now growling stomach. I clutched it in hopes of quieting it down but the rumble was still audible.

"Apology accepted. Can't wait to hear what was said," Karen replied and took her chair.

I couldn't find a place to focus except on Wyatt. He was striking in that way that keeps your eyes glued to him even after you realize you are staring in a manner verging on rude and spooky. Wyatt was not model gorgeous, or even actor handsome. He was manly. "Man-nificent," as Jillian would put it.

"You must be Ellen Patterson," he said walking over to take my hand. "I'm Wyatt Knight. May I call you El?"

"Yes, you may."

My heart was thumping and I felt myself beginning to blush. I shook it off thinking that I'd had too much caffeine and not enough food. No more add-shots before breakfast, especially if there's no breakfast before lunch.

"Nice to meet you, El." Wyatt's left hand covered my right before we broke the handshake. Breaking his glance was much more difficult. The handsome, successful, straight, male executive in Hollywood is a rare commodity. Add tall, fit and with a full head of hair to that list and it's nearly non-existent. I was looking at a unicorn.

As Wyatt went back to his seat, I noticed Karen looking at the two of us, eyebrows raised as far as the Botox would allow.

"Where's the rest of the gang?" Karen asked.

"They're on their way, bringing in the latest specs and breakdowns. New York was emailing them over. And Craig should be bringing in lunch any minute." Wyatt's smile was laser bright and his blue eyes beamed under Hugh Grant-esque, floppy black-brown hair. Gauging by Karen in her heals, he was at least six-one. I like tall men. Lord. Where did that come from? I am with Tim. I live with Tim. I love Tim. And I would be working with Wyatt. As attractive as I found him, nothing would ever happen. I could indulge in a fantasy or two today but after that, no more.

"More water, ladies?" Wyatt asked.

"Water would be wonderful." Jesus. Did I actually say that?

"Wonderful," Wyatt smiled back and got up to grab a bottle hidden in a cupboard. He walked it over to me. "There you go, El," he said with a wink.

A wink. Good. I'll just focus on his cheesy qualities. But that cheeseball did make me smile. Luckily, the rest of the GFE team came barging in so I wouldn't have to worry about saying or doing anything dumb, at least for the moment.

"God, Karen, you look better and better each time I see you," said Bob Berger. Bob was the big kahuna at GFE, in spite of his stature. A short, round and folliclely-challenged man in his fifties, Bob has been around the block and was a huge fan of Karen, like most men his age. "Damn. How do you do it? And can you tell my wife?" Bob finished with a hearty chortle that continued a bit too long, then turned into a series of hacks. The guy had ho-ho-ho'd himself right into a coughing fit.

Karen, always the class act, smiled broadly with an, "Oh, Bob, you rascal." Then deflected the inappropriate attempt at flattery by turning the attention to me. "Bob, this is Ellen Patterson."

"Nice to meet you, missy. We've heard a lot of great things about you. You're the deal breaker, you know," Bob croaked out between coughs and pumping my arm.

I looked over at Karen, whose kind veneer was slipping into shock. Inappropriate she's used to; unprofessional she rarely tolerates.

"El, you should also meet Gary," Wyatt directed, taking

charge where Bob should have, were it not for the phlegm. "Gary is our COO."

"Gary Wilson. Nice to meet you, Ellen," Gary said, forcing a smile. He was the slight, quiet, uncomfortable type. Most likely a former high school math nerd, Gary didn't make eye contact with either Karen or me. Then there was an explosion in the room.

"God, those fuckers took forever to come through on email," said this bulging, mother-to-be with an armful of papers.

"And this is Arlene Freeman. Executive VP of Development. Arlene, please meet Karen Ellis and Ellen Patterson." Wyatt delivered this introduction in a manner that exhibited his confidence and future power.

"Great to meet you, Patterson," Arlene shouted and she pressed her moist palm into mine. "Hey there, Karen," she said with a wave as she walked over to shake Karen's hand. "Shit!" she said, grabbing her belly. "This boy's a fucking little kicker. Two more months, though, and he's evicted. Got my date set at Cedars and can't wait. Where's lunch? We need to eat." Arlene was a giddy steamroller. Of course, I liked her immediately.

Karen and I exchanged glances as we gathered around the table to hear the presentation. Unlike their introductions, the GFE group was smooth in their approach to business. That is until Craig clattered in with lunch. Without surprise, Karen's order was wrong, but we made due. I gave her half of mine.

The presentation continued as we ate, with Wyatt taking the lead. He had a natural ease that was terribly sexy. I had to work to keep focus on what was being said rather than what was catching my eye. The conversation had something to do with me, he didn't.

Lunch meetings are always a bit humiliating because, inevitably, I will be asked a question the moment my mouth was full. This day was no exception.

"So, El," Wyatt said the moment I shoved a forkful of salmon and spring greens into my mouth, "we want to offer you an associate producer position on the show. No one knows Karen like you. Your input into segment and show ideas would be invaluable."

I just sat there with my mouth full of food and all eyes on me, cursing the fact that I ordered a salad. I should've had the penne. Lunch meetings and first dates follow the same ordering guidelines: Nothing involving strenuous cutting or twirling, which may splash sauces or the like onto clothes; easy to chew so as to appear delicate, not bovine-like whilst masticating; and avoid leafy greens, which tend to get caught in teeth. Clearly, I failed with this order.

I remained motionless for a moment. How exactly does one handle a situation like this? There you are, cheeks bulging with lunch, four executives, one assistant (Craig somehow invited himself to the meeting and a free meal), and your boss staring at you, waiting for a reaction as they offer you a key position on a hot new talk show. Does one chew? Swallow it whole and hope for asphyxiation, or spit the wad in the flimsy paper napkin kindly provided by the restaurant? I chose to chew quickly, swallow hard and prayed for a good death.

"You'll have to excuse me," I said, with a fair chunk of salmon hovering over my windpipe. "I wasn't expecting anything like this."

Karen smiled at me warmly, like a proud stage mother approving my performance.

Wyatt continued with, "How could we do the show without you?"

"I'm very flattered," was all I could manage, still trying to swallow the remaining fragments of my twenty-dollar salad.

"I must have you there, El. Don't let the associate title fool you. You are *my* producer. You know what I want better than I do. I need you in those meetings making things happen, bringing me the right story ideas, making the show the best it can be," Karen asserted.

I placed the fork on the oversized white plate and must have miscalculated the landing somehow because the silver utensil launched a well-drenched piece of lettuce at my shirt before hitting the ground. How absofuckinglutely perfect. Unfortunately, every once in a while, the middle school klutz in me decides to make an appearance, and only at the most humiliating of times.

With all eyes upon me, I did my best not to overreact. With as much poise as I could muster, I picked up the fork from the ground. Karen slyly handed me another napkin.

"Thanks, Karen," I said, both for the paper and her words. I was moved by her verbal display and how much she wanted me to be a part of this. But, before I could give my reply, I noticed her staring at me. She looked at my shirt, then at me in the eye, then back at my shirt; the signal any true friend gives when there's something amiss. A tomato chunk had found its way to my right breast. Thank God I wore black. It's chic, slimming and forgiving.

I removed the produce with nonchalance and set it on the side of my plate. I brushed the offended area with my paper napkin, and it left a pathetic trail of white, pulpy lint. Damn that Craig for not bringing in the linens. The matter was growing worse with each attempt to remedy it.

In a kind effort to distract the crowd from my boobage, Wyatt cleared his throat and said, "And if the show does go to New York, we will of course pay for your relocation."

"New York?" I coughed out, finally looking up from my tit. I glanced at Karen who was staring down at the table. "New York?" I asked again, looking at Wyatt.

"It hasn't been decided yet, but there is a strong chance the show will happen there. Easier talent bookings," Wyatt explained.

"How can there be easier bookings in New York when all the talent lives in L.A.?" I questioned to no one in particular.

"See? This is why I need her. She asks all the right questions," Karen interjected.

I just looked at her with my eyebrows together. I can do that. No Botox.

What the fuck had she gotten me into? New York? Why not Istanbul? Talent bookings there must be a breeze.

"It's logistical," Arlene explained. "Morning news shows prime them, then they are ripe for our taking, going deeper into whatever agenda they are promoting. New York is open for a thinking, feeling, fucking fantastic talk show. None of this Kathy Lee-Kelly-and-The-View shit. We want gripping, gritty, inspiring, provocative, profound and profane things on the air."

"At ten ayem?" I asked. "You think America is ready for that?"

"Yes," the GFE gang said in unison.

The GFE-ers went into detail on how they saw the show developing. They passed around the title cards, set design, potential show ideas; they even played a theme song. Karen was entranced. I hadn't seen her this enthralled since she was up for a supporting role in a Scorsese film. Unfortunately, they went with someone else. Someone younger.

"I love it," Karen said straightly. "I love it all."

The GFE team smiled and nodded to each other.

"Now," she continued, "I just need to know if I should put my house on the market and start looking for a home in New York, or if we are going to stay put."

"We should have an answer by the end of March if not before. They're still crunching numbers," Wyatt stated.

Karen stood up. "Send the contracts to Howie and let's put this to bed."

I think they had to stop themselves from breaking into applause or high-fives. Karen went about the room thanking and hugging each exec. Gary was especially uncomfortable. When she was done with them, they came along to me, shaking my hand, congratulating me, welcoming me aboard. In between handshakes, I dusted my breast; the lint almost vacated. Wyatt was last to come to me.

"Nice to have finally met you, El," he said with that commanding smile of his. As he shook my hand, I felt a warm rush run up my arm. "I look forward to working with you."

"Great," was all I could manage. I started toward the door with the rest of the GFE crowd and Karen when Wyatt took my hand again.

"As a matter of fact, we should have dinner. Get to know each other better. I'd like to hear your take on things."

"Sure," I said, very unsure of everything at that moment.

"Tomorrow night?" he asked.

"Fine." I had gone monosyllabic.

Wyatt smiled. "Great. See you tomorrow, then."

I nodded as I slipped out the door with Karen. I drove us back to her house in silence.

"Are you okay?" Karen asked as we entered the abode.

"I don't know," I said with a sigh. "This is a lot to take in."

We walked into the kitchen, and I took a seat at the island. Karen watched me as I sat, then grabbed a bottle of champagne out of the fridge. She threw open the French window above the sink and popped the cork out of it, sending it flying into the hillside. She took two Fabergé flutes from the cupboard and poured the bubbles into them. She placed one in front of me and took a swig from her own.

"I'm sorry," she said.

I looked at her, utterly nonplussed. "For what?"

"For today. I thought this would be a wonderful surprise. Now that I think about it, it was really kind of inconsiderate."

"Oh, Karen, no it wasn't. It's a bit overwhelming, that's all. Not just the position, but New York. Why didn't you tell me?"

"That's the inconsiderate part. Sometimes, kiddo, I forget you have a life outside of mine. That's kind of shitty." She went into the pantry and brought out Kettle Chips and Peanut M&M's. "Here," she said. "I think we need these." She opened up both bags and passed me the M&M's—my personal form of Valium. "I'm sorry I sprang this on you like that."

"This is an incredible thing, Karen. I'm really happy about it. Really. I know I'm not exactly exuberant, but I am happy. Totally excited," I said, a little too flatly.

"I can tell," she deadpanned.

"It's just..." I took a mouthful of champagne and swallowed the tears that were welling up unexpectedly.

"El, what is it?" Karen asked, placing a comforting hand on my shoulder. "Tell me, kiddo," she said softly. "What's going on?"

And there, on the island of an ocean-blue kitchen high on a hilltop in Bel Air, the haze lifted and it all came into perspective. What was wrong. What was really wrong with me. And it was everything.

L.A. might be the only place in the world where you can have it all and still be miserable. I might not have had all of it—

obviously without fame, fortune and flawless beauty—but I had a great job; a handsome, employed boyfriend; good friends—my friends, not Tim's; a roof over my head; food in the fridge; and money in the bank (debt up to my eyeballs but, you know, I'm American). Yet, with all that I had, there was a feeling of needing more. Something was missing. There was an annoying want that I couldn't place. And then I realized the size of the hole I had inside me.

"You know," Karen said with a slight slur. We were nearly finished with our second bottle of champagne and contemplating our third as we ate dinner delivered from The Ivy in front of a roaring fire. She had cancelled her dinner plans so we could talk. The candle flames fluttered around us in concert with the fireplace and Sting crooning somewhere in the background. Karen's musical selection, not mine.

"Ooh, was that thunder?" Karen queried. The rain had started shortly after we arrived back and had not let up since. This, too, was unexpected, but always welcomed as far as I was concerned. Nothing like a good cry in the rain.

"What was I saying?" she asked.

"You know," I answered.

"No, I don't. If I did, I wouldn't have bothered asking, El."

"No," I replied. "You were saying, 'You know.' That's where you left off."

"Oh, yes. Sorry. Well, you know, relationships are complicated. Take it from me." She gave a knowing chuckle. "Three marriages, three divorces, numerous co-habitations and several broken engagements, but absolutely no children. Success? Failure? It just is what it is. I've known deep love and tragic heartbreak, but I don't have many regrets. Maybe husband number two. He was a real shit. Anyway, the one bit of advice I have for you is: If you're not happy with Tim, move on. For chrissakes, El, move on. The most important thing in life is to be happy."

Sage words that sounded oversimplified, if you asked me.

"But I didn't even realize until today that I wasn't happy," I said. And it was a shock to my system at what an odd revelation that was. I suppose I knew I wasn't terribly overjoyed or completely content, but I thought everything was fine. Not perfect, but fine. I mean, how often do we ask ourselves if we're happy? Other people may—usually when everyone's had a few cocktails and wants to avoid talking politics and industry—but, if you aren't depressed or on medication for it, you usually answer *yes*. "Maybe I'm just overwhelmed by the offer. Maybe it's just that," I responded, hoping it could be true.

"So, all that blubbering in the kitchen was just about being a producer on my show?"

"Maybe. Maybe it's PMS. NYC. I don't know." I trailed off in thought, slightly disgusted with myself. What the hell was wrong with me? I should be dancing on tabletops right now, not crying in my champagne. I was offered the position of Associate Producer on Karen Ellis' new talk show. Anyone in her right mind would be over the moon. Not me. Even this didn't make me happy. Perhaps I should be medicated. Go on some sort of anti-asshole prescription. Right now, I'd do anything to make this angst go away.

Karen let out a deep sigh. "I'm going to ask you a hard question, kiddo."

"Okay," I replied, bracing myself by draining my glass.

"Are you still in love with Tim? Because you hardly mention him anymore or what you two are up to. Is he still the one you want to build a life with?"

I shrugged. "Up until about six hours ago I thought so. Now…" I ended the thought with a shrug.

"Ellen, if you don't know that says it all. If you have to think about whether you're in love, you're not. If you have to wonder if you're happy, you aren't. And if you aren't in love or happy with Tim, why stay?"

Karen was very matter of fact, and I adored that about her. Except at this moment. The one thing I didn't need was a hearty dose of honesty and pragmatism. I would've rather had another bag of M&M's. The tears began again. She is going to make a great talk show host.

"Oh, honey," Karen said when she saw the drops falling. She handed me a box of Kleenex. I blew hard. I took that Claritin a little too late.

"It's not that simple, Karen," I finally answered. The tears and mucus now wiped away, I returned to what was left of my dinner and busied myself there. I poked at a black pepper shrimp with my fork, almost to see if I could wake it. I play with my food when I don't bite my thumb or twist my hair. I looked over at Karen who was holding me in her gaze, waiting for me to continue. "Okay," I said. "It's like this…I've made this investment. An investment in Tim. In us. For nearly five years, I've nurtured this investment—"

"And you're waiting for it to pay off?" Karen interjected. It was more of a rhetorical response than a question.

I nodded. "Is that so wrong?"

"Take it from me, El," Karen offered gently, "not all investments pay off. Some are such a huge risk that you can lose everything if you hold on too long."

She filled up my glass and hers, and then the bottle was as empty as I felt. Outside, the thunder grumbled and a flash of lightning broke from the sky. The rain pelted the windows as the fire crackled and popped. Nights like this in Los Angeles are few and far between. They're a beautiful way of telling us to slow down and soak up life. But we generally ignore them. Bitching about how it screws up everything from traffic to our hair. I love the rain. But, tonight, it's echoing my sadness.

"So, what should I do?" I asked, dabbing a tear.

"I can't tell you that, kiddo. You have to come to that decision on your own. But, if the show goes to New York, will you come?"

"I don't know. We haven't even started talking about money or anything."

"The money will be fine. You know I'll take care of that. And we'll pay for your move and a realtor to find the right place for you. Something Pre-War, I'd like to think."

"Pre-War? Which one?"

"New York real estate terminology," she said, waving the question away. "Anyway, will you go to New York?"

"Well, I…I don't…"

"Don't mull it over, El. Give me your gut reaction! First thing that pops into your head. Would you go to New York?"

"Yes," I said without thinking. And I meant it.

Karen smiled and raised her glass.

I was shocked by my own admission and the certainty with which it came. New York? Natives of Los Angeles never consider moving anywhere else in the United States, especially New York. I couldn't have a car in New York. And I love my Jetta. Okay, I could have a car, in theory, but with the traffic and parking nightmares, it's just easier to hail a cab. And I would be hailing cabs. One time on the subway was enough for me.

"So, what does that mean?" I asked, praying she had the answer.

"I suppose it means you have some thinking to do, kiddo. Lots of thinking," Karen said, rising from the pillow on the floor where she was sitting. She took the bottle and our plates into the kitchen, Ruth long gone.

"Tea?" she shouted from afar.

"Please."

A cool draft blew across the floor. Karen must've let the dog out. I pulled myself up and onto one of the sofas, and wrapped myself in a cashmere throw. If you're going to have an existential crisis, Bel Air is really the place to do it.

The rain continued to kiss the windows and I wondered where Tim was right then. Surely, it was raining in Seattle. Is it ever not? What was he doing? Who was he with? What was going through his mind? Did he miss me? And then I realized how long it had been since I missed him. And that felt awful.

In the beginning of our relationship, the periods of separation were torture. Teary goodbyes. Nightly phone calls. Incessant texting. Long, mushy emails. Phone sex. Then, the time apart became a part of our rhythm. Another film on location? Let me know if you need help packing. Now, we don't bother calling each day. We text or email only to remind each other of one task or another. Mostly to me: *Did you pay the property taxes?* Even FaceTime is rare. After being behind the camera all day, he doesn't really enjoy being on one. The last two films Tim had done on location, I hadn't even flown out for visits. It was easy to blame it on my work schedule. Or claim our relationship was so stable we could handle the time apart. That was much nicer than admitting that neither one of us cared. It's midnight on a Friday; do you know where your boyfriend is? Nope. What's worse? I didn't even care.

Karen and I watched half a movie while sipping our tea. I was suddenly utterly exhausted by the day, the cry and the antihistamine I was on.

"I'm going to hit the hay," I slurred to Karen.

It was decided halfway through the first bottle of champagne that I would spend the night. There's a guest bedroom off my office that has become "El's Room." It's where I stay to housesit when Ruth is unavailable, allergy-proofed for my benefit.

"Sleep well, El. And sleep in," she said as she patted my hand. "I'm up early for yoga then lunch with the girls, so stay as long as you'd like. You know you're always welcome here."

"Thank you, Karen. For everything," I said.

She pulled me into a hug and said, "No need for thanks, my friend. No need for that."

I found the light already on in my room. Karen had laid out a pair of silk pajamas, slippers and left a note:

> Sweet dreams, kiddo.
> You'll see it all fresh in the morning.
> xoxo,
> Karen

On the nightstand, I found a pair of B vitamins, a tall bottle of Evian and a banana—Karen's foolproof hangover antidote. I peeled open the banana and checked my iPhone. No new messages. I don't know why I was surprised by that, but I was. It made me feel lonely. No one knew my news yet. Still, a message from someone, just to say *Hey* would have been nice.

I peeled off my clothes, slipped into the PJs and slid into the slippers. It was like being draped in a cool cloud and standing on air. I was feeling better already. I was probably making too big a deal over this. It's just a promotion. A fabulous promotion, but a promotion nonetheless. People get those every day. And this was merit-based. I earned it. I owned this. So, why wasn't I shouting from the rooftops? I should call Tim and tell him, then gather the girls for a celebration. I was going to be a producer! I actually did have a career! This was worth a night on the town, a private table somewhere fabulous, way too much drinking and dancing. So, why wait? Perhaps because it was after one in the morning. A call now would be impolite. Still, since I've already had too much drink, I might as well dance. I took my phone and connected it to the room's stereo, and selected Prince's *Purple Rain*.

"Let's go crazy. Let's get nuts."

I bopped myself into the bathroom to peel out my contacts and ready myself for bed. Feeling good for the first time since the news hit, dancing around like a dork, glad that no one could see me behaving like a fool. But whilst brushing my teeth, it occurred to me that Wyatt had asked me to dinner on a Saturday night. A Saturday night and I said yes. I said yes to a dinner on a Saturday night, like I was a wallflower. Showing myself up as one who had no plans and an inactive social life built around an absent boyfriend, wasting a rare holiday weekend like a loser. Jesus.

Then, as I was rinsing, it dawned on me that no one has a business dinner on a Saturday night. Why would Wyatt even ask something like that? Unless he…oh, man.

I had a date on a Saturday night with a man who was not my boyfriend.

Holy shit. I had screwed the professional pooch.

Chapter Three

It took some effort to open my eyes. My lids were heavy and swollen from crying. Sally's barking, and Karen's attempts to hush her, caused them to open. When I glanced at the clock, it showed a blurry seven. I stayed in bed listening to the rain, surprised that it had lingered overnight. I tossed and turned for another hour then, when it was apparent I wasn't going to sleep, I drew myself a bath and soaked in it until I pruned. Avoid. Avoid. Avoid. So much easier than to face things.

My brief euphoria had faded. I had that hard-cry hangover, surely assisted by the antihistamine-champagne combo one should always steer clear of. My head was murky. Caught in that peculiar moment when you realize what you wished for has arrived, and you are simultaneously overjoyed and overwhelmed, completely delighted and absolutely daunted, all of which brings about intense lower-intestinal gurgling. Things were now in motion; that was certain.

I pulled myself out of the bathwater accepting that I was now an executive. Executive decisions were warranted. The first was to figure out how to tell this to Tim, Jilli and the rest of my friends. The promotion was one thing. New York was another.

On the verge of thirty-two and still an assistant, I had considered myself washed up. I secretly resigned myself to the situation I was in—a lifer. Carol Ann. I watched my friends grow in their careers, happy for their success but wondering about my own. Like if or when it would come.

Without many options I could see, I thought I would continue doing what I did until I got pregnant—after getting married, not before. I'd take time off to deal with a newborn, find an affordable nanny (I've seen the toll taken by kids and know that good help was worth paying for, after all, mommy needs a break and a happy hour), then recover from the tummy tuck and breast reconstruction I feared would be necessary after seeing the state of my mother's body after two kids and knew I would be lucky to survive one—I might have gotten my father's allergies, but I inherited Kitty's skin.

Then, I'd probably drag out my maternity leave until I came up with an alternate vocation. Maybe go back to school and become a shrink. Total job security with that in L.A. Although, listening to the annoying complaints of Hollywood wives might not be worth the four hundred per hour I'd overcharge them. Maybe I'd get certified as a yoga instructor or the like, go into business with Em. These were the thoughts that drifted through my mind when I wondered what the fuck was I doing with my life. But then BOOM! Now, I don't have to worry about a Plan B. Now, I have a bona fide career. It even comes with a future. Success was surely around the corner.

I pulled my damp hair back into a ponytail, threw on yesterday's clothes and left Karen a thank-you note. Once I reached Sunset and got a strong signal on my cell, I called Jilli.

"You're kidding me, right? You still want to do lunch, even though it's raining?" was Jilli's response. It was nearing eleven and she was still in bed. Whether or not she was alone, I wasn't sure.

"It's rain, Jilli. Not frogs falling from the sky. I think we can handle it."

"Driving in the rain is so annoying. This is going to suck serious ass, El." Jilli was not a morning person. I heard her sigh. "Fine," she said after a pause. "Let's meet at The Grove then. That's more or less in between us."

Jilli lives in Glendale to be closer to the studio where she works. We were less than twenty miles from each other, but it might as well have been two hundred. The negotiations of where and when to meet were always a part of any plan. She knew she was on the losing end, being the one Eastsider in our group.

"Want to do that French place?" she asked.

"Can we meet at Du-par's? I could do with some pie. Jilli, you won't believe what's happened."

"Pie? It must be big. Holy fucknuts! You're going to leave Tim, aren't you!"

"Jillian, no. Jesus."

There were times I swore Jilli could read my mind, my deepest, darkest thoughts, and it freaked me out. Because if I went to New York, I would in fact, in a very literal sense, leave

Tim. As far as actually breaking up with him, I couldn't think that far ahead. I was still in an antihistamine haze.

"Okay," Jilli said. "So, is this one of those things that if I ask what it is now you'll tell me, or will you make me wait for a face-to-face?"

"Face-to-face."

She let out a sigh. "Fuck. Then I'll get my shit together and see you at noon." Which really meant twelve-thirty.

Jilli and I ended the call and my cell immediately rang again. I figured it was her and didn't bother confirming. I pressed the answer button on my steering wheel and said, "You're so not getting out of this."

"I wouldn't want to."

It was a man's voice. The Caller ID read 'Private.'

"It's Wyatt," he said before I could ask. "Did I catch you at an okay time?"

Shit.

"Hi, Wyatt. Yes. Sorry. I thought you were someone else. I don't usually…"

"Sounds like we're still on for dinner tonight. Eight o'clock sound good?"

"Um, sure."

He sounded sort of businesslike, so maybe this really was work related.

"Where are you?" he asked.

"I'm in my car coming down Olympic."

He laughed. "No, silly. I meant where do you live? What side of town are you on?"

He called me silly. That wasn't businesslike. Before I could recall where I lived, a huge, black Range Rover, still donning the dealer logo in place of a license plate, cut into my lane without regard to my safety or the slickness of the road. The bastard didn't even use his turn signal.

"Mutherfuck!" I exclaimed as I slammed on my brakes, blared my horn and slid on asphalt, narrowly avoiding the earth-killing, gas-guzzling behemoth, fortunate that there wasn't a car in the lane I was veering toward. "Asshole! Mutherfucking asshole!" I screamed out. I rolled down the window and let my middle finger serve as exclamation to my point. Wyatt kept repeating, "El, are you okay? Ellen, is everything all right?"

"Yes. I'm fine. Just some SUV-driving bastard thinking he owns the road. They should be outlawed, those petroleum-sucking, ozone-depleting catastrophes!"

"You drive a Prius, I take it," Wyatt surmised.

"No, a Jetta," I replied contritely.

If you've been in one accident, you gain a life-loving respect for German steel and engineering. I've been in two, neither my fault, and while I would love to own a hybrid and save the planet, I'd much rather own something that can absorb an impact and save my ass. At least it's a sensible sedan with re-spectable gas mileage.

"I'm in Venice, by the way," recalling his last question before I was nearly Rovered. I answered trying to sound somewhat professional, attempting to regain a bit of dignity.

"Great. I'm in Manhattan Beach. I'll zip up and grab you about seven-forty-five. How does Ivy at the Shore sound?"

"I had Ivy last night," I blurted. Like that mattered. When will I learn to think before speaking?

"Oh," was Wyatt's response.

"But I don't mind having it again. I had Ivy Ivy, not Shore Ivy." Jesus. I must have Tourette's. I should really see someone about this, get properly diagnosed. There has to be a pill I could take to save me from moments like these.

"No, no. That's fine. I'll just think of something else and surprise you. Sound okay?"

"Sounds perfect," I cooed. So not businesslike.

We said our goodbyes and I floated on a cloud all the way to lunch with Jilli, who brought me crashing down to Earth.

"So, out of the blue she just drops this on you? Like you can just pick up and move your life three-thousand miles away at the snap of her fingers?" Jilli said as she pushed herself back from the table. "That's some fucking nerve."

Jilli is allergic to bullshit in any form, unintentional or otherwise. Catholic girl-school educated, she had survived nuns and could take on anything. As she spoke, her bright blue eyes flashed under her near-black hair that was recently cut into a chic shag. The style complimented her angular features and flawless, creamy skin, but she hated the new 'do, having gone in for a mere trim and ended up with a new 'look.' "Here's some advice," she said when I met her at Chateau Marmont to inspect the damage, "never become friends with your hairstylist or your psychic. It just fucks everything up." Jilli was always to the point.

I sat up straight, feeling the need to defend Karen. "It wasn't like that, Jilli," I asserted.

"Bullshit. It's exactly that, El."

Maybe it was, but in the nicest possible way. "But, if the show goes in L.A., just think what that would mean for me."

"El, did you think what it would mean if the show tanks? In L.A., you'd live. You'd survive it. But say you move to Manhattan and the show's a stinker. They cancel it after six weeks. What then? Are they going to pay to relocate your life back to L.A.? Would you go back to being an assistant? No, wait. Karen will have already hired another assistant, since you will be busy acting as a producer. So, you'll be stuck in New York with no job. Sound good to you?" Jilli took a sip of her Diet Coke. "We should really be having a cocktail with this conversation, you know?"

"Okay, I didn't think that far ahead," I sheepishly admitted. "But can't I be excited for a few minutes about this chance? Jesus, Jilli, this is supposed to be a good thing." And I was doing my best to feel that way about it.

"Sure, be excited. But then you have to make some practical decisions," she countered. "It's great, El. It really, really is. But is it right for you? That's what you need to consider."

I wanted to be mad at her, but she had a point. I tried to talk but couldn't get a word out. I just dragged a fry through the ketchup trying hard not to consider the phenomenal amount of thigh dimples on my plate. Under these circumstances, fat, starch and sugar are completely necessary to keep brain and mood function steady. Jilli watched me quietly. She knew better than to push much harder.

"Hey," she said with a soft tone. "I just don't relish the thought of you moving a million miles away, that's all."

"No, you're right. I haven't thought about a possible downside. I just got caught up in the title. Producer. Associate Producer. Whatever. It just sounded…like I had finally arrived." I forced a smile.

"I know, El," Jilli said. And she did know, all too well.

Jilli and I met nearly eight years ago when we both were working at that awful studio, the one with the rodent running it. We were at the bottom of the food chain in neighboring cubicles, making copies, fetching coffee. We did our best to make the most of it.

Jilli and I hung out in a posse with four other assistants: Emily, Claudia, Teresa and Remi. In our first year in the industry, we went everywhere together. No premiere party or hors d'oeuvres platter left unturned. We thought we were networking, being seen in all the right places, sure the stratosphere was our limit.

Jilli and I once fantasized about having our own production company, Jell Films. Jilli insisted the receptionist would answer the phones with, "J'ello." We had epic plans to take over the town but, before the fantasy could be fulfilled, the job offers we got wound up putting us in different directions. A few of us suffered burnout and our rises to the top slowed, or collapsed completely.

Emily left the industry after receiving two ulcers and a year-long bout of insomnia. She is now a Pilates instructor and owns a private studio in Brentwood. There, she trains studio wives and has become quite successful, quoted in magazines and making local TV appearances. Claudia and I thought leaving the studio system would increase our chances of making the right connections, and we continue our illustrious careers as assistants. Teresa segued into publicity because it was the surest way to go to all the premieres and parties, and get the gossip first. Remi wanted something creative but without a heavy weekend read and is now a casting director.

I was the first to move on, and what I thought was up, taking an ill-fated job with a red hot, on-the-rise film director who turned out to be a one-hit wonder that cost the studio nearly a billion dollars on his next two underwhelming films. Jilli's the only one who stayed in development, too stubborn to give in. She's stuck it out and worked her way up to Director of Development at another studio, though she should be a VP by now—something we both know and don't talk about.

Two years ago, Jilli was attached as a producer on a script she brought in to one of the many vanity production companies under her studio's umbrella. Through some political man-euvering, her boss undid that deal and took a producing credit herself. Jilli's never quite gotten over that, and has been plotting revenge ever since.

"Seriously, the film had like eighty-seven producers on it. She couldn't spare one more title?" Jilli fumed when the dirt went down.

The movie came out last Thanksgiving and tanked. Jilli knew it would've been a blockbuster if she had kept shepherding it. I believe her. But that's the problem with development. Art by committee never succeeds. You can't please everyone and, when you try, you're doomed to fail.

In spite of the different directions we've ventured in, the posse of ours is still close. I talk to one, if not all, of them every day. Texts are incessant and we meet on a semi-regular basis, forcing a mandatory meal when someone has news, or it's just been too long since we last saw each other. We know the sad fact is the only way to keep relationships going in this town is to schedule them.

The lunch plates were cleared and I ordered a slice of pie.

"What does Tim say about all of this?" Jilli asked.

"I haven't told him yet," I mumbled through peaches and crust.

"Why the fuck not?"

I shrugged and swallowed. "He'll be home soon. I'll tell him then."

She shook her head. "I'm not getting this. Why would you wait on something like this?"

"There's another problem," I admitted.

"Lay it on me," Jilli replied.

"I have a date tonight with one of the executive pro-ducers."

"I'm sorry. Say that again."

"He asked me out yesterday at the meeting. 'Dinner tomorrow night.' I said yes. I think it's just business, though. At least that's how he pitched it."

"Business?" Jilli laughed. "It wouldn't fit into that category with a shoe horn and lubricant. You have a *date* date. And you have a boyfriend. And you are about to shit where you haven't even started eating yet. El, where's your head?" Then she leaned in and asked, "Who is he? What does he look like? Christ, now I need a slice of pie. We really should have had some cocktails for this."

Over dessert, I told her everything. We continued our conversation through a mini-shopping spree. When you've been offered a new job and have a date, a new ensemble is warranted. And Nordstrom was having a sale.

"Mother of God," Jilli said as we pushed our way around the paparazzi. "You'd think you can avoid this shit by skipping Robertson, but all it takes is one celebutard to fuck up a Saturday, even with the rain."

As is happened, Rhiannon Shaw decided to visit The Grove, and her assistant surely tipped off the paps. Rhiannon was the cokehead *du jour*, taking her fame as a poptart and sometime-actress to mean she could get away with all sorts of shenanigans. She's screwed half of Hollywood, has the Valtrex prescription on Smoking Gun to prove it. She just celebrated her twenty-first birthday last week. Will these girls ever learn? Didn't the summer of Lohan or Britney's implosion teach those kids anything? At least this one keeps her underwear on.

Paparazzi were a plague on L.A. We weren't allowed to shove them, run them over, or even call them names—at least that's what Meaghan, Karen's publicist told me after I openly referred to them as 'pigs and vultures' when Karen and I were surrounded by their cameras on a day out in Beverly Hills. The things celebrities go through just to see the dentist. We had to tolerate them like pigeons or cockroaches. They seemed to multiply in the same manner. You found yourself scurrying to avoid such vermin, as if to avert exposure to some contagious disease. Only being ogled by Warren Beatty causes the same need for a shower as being in the presence of those slimeballs.

There's certainly a special place in Hell for them.

Jilli and I finally made our way through the fracas and onto doing more damage to our credit cards as we continued our convo. As it turned out, Jilli knew Wyatt professionally years ago, back when he was an agent at CAA and dating a junior lawyer at one of the top entertainment firms.

"He's not a complete schmuck from what I recall. Wasn't one of those Young Turk wannabes. He's on the TV side, so I don't have much on those folks. I can ask around if you'd like," she offered.

"No. That's okay. Doesn't matter anyway. I have a boyfriend, right?"

"Yeah, right," Jilli smirked.

We were walking back to the car park through the pseudo-streets of The Grove when Jilli just walked into traffic, not waiting for a clear opportunity to cross the street, testing the pedestrian laws, causing cars to stop short and slam on their brakes. Never a wise thing to do, especially after a rain.

"Jesus, Jilli," I shouted as I ran after her, the cross-traffic now at a dead stop. The other cars would not go until I went; L.A. is way too litigious for chance.

"Where did you learn to cross a street?"

"Must be the New Yorker in me," she smirked.

"You're a native of L.A.," I reminded. She grew up in Pasadena, one of the more Republican areas north of the Orange Curtain, and she's been rebelling against it her whole life.

"Yeah, well, I've been sleeping with a New Yorker for the last few weeks, so…"

"Anyone I know?"

"Not yet," she replied. "By the way, what did Tim get you for your VD?" Deft change of subject that did not go unnoticed.

"Nothing."

"Seriously? He let another February fourteenth go by gift-less? Did he at least send a card?" she inquired.

"Nope. Not even a text."

"No wonder you aren't telling him. You know," she said with her hand on her hip, "I am probably the least sentimental, most unromantic woman ever born, but even I would not tolerate him forgetting Valentine's Day. Especially considering how long you've been together. It's bullshit."

"It's Tim," I shrugged. "He's just not a Hallmark kind of guy."

"Copout. You have my permission to shag Wyatt senseless. Tim owes you a good time. Wyatt may be the man to give it to you."

"You are terrible," I laughed.

"So bad I'm good," she smiled and hugged me goodbye when we arrived at my car.

"Call me the second you get home tonight," she called out as she walked to her unfortunate mode of transport—a Range Rover...like the one that nearly killed me earlier.

"Aren't you going to be on a date?" I shouted back.

"It's completely interruptible."

What Jilli didn't tell me at the time was that her long-plotted revenge against her evil ex-boss was well into effect. She's a Scorpio and prone to secrets. Eventually, though, she spills them all to me.

Meanwhile, I had to decide if I was going to be keeping this a secret from Tim. He had sent me a text while we were at lunch: Call me, babe.

I tried to remember the last time he signed off with *Love* or a series of exes and ohs. Maybe his Christmas card to me? I couldn't recall. All those little niceties seemed to have faded over time.

"You didn't call me last night," he said.

"Was I supposed to?"

"Kind of, I guess. Just would have been nice to hear from you."

"Same here. Your phone can call out, too. Right?"

"Yeah, yeah. What are you up to?"

"Driving back from lunch with Jilli. Then I have a dinner tonight." That admission caused me to wince. "What about you?"

"Heading over to the local bar. Shoot some pool or something. Film's going well. We might actually finish ahead of schedule, if you can believe that."

This is how boring our conversations had become. I must have of tuned out at some point.

"Did you get a decision, El?" Tim seemed to repeat.

"Sorry?"

"About Vancouver. Are you doing the film with Karen? Because, if you are, maybe you could make a stop here."

"I can't. There's just too much going on here," I said.

"Like what?"

"Stuff, Tim. Work. I have a lot to do. Do you really want me to rattle off the list?"

"Never mind," he relented.

Never mind indeed. We finished up our chat with exciting repartee about not much, then I finally excused myself by saying, "Babe, I'm nearing that spot on Olympic where I might lose you. Have fun tonight and I'll talk to you later okay?"

"Okay, babe. Have a good ni—"

And then the call dropped. There was no need to dial back and finish the goodbye. That was as good as it was going to get. I started to see that I wanted more than that. Much, much more.

Chapter Four

As I was giving Wyatt directions to my house, it hit me that I was giving him directions to where Tim and I lived. This was growing increasingly awkward. I thought about cancelling, but that might seem rude, right? After all, we were going to be working together and I didn't want there to be tension between us. But how does one go about getting rid of sexual tension? The only way I knew to quell it was to get naked—not exactly prudent here. Like I said, awkward. I couldn't take anymore time thinking about it, though. I had to find shoes to go with the new skirt I picked up that afternoon.

The rain had stopped, but I wasn't sure about wearing strappy, high-heels. I go open-toe as much as possible, and have a hard time finding rain-friendly options. After digging through my closet for a good twenty minutes, I found a fabulous pair of sling-backs that I always forget I own. The soft gray skirt was straight and ended below my knee. I coupled it with my black cashmere cardigan that I hung open just so when I left the first three…two…three…what the hell, three buttons open. The gold cross my grandfather gave me peeped through the opening. That should keep us both honest.

I tied my hair back at my neck. With the side part, it was professional, and just a little sexy. The dangling pair of Celia's earrings added just the right touch of chic. The earrings are mine, actually; she made them for me as a Christmas gift.

Celia was once one of us, but she decided that if she was going to work hard at making a career, it might as well be for something she loves. She got that smart after a year in the industry and started designing jewelry. Now, she is super successful and lives in New York. I smiled at the thought of hanging out with her again if I moved, then shook that thought from my head and smoothed out my ensemble. I felt lovely. Then the home line rang.

"Yes," I sang into the phone, thinking it was Wyatt at the gate.

"Oh, so this is a working number." It was my sister.

"I'm in a hurry, Gwen. What do you want?"

"A call back would be nice. Really, are you *sooooo* important you can't call your mother or sister?"

What's the point of having caller ID if you don't use it? I silently scolded myself.

"Actually, Gwen. I do have a lot on my plate at the moment."

"Oh, and I don't?" my sinister huffed.

"I take it you're with our mother now." Gwen always performed in that manner when sitting by Kitty's side.

"As a matter of fact, I am. I just brought her back home from the hospital." She paused for effect.

I would've rolled my eyes, but I thought it better to keep them focused as I retouched my mascara.

Kitty likes to visit hospitals now. She does this whenever she feels she's not getting her fair share of attention. This little trick of hers has been going on a great deal in the last year. My stepfather died of a heart attack about eighteen months ago; were it not for the open casket, I would've figured he faked his own death. Easier than a divorce. Sadly, three months later, my grandmother, Kitty's mom, passed. The attention that came with being "a widow and an orphan," as my mother liked to describe herself, had recently begun to wane. To be center stage again, she's taken up faux alcoholism (she only drinks when people are around; no need to do it without an audience) and hypochondria.

"What did Kitty come up with, I mean, down with this time?"

"She had walking pneumonia, and you weren't even there for her," Gwen said with forceful drama. "Mom could have died, Ellen."

"She had walking pneumonia, Gwen. 'Walking' implies being ambulatory. I'm sure they just gave her a bunch of antibiotics and sent her on her merry way."

"Walking pneumonia can be very dangerous at mom's age, Ellen."

My mother is fifty-one years old. Kitty got knocked up with

me shortly after high school. This was before being a single mother was chic in suburbia. I think she did it to trap my father. Being from a small town and Catholic families, marriage was the solution both clans chose for them. Kitty makes sure that I am fully aware her life did not turn out as she planned, and it's all my fault.

"And," Gwen continued, "she might have to have her implants removed. The x-rays showed possible leakage."

"Implants are supposed to be removed every ten years or so anyway. It's maintenance, not a mastectomy."

"Oh, and in your spare time, between fetching coffee and hailing limos, you've become a doctor? You know, you don't know everything, Ellen."

I can't believe her. She's almost twenty-nine, but remains the annoying ten-year-old I grew up with and grew to loathe. Can you picture the flying monkey with me? Just put a blonde wig on it and you have my sister cold.

"Gwen, I work in a town full of fake tits. You pick up this information in general conversation. Kitty's going to live. Trust me. But, I can't chat anymore. I've got to go."

"Well, don't bother saying goodbye," she said, and hung up on me.

And they wonder why I don't stop by for dinner.

My sister moved to Colorado for a brief time. Everyone was shocked; no one thought the umbilical cord could stretch that far. But Gwen believed in the myth of *Men*ver. After two years, in which she did not meet Mr. Right, she moved back in with Kitty and transferred to CSUN to finish up her business degree, which she quickly applied to Real Estate. Now, she lives down the street from Kitty with her fiancé Daryl. Yes, my younger sister is engaged after a yearlong courtship. She and Kitty love to rub that in.

My mother and sister are two people I would not want to ruin any good news with, so I wouldn't be telling them about the talk show until the ink was dry on my contract and we were in production. Kitty would find a way to disparage the show and my position, and Gwennie would likely accuse me of trying to upstage her before the wedding.

The phone rang again. I saw the number on the phone's display and, instead of ignoring it, I faced the dragon. Kitty was in the midst of a long, hard and well-acted cough when I picked up.

"How are you feeling, Kitty?" I asked, skipping the hello.

"For chrissakes, Ellen, call me Mother. I'm fine. Just fine. I will have to have surgery on my breasts, though. They want to rule out cancer. But I'm sure I'll be okay."

When I didn't react to the C-word, she rustled up a few more coughs.

"I just don't want you upsetting your sister like that. You two should get along. My mother's heart would break hearing you two go on like that."

I rolled my eyes so far back on that one a contact got stuck. "Shit," I whispered, trying to dislodge the lens.

"Don't use that language!" Kitty shouted.

Rather than go into the discussion about how old I am and that I could use any goddamn language I fucking well pleased, I just put on a saccharine smile and said, "Kitty, I have to go now. I'm expecting another call. I'm glad you're feeling better. Take care. Give my very best to Gwen. Bye!"

As I was hanging up, I heard her say, "You should come see your mother before she dies!" Kitty is expert in putting the 'fun' in dysfunction.

A moment later, phone rang once more. It was Wyatt was calling from the gate. He was spot on time.

"I'll be right down," I said into the receiver.

"Buzz me in. A gentleman greets his date at the door," he said into the callbox.

Definitely not businesslike.

"Thanks, but I'll be right there." I put the phone down, checked my lipstick, grabbed my coat, purse and keys, and dashed.

As I approached the gate, I saw him pacing behind the bars of the barrier. He reminded me of caged panther—his black Prada coat catching the reflection of the streetlight. The clacking of my heels on the concrete brought his attention to me. He gave me that smile, and I tingled. Then I took step that didn't stop.

I slid on the slick cement on one sling-backed foot for a good, long yard. It probably took all of a second, but it felt like an eternity as my fate hung in the balance. Would I fall flat on my ass, or would all that Pilates and yoga pay off, and I would find my center, use my core? Ass over teakettle—not here, not now. I watched Wyatt's eyes widen as I defied gravity and steadied myself in a much less than graceful manner.

"Whoa," was his reaction. "Are you okay?"

"Still standing," I smiled back, straightening out my skirt with a quick check to make sure I didn't split a seam, and tossing my ponytail back over my shoulder to regain the rest of my composure. Of course, I think I've only worn these shoes once or twice. Not nearly enough to bring traction to their soles. I made it to the gate without further incident, taking dainty, baby steps as a precaution.

"You look amazing, El." He held out his elbow. "May I? The steps are still wet."

I wanted to decline, to keep things businesslike, but I couldn't trust my shoes. Or the weakness in my knees. I placed my hand in the crook of his elbow and felt the hard bulge of his bicep. Nice. His BMW X5 was parked in the red, a total pet peeve of mine, but I let it go; there wasn't another space open on my block.

He opened the *space gray* door for me and, as I got in, he said, "I realize that I'm driving a gas-guzzling, earth-killing SUV, but since your car sucks petroleum, too, I thought you could deal." I tried not to smile at his mocking of me, but failed. "Besides, it's a diesel. A little better, right?" When he got behind the wheel, he continued with, "I thought we would go to Shutters. Is that all right with you?"

Shutters is a hotel on the boardwalk in Santa Monica. Two restaurants, one lovely view of the Pacific, and nearly two hundred rooms with beds in them. What else could I say but, "That sounds nice."

We were relatively quiet as we drove. Never once have I been picked up for a working dinner. I could no longer deny this was a date. I kept my eyes forward, hands folded in my lap and listened to the music. Bowie swirled through the speakers. I assumed satellite radio, then noticed his iPhone connected to the stereo. *Young Americans*. My favorite Bowie album. I couldn't complain, nor say I wasn't impressed.

"He'd have been a great guest for Karen, don't you think?" Wyatt said, ending the silence.

"Pardon?"

"David Bowie would have made a great guest for Karen's show. Didn't he and Karen date during the whole 'Serious Moonlight' thing?" he asked.

"No. She was married to Danny Beardon, the director, then. Everyone always gets them confused. They were both blonde, British and reportedly bisexual. And, sadly, they're both dead."

I have acquired vast knowledge of pop culture history that was way before my time through Karen. It really sucked to grow up in the nineties. I would take Duran Duran and John Hughes over Nirvana and Michael Bay any day.

Wyatt smiled and said, "I see again why Karen wants you on board."

I grinned back at him then quickly returned my stare to the road. We might be talking business, but I was blurring professional and personal lines.

I don't cheat. I never have. But, more than once, it's happened to me. Even knowing how bad infidelity feels, thoughts of waking up in those soft Shutters sheets with Wyatt kept spinning in my mind, no matter how I tried to shake them loose. Bowie's croon didn't help the matter.

All night—she wants the Young American.

How is it possible to be so drawn, so animisticly attracted to someone you've spent maybe two hours in the company of? It's absurd. It's embarrassing. It's impossible to ignore. And it's totally annoying that it's happening now, when there's so much in question. Will the show go in New York and would I want Tim to move with me if it did or would I want a fresh start altogether? Too many fucking questions. I felt a migraine lurking. But, the chemistry I was experiencing with Wyatt was the worst of it. I was afraid to look at him. And dared not speak.

"You're awfully quiet," Wyatt said, speaking over the music.

"Am I?"

Wyatt only responded with an eyebrow raise.

"I suppose so," I admitted. "I just…I've never had a colleague take me to dinner like this."

"Oh. We're going to keep this strictly business?"

"I think we have to, don't you?" I asked, not sure of the answer I was hoping for.

"If you say so," he said in a manner that showed he didn't buy the weight of my conviction.

"Wyatt, I have a boyfriend. I live with my boyfriend."

"Then why are you here with me?" he asked. I noted the confident smirk on his face.

"That's a very good question, and I've been asking myself that all day."

"Did you give yourself an answer?" he posed directly.

I shook my head. Then I found myself asking, "Why did you ask me out?"

"That's a question I've been asking myself all day. Maybe tonight we'll find the answers."

Jesus. I was in trouble. Ass over teakettle for sure.

We pulled into the valet of the hotel, relieving us of further discussion. Wyatt came around the car to meet me and took my hand like it was the most natural thing in the world to do. I responded in kind. We walked into the hotel lobby and up the stairs to One Pico. When we reached the restaurant, the host greeted him by name and brought us to our table. As soon as I laid the napkin in my lap, champagne appeared and caviar was served.

"This is a celebration, isn't it?" he asked me. "I wanted to do this right."

And he did. This was exactly the kind of thoughtful touch I had always wanted. Dreamed of. Longed for. Craved. From Tim. Not a co-worker. That nasty little caveat Jillian mentioned about defecating where one dines kept ringing in my head, and made me look sideways at what I was about to ingest. So glad he didn't order pâté.

"Tell me about yourself. I only know you by reputation," he said as the waiter poured champagne into my glass.

"And what does my reputation tell you?"

"That you're a straight shooter. Completely on top of things. You are a professional who is respected and admired. Even the toughest in town have a soft spot for you."

"Are you talking about me or Karen?" I inquired.

"You, silly." That was the third time he called me that. I was liking it less and less. "And you've worked for some tough people."

I did seem to have a way with the criminally insane. Or at least those who qualify as certifiably narcissistic. Bosses in Hollywood are similar to dogs or killer bees; as long as you don't express panic or fear, you are safe in their presence.

"We should probably keep this in perspective, Wyatt. I'm an assistant, plain and simple. Some people might assume my job is easy, that anyone with half a brain could do it. We both know it takes a bit of skill and some savvy to do my job well. But, I'm still just an assistant. My reputation is a reflection of whom I'm working for at the moment I'm working for them. In this case, it's Karen who makes my reputation seem so strong."

"That's where you're wrong. I went all the way through your résumé, called everyone, well, almost. It's you they like. Bev Watson fucking loves you, by the way. Of course, there was that little scandal," he said as he looked into his lap to adjust his napkin.

I actually cringed at the mention of that. Shit. Will it ever go away?

Remember that hot, up-and-coming director I mentioned earlier? I suppose now's the time to tell you about him, my experience with the clichéd aspect of Hollywood and the egomaniacal employers who dwell there.

Jon Tatum was the It Boy who took Sundance by storm about seven years back. His grandfather was a huge television producer, as was his father. Jon wanted something more: Movies. His family's money bought him into the right film school, into the right internships and funded his 'groundbreaking' student short that was, over a few years, developed into a full-length independent feature that somehow got into Sundance. The right publicist started the appropriate buzz that eventually got his rather mediocre movie right smack in the middle of a distribution bidding war that made headlines and secured him a three-picture deal with the rodent-run studio I toiled at.

At that point, I was suffering as the assistant for two junior development execs at the studio's big budget banner, Stonebridge. It was a half-step up from office assistant. Coffee-fetching and copy-making were still involved. My job description also required me to fill any more important desk emptied by illness or vacation. The banner president did not like "the trolls from the temp pool," as he so kindly put it, working in his office.

I was covering for the receptionist, who had come down with the brown-bottle flu caught at happy hour the night before, when Jon came in. He had all the swagger of someone who believed his own bio. Full of himself was an understatement; he was a good thirty-pounds overweight. Though he tried to cover it with additional bravado, I could tell he was nervous.

He was there to meet with his new bosses and had to make an impression for this crucial phase of his career go smoothly. He struck up conversation with me as he waited to be called in. I felt the need to entertain Jon since no one had come out for him. Not even to offer a beverage. The president's assistant kept IM-ing me to let him know that it would only be another five minutes. When twenty went by, Jon assured me he knew he was being kept waiting to be reminded of his place in the industry and to bring down the swelling of his head.

"Is it normal-sized yet?" he asked, patting his noggin. I laughed.

When Jon finally went in, he flashed me the thumbs-up as he walked by. I laughed again.

Sadly for Jon, what his family's money couldn't buy were good looks. He was already balding in a less-than-distinguished pattern. His pasty skin denied that L.A. was his birthplace, and his doughy body was not helped by his sloppy fashion sense. Fortunately for him, there were still plenty of women in L.A.

who shagged for status. Those emaciated masses, deranged from a lack of nutrition and desperate enough for any brush with success, were happy to serve as arm candy and service their suitors in hopes that they would be put in the next film, get a new car, perhaps a shopping spree, or at least go to the hot spots and a few good parties where they might meet someone even more famous and/or successful. Famous men really aren't that particular.

In a short time, Jon had gained a large reputation as a womanizer in the tabloids and blogs. He slipped me his card on his way out of the meeting. I winced at first; somewhat disgusted at what I thought was a sleazy attempt at a hook-up. Did he take my politeness as flirtation? Gross. When I went to toss the card in the bin, I noticed he had written something on the back:

I need an assistant.
When can you start?

Completely relieved, I called him that afternoon. We discussed terms ("I've never had an assistant before so you tell me how it works."), and salary ("They are giving me a shitload of money, so I'll pay you double what you are making there, as long as you aren't making a hundred grand."), and the fact that I had aspirations to produce ("Cool."). I started the following week. Two weeks' notice wasn't required since he was part of the studio 'family.' My bosses weren't all that happy, but the banner prez was pleased Jon was pulling from his team.

At first, Jon was a nice guy, professional and respectful. That lasted about three months. As his buzz continued, he evolved into an egomaniacal tyrant who believed the legend that his PR firm created. Not only that, he was a truly crap director. On his first studio film, we were two weeks behind schedule, in spite of the overtime, and six million over-budget five weeks into the twelve-week shoot. It was a nightmare. That was also where I met Tim and The Crew. The chance to flirt with Tim was the only reason I didn't quit. By the end of the shoot, Jon's career and reputation were in the toilet, and Tim and I were in love.

When the film bombed, which surprised no one but Jon, he went off the deep end. Booze, bud and anything illicit fueled his petulance and paranoia. The only thing healthy about him was his ego. Then again, even that was bloated.

We were in pre-pre-production on the second film when things started going south at an even more dramatic rate. Jon didn't like that I had a boyfriend, that I actually wanted to go home at the end of the day, that I wasn't available to "hang" after work, or that I was "fucking below-the-line." I'd already had enough of his insanity and made inquiries with a headhunter to find a new job. I was meeting with her Monday morning. It was the Wednesday night before when all this went down.

"What do you see in that camera boy that you don't see in me? I'm a director. Do you know what I could do for your career?" he asked, seated at his desk in the home office we shared. He didn't want the suites the studio had offered him, believing they would be bugged, which could've been true. So, we converted a double-room upstairs to serve as a workspace. I was finishing up the notes I took from that afternoon's meeting, doing one last spell check before I pressed *Print.*

"Tim's a nice guy, Jon. You know that. Besides, you like actresses, models and Playboy types." I thought he was joking— just being his usual, sarcastic, arrogant self—so I joked back. I was wrong.

He came up behind me as I was collecting the notes from the printer and put his hands on my waist. I could feel his breath on my neck. Even worse, I could smell it.

"You know I've always had a thing for you, El," he said in a low, slow tone.

My stomach knotted. I stepped away, ignoring him, hoping that would be enough, figuring this behavior was from a new combination of pills and pot. Once he sobered up a tad, he would realize his rudeness. Again, I was wrong. He stepped in front of me, grabbed my shoulders, pulled me toward him, attempting a kiss. Now, I was pissed.

Jon was about six feet tall, but a soft six feet. I reached for his arms to push away from his hold and found myself squeezing bags full of Cool Whip where his biceps should have been.

"Let go of me, Jon," I said through gritted teeth.

"Not yet," he said and pulled me toward his face, lips parted, and tried to kiss me once more.

I gave him a shove, this time at his chest, and found my hands on moobs. My stomach began to reverse. "Knock it off, dammit!"

His eyes were glazed. I couldn't tell if he was on uppers or downers, or a combo of both. Oddly, I wasn't scared, just super fucking annoyed. He was too pathetic, too slovenly sad, to be threatening. Besides, I actually lifted weights.

"Jon, just what the actual fuck do you think you're doing?"

"I'm taking what's mine. I pay you. You're mine."

"I'm your assistant, not your piece of ass. Get your hands off me, right now!"

He didn't move. I repeated my request. When he failed to respond, I slapped him across the face. Hard. It was a good smack and my palm buzzed from it.

"Ow!" he whinged in a girly way. "I can't believe you hit me. I could sue you for that."

He retreated to his chair, still holding his cheek.

"Seriously? Let's go over your list of sins: Sexual harassment, false imprisonment, hostile work environment—and that's just for starters." I grabbed my purse and jacket. "Consider this my resignation. Asshole."

As I headed toward the door, he started crying. Yes, crying. Blathering on about how nobody loved him, that he was a hack, his career was in the gutter and that he needed me to help him get his life on track.

"Stay, El. I really need you," he pleaded.

"What you need, Jon, is professional help, and a good, long stay at Betty Ford," I said and walked out.

On my way home, I called Jilli to get her advice.

"Jackpot, baby. You just hit it. You might have to make a police report, though. I'll meet you there. Beverly Hills or West Hollywood station?" She was a little too excited about this.

"Can't I do that in the morning?"

I was meeting Tim's parents that night for the first time. I was going to be late as it is. Besides, I needed time to think about what had happened and what I was really willing to do about it. In spite of being a native, I'm not litigious by nature.

I went to dinner and didn't tell Tim what happened with Jon after we dropped off his mom and dad at the hotel. Tim went ballistic. I had to stop him from driving over to Jon's and going caveman on him. I have to admit I found his reaction completely sexy. Not very feminist of me, I know, but it was nice to have a man willing to defend my honor.

The next morning, I contacted Jon's attorney. The last thing either of us wanted was this matter on public record. A check for half my annual salary was delivered to my apartment three hours later with a letter stipulating that, by accepting the money, I agreed to not talk about the 'incident.' Looking back, I probably should have filed the police report, but I was naïve and still hoping for a Hollywood career.

That payout did not stop Jon from blabbing, however. He invented some tall tale about how he had to sack me after I became sexually obsessed with him. Jilli heard about it through the assistant grapevine and called me immediately. I called Jon's lawyer again, the other half of my annual salary was sent to my door with a written apology, and Jon was put into rehab. From the payouts, I was able to make a serious dent in my student loan (film school isn't cheap, and a private one is an extravagance), put a down payment on a new Jetta and money into savings, which was paramount since I wasn't sure if or when I would ever work in this town again. Thankfully, I wasn't tarnished by the Tatum Trauma. It's more or less an innocuous ink smudge on my CV.

Since we are going through my résumé, I might as well mention that I was next hired by manager/producer Victor DeMatteo. Victor had been in music for three decades before being fired by his biggest client and by-then business partner, Jade. With a multi-million-dollar settlement from the parent corp of their music company, Vic decided that—instead of retirement, as the industry as a whole truly hoped he would—he wanted to become a movie mogul. He wasn't quite there, but hired me for my bit of experience. Once again, I saw my shot at getting closer to producing. You'd think I would have learned by then.

Vic didn't realize that the movie-making process was a long one. He had optioned the bio of strung-out, 60s sweetheart Yvonne Bright, and wanted to make that into a blockbuster feature. He didn't figure that he needed to find an interested studio, hire the right writer, attach bankable actors and sign a director the studio and the actors all agreed on, get the script and budget approved, wait for the director's schedule to align with the stars', hope that the locations you want/need fit into the budget and schedule, and that no one has dropped out, got sick or pregnant. Then there was post-production, audience research and, God forbid, re-shoots.

Victor couldn't understand how, back in the day, a music video could be shot in twenty-four hours, and a feature would take months to film rather than a couple of weeks. He grew increasingly frustrated at the glacial speed of filmmaking and went back into music management.

I like the music business less than television.

As a bonus, Vic was a screamer. His temper was ignited at the slightest provocation, or for no apparent reason at all. Only once was his ire specifically aimed at me.

He called me late one evening from Miami, where he was courting a young singer, one he thought would be the next Jade, or Latina version thereof. His upset? That he had been given a junior suite rather than the full we had reserved. Even though he was all of 5'5" (an inch shorter than yours truly), Vic was not the type of man to stay in a junior suite. He called me from the lobby screaming, angry over the fact that they couldn't get him a real suite that night, and that I should call the manager, who was standing right in front of Vic.

"Do you really think a call from me would be more effective than you yelling at him in person?" I asked pointedly. The fact I didn't say, "Sir, yes, sir," immediately meant:

"You don't fucking know how to do your fucking job, and your fucking job is to take care of me. Did you fucking confirm the fucking room before fucking I left?" I was holding the phone a good four inches from my ear to save me from perforating the drum.

"Yes. I confirmed everything yesterday after lunch." Vic was on an early flight the next morning, so I confirmed the car pick-ups and room reservation the previous day, standard protocol. Like I said, an assistant's job is not rocket science.

"Did you confirm it again before I landed?" he barked.

"No, Vic, I didn't." I've never had to reconfirm a 'yes' with a five-star hotel before or since. You can generally take them at their word.

"Then what the fuck have you been doing all day?"

"I've been busy setting up the meeting for you in New York with the director, writers and lead actress."

Vic made the mistake of offering Sarina Adams a co-producer role on the film, which she took too literally. When she wasn't invited to a conference call with the director, she felt she was being snubbed.

"For some reason, Sarina didn't want to go, Vic. She didn't think you really wanted her there. You were on the plane and not reachable, her agent's vacationing on some yacht off Greece and her manager was recently sacked, so I was the only one I could think of to talk her into going. I spent most of the day convincing her that you did really want her there and, somehow, I convinced her that was true. I figured that a priority since you, the director, the development execs and the writers were all going to meet in New York for her to read with Sean Michaels."

Sean's the golden boy of box office who Vic begged to play Yvonne's lifelong love, Eddie Mann. He was stuck in Manhattan finishing up a play, so everyone had to go to him.

"Just so you know, Victor, Sarina's on her way to Manhattan as we speak, excited to meet with everyone."

Vic was quiet for a moment, not sure what to yell about next. He cleared his throat. "Well, I should probably call Sarina so she has a message from me when she lands. I'll talk to you later."

The hotel kindly admitted their error, which was due to an overbooking and extended stay of another music impresario and his epic entourage. The hotel manager assured me that Vic would be upgraded to a luxury suite the next day, and the first night's stay would be on the house, something he had told Vic upon his arrival.

When he came back from his trip, Vic acted as if nothing had happened. I couldn't let it go. I told him if he ever acted like that with me again, I would quit on the spot. He said he would do his best, but no apology ever came. Just the monogrammed Tiffany stationery he got me for my birthday, two weeks belated. Shortly thereafter, I handed him my two weeks' notice, handwritten on monogrammed Tiffany stationery.

From Vic, I went on to work for Karen. It took me about a month to realize that she wasn't going to go into a conniption if something wasn't perfect or even just because she felt like it. Working with her was like being on vacation.

While I wasn't really tarnished by the Jon debacle, I will be forever linked to the downfall of a once-promising director. He's now doing Saturday morning TV shows with his dad's production company. I still have a physical reaction at the thought of him. Part of that is disappointment. It stung that it was still a murmur around town and that Wyatt felt the need to bring it up.

"You know the truth on that one, don't you?" I asked Wyatt.

"I know you got a pretty penny out of it, but I'm sure it was nowhere near enough for what you went through. I'd like to smack him around a little myself. But, I think he gets a pretty good ego bruising each time he walks onto that kiddie set. And, Hef's banned him from the mansion, again." Wyatt smiled. I didn't follow suit.

Wyatt had the upper hand, and that was something I did not relish. He knew much more about me than I did him. I was annoyed that I didn't Google him before dinner. I should've had Jilli do the reconnaissance, at least. I was more than a little irked when Wyatt told me it was Howie who had given him my résumé.

The evening began to taste sour. I should be with my friends right now celebrating, not here with Wyatt. I should have told Tim about the promotion and this stupid dinner. How would I ever explain this to him now? The guilt was making me cranky.

"You're quiet again," Wyatt observed, taking the last bite of his steak.

We had ingested the remainder of our meal exchanging only a handful of words.

"Sorry if I said something wrong. I should've skipped bringing up the whole Tatum thing," Wyatt said earnestly, looking me in the eye.

"It's okay. Everyone loves a tasty bit of gossip."

"Look, El, I wanted tonight to be fun. Celebrate the show. Get to know each other. I'm sorry it went off track. Can we start over?"

I nodded and attempted a smile.

We talked like normal people over dessert and more champagne, about life, not work or things Hollywood-related. I recognized that he kept my glass full while modestly sipping his as he told me where we grew up (Boston); went to school (USC); and we found that we had something in common in our future aspirations (we'd wanted to be producing feature films).

We moved into the hotel's lobby to sit by the fireplace and sip coffee. There, he told me he had ended a long-term relationship last summer. Had been dating, but no one seriously. Was the younger of two brothers with a sister a year younger than him who was getting married in the fall, making him the last single sibling at the ripe age of thirty-five.

I told him about my upbringing, leaving out the snarky details of its dysfunctionality. Gave him the basics of my relationship: Tim's name and how we met; the lack of elaboration and enthusiasm surely told him everything else.

It was nearing one when he brought me home. We sat in his Beemer not wanting the night to end. Then, he said what he shouldn't have, though I was somewhat relieved he did.

"I am attracted to you, El." He was looking me straight in the eye. "I make it sort of a rule not to get involved with people I work closely with. I thought you should know that."

"Okay," I said, waiting to hear what would come next.

"And I respect the fact that you are in a relationship. But...and this isn't easy to say...if the attraction I feel for you doesn't dissipate, I'm going to have a hard time being alone in a room with you."

"Well," I said, murdering the silence, "at least this is a problem we both share." With the tension now gone, I no longer had the adrenaline to dull the alcohol, and realized I was more than just a little buzzed.

"What are we going to do?" Wyatt asked.

"Hire an intern to serve as a chaperone?"

"I'm serious, El," he said taking my hand in his. My heart stopped, then pounded hard to catch up on what it had missed.

"I know, Wyatt." I knew I should've pulled my hand from his, but I couldn't.

"One more thing I have to know," he declared with seriousness.

"What?" I was ready to answer anything.

"You spell your nickname E-L and not E-L-L-E. Why?"

"What's the point of shortening your name by removing one letter?"

He laughed, removing some of the atmosphere.

"And my middle name is Louise, so it's also my first two initials," I finished.

"Ellen Louise Patterson. I like it," he smiled.

"Now you have to tell me yours," I dared him.

"James."

I have a rule, starting back in college, that I can't sleep with a guy until I knew his middle name and favorite color. We were just a shade away from that, and I had to keep my wits about me. Tim's are Michael and blue. I needed to focus on those.

"You know, I'm going to insist on walking you to your door," Wyatt said softly.

"Do you think that's a good idea?"

"I know that if we sit here a moment longer, I'm going to kiss you."

Wyatt leaned in to do just that when my iPhone vibrated. For a quiet mode it was awfully loud and I jumped when it shook and sounded. Tim's smiling face gleamed from the large screen.

"Shit," I said under my breath. Caught red-handed.

"Him?" Wyatt asked.

I nodded. What is it about men? How is it that they can be oblivious to most things right in front of them but, somehow, they can sense when another guy is interested in you and immediately become attentive, even when they are hundreds of miles away? With the continuing vibration growling, I had no choice but to answer it.

"Hello?" I said with Wyatt watching me, running his finger over my left hand as it rested on the seat. I wanted to let Tim know an engagement ring would come in handy right about now, but I didn't think this situation would really help build my case for making a lifelong commitment.

"Hey, babe. What's up?" Tim said loudly, obviously with a few drinks in him, and clearly audible to Wyatt.

"I'm saying goodbye to a friend. Can I call you back in a few minutes?"

"Sure, babe. Tell your friend I said hello," Tim slurred.

"Bye," I said softly and ended the call.

"Well-timed on his part," Wyatt said with the slip of a smile.

"A bit," I returned. "I should go."

Wyatt nodded as he reached up and touched my face. "I'll walk you in."

"No," I said a bit louder than expected, feeling my eyes go wide.

Wyatt smiled. "Yes. It just so happens, El, that you are a lady and I am a gentleman. I'm walking you up."

He got out of the car before I could move. I sat frozen. Stunned. Drunk. He opened my door. I still wasn't able to command my body to exit.

"Do you want me to carry you in?" Wyatt asked.

"No, no. I can manage," I lied.

"Just swing one leg out, then the other," Wyatt coached.

"Very funny," I snarked and finally removed myself from the vehicle.

He took my hand to assist me, as a gentleman would a lady. I searched a little too long for my keys, considering I was carrying a clutch. I fumbled a bit unlocking the gate. It was all so mortifying. I could feel his entertainment as he followed me to my door. *Our* door. The door belonging to me and Tim. Me and Tim. Me and Tim. That's all I could think of as I slid the key into the lock, ignoring the Freudian connotation. I also tried ignoring how much I wanted to kiss Wyatt. I turned to face him and met his blue eyes. Before I could say anything, he asked, "Aren't you going to invite me in?"

God, how I wanted to invite him in. All the way in. *YES!* I wanted to scream. "Uh…," was all I could mutter.

"Kidding," he smiled and leaned in to kiss my cheek. "I had a nice time tonight." When he whispered in my ear, his deep voice filled my body.

"Me, too," I whispered back.

He kissed my cheek again and my body trembled. Wyatt pulled away from me slowly and I felt the chill of the night as his warmth left me. He squeezed my hand as he stepped back and a smile spread across his mouth. The mouth that was just to my cheek. Then, that mouth parted to say, "Don't forget to call your boyfriend."

Chapter Five

"Jesus, El. Get the puss off, will you? We are on the red carpet in ten," Jilli said as she drove us into the parking lot of the parking lot where the huge white tent was pitched. I was on the verge of surviving the Spirit/Oscar weekend, but it could still go either way.

"No one will be taking our photo, Jilli." There's nothing sadder than having photographers drop their cameras as you pass. Would a courtesy flash kill them?

"Wrong, Ellen. I have a friend at *Los Angeles Magazine* working the line. We are so in. And, once one Neanderthal photographer snaps us, the rest will do the same," she grinned, and it was infectious. "There," she said. "That's better."

The Spirits Awards is the coolest event in all of L.A. Held the Saturday before the Oscars in a tent planted on a Santa Monica Beach parking lot, they are the most coveted tickets in town. These seats can be harder to get than those at Elton John's or *Vanity Fair*'s Oscar fêtes.

At the Spirit Awards, people wear jeans or a designer gown, and are on the verge of drunk before the cameras roll. You are spitting distance from the likes of George, Quentin, Julianne, Jennifer, Jake or the Jolie-Pitts, and any other A-Lister who was in an indie flick or twisted their agent/publicist/studio head/manager to wring out a ticket. Since Karen won Best Actress the year before and was presenting this year, she got me in, plus one. Since Tim was still on location, Jilli was my date.

As is tradition, it rained the night before, so there were a few puddles to bypass on our way down the red carpet, which was littered with the usual suspects. We were behind John Waters in the press line when I heard, "There you are!" which caused John to jump.

Karen was resplendent in a Prada dress and wearing Celia's jewelry. She towered over the other attendees in her four-inch Louboutins as she made her way back down the line to greet Jilli and me with hugs and air kisses.

"You both look absolutely fabulous," she complimented. Light bulbs were flashing in a blitzkrieg manner, and Jilli was striking subtle poses. Jilli and I were in loaned dresses and our best heels, with hair and makeup camera-ready. The show was going out live on IFC. We made our way down the red carpet with Karen introducing me to friends and the press as her producer.

Jilli's eyes went wild. "Forget *Los Angeles*," she said through her toothy smile. "We are so in *Vanity Fair*."

I shook more hands in those few minutes than I did the whole of last year. Jilli and I took our seats at the table as Karen went on to schmooze. I saw her accosted by Bev Watson and kept my eyes peeled, hoping that Anise would not appear—or worse, be seated at one of the empty chairs next to me.

"You know who's going to be here?" Jilli started, and then her eyes locked on something above my head. Before I could turn to see what caught her attention, a warm hand touched my back and soft lips pressed against my cheek.

"Hello, El," Wyatt greeted. I went completely blank. He laughed. "I was hoping you'd be happy to see me."

"Wyatt," Karen beamed. "You made it. I'm so happy you could join us."

"Oh, she's good," Jilli whispered to me.

Karen introduced Wyatt around the table and finished with, "Jillian Raines, El's best friend and a VP where, darling? I'm so sorry, I forgot."

"Director of development. Seventh layer of Hell," Jilli returned.

"I'm familiar with that company. They do interesting work," Wyatt charmed as he shook her hand. He took the chair next to mine and put his arm around me as he whispered, "I couldn't refuse Karen when she offered me the ticket. Hope you don't mind."

"Of course not," I replied, and looked over to Karen. She smiled and gave me a wink.

Waiters placed our lunch in front of us and our champagne flutes were filled as the show began. Cameras would come by for reaction shots, aiming for Karen. I feared I was in the line of fire, too.

Karen took the stage to present midway through. While she gave her little speech, Wyatt leaned into me, wrapping his arm around my shoulders and whispered, "She's great. Her show is going to go through the roof."

It took me a while to notice that he had kept his arm around me. It took me a while to notice because it felt so right. It wasn't until I caught the camera lens that I understood no one else would consider the position remotely appropriate. Finally, his arm was removed as we broke into applause for the indie darling, Cassie Myers, who won Best Actress for her portrayal of a rebellious waitress/poet in *Rhyme Me, Dine Me*. Watching Karen hand Cassie the award was like witnessing a passing of the torch.

"She's the one," Jilli said during Cassie's speech.

"Who's the one what?" I inquired.

"Cassie. She's the one with the production deal. The one I've been meeting with. This is so huge. The film's going to be fast-tracked now." Jilli's smile spanned coast-to-coast.

Jilli not only had her revenge plan in action, she was looking to achieve her career goal of heading a production company. Jilli had heard that a young actress with a promising career was getting a company together and needed a partner to run it for her, but she didn't want anyone too old, or too "studio-fied", as she put it. Jilli was just right for the job. They'd had two meetings so far and were getting on like houses on fire. A saying you don't use in Malibu, by the way.

"Did you have fun?" Karen asked as I walked her to the waiting sedan. After the show, she had made her quick-but-polite goodbyes. She never stayed too long at events like these.

"You are a troublemaker, Karen Ellis," I chided.

"I prefer matchmaker. I thought he'd have a nice time. And that you would, too," she said as the driver held open the door for her.

"Sure you don't need me to come by tomorrow?" I asked every year if she wanted me to help her get ready for the Oscars, although, every year, I got the same answer.

"Kiddo, I have done so many of these award shows, it's no big whoop anymore. I've got it down to a science." This year, she added, "Kenny and Jeanine will be at the house early for hair and makeup, we'll have a light lunch delivered and a few glasses of champagne. Then, the car will bring up Howie and whisk us both away." Karen took Howie as her escort whenever she wasn't seriously dating anyone, which gave her the freedom to flirt with the winners and console the handsome losers. Karen knew how to have a good time.

"But," Karen said, poking her head out of the car, fortunate that the driver had keen reflexes and stopped the door he'd started to close. "I do have something I want to talk to you about on Monday. Remind me. I'll likely be sleep deprived, but we can go over it while I'm packing."

"Okay," I replied, my curiosity piqued. I watched her car drive away and headed back to the white-tarped palace. I had gotten lucky and gotten out of going to Vancouver. With all we had going on, it only made sense for me to stay. I kind of hoped that wasn't what she wanted to talk about; that she hadn't changed her mind and wanted me to go.

As I entered the after-party full of stragglers, I saw a tall, gorgeous blonde draped over Wyatt. Cassie and Jillian were having a tête-à-tête in the corner, but Jilli was keeping an ir-ritated eye on the blonde.

"It will be great to have you in New York, Wyatt. Charlotte is really looking forward to seeing you," the blonde said.

Wyatt saw me approaching and smiled a little too broadly. "Ellen Patterson, I'd like you to meet Constance Taylor," he said. And for the first time, I saw him flustered.

Constance stuck out her hand and forced a smile.

"How do you do?" she breathed. Her right hand had the consistency of an overcooked noodle, as though it had no bones. I pride myself on a firm handshake and her eyes bulged as I enclosed my grip.

"Nice to meet you," I smiled.

There was an awkward moment after our handshake broke and I turned my eyes to Wyatt.

"Um, ha," he uttered as he cleared his throat. "Constance, here, is a friend of mine, um, from New York. She's in town to meet Bob. She might be joining our New York office."

"If they play their cards right," Constance purred. Wyatt let out a noise, something resembling that of a donkey, but I believe it was meant to be a laugh.

"Yes," he said looking me in the eye. "Connie would doing PR for Karen's show."

Constance shot me a look. "So you're that Ellen," she said, somewhat accusingly.

"Possibly."

She leaned in and gave me a kiss on the cheek.

"I have heard so much about you. Karen's show would be my main project, if GFE closes my deal in a timely fashion," she said poking her bony elbow into Wyatt's ribs, causing him to wince. "It would be great working with Karen, though I'll miss my clients. I'm here today because I'm repping Anthony. He really should have won, don't you think? Hey, if you're free this week, I'd love to grab a drink or something. Can I get your information from Wyatt?"

"Sure," I said, somewhat taken aback by her change in demeanor.

"Wyatt and I are flying back to New York together Wednesday night. I was just telling him how much fun we'll have there, and he can see Charl—"

Constance was interrupted by Wyatt with, "I won't be there long enough for socializing. This trip is just to get the show settled." He took a step closer to me, as if to protect me from bullets or any other projectiles that might be launched.

"I thought you were going to be there for a week. That's what Charlotte said, anyway. I thought for sure we'd all get together for dinner over the weekend. Unless you and Charlotte wanted to catch up on your own."

I wanted to ask who this Charlotte was but didn't have the chance, though I did have suspicions.

"If Charlotte and her boyfriend want to have dinner, I'm sure she'll let you know. But I'll be busy working. Maybe we can grab a drink between my meetings, if you are so anxious to see me." Wyatt went big brother on her again, and shot me a smile. I couldn't muster a return.

Jillian came over to put an end to the awkwardness.

"El, I wanted you to meet Cassie."

Cassie, a petite brunette, shook my hand with a smile. "Karen totally rocks," she said. "I so hope she'll play my mom in my next movie. It's the first one I'm producing and it's going to be such a strong role. Total Oscar material." She was so earnest it was endearing.

Jilli nodded proudly. We gave the courtesy introductions so everyone met everyone, then Jilli's focus went back to Cassie.

"So, at the hotel on Tuesday?" Jilli asked.

"Yeah, for sure." Cassie gave Jilli her room info and said, "Later," to us.

"We ready?" I asked Jilli, perhaps a bit louder than necessary.

"Yeah," she said. "Let's grab the gift bags and go."

"You two are leaving?" Wyatt looked disappointed. "I thought we could go over to Ivy at the Shore for a gimlet or something. Or The Lobster for an early dinner?"

"Not me," Jilli said. "Gotta get home and get ready."

"Date?" I asked her.

"How'd you guess?" she quipped.

I smiled at Wyatt. "I'll see you later then."

I grabbed my swag and waved goodbye to Constance, who had made her way over to chat up the head of Film Independent.

"I can't coax you into a cocktail?" Wyatt asked. "This may be our last chance to get our ideas down before I fly to New York."

"Jilli's my ride. I should go with her. Honor the girl code," I explained.

"I can take you home." He was so persistent it was hard not to let a smile slip.

"Just fucking go with the poor guy before he drops to his knees and begs," Jilli blurted.

Wyatt's eyes went wide.

"You did meet my best friend, Jillian Raines, didn't you? She's kind of shy and quiet," I grinned. "But I do need to get home." If only to keep some integrity about me. He offered to walk us to Jilli's car.

Jilli walked ahead on a call while Wyatt and I trailed behind. I was glad he was quiet. If he asked me to go with him again, I would have said yes.

The air at the beach was clean and crisp. The sun hung low in the sky, accompanied by a few remaining clouds. Dedicated joggers and Rollerbladers kept rhythm on the boardwalk. Seagulls squawked and dove for remnants left by determined tourists. But, as I walked alongside Wyatt, I couldn't shake a certain pebble in my shoe.

"Can I ask who Charlotte is?"

"Charlotte is my ex-girlfriend."

"And she's in New York?"

"Yeah. With her new boyfriend. Connie knows her because she's best friends with my sister. Connie moved to New York the year before and, well, she and Charlotte became friends."

"That's nice," I deflected.

"If that's a euphemism for 'awkward', then, yes, it's nice." We arrived at the Rover. "See you when I get back from New York?" he asked.

I nodded and he put his lips to my cheek. He told Jilli that it was nice to meet her. She said likewise, and then there was nothing left to do but for me to get into the SUV and for him to walk away.

Walking in to Karen's dressing room, I found her standing in a sea of suitcases and well-organized piles of clothes as she gushed to me, "You'll never guess who I just got off the phone with."

"Who?" I asked handing her the mug of tea.

I took a long swig from my latte. It was the morning after the Academy Awards and I had made the mistake of going to a viewing party with Remi that ended up getting us into one of the after parties, and stayed out well past my bedtime. There were two additional shots of espresso in my cup to help prop my eyes open.

In spite of whatever time Karen made it home, she got up bright and early to read the press and see herself replayed on TiVo. Now she was on to packing for the film. Karen never waited 'til the last minute for anything, but I was about to discover her motivation to get a move on.

"Billy Harding," she sang. Her smile nearly reached her ears. I wished I could've returned her enthusiasm, but I knew Billy's reputation too well.

"Oh," I said, trying to sound interested. She was going to be working with Billy in Vancouver.

"He was so sweet to call. He said he saw me on the show last night and blah blah blah," which was Karen's abbreviation for a litany of compliments. "Then he told me that I was the only one he wanted in the role and how excited he was to be working with me. Isn't that charming?"

"Very," I lied.

Billy Harding was my nightmare. The quintessential Hollywood addict bad boy, when Billy wasn't on booze and coke, he was onto hookers and co-stars. Fresh out of rehab, and looking like a new man thanks to a team of personal trainers, hair transplants and a chemical peel, this film was Billy's comeback. And, at fifty-five, you don't get many more of those.

"He sounded so good," Karen continued holding up sweater after sweater, putting some into her case and others back on the shelf. "Seven months sober. He's past the crucial first hump," she assured.

One husband and two boyfriends of hers had standing reservations at Hazelden. Karen had expertise in both attracting and detoxing addicts.

"Isn't it twelve months they are supposed to wait until they get into a relationship?" I asked nonchalantly. Karen shot me a look. "What?" I asked innocently. "Isn't that what they said in that Sandra Bullock movie?"

"I'm talking about his career. He's doing really well, and that should be acknowledged."

"You're right. I'm sorry." Shit. She's going to fuck him. I just knew it. I decided to change the subject. "Now, we have that meeting set to discuss the first ten shows' themes while you are away. Production said you would have that Wednesday off, but do you want to hammer out your ideas first so I can send them to the team before the call?"

Karen tilted her head and gave a proud smile. "My producer," she beamed.

"Stop it," I said, rolling my eyes. "Seriously, I think that would make the call more efficient. I know how you hate being on the phone too long."

"Kiddo, that's why I have you. Yes, we will do the list. Yes, you should send it to them before. But, no, after we go over the list, I'm done. I have a movie to do. And since that will be my day off, I'm taking it off and leaving the rest to you." She stopped for a moment and looked at me. "You know, you were supposed to remind me that I had something to talk to you about," Karen said as she held up a skirt in front of her then tossed it in the 'to go' pile.

"That's right. I totally spaced. What's on your mind?"

"Well, I've been thinking. How about you and I starting a production company for this venture? We could produce other stuff as well. I mean, I can't just completely quit film. That would be fucking insane."

I choked on my latte. As soon as I was able to speak I said, "Wow, Karen. Are you serious? You want me to be…"

"My producing partner? Yes, kiddo, I do. I've always known how lucky I am to have you on my team. And this isn't completely altruistic. You have an eye for material. You know all the players, have good relationships and you are ready for this. It's a business move, El, not charity. And I think it would be fun. Together we could do some great stuff. What do you say?"

"Yes. Yes! That would be fantastic." I was grinning so broadly, I thought my mouth might rip.

"I've even thought of a name. How about KEEP Productions? That's our initials put together. Karen Ellis and Ellen Patterson. K-E-E-P. Kind of clever, don't you think?" Karen queried, giving me a nudge.

"Very," I beamed and gave Karen a tight hug. She squeezed back.

"I'll have Howie and the lawyers get on it. Do you have an attorney yet? I hope so. You need one. You're in the bigs now, kid." She gave me a nod and continued with her packing. "As soon as we know where we're going to be living, we'll hire your replacement. Honestly, you'd think they'd give us an answer by now."

"Wyatt's talking to them about doing it in L.A.," I said without thinking. "Um…well…I think that's what he mentioned." On a long call we had before the Oscars aired.

"You two are working well together," she said, looking at me slyly.

"Yes, but…" I started.

"Don't worry, El. You're a smart girl. You'll handle this right. And do keep me posted on the outcome. I don't really care where the show goes at this point. I just want to know. And it seems my girl has the inside track," she finished with a smirk.

I knew I must've been three shades of red as Karen turned back to look at which dresses she might take. It was customary for her to take four bags for a two-week trip. I took a deep breath hoping to inhale my composure. Jilli did give me the name of an attorney she used to date. I had spoken with him on the phone once, but had delayed setting up a face-to-face. Meeting with a lawyer was always something to dread. But now, I couldn't wait to talk deal points and backend and…*Oh, my God! I'm going to be a real producer!* I screamed in my head. Ideas raced through my mind. A list of scripts in turnaround we might option. Writers I wanted to meet. Visions of Karen and me in meetings, on set…This was it. Really it! My life had arrived. A little tattered from the delays in shipping, but it was here.

I started to call Jilli to tell her the news, but then stopped myself and put down the phone. The talk show was one thing, but KEEP was exactly what she wanted for herself. And if things didn't work out with Cassie like she'd hoped, it would be salt in a deep wound.

Once again, I hid my good news rather than announced it. Suddenly, instead of being the girl who would send out a group email when I found a good jeans sale or a cupcake worth noting, I was a woman keeping everything on the Q.T.

For the first time in my life, I had secrets, and they weren't even juicy or shameful. I couldn't understand why I had gone mute, unable to distinguish it as either a form of madness or maturity. But there was one thing certain: There would be no way I would turn down New York if that's where the show would go.

Sadly, I had another replacement to find rather than my own. Ruth's mother fell ill and Ruth had to go to San Antonio to take care of her, not sure when or if she would return. I helped Ruth create a bible for her replacement, since she couldn't stay to train. Karen offered to keep the door open for her here, or in New York. We just hoped that Ruth's mother would get better.

Ruth's departure also meant no one to watch Sally while Karen was on location. I called in my film school bestie, Gabe, to housesit.

"Just stay out of her closet," I jokingly warned. "I don't want to see her smalls on Perez Hilton."

"Please, El. I'm not that much of a 'mo."

Gabe was in the Masters program while I worked on my BFA, but we found ourselves in many of the same classes and bonded quickly. A tall, handsome, Texas-bred Southern gentlemen, many of our classmates assumed we were a couple, but I was missing a vital part of anatomy to make that relationship possible.

Gabe worked as a freelance editor cutting other people's films while he pieced together a documentary on his favorite actress, Tallulah Bankhead. He just got back from doing "research" in London and needed some extra cash.

I told him the latest, including the KEEP news, as long as he promised to keep it all a secret. Being the dear friend that he is, he screamed, "This is the greatest fucking news ever! Can I stay with you in New York? I have research to do there, too."

Why I could tell Gabe so easily but not Jilli or the rest of the posse didn't make much sense. I had always enjoyed and celebrated their successes, and I knew they would do the same for me. Maybe it was the timing. Mine seemed to be off. I hoped the change to Daylight Savings would sort that out. Longer days would actually be a blessing.

I never thought I'd hear myself say that.

Chapter Six

How is it possible for me to be late to a brunch five minutes from my home? That has to be some sort of special skill.

"Where are you?!? We lied and said that you were in the bathroom so we could get seated on the patio. They're growing suspicious. Hurry, hurry, hurry!" It was the girls on Jilli's speakerphone shouting and laughing. I looked at my dashboard clock. It was ten-fifty-eight. I was on time. Ish. But how the did they all get there early? That never happens. Especially with Jilli coming from the other side of the world.

"I'm nearly there," I promised.

All I got back was a chorus of "hurryhurryhurry," before they hung up.

With Karen safely on the plane to Canada, Gabe fully trained on dog duty and how to navigate the entertainment system without screwing up the settings, and me with a slew of maids to interview on Monday, I took Sunday to meet with the girls. As much as I adored them, what I really wanted to do that morning was sleep. Hibernate. Hide. It was my last free weekend before Tim returned home, and I had to fortify myself for that.

I entered the restaurant and heard the laughter of my friends before I saw them. They were beautiful, animated, and obviously on their second mimosa.

The girls were jovial. Except for Jilli. She was sitting behind dark glasses with a drink in her hand and a scowl on her face. I could feel her bad mood before I got to the table. I gave my hellos and hugs, and took the empty seat next to Jilli. Cautiously, I leaned over to give her an embrace. She returned a light pat on my back. Her chill equaled that of the breeze. I pulled my Vince around me tighter. Karen is endlessly generous with her hand-me-downs, and I had worn this shawl-neck to near threads.

Jilli was not a morning person, not by a long shot, but rarely did I get the business end of her prickly side. I brushed off her mood easily, figuring she would soon thaw on her own. I was ready for a drink and, being wonderful friends, they had one waiting for me. I find noon to be a more respectable time to imbibe at brunch, but the girls made eleven seem perfectly acceptable.

"Cheers, ladies," I said. We merrily clinked glasses. The pulp of the fresh-squeezed juice and the booze's bubbles tickled my throat. I had to take a second swig to calm it.

The waitress zipped over ready to take our orders before I could even open my menu.

"I'll have another," Jilli said, holding up her glass before the waitress or anyone else had a chance to speak. "As a matter of fact, just bring another round. We'll order the food when you get back."

The waitress smiled at Jilli and disappeared.

"Cell phones are off, right?" Remi asked. Everyone nodded in return. I quickly reached for mine and set it to vibrate. The next two hours were sacred time and we would not allow disruptions. It's just a shame the rest of the diners did not feel the same. The annoying omnipresent cellphonic cacophony of Los Angeles had made its way to Venice and the Rose Café. The man behind Jilli was having breakfast alone but conversed with a friend on his earpiece, giving him the appearance of talking to himself, and talking rather loudly. So loudly, in fact, we were treated to every lascivious detail about his conquest the previous evening. Jilli had heard enough.

"Dude, seriously. None of us want to hear how you banged her sideways against the wall, okay? It's an image we can all do without, especially at breakfast. So, keep it down, will you?" Jilli directed.

The dude was about to give a macho reply, but he examined her posture, and the pleading eyes of the rest of us, and decided against it. He told his friend he'd call him back and asked for the check.

Jilli sat back with a self-satisfied smile. The rest of us breathed a sigh of relief, especially when the waitress appeared and doled out our drinks. We gave our requests for overpriced pancakes and egg whites, then settled into conversation. I took solace in knowing that the last thing we would talk about was work. Something I was happy to keep avoiding.

"I'm being haunted by ghosts of dicks past," Remi said in a loud whisper, hunkering toward the table so all of us could hear, but the rest of the patronage would be spared. "It's like every guy I've dated has decided to call. I should really change my phone number. And email. Maybe sage my bedroom. Do you suppose getting a new mattress would help?"

"Well, at least you're being haunted," Claudia chimed in. "When I end an affair, they stay gone. And I haven't had it in so long I'm getting carpel-tunnel in my right hand. Do you think I can still get that covered under Worker's Comp?"

The lovely thing about this group of friends is that they were not industry-obsessed. We had other things to talk about: books, music, gallery exhibits, parties, gossip, diets, sample sales, relationships, sex. Obviously. We'd get around to heavier topics. Eventually.

"Are we all going to Vicki's wedding shower?" Teresa asked.

"I think we have to," Emily said.

"It's going to be like passing a traffic accident. You don't really want to see it, but you can't help craning your neck for a good view," Claudia noted.

Remi rolled her eyes. "Do you have any idea how much they are paying for this little get-together? I'm going just to eat and drink my way through what Vicki owes me in unpaid dinners and unreturned sweaters. Puck himself is catering. I won't eat for at least a day before. Nothing solid anyway."

Ah, sweet revenge.

"You couldn't pay me to go," Jilli responded.

"You have to go, Jilli. I'm going to need your help deflecting the bullets," I pleaded.

Vicki had asked me to be a bridesmaid and I turned her down. She was sort of on the fringe of our group back in the day. We worked at the same studio and she tried hard to be a part of our odd little clique but was a square peg to our well-rounded set.

Vicki worked as a receptionist at the studio while she searched for her big break, or at least some juicy gossip. She was the one who called in sick on the day I met Jon Tatum. Vicki truly resented that I "stole" her job. And later resented the payout I got from it.

Vicki went on to be a personal assistant to a retired mogul who was a heavy hitter in the philanthropic circle. From there, with the connections she made, she became a professional organizer, and had a booming business. I always thought Vicki had missed her calling. She was total agent material, which, sadly, is not exactly a compliment.

Vicki's true objective wasn't climbing up the professional ladder. She wanted to marry well. Her determination was unwavering and is about to pay off. Last spring, she got engaged to über-manager/producer Llewellyn Johns after organizing the dissolution of marital assets when his first marriage came to an end. Coordinating both moves and the estate sale of the items neither or both wanted, Vicki and Llewellyn found they were a match. She promptly folded her business and took up residence with him in the Palisades.

I was surprised that she had asked me to be in her wedding party. She has her connections, but friends were few and far between. I did wish her the best, always hopeful that someone will find a happy ending in this town—outside of a massage parlor or romantic-comedy. The unfortunate thing was Vicki's last name was Hasser, and she intended to hyphenate.

While we would celebrate Vicki's achievement, or at least have a free meal on her soon-to-be hubby, we would not be joining the happy couple in Jackson Hole as they exchanged vows on some rented ranch. As Jilli so eloquently put it, "If I wanted to spend four days on Brokeback Mountain, I'd queue it on Netflix." This alluded not only to the scenery at the nuptials, but the persistent rumors that Llewellyn enjoyed being fellated by young male actors every now and again. Vicki's insistence that we refer to him as Lew did little to butch up his image.

We continued debating what gift from Vicki's pretentious registry to go in on together. I felt confident that I could skip talking about the talk show altogether and steer my friends' focus on the latest lovers, scandals and who would share what dessert. The conversation easily swayed from Vicki to the pros and cons of colonics, overdue vacations and the best new place for a mani-pedi when something truly awful happened. Anise.

"Oh, my God, El. Drinks! We must have drinks! Celebrate this great news!" she sang as she slinked toward our table. "Why didn't you tell me about your producer-ship with Karen? I had to hear about it from Bev."

I winced as she went in to hug me and caught Jilli rolling her eyes.

I did the polite thing and introduced her to the girls. She pointed out the two friends she was with, mentioning, "Elaine there is a stylist. Great discounts and first dibs at sample sales. You two should meet, El. But we really do need to celebrate. Call me and we'll go someplace fabulous…on me, and, well, Bev, too. I can expense you now!" She then blew kisses—something I hadn't seen performed live by anyone older than two—and left.

Merde. It was starting. The grand suckupification that occurs when an assistant makes an ascent. Your name is now classified in other assistants' contacts with an asterisk. This denotes you are worthy of any favors, asked or unasked. You are put on better guest-lists in hopes that you will remember the do-gooder kindly and one day return the favor, or at least their phone call. After all, you were once one of them.

You are also added to the holiday gift lists, if you weren't there already. News of your new position will filter through to the retail industry where you'll be pandered to by sales clerks in all the top shops—because catapulted assistants rarely keep their wits or their new income stratum about them.

The thought of this made me itch. Anise's display was also rash-inducing, but I shook it off. No matter how much smoke might be blown up my posterior, there would be little chance of my head inflating beyond my hat size. First, I'm not very social with other assistants. They've become increasingly younger as my tenure's endured and drinking all night at the club *du moment* was no longer my cup of coffee. Exposure to any of their flattery would be as accidental as Anise's. Second, and more importantly, I was lucky to have five friends who would easily keep reality about me.

"Fucking Fennel couldn't keep her trap shut, huh?" Jilli

deadpanned. Jilli couldn't stand Anise after having to deal with her and Bev on a film last year. Jilli refused to call her by name, instead choosing similarly flavored food.

"Don't worry, I told everyone, anyway," Claudia beamed. She looked at me with expectant eyes. Her brown leather blazer toughened her narrow frame. Her caramel colored curls were full and buoyant in the light breeze. She was donning tortoise-framed glasses, which made her look serious and severe until you reached her smile. Even working for that battle-axe boss of hers had not diminished Claude's shine.

Claudia had called me the week after the GFE meeting occurred. "Tell me I can have your job," she groaned into her cell phone. "Are the rumors true?"

She was calling from work but didn't want her boss to see her phone line lit up. Claudia is employed by one of the more horrible producers in Hollywood, Donna Hersh. Most of Donna's assistants lasted less than forty-five days. Claudia has been there six months, and the signs of wear were showing.

"What rumors?" I asked, trying to play dumb. Only Jilli knew at that time, and I was certain she wouldn't tell.

"Well, word is you are going to be a producer on Karen's new show. It's all over town."

"I highly doubt that anything to do with me is all over town." I hated being fodder on the grapevine. I was realizing I still had a severe case of PTSD—Post-Tatum Scandal Disorder.

"When an assistant goes from zero to producer, it spreads faster than wildfire or herpes in this town. You know that," she quipped. "Can I have your gig when you go? I need to work for someone nice for a change."

Poor Claude had an amazing knack for going from one asshole boss to another and found herself stuck in a perpetual assistant position, never really moving up the ladder in spite of all the promises she was given if she stuck it out. And she was unsure of how to get off that nightmare carousel.

"Nothing is final yet. You know how these things go." I had no plans to count chickens before they hatched.

"Fine, be that way."

I asked her to keep quiet and that I would tell everyone at

once next time we all got together. So much for that. I was being served up as gossip á la mode.

"It's spectacular news," Remi cheered, holding up her mimosa in my honor. Her Spanish eyes flashed as she smiled. Her long, black, wavy hair was disciplined into a knot at the nape of her neck, which was wrapped in the warmth of a cream cashmere scarf. She looked as though she belonged on the deck of a boat. She was very Kennedy-esque in spite of her Castilian roots. "We were waiting to see if you'd say something, and—"

"True to form, you didn't," Teresa interjected.

"Glad I did, though. Don't be mad," Claudia pleaded.

"I'm not mad," I assured.

"Good news is meant to be shared," said Emily.

"I know. I'm sorry I didn't tell you. I'm still getting used to the idea," I admitted.

"Bio and a good headshot. You have to get those done, like immediately," Teresa ordered. "Let me know if you need any help with that." Tess, never ever Teri, with her strawberry blonde hair and blue eyes, reminded me of a spring nymph. She covered herself religiously in Marc Jacobs, serving as our resident clotheshorse and fashion plate.

"I just want your job. Please, just give me your job," Claudia begged, squeezing my hand.

"Don't let the stress get to you, El. I don't want you working yourself into an early rehab," Emily smiled before popping a berry from her fruit bowl breakfast into her mouth. She had the grace, poise and posture of a ballerina—thanks to the endless hours of Pilates and never touching an animal product—and the wiry blonde hair of a disco goddess. She glowed without a stitch of makeup. But I'd like to think her fuchsia sweater helped today.

Jilli smiled but remained uncharacteristically quiet. I suspected a hangover but remembered that Cassie had cancelled her last meeting with Jilli, and I hadn't heard about a rescheduling. Perhaps this group adulation stung a bit. I just wasn't prepared for her to bite back.

"Tell them the best part," Jilli commanded before finishing her fourth mimosa by my count.

Everyone looked at me as I searched for the better end of this deal. Nothing came to mind but KEEP, which I was definitely not going to share under the current circumstances, so I gave a weak smile and a shrug.

"Go on," Jilli challenged. "Tell them the rest."

"Oh," I said, figuring I had finally copped on to her sarcasm. "The show might happen in New York."

The girls twittered their hopes that I wouldn't have to move, along with supportive assertions on how exciting New York could be. Claudia seemed less interested in my old job.

Jilli smirked to herself, then corrected, "No. Tell them about Wyatt."

It was a slap in the face, my best friend betraying me with such abandon.

"Does she mean Wyatt Knight?" Tess asked.

"Used to be an agent?" Remi continued.

"Now he's at GFE. That's right. I saw his photo in *Hollywood Reporter*. Some premiere party or charity thing. Way hot," Claudia added.

"Am I that far out of the loop?" Emily asked.

"You should've never stopped reading the trades," Remi chided. "He used to date that hot broad entertainment attorney. Shannon something."

"Charlotte Anderson," Emily blurted, like the winning answer to *Who Wants To Be A Millionaire*. We all looked at her with amazement. "What?" she continued. "She was a client of mine until she moved back East last year."

I was somewhat perturbed by the fact my friends knew so much about Wyatt. Had I known, I would have called them before that first dinner.

"So, what about Wyatt?" Tess queried. Then, as if a light bulb had gone off, she leaned in and whispered, "Oh, shit, did you and Tim break up because you might move? Are you sleeping Wyatt?"

"No!" I defended.

"Not yet," Jilli laughed. I shot her a look, hurt and completely pissed off by her cruelty.

"Details!" my friends squealed in unison, while Jilli sucked what was left out of her glass.

"There's nothing to say. We had dinner a couple of weeks ago. And Karen invited him to the Spirit Awards. That's all. Are we going to order dessert? Anyone want to share?" My attempt to change the subject flopped.

"That's who was hanging all over you on IFC," Emily stated.

"I only saw his back and assumed it was…oh, what's his name…your friend, the mayor of The Abbey…" Remi stammered.

"Gabe," Claudia said rolling her eyes.

"Looked very chummy," Tess said, confirming my concern. Tess missed being at the awards. She was in London on a press junket for a client's film, but she had the show TiVo'd.

"I'll say," said Jilli.

"Okay, enough of this. Might as well dish it, if that's the only way we can get Ellen to open up. Relationship reports, ladies," commanded Remi. She raised her hand to start it off. "Seeing three guys. All of them younger, two of them actors, none of them serious. And they are all a little too in touch with their feminine side, you know? One asked me to join him for a pedi."

"Is the metrosexual thing still happening?" Emily asked. "I thought that was over."

"There's no such thing as metro. Tell him to suck a dick already and get it over with," Claudia interjected. "Said the miserable one failing with online dating."

Claudia turned to Emily causing the accounts to go around the table in a clockwise manner, ending with me at high noon.

"Happy. Talking about moving in together. Ron thinks that's the important next step, but I don't want to play house. Besides, I'm looking to buy a house. Ron already owns so that makes the situation even stickier. But, we're happy." Emily smiled then turned to Tess.

"Still dating Dane, going on month seven. Absolutely losing interest. His children are total brats. Complete turn off." Tess turned to Jilli.

"Just hanging out and having fun." Jilli avoided these

reports. Whether she was hot and heavy with someone or not, she always gave the same reply.

"Can we please have the full scoop for once, Raines?" Tess pushed. "I mean, this pat answer is horseshit. We are friends, right?"

"Fine," Jilli said with a sigh. "If you really want to hear it, I'm having an affair with a married man."

"Jilli, no," Remi said with concern not judgment.

"Yes. And why not? Men are lying, cheating bastards, anyway. Might as well be what the bastards are lying and cheating about."

"He won't leave his wife for you, you know," Emily cautioned.

Jilli winced. "I wouldn't want him to. Look, it's just sex. I don't have time for a relationship and this is working for me just fine. I think of him as a walking, talking dildo."

The girls looked at each other, deciding silently that rationalizing with Jillian would be fruitless.

What Jilli wasn't mentioning was the married man was Selma's husband and that this was all part of a plan. This was part of getting back for getting screwed over. Jilli took what Selma did as a personal hit instead of a professional attack. Sleeping with Selma's husband was about as personal as you could get.

The girls reminded Jilli to tread with caution, and then their eyes settled upon me.

"Do I really have to?"

They nodded like Bobbleheads. Jilli motioned to the waitress for another round of drinks; everyone but Jilli and me changed their orders to straight OJ. I took a sip from my glass and brought them up to speed as fast as I could about Wyatt and Tim. When I finished, it was quiet except for a cell phone ringing in the distance.

Remi and Tess exchanged glances. Claudia folded her napkin.

"Well, I think this is exciting," Emily cheered. The rest of the group, slack-jawed over my newsflash, looked at her with consternation. "What? It is," she defended. "Everything is open for you, El. Love, career, life. Wow." She finished with a heartfelt smile and I had to laugh.

"Thanks, Emily," I replied.

I heard Jilli mutter, "Good Christ," under her breath before downing mimosa number five.

I looked around at my friends, so beautiful and stylish, and successful-ish. We all worked hard and wanted so much. Up until this moment, I had been the stable one, in both my job and relationship being the longest held and both seemingly going well. I could see that my news affected a few of them.

In all honesty, we were all struggling with our adulthoods on one level or another. Only two others had committed relationships, and those weren't without their troubles. We all rented, though Tim was my landlord; Emily was determined to buy real estate whether the market was set to crash again or not. My friends leased, never bought, their behemoth SUVs—Jilli had the Range Rover, Remi a Land Rover; Teresa had a black version of Wyatt's X5; Claudia, a Cherokee, and Emily a hybrid Lexus. It looked like a military operation was going down whenever they all parked together. I never got why so many women in L.A. wanted to drive such large vehicles, and I'm the size queen of the group. I'm only two months away from owning the Jetta outright, and look forward to that day when the payment goes away.

My friends and I had exited our twenties with none of us having been married or even engaged. We weren't really tied down to anyone or anything, even though we attempted to anchor ourselves in some way—mainly to each other. It made for a confusing blend of liberation and trepidation. And my news was adding to that bewilderment.

Our situation was not atypical in Los Angeles. Women here seem to be more active in seeking out Botox than a boyfriend, a promotion rather than a proposal, a home to own rather than a husband to belong to, a Chihuahua to carry about instead of a child. We hunted our next job, project or client, but not love. We wanted that to come to us. Like it did for Cinderella, Snow White, Sleeping Beauty or Molly Ringwald in a John Hughes movie. We didn't want to have to work for it because we had to work so hard for everything else. We wanted love to simply *happen*. Now that we were in our thirties, it was a little late to finally realize fairytales and *Sixteen Candles* had really fucked us up.

For some reason, we couldn't admit aloud that what we really wanted—more than a closet full of Choos, a house in the Hills, a raise or promotion—was love. True and deep. Just like John Hughes showed us it could be. After an unhappy ending—and a bottle of wine—the honesty would flow. The truth always comes out, at the end of the day. Especially after a shitty one.

Everything my friends had accomplished would gladly be given up for a man who was good and loving and wanted to take care of them. Someone they could relax with, be themselves with, rely on. But the pursuit of that prize was not as easy to accomplish as the quest for the next marker of success or status. A guy could always be found to accompany you to the premiere, attend the party, you could find one to dine with, to sleep with, but not always one you'd like to wake up next to.

Sadly, Mr. Right Now would have to serve as sufficient until the charming prince arrived. By this point, we were out of the practice of trusting and believing something really good was waiting out there for us. Eventually, the optimism fades.

I admit that I felt lucky, relieved even, that I didn't have to go through the dating gamut my friends suffered. "If I could just find a guy like Tim," they would say, and I'll admit that made me feel proud. I had something others yearned for. And, maybe that's why I clung on to it as long as I had. But now they saw that I was unsure about it. When exactly does pride goeth?

In order to change the subject, I mentioned dessert again. No one was interested, but it did get the conversation to shift, this time to gossip on former co-workers and the opening of a new hot spot owned by one of Tess' clients that she would get us on the list for. We pretended that we would all meet there for a night together, but knew the doors would be shuttered before we would be able to coordinate our schedules. And then it was time to go. We settled the check, handing the poor waitress six platinum cards with which to divide the bill. We made our goodbyes at the table.

"You aren't letting her drive, are you?" Remi whispered to me when we hugged.

"No. I'll sort her out."

"Good," Tess added as we embraced.

"I gotta pee," Jilli declared as she grabbed her purse.

In the bathroom, I convinced Jilli that I could not survive without a boardwalk churro and I needed her to accompany me. It was the only ruse I could think of to keep her from getting in her Rover. One could not be direct with Jillian Raines when she was in such a mood and alcohol was added. She wasn't irresponsible, just acutely obstinate. I had to prey on her need to be needed, and constant craving for pastry.

Jilli and I made idle chitchat on our walk over Rose Avenue to the ocean, trashing one-note actresses and doughy actors. I was still hurt and a bit angry at her behavior, but I could feel her regret. Jilli was not someone I could remain upset with. I knew her too well, and she me.

I wanted to ask her about how things were with Cassie but thought better, in case it had all gone pear-shaped. Once we had the comfort of that warm, sugar-coated stick, we would say the things needing to be said. Until then, we were slowly sobered by the cool air. Our high-heeled boots stomped the pavement, giving a rhythmic beat to our journey. She passed her arm through mine and linked our elbows together.

"I can't wait for spring," she said.

"Me, either," I smiled. I did love my friend, no matter what a bitch she could be.

We took up residence in an upscale ice cream parlor to get some overpriced-yet-organic coffee.

"I'm sorry," Jilli said softly as she stirred her almond-milk latte.

"What's going on, J? What brought on the mood?"

"Andy," she said softly. Andy is Selma's husband. He's also president of Picture Motion Films, the West Coast's "independent" mega studio. No film at Picture Motion had a budget over ten million, and they've all brought in a profit of no less than fifty million. He was in his forties, successful and fit, but his clever humor made him more attractive than his looks alone.

"What happened?" I asked.

"He told me he's in love with me, and he's going to ask Selma for a divorce."

"And that's not what you wanted?"

"Hell, no! I wanted her to find out, absolutely. I would relish the poetry of having her know I was fucking her husband because she fucked me over. But I did not want him to leave her. Not for me, anyway."

I stared at her for a moment and it clicked. "You've fallen for him, haven't you?" Jilli didn't say a word, but I knew I had hit it. "Oh, Jilli. They don't have kids, do they?"

"Do you really think I would plot something like this if children were involved? No, they don't have kids. She's too toxic to house a viable egg."

Selma now runs a division of Galaxy Studios, ironically the family film and animation banner.

"What are you going to do?" I asked, concerned for my friend's heart and career.

"End it. What else can I do?"

"If you love him, you might want to stay with him."

"He cheated with me, El. He'd cheat on me. Isn't that how it goes? It's too complicated, anyway. It's got to end."

"I'm sorry, Jilli. I really am."

"Don't be, I did it to myself. And I'm sorry for being such an asshole this morning. I didn't mean to take it out on you. But he dropped the 'I love you' bomb on me right before I left."

"It's okay. I can handle it."

You can't have friendships this long and this real without the occasional feather ruffling. There are times when you need to take things out on the ones you love. It's not exactly the most grownup way to handle stuff, but sometimes pushing a friend away is the only way you're able to reach out for support.

Jilli and I took our time walking back. She was completely sobered up, not only from brunch, but her affair. She told me that she and Cassie were meeting the next day. Cassie had gotten the stomach flu and needed to recover so they wouldn't have to hold the meeting with the bathroom door between them. Jilli was excited and scared, and I knew exactly how she felt. Too much coming at you at once takes all the fun out of it. I wished her luck for the meeting, for ending it with Andy, and gave her a long hug before parting.

"I love you, Jilli," I said as I embraced her.

She tightened her squeeze. "I don't know what I'd do without you, El."

Chapter Seven

When you fall in love, you hope that will be it. You're done. You found your One and "happily ever after" is just around the corner. Not in L.A.

In L.A., first comes love, then comes living together, then comes the struggle to get your career to where you want it to be before you can even think of engagement or marriage. Or maybe that's just Tim and me. Either way, it's annoying that there's always a delay. Traffic or a guild strike or mudslides on PCH; there's always something getting in the way here. Right now, it's a pair of fake tits the size of soccer balls trying to bump their way in front of me at Starbucks. Usually boobs like that are found at Coffee Bean or Peet's. They must have gotten lost. Or confused. It should all be much easier than this. Much easier. I'm sure the owner of those soccer balls finds it easy.

"Shit," I shouted as I slammed on the brakes to miss the hatchback-something-or-other that stopped short to avoid being crushed by a bus. The day was off to a shit start altogether. Tim was coming home. I can't say I was too happy about it. First, having to set the alarm to wake up early on a Saturday morning, and now having two dollars of my five-dollar latte spill on the floor. At least I was in Tim's Cherokee. I didn't want to risk damage to the Jetta. Driving through LAX is like playing bumper cars. You'll see at least two fender-benders on your way to get-ting where you need to be. As long as you aren't in one, you're a winner. The Cherokee was a semi-Urban Assault Vehicle and made people think twice before cutting me off. And, since I was fetching him, it was only fair that any dent incurred should belong to his vehicle. While he wouldn't be happy about the mess, the coffee spill was better than a collision.

I made it around to the American terminal without further incident and, for once, when I pulled into the passenger pick-up, Tim was there ready and waiting, looking as though he was posing for J. Crew. His sandy blonde hair, blue-gray eyes and tan would let you believe he was from L.A., but he's an East Coast boy, just like most of his friends here. You can tell when he says my last name. It's not Patterson, but *Paddahsun.* He smiled broadly when he saw me pull up. I smiled back. It felt good to see him. And it felt good to feel that.

With Wyatt away and Tim back home, I could focus on my personal life without distraction or escape. And see if I could salvage it. Wyatt was still in New York. His trip was extended another week and I wondered if he would make a point to see Charlotte, with or without her boyfriend. I shouldn't care, considering my boyfriend was now sitting next to me, but I couldn't help but be curious.

I had tried to be good. Wyatt and I only exchanged a few (dozen) emails since our parking lot goodbye, and two phone calls, but we succeeded in keeping it professional. Mostly.

Wyatt was the closest I'd come to cheating on Tim. And it was eating at me. Admitting all of it to my friends had made it too real. Remorse over my crush was like a slow tsunami. The closer to Tim's homecoming, the worse I felt.

I started calling around, in a co-dependent state, to find someone to spend money with. Retail therapy is cliché, but it's also a happy distraction. Jilli couldn't; she was bogged with work and meeting with Cassie on the sly. Things there seemed to be back on track.

"I can't complain," Jilli said. "She's not bad for an actress. And the script she's optioned is great. Karen should consider it. The role is Oscar bait."

Jilli sounded much better. But, we weren't talking about Andy. That was a subject she didn't want to discuss.

Tess came to the retail rescue. When I explained my angst, she offered to join me at Neiman's after work. I used my sister's impending wedding as an excuse to shop. It was three months away—Gwen had to be a June bride—but a dress for that seemed like an item I could rationalize a splurge on.

"Aren't you going to be wearing a bridesmaid's uniform?" Tess asked in the dressing room.

"During the ceremony. Not a moment after. That was the deal I struck when I saw the monstrosity she selected," I explained.

After the overspend, I told Tess about my existential crisis at Karen's and how I had been trying to figure it all out since then, waffling between staying with Tim and wanting to leave, now in a panic with his return looming.

"I still love Tim, but I'm not sure what that means anymore," I admitted.

"Of course you still love your boyfriend, you idiot," Tess chided. "You wouldn't be with him if you didn't love him."

We were sipping martinis and nibbling on appetizers in the upstairs bar. Tess had demanded a drink after she helped me find the perfect dress: blush-colored, sleeveless frock with an empire-waist and flowy, flirty skirt that landed below the knee. The daringly plunging neckline gave a contrast to the demure silhouette. It was soft and feminine and something I would wear again. For $700, I had damn well better.

"If you weren't happy with Tim, you would've left him a long time ago. You know that," Tess continued.

"I suppose," I muttered.

"Look, El. I have to say that I don't have all that much sympathy for you here."

I couldn't believe my friend said that. Jilli maybe, but not Tess. "What do you mean?"

"You don't even know how good you got it. You have this gorgeous boyfriend you live with, totally committed for how long now? You have a life with him, El. Full of things like vacations and sailing, and weekends with friends. It may not be glamorous, but it's consistent. He loves you so much, but you don't see it because he hasn't proposed yet."

"I know he loves me," I defended.

"Do you? Do you know what the rest of us have to go through just to find a guy we wouldn't mind having breakfast with, in public? You saw how long it took me to find Dane, and that's a package deal. Not only do I get his kids but his bitter ex-wife and the mood swings that go with it. What about poor Claudia? When was her last relationship? Seriously, El, you would be an idiot if you left Tim for another guy."

"I'm not that dumb, Teresa. I wouldn't leave Tim for Wyatt. I would go because I'm not happy."

"There," she said, pointing at me, almost forgetting to swallow her drink. "That's just it, El. You should be happy. You've got what every woman in L.A. wants. Hot guy, cool job and fabulous friends," she said, giving herself a Vanna White with her hands. "Do you get that?"

"That you are fabulous? Yes, Tess, I do," I grinned.

"Not what I meant, but thank you. You have to get happy. Because if you aren't happy now, being single isn't going to make it all better. It's better to be unhappy in a couple than unhappy and alone. Trust me."

I knew things weren't going so well with Dane, but I didn't expect a lecture like this.

"And those are my options? Unhappy and unhappy?" I snarked back.

"If you don't figure things out, then, yeah."

Figure things out? Wasn't that exactly what I had been trying to do? It's not like I had the luxury of going off to a mountaintop to meditate like Buddha until the answer came. Nothing would please me more than to take a moment to ponder my future and the meaning of life, but I couldn't even make it to the bathroom without a disruption. Shakyamuni didn't have the burden of an iPhone on overload. Even my home phone was ringing off the hook. I was just spent. Absolutely shattered. And now, Tim was back.

I did tell Tim that I had some news to share when he got home. And he was okay with waiting to hear it. I wasn't exactly comforted by the absence of his curiosity. I could be announcing a need for a drastic surgery or an affair. Hello? Yet his lack of need-to-know had made getting on with things less complicated. The contracts had come in. And I still had to find someone to replace Ruth.

"Glad to see you tidied up the place for me," Tim said when we walked in the door.

The jerk. Granted, there were piles of unsorted mail, magazines and scripts lying about. Some dishes resided in the sink. A collection of coats and sweaters were displayed over the dining chairs, and a few pairs of shoes were on the floor. Okay, the place was a little disheveled; but rather than garner criticism, it should've illustrated the kind of week I had.

"The maid quit," I retorted.

"Huh?" He never got my sarcasm.

Typically, I'm a neat girl—fastidious bordering on anal— but by the time I got home from my long days of trying to be an assistant and a producer, and interviewing maids, I just didn't have the energy to be one myself. Unlike Tim, I have always been a big proponent of having a housecleaner; he was too cheap to hire one, "Since we are never home anyway." Meaning him, mostly—leaving me to vacuum, dust and lead with the laundry.

Instead of coming to my own defense, I just blew it off with, "Are you hungry?"

Tim walked over and wrapped his arms around me. "I'm starved," he exhaled into my ear and then kissed me deep and long. His broad shoulders land just over mine. We fit well that way. He kissed my forehead and cheek and pulled down my turtleneck. He ran his tongue lightly up my neck. Chills ran down my spine. "I missed you, babe," he said, holding my face in his hands, locking my eyes with his.

"I missed you, too," I said before he pulled his mouth to mine. And it wasn't a lie or even an exaggeration. This was the Tim I missed. The Tim hungry for me. Passionate for me, like he was in the beginning. We stopped kissing long enough for him to pull off my sweater, and me to pull off his.

"You aren't wearing a bra," he smiled.

I couldn't find one in my semi-asleep state that morning. The night before, Gabe and I went to a gallery opening and ended up at an after-party that got me home well after three. I don't know what time Gabe got in, but I reminded him to get back to let Sally out so he didn't have messes to deal with.

Facing the morning to meet Tim, I felt put upon rather than excited. Now, I was feeling more connected. Even though much had changed in the last few weeks, a few moments in his arms and with his lips I recognized myself again. I remembered who I was with him, and who he was to me.

He cupped my breasts in his warm hands and kissed me again before leaving my mouth and trailing down my neck with his tongue. I was melting. Wet and warm and wanting more of him. I reached down and caressed the denim that restrained his erection. He let out a soft moan and pulled me down to the floor and on top of him. As we kissed on the awful gray carpeting that came with the terrible townhouse, I writhed with him beneath me. The friction of our jeans was combustible and protected us from rug burn.

"Let's go upstairs," I said.

He shook his head no, looked over at the chair, then at me. I knew what he wanted and obliged. The soft leather was cold on my bare back, but I knew that would be temporary. Tim was on his knees before me. He undid my jeans. I arched my back as he made me naked. He ran his hands up my thighs and parted my legs, then his tongue worked its magic.

The orgasm took my breath from me. Tim stopped, unbuttoned his fly and slid down his pants. He pulled me to the edge of the chair and entered me slowly. I met each motion with rising hips. I pushed myself up to meet his mouth. We moved together perfectly.

I loved the sound of his orgasm. Masculine and vulnerable. We were locked in a tight embrace. My arms and legs wrapped around him as the aftershocks continued. I quivered as he ran his fingers down my back. He smiled at my reaction.

"That's what I missed most," he said, kissing me once more.

I ran my fingers through his hair. Every part of me was electric and alive. I always remembered how much I missed making love when he got back.

Our sex life had always been good but, over time, had grown a little predictable. It took a downturn last year when he suddenly waited for my first orgasm rather than my third to come. I found that unforgivably rude. I thought the response to my climax got him too excited and blamed myself for his early arrival. I decided I would hold back some, but it is incredibly difficult to fake *not* having an orgasm. When that became too complicated, I took another tack. Rather than exclaiming, "Oh, God! Oh, God!!" I would say, "Don't you dare come. Do you hear me? Not yet!" Not very erotic, or effective for that matter. I felt robbed and it pissed me off to no end that I was being punished for being multi-O'd.

"Do you know how many men would love to have a woman orgasm as easily as I do?" I blurted in post-coital frustration.

"And you came already. I don't get what you're so upset about," he retorted.

I was incredulous. "Tim, if you could have multiple orgasms would you be happy if I cut you off after one?"

He was quiet for a minute, seeming to examine the ceiling for cracks or doing the math, before giving an understanding nod. After that, I usually got two.

We made our way upstairs and napped in our bed, tangled in each other. We made love again, ordered in Chinese that we ate naked on blankets laid out on the living room floor (Tim threw on his jeans long enough to get the door). Feeding each other with chopsticks and sipping wine, the insta-light fireplace —one that ignites by the flip of a light switch—kept us warm. Another tacky part of the townhouse, but it worked.

It was our version of a picnic, something we had done since we first started dating and were too broke to go anywhere fancy. For us, romance was dinner on the living room floor. Just us, bathed in afterglow and candlelight. And tonight, it felt like we were back at the start. In love. At least three orgasms. And nothing else mattered but being together.

We finished dinner and kissed and cuddled. Spooned together, watching the fire dance, I almost felt content.

"So, what was this thing you were going to tell me about?" Tim asked as he ran his fingers through my hair.

"It looks like the talk show is going to happen," I said softly.

"Are you going to stay with her if she does it?" he asked.

"Of course. Why wouldn't I?"

Tim shrugged his shoulders. "Didn't think TV was your thing. You and Jilli talked about producing a film together one day."

"Ages ago."

"So that's not something you want to do anymore? You're

happy being an assistant?"

A chill hit the room. I pulled the throw from the sofa and wrapped it around me as I sat up and away from Tim.

"Want me to turn up the heat?" Tim asked.

"No," I said, feeling the irritation rise. As easy as it was to fall into the habit of loving him, it was just as easy to be pissed off by him.

This was a sore subject between us. Tim had a 'career.' I had a 'job'; something he saw as temporary until something bigger or better came along. Even though bigger and better had arrived, I was still completely annoyed by his attitude, and copped one of my own.

"Tim, does it bother you to tell people your girlfriend is an assistant?"

"What?"

"Would it make you happier, prouder if I were something else? In development? An agent? Real estate even?"

"Babe, what are you talking about? Wait. Are you getting your period?"

I shot him a *You must be fucking kidding me* look.

"I'm serious. I'm not trying to be a dick," he said. "I just want to know how we went from a nice, naked evening to the verge of a blow up?"

Breakup, I thought. *We are on the verge of a breakup!* But I didn't say anything. I just wrapped the blanket around me tighter. Like a straightjacket.

"Hey," Tim said softly. "Come here."

"No," I replied flatly.

He didn't ask a second time. He simply moved over and took me in his arms. He kissed the top of my head and rocked me gently. Rather than surrender to his attempt to soothe me, I stiffened and began to feel the constriction of claustrophobia.

All I had to do was open my mouth and tell him my good news, this great opportunity Karen had served up. I could tell him about Wyatt and the possibility of moving to New York, and how maybe this was the natural end to our relationship. All I had to do was open my mouth. I did, but only to take a sip of wine after I broke from his embrace.

"What?" he asked.

I wasn't sure what I was going to do or say. I just parted my lips and let the words flow. Whatever would come out, well, I would deal with it.

"Karen wants me to be a producer on her talk show," I stated.

"You're kidding me," Tim replied with excitement. "That's great, babe." He let out a laugh and squeezed me hard, kissing my cheek. "When did this happen?"

I told him about Karen's surprise admission. The meeting. Even the unfortunate salad launch, which made Tim laugh, knowing my klutzy side all too well. I started to go into the rest—meaning Wyatt and New York—but stopped short of that, skipping the production company news altogether. I just didn't want to go there yet. Yet again.

Tim gave me a kiss then simply asked, "Why didn't you tell me about it when it happened?"

I shrugged. "It was so out of the blue, you were coming home soon, and…it's not a done deal yet. She hasn't finalized her contract. I haven't begun looking at mine."

"Still, I wish you would've told me, El," he smiled. "That's really huge news. Ellen Paddahsun, talk show producer. Has a nice ring to it, don't you think?"

I smiled politely at his comment. Yes, I thought. Much better than Ellen Patterson, *Assistant to Karen Ellis*, as I'm listed on IMDb.

"Tim?"

"Yeah, babe."

"Let's just keep this between the two of us. I don't want to jinx it, or make a big deal out of it until everything is settled. You know how this business is. It could fall through, and then I'd have to deal with all the questions." The thought of having this discussed with or by his friends made me wince.

Tim smiled at my request and supported it with an affable, "Okay, babe."

And that was it. By the next morning, it was like I had never mentioned it. We immediately started into our routine, the weekend version at least. We made love in the morning (we always made up for lost shag-time when we returned from location) and then he forced himself out of bed for a run. Unlike me, Tim was not a gym rat. It was only running, sit-ups and push-ups for him, and that's all it took. Men are so fucking lucky.

While he was out, I stayed in bed pondering the options for the day, the week, my life ahead. I rolled over and put my face in his pillow, breathing him in. His scent brought me comfort.

The life I had with Tim was comfortable. But, is that a good thing? For shoes, sure; but I was afraid it spelled malaise in a relationship. When does comfort become complacent? Complacency was what I feared most.

I didn't want to just wander through my life, which was what I realized I had been doing until Karen made me this offer. I didn't want to wander through life; I wanted to live it. With passion and adventure, or at least a modicum of awareness. I wasn't sure if I could do that with Tim. Our desires and senses of adventure were growing more and more apart. Camping, sailing and hiking just weren't doing it for me anymore. I wanted something more…sophisticated, challenging, exciting out of life.

Tim and I had begun compartmentalizing our social lives long ago. I went to art shows with Gabe, to premieres and parties with Jilli or Claude. With Tim, I went to barbecues or museums, but he grew bored at more avant-garde exhibitions. He was allergic to the red carpet. He didn't mind the movie, just the press before it and party that followed. He didn't adapt to my interests as well I as I did to his.

I get seasick, but I own a pair of deck shoes. I have asthma and allergies, but I still sucked it up and hit my inhaler to make our hikes trouble-free, popped pills to tolerate the cats that all The Crew own. I would rather stay in a hotel than a tent, but go out of my way to prepare gourmet meals on a Coleman so we'd have something more to look forward to at the end of the day than turkey dogs. What was wrong with wanting a little room service? A few spa treatments. A courtesy wake-up call. Well, perhaps I got that.

The question I was really having trouble with was: What would happen if the show wasn't in L.A.? Would we commute and have a *relay*tionship, going back and forth from coast to coast? I simply didn't see Tim moving with me, even though that's the coast he's from. More to the point, I didn't see me staying here for him. This was going to take some time to figure out. Maybe a shower would clear my head.

I dragged my naked body out of bed and turned on the taps. As I stood under the hot water washing my hair, I recalled the first time I knew I really loved Tim. Not just being in love with him, but feeling deep, solid, unconditional devotion.

We had been together over year and had both fallen sick with a wretched stomach flu. We were at my place when it struck, first him, then me. He was stuck there, in my small apartment, too sick to drive to his place less than two miles away. For three days, we thought for sure we were dying, sometimes hoping we would. Something like that truly tests the mettle of a relationship, and one's plumbing.

We were still weak from the illness, but I had foolishly thought that I could manage a shower. I attempted to shampoo my hair, which hadn't been cleaned in days, but wasn't able to lift my arms long enough to scrub my scalp. We had been surviving on ginger ale, saltines and chicken broth kindly delivered by the gentlemen who ran the liquor store across the street, who took pity on my tearful pleas. They brought the extra Charmin, too. It was enough to keep us hydrated and alive, but not enough to build strength.

I sank to the floor of the tub and let the shower pour over me. I sat there and sobbed in that way you do when you are so ill that your skin aches and your teeth hurt, even your hair is in pain, and you can't think of anything better to do than cry about it. All I wanted was a moment of relief from the discomfort, and the ability to perform the simplest maneuver of hygiene.

The next thing I knew, Tim was there. He sank to the floor behind me and straddled me. Without saying a word, he slowly washed my hair and then my body. Then, without a word, I bathed him. We crawled out of the bathroom and into bed, and drifted into a wet-headed slumber, entwined together in exhaustion. We woke in the same position the next morning, looking rough, but feeling better.

That is love. Not the glamorous, rose-fettered version, but the true root of it. I had forgotten the dregs our relationship had survived. That's not easy to find. I don't know that it would be easy to leave. What we had was good. It wasn't the greatest love of all, but it was more than most had. Just ask Tess. And there's no guarantee I would find someone who made me happier.

The chemistry I had with Wyatt was concerning, though. It was a sign of trouble. Outside of the flirtation I had going with my trainer, I don't notice other men when I am in a relationship. It's like the attraction factor was blocked by commitment. Marco is hard to ignore, especially when mounting me to perform a deep stretch. Wyatt should have been easy to dismiss. That he wasn't, and feels the chemistry, too, says something.

But could I really leave Tim for someone as shiny as Wyatt? Would Wyatt still love me after three days of the runs and vomiting so violently it causes incontinence? It's easy to want someone when everything is sunny. But if you can still find someone desirable after a veritable shit storm, that's the real deal.

By the time I stepped out of the shower, I decided I would tell Tim about New York. We would decide together about the job, and what we would do if the show did require a move. He deserved that. Tim and I were a *we*. I was wrong to have shut him out. That was selfish and controlling and beyond unfair. And disturbingly like my mother.

I had let my attraction to Wyatt deter me from what I knew was true: I belonged to Tim. I belonged with Tim. And with this realization, the monkey that had been latched on my back for the last few weeks leapt off and scurried away. B-bye, you little bastard. Buh-bye.

Newly released from my jail of confusion, hair dried and makeup applied, I went downstairs to tidy up. After all, it was my mess; I needed to deal with it. All of it. I put my "Groovy" playlist on the Bose Karen had gotten me for Christmas and pre-pared to clean house to the rhythm of disco, soul, funk and punk. I turned the volume up, got down to the boogie and went to work. When Sly and the Family Stone commanded me to, "Dance to the music," I did.

"Hey," came out of nowhere and I shrieked.

I turned around to find Tim standing in the entryway, sprinkled in perspiration, trying not to laugh at the unbridled booty shaking he had caught me in the middle of.

"When you're done with your dance off and I'm out of the shower, The Crew's meeting up at Randall and Tab's for chili. Kent called while I was on the run. I said we'd join them. Okay with you?"

No, it was not okay with me. The Crew had just spent eight weeks together on location. Couldn't they bear to be away from each other for a weekend?

One of the more annoying aspects of a relationship is having to take on his friends and their wives. Yes, we were the only unmarried couple outside of Valerie and Roger, who recently got engaged. Val and Roger were sweet, Randall and Tab were tolerable, but the rest of that lot bugged me to no end.

"Tim, we have so much to do around here. Laundry, grocery shopping…"

"I can do all that tomorrow, babe. Let's hang with our friends today. You haven't seen them in ages. What do you say?"

I doubted he wanted to hear what I had to say—that it was like a vacation not having to socialize with them; that they were his friends, not mine—but, it takes too much effort to fight it, so I just said, "Sure."

He kissed me and pulled me in for a spin to the music before he disappeared upstairs to get clean. He would drive, so I could drink. And that was the only upside I could see to my day.

Chapter Eight

Wine. I needed wine. But first, I'd have to fake-smile and say hello to everyone. Even Liza. Tim promised we'd only stay for a couple of hours and I was going to hold him to that. Even if it meant faking an asthma attack.

Tim took my hand as we walked from the car, almost as if to drag me in. The only time I ever walk slowly is when we are headed to a Crew gathering. In his other grasp was the bag of beer and wine we brought. There's only so much Bud Light and Merlot a girl can take.

"Sure you don't want to tell them your good news?" Tim asked one last time.

"Positive," I stated firmly.

He squeezed my hand as if he understood. He didn't. How could he?

This was the mistake I made early on, when I was stupid in love—letting Tim believe I liked his friends. I tried. Believe me, I did. I got along with the guys because it was the guys I met first—on the Jon Tatum film—and sets are like summer camps in that everyone learns to get along, to the point where, sometimes, you actually do.

The guys are guys. They are harmless and sometimes entertaining. Their "women", as they are prone to call us, are another story.

The *hens*, as I referred to them, were not as easy to take. And they certainly didn't take to me. They clucked around, huddled in cliques. Electric women hung out without Electric women. The few Grips griped with other Grips. Camera hung out with Camera, DP, UPM and AD. That's where I was placed.

I was the last to come into their fold. Tim was the new guy to begin with. The Tatum film was his second with The Crew, and I was his first girlfriend. It turned out that most of the hens had tried to set him up with someone they thought was more suitable to him, and them. I wasn't what they had in mind in that I had my own mind. I came in, swearing like a Teamster, knowing the jargon, and giving zero fucks about Pinterest or *Dancing with the Stars*. I was odd woman out. And I didn't realize that the sexes were separated at these functions. There were times wherein the genders mingled, and there were times we were to be relegated in separate corners. I guess where I made my fatal faux pas was when I got bored with the conversation in the kitchen and went out into the living room to chat with the dudes. They weren't so easily offended by the fuck words.

Valerie and Tabitha were the noted exceptions. Tabitha was an elder amongst the hens, and also Canadian, making her an odd bird, too. Valerie's just about as nice as they come. Our friendships, while genuine, were based on the commonality of having to be together so often. If we didn't have that anchoring us, we'd have drifted apart long ago.

We approached the Studio City, ranch-style house that was Randall and Tabitha's abode, and I checked my watch to be certain of the two-hour mark. Their home became The Crew's main hangout when they bought it a year and a half ago. It was a typical three-bedroom-two-bath stucco box, with AC but sans pool, something one really needs to survive a summer in The Valley, and why they were able to afford it.

And, yes, this group really does refer to themselves as "The Crew", a name that held little irony since that's what they were comprised of: Members of a film crew—a gang of Teamsters, a couple of DGA guys and one ACS. Barbecues, holiday fêtes and Super Bowl parties were just a few forms of torture endured at these gatherings.

The front door was open when we arrived. I took a deep breath before we let ourselves in. Just two hours.

We were greeted with "Hey" and "Tim! El!" by the guys. The rest of the room turned to look at us. My cue to throw on a smile and appear delighted. It appeared as though Randall and Tab were hosting the wrap party. About thirty people crowded the house, including faces I didn't know. Must be new crew. Unfortunately, something old had shown up, too.

"What do you mean it has meat in it? I don't care if it's turkey. Turkey is not a vegetable. Turkey has a face. I mean, how hard would it be to make vegetarian chili? Just leave out the animal flesh. God, Randy. It's not like you didn't know I was coming."

It was Dori. I would be spending my Sunday with that chain-smoking vegetarian bitching about chili.

Her bark came from the backyard where she was outside sucking a cig, shouting into the kitchen through the screen of the open window. Her voice had cut through the music and din of conversation to pierce my ears. I could see her through the crowd as we made our way in. She blew out smoke with, "How long have you known me, Randy? Ten years. I've been vegetarian for twenty. How could you not know I don't eat meat? Seriously, now I have nothing to eat."

Peppered throughout the party were the ubiquitous platters of crudité, hummus and pita, cheese plates, chips and salsa and guacamole—standard wares put out at every gathering in L.A. I could clearly see the various arrays as Tim and I made our way over to greet our hosts.

Chain-smoking vegetarians are far from rare in this town. Just about every size-two is one. Surviving on nicotine, Diet Coke, sugarless gum, dressing-less salads and cold-pressed juices, getting protein from Jamba or half an energy bar, they are proud to be "meat-free" and typically drove a Prius. They will gladly regale you with their nutritional knowledge as they puff away on a ciggie to kill their appetites; their looks and life executed later, slowly over time. The annoyance brought on by someone so 'health conscious' as a chain-smoking vegetarian was more than I could take on most days. Dori took it to another level.

Far from Zen, Dori doesn't exactly fit the typical vegetarian image you might conjure. For one thing, she doesn't have that 'glow' most are accused of emitting. Her skin has more of a yellow-gray hue. I suppose that's from the excessive smoking and lack of proper exercise. I always thought vegetarians were sort of required to do yoga, Pilates or Tai Chi, with regular hikes up Runyon in between cleanses. The most I saw Dori exercise was her right to protest.

"Sorry, Dori," Randall said as his round, wire-framed glasses slid down his nose. He pushed them up then took a long pull from his bottle of beer. Randall's tall, thin frame hints at his propensity for anxiety. His long sleeves hide eczema. Right now, he's trying hard not to show that nervous side. He hates being called Randy, and I have an idea Dori is doing that for effect. "We weren't expecting you when we planned this. It was just going to be The Crew and—"

"Well, isn't that nice. Maybe I should just go then. But what about other people who might be vegetarian, Randy? Liza, for example. Shouldn't she have a meat-free option?" Dori huffed.

Liza was one of those vegetarians who ate fish, remaining a *vegetarian*, never using the term *pescetarian*, which I always found irritating. I mean, I've never seen a salmon tree or sea bass bush, have you? Even though Dori and Liza differed on what constitutes meat, it didn't stop Dori from coming to Liza's defense; she had a point to make. It was a kind gesture, I suppose, but Liza is known for only eating raw veg at parties in order to highlight her 'willpower', still toying with her high school eating disorder while reminding the rest of us, "Bikini season is just around the corner." She starts that campaign in October.

I watched as Dori secured a hand on her hip, a sign that her patented diatribe was about to be unleashed. She waved about the cigarette in the other as she went on (and on) about the negative aspects of a carnivorous diet, focusing specifically on the intestinal effects.

If Dori smoked American Spirit or some other sort of natural, organic or herbal cigarette, it would be one thing. Unlike other CSVs who chose a "Light" to light up, Dori smoked Marlboro Reds. And if Dori didn't want to eat anything with a face, shouldn't "Little Debbie" products count?

Emily, a vegan herself, told me that there's no such thing as an overweight vegetarian. They are mythic, like Nessie or Big Foot.

"Please," Emily ranted. "How can anyone get fat on fruits and vegetables? Deep-fried mozzarella sticks aren't part of the program. Just because it's meatless doesn't make it fair game. Cheese pizzas, Diet Cokes, fries and hot fudge sundaes do not a vegetarian make." Emily can get on a soapbox when it comes to health, too. But she makes a more credible expert.

Dori is not part of The Crew, which makes having to tolerate her even more taxing. She sort of wandered into our fold like one of Tab's strays. Dori befriended Tabitha when they were neighbors at the apartment building Randall and Tab resided before they bought the house. Over time, she became a fixture at their parties. For the last three years, we have listened to Dori's endless lectures about the cruel treatment of both animals and smokers, and how meat is the devil's byproduct. I honestly have no idea what she does but bitch and complain and, even though she is quite good at it, I can't see how that pays the bills.

"Vegetarian, Randy," she bellowed. "Do I need to spell that out for you? It makes me question your integrity as a pet parent. I mean, how can you really love your cats when you eat animals? How do you think they feel, Randy?"

"Well," Randall started. "Our cats eat birds. Turkey's a bird, so I think they will be all right with it."

That very-unlike-Randall remark set Dori off on another tirade, this time about allowing the cats outdoors. I felt a migraine creeping up my neck, heading toward my frontal lobe. I needed that wine.

My typical M.O. for these events is to drink until I get perma-grin to make it appear as though I'm having a lovely time. Fortunately, I'm a lightweight, so that doesn't take long. Then, I will force congeniality, endure banal conversation and make the best of the situation. Because, in a relationship, that's what you do: Tolerate his friends, and appreciate yours more.

I once hoped I could blend my tribe and Tim's, trying hard in the beginning to make that happen. Back then, the posse came to Crew parties and did their best to mingle. They soon understood why I was so desperate for them to come along. After Tim and I moved in together, I hosted cocktail and dinner parties, hoping to keep my friends in the mix. One by one, the girls permanently bowed out. Emily was taking classes for her certification. Tess had events. Remi was always going out of town, and Claudia had coverage to do for weekend read. But, funnily enough, if I invited them to do anything not related to Tim's friends, they were completely free. I took their hints and stopped torturing them by asking. Jilli didn't bother with the soft excuses. She put it more bluntly with, "I know you and Tim are Siamese now, fused together at the pelvic region and all, and I get that you have to do things with his people, but—as much as I love you, El—no fucking way. I'm just not up for suffering through another IATSE fest."

I could never blame my friends for abandoning me. I brought it on myself. I chose to play the role of the dutiful girlfriend. I chose his friendships over mine. His comfort over mine. His wants over mine. It was beyond idiotic, complete rookie moves. I shan't make the same mistake again. Love may be blind, but it doesn't have to be asinine.

Before I put my purse and jacket down, I felt my iPhone vibrate. I absentmindedly checked it out of habit, half-thinking it might've been Jilli. But it was a text from Wyatt. I shielded the screen from Tim.

Back Thursday night. Lunch on Friday?

Before I could reply with a polite decline I heard my name.

"El!" Tabitha squealed as she ran toward me. "So good to see you," she said, hugging me hello. "It's been so long. We missed you at Liza's birthday. You shouldn't work so hard," she continued while hugging Tim.

I only worked hard at an alibi. I don't do hen gatherings as a rule. Hen gatherings are Liza's events. She thinks of herself as The Crew's cruise director and feels it's important to have the women get together when the men are away. I couldn't disagree more. I can't use the going-out-of-town excuse with them easily, and I can only be sick so often. As far as the hens are concerned, Karen tends to overload me with random, last minute duties— like actually enjoy my time off.

Tabitha led us into the party, linking one arm with me and her other through Tim's. She jovially rambled about planning a sailing day once the weather got warmer. A sturdy redhead standing at five-three, she contrasts Randall's elongated frame. Tab and Randall are both forty-one, and age is about all they have in common.

After having an on-again-off-again, long-distance romance for more than a decade, they finally tied the knot nearly seven years ago, and they've been in marriage counseling for most of it. They had a split last summer. Everything kind of came to a head when Randall went to some sort of self-help seminar; he's currently in the middle of becoming a new man. Tabitha told me, "If I wanted a new man, I'd get one with a bigger dick, and one that wasn't so quick to fire."

They went through a three-month separation, which was as long as the lease on Tab's Santa Monica sublet, after which she moved back into their home. While they were apart, she and I would meet on occasion for cocktails or coffee walks along the beach. Tab was always nice and she clearly needed someone to talk to. She admitted that, after she moved out, she had started seeing a guy from work, and swore me to secrecy. Tim was on the other end of it, patting Randall on the back while he got teary over his beer.

Tab's affair was short-lived and never consummated, only because the guy couldn't get it fully up. She said the attempt at adultery was a mistake, but it helped put her marriage in perspective. Now that she and Randall were back together, things were going well. Or, at least, that's how it appeared. Who really knows what's going on behind closed doors? And do you want to? I didn't. Especially because they were 'working hard' to start a family. Like many in L.A., they didn't think they wanted children, until both of their clocks started buzzing with alarm. With that fertile window almost shut, Tab and Randall decided to get a move on procreating. She made her way to him when he was on location, not wanting to let an available egg go to waste.

We continued chatting in the kitchen and Tim dutifully poured me a large glass of the Pinot Noir we brought. I filled my mouth with the wine. Anesthesia. Tab was telling me about her new job as she pulled out a can of soup from the pantry. She rambled non-stop while she took a small pot from the cupboard, opened the tin, plopped its contents into the pot and onto a burner. She took a pause from her storytelling and shouted out, "Dori, honey, we have lentil soup for you to eat. Organic. Vegan. It will be done in a sec."

"I was really looking forward to having chili," Dori grumbled as she put out her cigarette with her Birkenstock. Yes, a real, live Birkenstock. The most unflattering footwear ever created, and Dori wore them everywhere and with everything. Today, she wore them with socks.

Her ensemble was completed with less-than-flattering, draw-stringed pair of flowy pants in what I hoped was meant to be a cream color, and not just dingy from time. To complete the costume, she donned a frumpy sweater. Her limp, mouse-brown hair rested shapelessly at her shoulders. She never bothered with makeup, not even the cruelty-free lines. Dori was one crunchy girl. I wondered why earthy women tended to shy away from anything resembling fashion. Can't hemp be made into something flattering?

I felt a tap on my shoulder and turned to find Valerie with Roger standing behind her.

"Oh, my God, El, you look amazing," Val gushed, sweet as sugar.

I noticed Liza did a double-take hearing Valerie. She was in my line of sight when I leaned over to give Val a hug.

Valerie's blue eyes danced under the bangs of her straight, blonde bob. Roger took a step toward me in his Tevos to kiss my cheek hello. Roger's the ultimate nature boy and Val's boyfriend. Fiancé, actually. Why is that the one F-word I can't say? His wavy locks are a little longer than they should be, but that just adds to his easy demeanor.

Roger and Val are the couple I enjoy double-dating with most. Usually, we'd go on day-hikes together, or something else inexpensive. They are saving for a house and now their wedding, and avoid spending money whenever possible. On our hikes, we'd let Tim and Roger trek ahead while Val and I would talk about our relationships, and how long we'd be willing to wait for that deeper level of commitment, one involving thrown rice and too-sweet cake. She and Roger had been together six years, and we aren't talking off-and-on. So, when they got engaged, I was truly happy for them. But that left Tim and I as the only couple in The Crew not to be legally joined, not even by real estate. Perhaps that was the first sign of my apathy. There came a point about a year ago when I couldn't ask the Tim-where-are-we-going question anymore.

For now, we weren't going anywhere. The options were limited. Stay in the kitchen or move to the living room, but the backyard was quickly ruled out. The smoke from Dori's cigarette crept through the window screen and into the kitchen. I thought about hiding out in the bathroom for a bit and Facebook the boredom away. But that was juvenile. Besides, the litter boxes of Tabitha's three cats resided there. One in each loo. No matter how diligent the owners might be, three cats are hard to keep up after, and neither Tab nor Randall were tip-top on the house-keeping tasks. They did a cosmetic tidy before these events, but the boxes always seemed to be last on the list, or simply missed. I had to hold my breath and pee as fast as possible when my bladder would no longer wait. If I undid my jeans before walking in, I could whiz, wash and zip all on a single inhale. Valerie excused herself to do just that, wise to be wearing a skirt. I busied myself with the wine bottle, refilling Tabitha's and topping off my own.

"Hey, El," I heard in a thick Jersey accent that could only come from Kent. I gave him a hug hello then felt the air turn icy, which meant one thing: Liza.

Kent's friendship with Tim makes Liza, his wife, my best frenemy in the group. We all have one of those, don't we? The bitch you are obligated to befriend because of your boyfriend's buddy. I could tolerate her at first but, over time, her controlling nature and endless insults have worn thin.

"El, hi," Liza said in her shrill voice, faking it enough to sound like she's happy to see me. That's been well-rehearsed over the years. "Wow, you look like you can use all that wine. Long week?"

And that's a sweet greeting from Liza. What exactly does one say to that? *Gee, Liza, looks like it's time to do your roots again*, came to mind, but I bit my tongue.

She pursed her lips into something of a smile and wrapped herself around Kent, a great big bear in a Baldwin sort of way. A peroxide blonde who insists on spiking up her overly-bleached, boy-short hair in a Jennifer-Lawrence-meets-Billy-Idol manner because this exemplifies her "feisty, playful nature."

Her phraseology, not mine.

Jilli described her another way. "She's kind of got that Jamie Lee Curtis thing, you know?"

I love Jilli.

What they say about opposites attracting is fully illustrated with Kent and Liza. Kent is kind, funny, easy to talk to and the reason why I put up with Liza to the extent that I do. I've always been confused by their relationship. Long ago, he gave her the reigns. Something he's been trying to get back, recently. Liza was the type to make very clear, in front of all of us, that she could have any many she wanted, and Kent was lucky she chose to be with him.

I think he felt less lucky two years ago when they came back from their honeymoon fighting because Liza didn't see why their kids should have his name, or why she should for that matter. A topic I think would have been more prudently discussed prior to the wedding, but that's just me. I mean, keep your name, take his or hyphenate, but at least let the guy know which way you are heading. As she explained it—in an attempt to quell our bewilderment when the matter was revealed at a Crew dinner party—her dad's the last of the family name and, since he only had girls, it was up to her as the oldest and first married to save it, carry it on with her children. Which would make sense, I suppose, if her last name were anything other than Johnson.

They fought again when Liza told Kent she wanted to wait a few more years before having children. All that fuss about kids and last names, and it turns out she's not sure if she wants any. Again, something to mention before you marry, no? They do their best now not to bicker in public, or bring their grievances to Crew gatherings. Liza paints them with a happily-married veneer. Occasionally, a crack appears, but she usually covers by taking a dig at me.

Like when we went camping with them in Joshua Tree in an attempt to teach me how to rock climb. Tim learned from Kent a few months prior on one of the guys' trips. He was attempting to give me instruction along with Kent's guidance, but his sounded more like criticism. I had to shout down, "You know I love you, honey, but I really need you to shut the fuck up."

Kent was a good teacher, but Liza felt the need to chime in. He must have felt my frustration through the belay because he turned to her and said, "You're not helping her, Liza. Just let us do it." With words of encouragement, and promise of a whiskey as soon as I made it down, I overcame my fear of falling, and made a thirty-foot climb.

That meant the three of them spent the better part of the morning staring up at my ass trapped in a harness. Couldn't have been the most flattering view, which Liza made sure I knew.

"You should really think of taking barre classes. They really help tone up your backside," Liza encouraged as we were walking back to our tents. Sweet little things like that are what endear me to Liza. For the record, her ass is pancake flat. This baby is proud to have back.

It's never a nice feeling not to like someone, let alone loathe them. Hatred is an ugly emotion that easily oozes out of me whenever I am in Liza's presence. It's almost like I'm allergic to her, but Benadryl wouldn't work against her brand of venom. Liza works hard to provoke me. She's that annoying type who's always stepping into the spotlight, stabbing a flag in the center of attention, with off-putting, former-cheerleader pep. Liza made a point to seize each moment like it was a life or death situation, competitive about everything. She had to know more, do more, make more, have more, and do it all first and better than the rest of us. I tried hard to find something redeemable about Liza, but have repeatedly failed.

I wanted to stop the conversation before there was carnage than the blood drawn from biting my tongue. So I smiled at Liza and said the appropriate, "So good to see you," while looking at Kent. "Now, where did I put my boyfriend? Oh, there he is." And I made my way over to Tim.

I leaned into Tim and he put his arm around me. My head throbbed as I surveyed the gathering. From the kitchen window I could see Dori outside lecturing poor Val about something. Lit cigarette waving in the air. Hens were clucking in the corner of the living room. Men were gathered on the sofa, immersed in ESPN. I was ready to go, and we had just gotten there.

Relationships are strange little creatures in and of themselves, let alone taking into account the components that make them up. And, in this group, you'll see the variants of couple-dynamics that abound. Roger and Valerie have a simple relationship, happy with what they have and take each day as it comes. Liza longs to be in a power couple, and drags Kent along with her in that pursuit. Tab and Randall try to achieve the fairytale, fail repeatedly but still try.

Tim and I are someplace in the middle of all that. We want it simple but have things complicated by our work and, while we both know that "happily ever after" is not realistic, we still seem to struggle with, "Happy now?" Such a question is hard to answer at one of these soirees. Spending the rest of my life with Tim was what I had hoped for. Planned on. Spending the rest of my life with his friends as well—well, I tried to keep that thought out of my mind.

In case you care, because everyone in L.A. seems to, I'll tell you what they all 'do' in The Crew. Randall is the Gaffer, or Chief Electric (that's the department that sets the lights and runs the, you guessed it, electricity). Roger is the Best Boy Electric, sort of second in command. Such silly job titles in film. Gaffer. Best Boy. Key Grip. Loader. First AD. DP. UPM. And they are all at this party. I'll continue, and include the gals of this group, who aren't in The Industry, thus making them 'civilians.' That's what we call you if you are smart enough to avoid the hypnotic glow of Klieg lights. That's nicer than what the trades call you— a 'non-pro.'

Tabitha is in marketing and now works for a corporate housing company. She also paints and sculpts—really badly, but you have to appreciate her passion for it. Valerie is kind of finding herself. She started back at school to get her Master's degree; she wants to be a speech therapist, an occupation much more difficult to get into than one would imagine. She's temping to make ends meet in the meantime.

Kent is the First AD, or Assistant Director, who kind of helps pull all the crews together with Al, the Unit Production

Manager, and keeps the film on schedule, directing the crew rather than the actors. Al's wife, Renee, doesn't really work, or speak to me for that matter. Renee wants to be a producer and is constantly pushing one script or another on someone. She belongs to Independent Cinemakers, a group of wannabes who 'network', an annoying euphemism for bugging people while trying to break into the industry. Renee's hated me since I turned down a script she intended to produce; she thought Karen would be perfect for it and hoped to attach her for the lead role. The script, written by a friend of hers, was so poorly executed that no script doctor in Hollywood could bring it to life; it would be best to just set it on fire. I didn't tell her that, of course. I just said that Karen had another similar project in the works. She took it personally and hasn't said more than four words to me since. That's one of the perks of my job: Befrienders—those who engage me because of whom I work for. They adore me until I can't do anything for them.

Liza and Renee are close. They obviously have something in common, besides badly cut short hair. Renee wears her black locks in a Demi-in-*Ghost* style that keeps threatening to make a return to fashion, but never quite does. Even JLaw couldn't make it a trend. Renee is thirty-eight but looks older, and is verging on mutton-as-lamb territory. No one should shop at Forever 21 after they turn twenty-one.

Liza is a political animal. She sees friendships as ways to get Kent another rung up the ladder, and Al would be part of that plan. Liza thinks Kent should be directing by now, and has repeatedly pushed him to make a reel so she can submit it to her agency. What she hasn't grasped is that Kent is very happy to stay an AD, and is making a steady living at it.

Liza works in advertising and a product that addresses feminine itching is her top client. It brings a smile to my face when I see one of her ads. She's not on the creative end, though. She coordinates; a client manager or something that requires a lot of lunches. Still, I always make a point to tell her when I've seen one of 'her' commercials.

The couple rounding out the core of The Crew is Gordon and Mavis. Gordon is the DP, or Director of Photography, also known as a Cinematographer. Basically, he is the maestro of the camera crew, grips and electrics. Since Tim is his camera operator, Tim works closest with Gordon, and wants to be Gordon one day. Mavis was a journalist back in their native Australia. While she'll take a freelance gig every once in a while, and flirts with the idea of writing a novel, she's happy just to throw fabulous parties and feed us well with food, wine and stories. Her fêtes hold mostly their expatriate friends and are much more tolerable to attend. Usually, it's just Tim and I invited, and not the rest of The Crew. It's nearly impossible to have a bad time with a bunch of drunk Aussies. She and Gordon come on occasion to Crew parties. I was kind of surprised to see them there. But glad. At least I could have a normal conversation with them.

And that was the real problem I had with this gang. Everyone was college educated, but the scope of topics was limited. I can only guess what the men talked about on their own, but the women generally discussed shopping or the TV show they were all hooked on. When we indulged in co-ed conversation, we hit on about four subjects only:

1. Camping
2. Sailing
3. Films
4. Vacation plans that didn't involve camping or sailing.

Politics, religion, sex, philosophy or anything at all interesting were subjects frowned upon.

"Those aren't appropriate matters to discuss in polite company," Liza once admonished. And with those rules noted, quite simply, I had nothing to say. I learned from years of trying to bring up more exciting matters to debate, and alienating the lesser skilled forensic artist, that it just wasn't worth the stony silence.

Instead, I would indulge in some fun by tossing four-letter expletives into conversation with the hens from time to time. The other women in the group didn't seem to have my affinity with, or mastery of, the word *fuck*. Bricks were shat when I let an

F-Bomb fly, and I took a sick pleasure in that. Tabitha and Valerie would try to play along and let one go every now and then, blushing as they did, and Mavis would let them flow after a few glasses of cabernet; she was, after all, Australian. But never Liza. She was above all that, often accusing me of being crass. I stopped short of calling her frigid.

As the party progressed, the pockets of people mingled. Several of the men stepped out into the backyard to smoke cigars. Dori enjoyed the carcinogenic company. Tab took Val and me into the second bedroom, which served as her studio, to show us her latest painting. It was less hideous than her last, but why she chose such a harsh color palate as tangerine, cobalt and dirt I'll never understand.

Some of the other hens followed in and conversation bustled. I stayed until going on a cruise was mentioned. Trapped at sea for a week with The Crew? I felt seasick at the thought and snuck out to get some air. On my way, I ran right into Liza and Renee.

"I saw you on TV, El, at that tent ceremony. And I had to ask myself, who was that man with his arm around you all night?" Liza grinned.

"He's a colleague of mine and Karen's," I said directly, without a flinch.

"A very friendly colleague for an assistant to have." She stared at me. Renee shared the same smug expression.

"No different than when you perch yourself on Al's lap," I smiled. "Just as friendly as that."

Both Liza's and Renee's eyes glazed a bit. But, always the cool customer, Liza held her smile and continued into the room to take over Tab's show. Renee followed like the Boston Terrier she was.

Now I really needed air, and another super-sized vino. I walked out of the hallway and into the crowded living room, and caught a glimpse of something quite surprising.

"Tim! Oh, my God. Tim, I can't believe it's you," squeaked the high-pitched voice of the twenty-ish blonde approaching my boyfriend. I watched her trot over to him and go up on tiptoes to wrap her arms around his neck for a hello squeeze. Then she ran her hand down Tim's arm in a knowing way when she broke from the embrace. I stopped dead in my tracks. A pit grew in my stomach, and the cold feeling of realization filled it.

I stepped backed into the hall to shield myself from view, and to watch more. Tim smiled at her and looked around, not so much to find me, but to see me before I saw them. I tried to keep myself hidden and gnawed my thumb.

The blonde didn't speak to Tim as much as she gushed. "It's so good to see you," she said and coyly flipped her extensions over her shoulder. They landed in the middle of her back, cheaply done without a proper trim to blend them in with her own. With the fake tresses removed, I noticed the huge amount of silicone protruding from the plunging neckline of her too-tight top. It was maybe sixty degrees as the evening took over the afternoon, and this girl was wearing a top that was both cut high and low, exposing her midriff and cleavage. Her second-skin jeans were slung low on her hips. A jacket or sweater nowhere to be found. Her glossed lips spread into an open smile as she looked adoringly at my boyfriend.

I couldn't hear Tim's response so I started toward them with purpose, curiosity and ire fueling my steps. Tim caught a glimpse of me approaching and visibly tensed. He forced an uncomfortable grin and said to the blonde, "Yeah. I'm here with my girlfriend, Ellen." He stressed the word *girlfriend*. I watched the blonde's reaction as he reached his hand out toward me.

She was pretty. Her face fresh and young. Her tits, however, made her look cheaper than her shoes.

"Hi!" she said to me in another squeak. Her broad smile exposed teeth that had been bleached to the point of appearing blue. Behind her was a pair of blonde bookends she had tag along. The bookends were whispering to each other and watching us.

"Hello," I replied.

"I'm Angie," she beamed and stuck out her hand. As I shook it, I wondered what else of mine that hand had pumped.

"Nice to meet you," I lied. I eyed Tim to clearly acknowledge the situation. He put his arm around my shoulders and stepped into me. A pathetic attempt at a show of loyalty. One that fell a bit flat. Something was definitely rotten in this Denmark. I've never had that feeling before with Tim. I wasn't going to ignore it.

"Wow, it's like such a small world," Angie rambled. "I ran into Kent and his wife at the airport. What's her name? She's so nice. Anyway, she called and invited me to come tonight, like out of the blue. Wasn't that cool?"

Very cool of Liza, indeed. Nothing Liza did was without motive. Especially if she had to reach for the film's crew list to do it.

Angie spoke again. "So, do you live around here?" She posed this question to Tim, her eyes locked on him. It was the "Ice Block", one of the oldest tricks in *The Competitive Woman's Handbook*. Nice try, sweetheart. Game on.

"No," I answered before he could, trumping her move. "We live in Venice." I stressed the *we* and smiled at her. The subtext of that response read: *I've been fucking him for half a decade. You don't scare me, little girl.* "Do you live around here, Angie?" *I'm going to be pleasant, but don't think I don't want to rip your extensions off and feed them to you.*

We were communicating on that frequency only women can hear; the undertone of our seemingly polite repartee screams out loud and clear to females, but men are completely oblivious to it. Two women can be hurling insults at each other all through a dinner, and their dates will never be the wiser. Liza and I did it all the time.

"No. I live in Redondo. But, like, all of my friends live in Santa Monica, so I've been thinking about moving there. A little closer to the studios, barely. But, like traffic sucks wherever, right? Might as well live at the beach!" She giggled, in that annoying just-out-of-high-school way she was a bit too old for. She used it here to purposely point out that *I'm younger and have bigger boobs than you. I'm uncomplicated and only looking to have some fun. I make him feel like the center of the universe. You make him feel like he forgot to pick up the dry-cleaning…again.*

"So, you drove all the way from Redondo Beach to Studio City for chili? That's nice of you. Isn't it, honey?" I mocked, enjoying Tim's discomfort.

"Uh, yeah," he sputtered.

"Angie. Is it Angie isn't it?" I smirked.

"Yeah." Her smile was fading.

"What is it that you do?"

"Oh, I'm a wardrobe assistant," she beamed.

"Of course you are," I said with just the right hint of disdain. Makeup, Hair and Wardrobe—the biggest flirts and gossips on any set. Some of them were good friends of mine, but I never trusted them with information I didn't expect to be shared.

Angie and I locked eyes for a moment. She no longer had anything to say. I broke the silence with, "Well, Angie, it was lovely to meet you. Maybe we'll run into you again." Which meant: *If you ever do see us, don't bother to come over and say hello.*

"Well, bye," she said. "See you on the next set, Tim."

"Yeah, see you," he said flatly.

I felt my nostrils flare. "I'm going to get my purse," I said. He didn't bother arguing or suggesting we stay another half-hour or so. He nodded and started to make his goodbyes. When I passed Liza on my way to my bag I said, "Your friend is here."

We walked to the car in silence, Angie needling me all the way. Bottle-blonde hair, fake tits and extensions. Did he find that attractive? That cheap, lap-dancer look? He was only thirty-three. A little young for a mid-life crisis.

Tim tried to break the ice by putting his arm over my shoulders. "Do you want to stop at Sage for dessert on our way back? I know how you love their—"

"No. I just want to get home," I said without looking at him.

He had cheated on me. To what extent I couldn't be sure. I didn't care. It didn't matter. After the tsunami of emotional reactions had passed—hurt, betrayal, anger, disappointment and sadness—I was left with one feeling: Relief. Relief that I didn't tell him about New York or the production company. Relief that I didn't have to ignore my attraction to Wyatt. Relief that there was an out, for both of us.

To avoid conversation in the car, I did something I never

do on the weekends or in front of Tim: I busied myself with my iPhone, returning emails, writing new ones, and responding to Wyatt's text with: I would love to have lunch.

To my surprise, I got a quick reply: Great. Can't wait.

I could feel Tim's tense awareness that I was too pissed to speak. For once, he was wise enough not to try to get me to talk. I might have gone all Naomi Campbell and hurled my iPhone at his head.

When we got into the townhouse, in a further effort to keep myself calm and distracted, I did something truly strange— I went into the kitchen and made cookies. Cookies! WTF? Anger makes me do peculiar things, but this was beyond odd. But I knew I had to stay occupied so I didn't say or do anything rash. Like baking was a lucid thing to do.

The homemade oatmeal-chocolate-chip cookies were Tim's favorite. I used to always have a batch waiting for him when he got home from location. This batch would be the last. A final act of love and thanks. Tim, and his little tart, had just made things a whole lot easier, and I was oddly grateful for that. I handed Tim a tray with a plate of the warm baked treats and a glass of milk. I kissed the top of his head and said, "I'm going upstairs for a bath," taking the glass of wine from the tray with me.

Tim sat there bewildered. I supposed he was waiting for some sort of outburst, or a we-need-to-talk type of statement. Sorry to disappoint.

I ran water into the tub, turned on some music and sunk into the water, breathing in a sense of calm. Closing my eyes, I let my mind drift. Drift to New York, to that night at Shutters. Setting up a production company. Seeing Wyatt again. Everything was going to be okay. I was filled with contentment. For the first time in weeks, I felt like all of it was going to work out perfectly. Then my eyes popped open.

Tim and I had been shagging like rabbits since his return. And we hadn't employed condoms since our first year…or the last time I was on antibiotics.

"Gross," I said aloud at the thought of his dick being in that bimbette and then in me. I got out of the tub and went to my iPhone. I dialed my gynecologist and left a message requesting the first available appointment.

About an hour later, Tim came upstairs and found me in bed reading a script on my iPad. He readied himself for sleep, then crawled in beside me and tried to snuggle up. I ignored him and swiped the screen to turn the page.

"Any good?" he asked.

"Not yet," I retorted.

"Thanks for the cookies. They were delicious."

"Glad you liked them," I said without looking away from my reading. Tim ran his finger up and down my arm in an attempt at seduction, or attention. So, I decided to give him some and closed the cover of my devise with a snap.

"So, this Angie," I started.

"Yeah?"

"Did you fuck her, or just make out?" I asked this calmly and quickly, without thinking if I really wanted to know the answer. Once it was said, I had to go with it and not flinch. I mean, you think you want to know, but do you? I was beginning to realize I might be better served believing he did something rather than have him confirm it.

"What?" he asked with surprise.

"Did you fuck her—and if you did, Tim, you'd better have used a rubber—or was it just making out? Or maybe she blew you and you thought it would be rude not to reciprocate. Which is it?" I posed the questions directly, without any emotion, and looked him in the eye until he answered. He was the first to blink.

"Why would you even ask me something like that?"

"Because I'm not a fucking idiot. Now, do I have to ask you again, or will you just tell me what went on?" I think my composure unnerved him more than my inquiry.

"Nothing went on, El," he said. "She had a set crush on me, that's all."

"Okay," I said and left it at that. I didn't believe him, but I wasn't sure to what degree he was lying.

It was my ego inquiring more than my heart. Liza knew something or she wouldn't have gone to all that trouble. She was the kind to befriend Hair and Makeup for the gossip. It didn't matter, though. I knew enough. A woman always senses when her man isn't being honest. Not that I could get all that holier-than-thou. Not with a lunch date set with Wyatt.

Admittedly, what was going on with Wyatt wasn't something Tim would approve of either. I knew the extent of my hypocrisy, but no bodily fluids were exchanged in my case. Sad to rest your integrity on something like that, though.

I rolled over and turned out the light. I could feel Tim frozen in his position, not sure what to do next. I finally felt him lie on his back. He let out a big sigh and said, "Nothing happened."

"I heard you the first time, Tim. Goodnight."

Chapter Nine

"You have got to be kidding me," Jilli said. Her mouth hung open as she mulled it over further. "Shit. Really? I never thought Tim would have the balls to cheat."

Jilli and I met up at The Newsroom on Robertson after she finished another meeting with Cassie.

"Your sympathy for my plight is staggering," I deadpanned.

"I'm sorry, El. Guess this makes you kind of even, though. Right?"

"Dining with Wyatt is not the same thing as blowing him."

"But you thought about blowing him," she countered.

I rolled my eyes.

"I'm just stunned that you didn't dump him on the spot. Baking fucking cookies? You can't be serious. You didn't even add some Ex-Lax to the batter or drop Visine in his milk?"

"I wasn't about to poison him. He's not worth the jail time."

"And what's the haps with Wyatt?" she asked, knowingly and knowing me too well.

"Lunch tomorrow," I said as nonchalantly as possible. "Hoping to drag it out of him if the show is going to New York or not. At least then I'll know if I should pack for a cross-country move or just one across town."

"You don't have to wait for that. You can move in with me. Stay as long as you'd like. You know that. You have a key for a reason, you know."

"I thought that was to discover your rotting, bloated corpse after I hadn't heard from you in a week," I snarked.

Jilli's only concern about remaining single was dying alone in her home by a freak accident or some undetected affliction, and having no one know until she stunk up the neighborhood. In such an unfortunate event, I was supposed to rid the place of the unmentionables before her mom saw them, and burn her journal.

"Fuck you very much, dear," she said, giving me a friendly

single-finger salute. "So, when are you going to end it with Tim?"

"I don't see the point in doing it right now," I answered flatly. After all, why move twice? "The Crew got another job that starts next month."

"You're not going to break up with him right before he goes to work, are you? Kind of a dick move, El. And that's coming from me. It's not fair to send him to the set upset."

"Please. I'll end it officially in a few weeks when everything's done and dusted with the talk show."

Selfish, I know. Coming up short on integrity? Sure. But I had always put Tim first. This had to be about me. It was my life we're talking about. It was about time I realized that.

"That's almost devious of you, Patterson. I couldn't be prouder," Jilli smiled.

We finished our dinner talking about other things. She still hadn't ended it with Andy, and I still hadn't told her about KEEP.

• • •

"What's the best way to break up with a man?" I asked Marco, my trainer, while looking at him in the mirror. He straddled me on the bench as he counted out my bicep curls and shoulder presses. His knees locked onto my thighs, his hands on my waist, his breath on my neck. It was such a nice way to burn calories.

Marco wrinkled his brow before answering, "Without sounding full of myself, I haven't had much experience being broken up with. Usually, I do the ending. And then it's generally by not calling back or showing up. Cowardly shit like that. Nothing I'm proud of, but it was better than watching them cry."

He positioned me into the next move and squeezed my waist to get me started.

"I suppose I don't need to stretch my imagination to guess why you are asking me this," he said in his imperfect English.

"I suppose you don't. Any advice?" I asked, pushing the weights over my head for the final rep.

"There's no good way to do it, El. Or no easy way. Are you

sure you want to end it?" he asked as he massaged my shoulders.

"Yes."

"For good?" he asked.

I nodded, looking him in the eye through the mirror's reflection.

"Then have your bags packed before you say anything and somewhere to go when you do."

Marco made sense. Jilli just might end up with a roommate.

"Thanks, Marco."

"You're welcome. Now, final set," he said and began counting me off. Halfway through he paused and said, "She waits until I'm engaged to break up with him. Jesus." And then we both laughed.

I had wanted to work up a good sweat before meeting Wyatt for lunch, so I had asked Marco to work me hard. Burn off some of that energy, that delicious tension. It didn't work as well as I had hoped.

"In keeping with our resort theme, how about lunch at Hotel Bel Air?" Wyatt asked charmingly through his cell phone that morning. I giggled to myself.

"Sounds perfect."

"You sound good, El. I'm looking forward to seeing you."

He made the reservation for twelve-thirty and said he'd meet me at the valet. He was waiting there as I pulled up. Without a word, Wyatt took me by the hand and led me to a booth, coveted territory at the Bel Air.

It was a crisp day. A few clouds lingered. The fireplace crackled, holding on to the last moments of winter before the Vernal Equinox. The afternoons were warming, the seasons were merging. Everything was changing.

Our appetizers were topped with doe-eyed glances and shy grins. Not knowing what else to say to break the ice, I asked, "How was New York?"

"It was good. I met with the network and pled our case for keeping the show on the West Coast, at least for the first season."

"My hero."

"Well, don't get your hopes up. They were pretty adamant,

but I got them to 'consider' it." He added the finger quotes to show their reluctance. "You don't want to move, do you?"

I shook my head.

"That's right. You've only lived in L.A. I sometimes forget I'm sitting next to a real, live, native Los Angelena."

"A breed so rare, Greenpeace has us listed as endangered."

He laughed anyway then asked, "Will you take the deal if we go East?"

I nodded. "This isn't something a girl would be wise to pass up," I said, looking him dead in the eye. He smiled back.

"I heard that you asked for revisions in the contract for a parachute if it tanks. Not that it will, of course. I'm impressed, Patterson. You are a smart cookie."

That was Jilli's suggestion. I should've given the credit to her, but I don't think she'd mind under the circumstances.

"And you were impressive on the conference call," he continued. "Good ideas. Strong presentation. You wowed them, Ellie. Wowed me, too."

I felt myself turn a shade of claret. It felt good to have the chance to test out my new role and have it turn out all right. I'm sure there would be missteps down the road—inevitable on a new path—but I was pleased that my first go it didn't go wrong, and that Wyatt noticed.

He had such a relaxed way about him that he put me at ease. I was able to enjoy our lunch without thinking about Tim or feeling guilt. I only felt good. Once my standard I'm-with-a-new-guy-I-like shyness wore off, we had flowing conversation without awkward silences. Wyatt and I had clicked early on, but this exchange was different. Something had shifted. Then I realized that we were happy to see each other. We had missed each other.

"What are you smiling about?" he asked, smiling back at me.

"Nothing," I said with my smile growing wider.

He reached under the table and found my hand. "Whatever the reason," he said, "it's good to see you smile. It's good to see you."

He held my hand as we walked back to the valet, and asked

them to bring my car first as he paid my ticket in spite of my protestations.

"Don't forget…lady," he said, pointing to me. "Gentleman," pointing to himself. All I could do was smile, squeeze his hand and breathe in his intoxicating scent, which was simply Kiehl's, but smelled so good on him.

"Are you warm enough?" he asked. I nodded. He ran his hands up and down my arms to warm them. Such a gentle man.

My car arrived with his behind it. He handed my driver a tip, then turned to me and said, "Let me know when I can see you again."

"I will." Before I could say 'Thank you,' or 'This was lovely,' he leaned in and kissed my lips softly. It was a warm, gentle kiss that lasted a lifetime and went through all of me. When we parted, neither of us said a word. Words weren't necessary. I smiled once more as he cupped his hand to my face. Then I pulled him to me and kissed him. Long and full.

"Who knows about all of this?" Gabe asked. He had noticed me walking on air when I got back to Karen's. I told him about lunch, the kiss, and then I had to spill the rest of the beans.

"Only you know everything. Nobody else knows about KEEP. I just think it's all too much to lay on everyone all at once."

"Or is it just too much for you?" Gabe inquired. I had forgotten how well Gabe knew me.

"Probably," I admitted.

"Ellen, this is all great stuff. You shouldn't have to shield your friends from it. Or Tim. You two…I don't know. He's a really nice guy. And hot. But he is J. Crew and you are Jil Sander. He's Gap; you're Gucci. He's Abercrombie—"

"I get the fashion analogy. Thanks," I said holding up my hands to stop him.

"You do things that you don't really enjoy just because he does and, Ellen, he does not do the same for you. When has he gone to one of my shows? Taken you dancing? Gone to one of Jilli's parties or hung out with Emily and her man? I can safely say once this side of never. What are you doing in a relationship like that?"

"You saw all that and never said anything?" I inquired, awed that he got it in one and it had taken Karen's offer to wake me up to it.

"Would you have believed me?" he asked.

No. I wouldn't have wanted to.

Gabe's observations, and the fact that my tongue had gotten to know Wyatt's, made it clear. I couldn't wait. Wouldn't wait. I would tell Tim it was over that night. There was always Jilli's sofa or my room at Karen's, once Gabe moved out of it, or Gabe's apartment until Karen came back. I had options. I could do this. A clean break. It was the adult thing to do.

By the time I turned the knob on the door to our home, my resolve was Herculean. I hadn't felt more certain about anything since kicking Toby Thompson in the balls for feeling me up on the playground in the fourth grade. Yes, I was ready to end this chapter of my life and turn to a new page. But then I opened the door and saw the most horrible sight.

Sitting on my sofa were Kent and Liza. I felt the color drain from my face.

"Hi, El," Liza cheerfully greeted, as if she were hosting me in my own home.

"Hello," I returned automatically as I walked in.

"Hey, babe. How was your day?" Tim asked, popping out of the kitchen with his hands full of napkins and plates. He gave me a peck on the cheek and said, "Let me grab you a glass."

Kent and Liza each held a goblet of red wine. A third sat alone on the side table of the leather chair. Brie and crackers and an assortment of grapes sat on the coffee table. Liza's doing no doubt.

"We were on your side of town picking up our new truck and thought we'd take you out for dinner to celebrate," Liza grinned. "Of course, we stopped by Gelson's on the way over for something to snack on since we weren't sure when you'd be home."

"How nice," I lied, taking the glass from Tim's hand and slamming a fair share of it on the first take. I nearly choked. Fucking Merlot. Liza's doing again.

"Have a seat, babe," Tim offered.

I'd rather stand. Or make a run for it.

"Al and Renee should be here any minute," Liza mentioned. "Should be fun." She turned to Kent. "Honey, don't you think you should give them a call, let them know El is earlier than expected?"

"They said they'd be here in thirty. It's fine," Kent stated, showing more authority with Liza than I could recall witnessing prior.

"Babe, have a seat," Tim suggested again, probably suspecting I was on the verge of imploding.

"Actually, I'm going to head upstairs to freshen up."

Good Christ. Did it not occur to Tim to give a girl some warning? That's why God invented cell phones, just so no one would have to walk into their home to such an unpleasant surprise. I started up the stairs without waiting for a response.

"Where would you like to eat, babe?" Tim called out to me.

If I heard 'babe' one more time I was sure my brain would bleed. "Anywhere is fine with me," I shouted back, trying not to sound too bitchy.

Kent had purchased a new Denali, which unfortunately had "enough room for everyone!" Once Al and Renee got to our place, the six of us got to ride in the same vehicle to dinner. I don't recall whose idea it was to go to Moonshadows in Malibu, when Venice and Santa Monica are littered with good restaurants. I put the blame on Liza, who longs for a 310 phone number, although now the best she can hope for is 424.

Rather than a mere five, ten or fifteen minute ride, I was stuck in the back of an S-U-Beast. Al rode shotgun while Renee told a riveted Liza of her latest fantasy project that she was sure would garner acclaim, if she could attach the right actors and get the funding—saying all of this loudly enough for my benefit. Tim and I sat in the back forty and, by the time we reached the restaurant, I was carsick. The headache and nausea were more pleasant than the company and conversation.

"You're pretty quiet. You okay?" Tim asked as we pulled into the valet.

I smiled at him, patted his hand and said, "What do you

think?"

"We have the script out to several investors. We're hoping to attach Cameron Diaz or Scarlett Johansson," Renee blathered as the server brought over the drinks.

"As if," I whispered before taking my double-vodka soda.

"I'm giving my notice at work," Renee continued. "There's just so much work you have to do as a producer before you even get to the set. I feel like I should get myself an assistant."

Shit. Here it comes, I thought.

"El," Renee said, acknowledging me for the first time that evening. "Where would one go to hire a crackerjack assistant? Do you have any friends looking for work?"

The only time Renee will talk to me is when she can find an insult.

"Generally, one would go through a placement agency. Crackerjack assistants typically start about seventy-five, more if you aren't offering benefits. Then there's the agency fee, which is usually about thirty percent of the annual salary."

"Seventy-five…thousand?" Renee choked.

"To start," I clarified. I was referring to executive assist-ants, those with years of experience. You know, the *crackerjacks*.

"You make the much?" Liza queried.

"Liza," Kent chided.

"No, no," I said and, for a moment, Liza and Renee looked relieved. "Like I said, that's to start. I've been doing this a long time now." I gave a Cheshire Cat grin. It was a low-class move on my part to talk earnings, but I couldn't resist. "Then again, if you wanted to go a little less 'crackerjack', as you put it, you could always put an ad up on Craigslist or the UCLA job board. I'm sure there would be lots of kids interested in learning from a first-time producer. Not everyone wants to start out at the top." Realizing I might've taken that too far, I softened it with, "You know, you can learn more with someone who's starting. It's a perk."

With Renee and Liza now sitting quietly, and my cocktail drained down to the ice, I was finally having a good time. It was nice not to give a shit. It was nice to get my digs in for once. I signaled our waiter and ordered another drink.

"So, Al. What's this next project all about? I hear it's in Phoenix," I smiled.

"The pilot is shooting in Phoenix. Re-shooting, to be accurate, since one of the principals was re-cast, the director was fired and the crew went with him. We are picking up where they screwed off. The series itself will be shooting in L.A. and the local deserts. We're lucky on this one. I think we'd all like to stay home for a bit," Al answered.

Tim squeezed my hand in accordance. When I looked over at him, he had puppy eyes.

"A series? As in TV?" I asked, trying to mask my sarcasm.

"Premium cable," Al corrected.

"Can't knock seven months of solid work," Kent smiled.

"Especially in L.A.," Tim said softly.

"Especially if we want to try for a family," Kent cooed. Liza shot him a look. Yes, I was finally having fun.

"And The Crew can shoot my film during the hiatus," Renee chirped.

"Wow," I said. "That sounds great."

"Meanwhile," Al continued, "We were thinking of getting in a little camping this weekend. Break in that Denali, right Kent?"

"Leave tomorrow, get back Tuesday?" Kent offered.

"You have my blessing," I replied. "I assume this is boys-only."

"Guys' weekend," Al confirmed. "Hiking, fishing, drinking." He laughed and Kent joined in.

"Sure you don't mind," Tim whispered as dinner was served.

"Not at all," I answered, syllable by syllable.

Kent and Liza dropped us off, and Tim and I entered the house in silence. It was only ten-thirty, but I was exhausted and couldn't wait to crawl into bed. Without a word, I started up the stairs.

"Don't you want to talk, El?" Tim asked. I stopped and turned to see him waiting at the foot of the stairs.

"When you get back, Tim. I'm tired."

"I can stay. I can tell the guys I'm not going," Tim offered.

"It's better if you go. Go and have fun."

"Fine," he relented.

I was asleep by the time my head hit the pillow. I didn't even feel Tim get into bed, which made sense when I didn't find him in it when I woke; though, it wasn't my alarm that roused me.

I went downstairs before the sun came up. A pillow and blanket were on the sofa. An empty glass and a bottle of Bushmills with a noticeable dent in it sat on the coffee table. Tim was clattering about in the kitchen ruining my Saturday morning sleep-in. He had time to pack and prepare for his trip last night, but why do it in advance when you can rush at the last minute?

I stumbled into the kitchen and noticed the blur of time on the oven's clock. It wasn't even five. I had to squint to confirm it.

"What are you looking for?" I grumbled in my it's-too-fucking-early voice.

"My thermos," he replied.

"You threw it out after the last trip when you left the rest of your latte sitting in it for nearly a month."

"Fuck, that's right," he sighed. "Sorry I woke you, babe."

How could anyone look so picture perfect at such an ungodly hour? Like a Madison Avenue lumberjack standing there in his hiking boots and Levi's with his gray flannel shirt open over a black tee. His was hair still damp from his shower and newly short from a haircut a few days before, making him appear boyish, almost innocent. But he was certainly guilty of waking me for no good reason.

"Don't worry about it. Have fun," I said, rubbing my sleepy eyes and heading back toward the stairs. Before I got two steps away, Tim grabbed my arm, spun me around and planted a huge kiss on my mouth. A brave man, considering I slept hard and didn't even take a sip of water before venturing downstairs.

"I can't leave with us like this," he said when we broke apart. I could feel his hurt. That should've softened me, but I didn't let it.

"Like what, Tim?"

"Like this!" he said, raising his voice just below a yell. "This. Us not talking. You pissed at me. Me pissed at you."

"I'm not pissed at you, Tim. And what do you have to be pissed at me about?"

"I'm pissed that you aren't fighting for this relationship, Ellen." I noticed that his eyes had dampened.

My hardness was melting, but I didn't say anything.

"You have to believe me when I tell you I didn't sleep with her, El. I didn't sleep with her."

"But something did go on between you."

He paused before answering. "We kissed. But it was only once. And it was only a kiss."

"And lying and cheating, Tim. And with someone as… Jesus. If I end up with a cold sore, I swear—"

"I'm sorry, Ellen. It was a mistake. It was wrong. And it will never happen again."

"How can you say that, Tim? How do you know it won't happen again?" I was hoping that he would admit that there were others before, or that he wanted to see other people. Maybe we could end things right here, and I could spend the weekend packing.

"Because it made me hate myself that I was unfaithful, even that slightly. But I was lonely, El. Two months without you and I missed you."

"Some substitute. She looks nothing like me," I said wanting to hurt him, as if that would assuage my own guilt. "If you missed me so much, why didn't you tell me? Why didn't you ask me to come and visit?"

"I didn't know that I had to ask after all this time. I thought you would actually want to visit me, that you might fit me into your schedule at some point and come out because you missed me, too!"

"The neighbor, Tim. Let's try not to wake him and the rest of the complex."

"Every other wife made it up there," he continued.

"But I'm not your wife," I reminded.

"Are we back to that?" he asked, throwing his hands up in the air.

"No," I said shaking my head. "Just go and we'll talk when you get back." This was too much. You can't really end five years in fifteen minutes. At least not in any neat or tidy way.

Tim walked over and sat in the chair. He let out a deep sigh and said, "Fight with me, El. Fight for us. Please."

"I don't want to fight, Tim. I'm tired. And you need to go. You don't want to be late."

He put his head in his hands. It was a sad sight. I had crumpled him into a ball. I walked over to him and put my hand on his shoulder. He grabbed my hand and looked up at me. Tears fell from his eyes.

"I can't leave like this," he said. I swallowed hard.

"Yes, you can. Go on the trip. Relax. Have fun. We can talk when you get back." I bent over and kissed the top of his head then went to the stairs.

"Are you seeing someone, El?"

I froze. Slowly, I turned around and took a seat on a step.

"I'm not seeing somebody, but I am attracted to someone else."

"That guy from the awards? Liza made a point of me seeing the show."

"She's always had your best interest at heart, hasn't she."

"She's a bitch, but she's married to my best friend. She thought she was doing me a favor."

"Like the favor she did you by inviting Angie to Randall and Tab's? We should send her flowers."

"So, is he the guy?" he asked.

"Tim, it's not about any guy. It's not even about the blonde. It's about us. I just don't think there is much of an *us* anymore. And maybe we should talk about that."

Tim called Kent and said he wouldn't be meeting them that morning. Maybe he would drive up later, lying that his stomach was a bit off. I made coffee and brought it into the living room. Tim rose and pulled me into him, hugging me tightly, not letting go. When he finally eased the embrace, I slipped through it and took a seat on the sofa.

Love is sort of like E.T. It might be dying a slow and horrible death, but the minute you start to believe in it, the heartlight glows. I had been so cold with Tim the past week, and I did it for spite, just to cause him pain. Punish him for not giving me what I wanted, or how I wanted it. I wanted him to feel all the loneliness and disappointment I had. Now that he did, it brought me no solace. It merely amplified my own emptiness and made me feel like more of an asshole.

In my mind, I had bolstered this to being a simple task of packing up and leaving, starting anew and leaving the past behind, but that was only because I wasn't factoring in my heart. No matter how things with Tim had turned out, he was still a huge part of my life. And pulling away from that, apart from him, was not going to be simple. It was going to be messy and painful and real. So, I had to come clean.

I told Tim about New York and KEEP. I downplayed Wyatt, because this really wasn't about him. This was about me and Tim and the two-months-shy-of-five-years we had spent together.

"Did you think I wouldn't go with you? That I'd expect you to stay here?" he asked.

"I don't know. Your career is here. Mine might take me there."

"Didn't you think we could make a bi-costal thing work until I found something there?"

"Tim, I didn't even see the point in trying. If after all this time you didn't commit to a future with me, why would we bother trying to make it work long distance? You wouldn't even buy this townhouse with me. Do you know how heartbroken I was over that?"

After two years of dating, meaning two years of me sleeping at his apartment while my underwear resided at mine a few miles away, I brought up the idea of getting a bigger place together. It made sense with the rent we were both paying and basically using only one abode. I said, "Just think about it… hardwood floors, backyard, fireplace. It would be nice to actually come home to a home, don't you think?"

Tim hemmed and hawed for a couple of months, then mentioned casually one morning as we waited outside Maxwell's for breakfast, "It might make sense to buy a place together."

I nearly burst into tears. To me, that was better than a ring. Marriages rarely last, but real estate? On paper, that's a thirty-year commitment. I was over the moon. But, over our egg whites and turkey bacon, Tim brought me back to earth.

"It will probably take about a year for us both to save up the down payment," he said before I could even open the real estate section. Obviously, he wasn't in a rush for us to be legally bound to each other in any manner. Still, I focused on the positive aspect. This was a step toward commitment, a huge commitment. The beginning of our happily ever after.

When Tim's father came into town for a visit during a business trip a few weeks later, we told him of our plan. He was very supportive. As we mused on the subject further, I thought how nice it would be to one day have a guest room waiting for him, but wondered how many more Marriott stays Mr. Davis would have to endure before that would occur. Two days later, though, I got a call from a very excited Tim.

"Babe, you aren't going to believe this," he started. Then told the tale that he and his father were cruising around the neighborhood and found a townhouse for sale by owner. His dad made an offer, signed a check for the down payment and, when he was calling me, they were finalizing the loan papers. "Babe, we go into escrow tomorrow. In sixty days, we move in. You are going to love it. It's awesome."

I hung up the phone and burst into tears. The dream I had of us buying a home together had been foiled by the kind gesture of Mr. Davis. There would be no weekend open houses to go to, no moment of simultaneous elation when we found our perfect place. I dried my eyes and tried to focus on the fact that we would finally be living together properly. But, I burst into tears again when I saw the place.

I called it the Sliver because it's a two-story, two-bed-room, two-and-a-half bath townhouse sitting on a busy street in Venice proper, which was the only upside it held. I don't know who the architect was but, without a doubt, he designed it on acid. The edifice was peculiarly shaped. The dining area actually came to a point. Tim had bought a two-story trapezoid, and very narrow one at that. And when I say narrow, I mean narrow. I'm five-six, and if I lie down in the living area and stretched all the way out, I could almost touch both walls. Almost.

The townhouse had nothing that we had talked about. No backyard. No patio. No hardwood floors. Not even a balcony. But it did have that switch-lit fireplace. And let us not forget the brand new, industrial gray carpeting that covered wall-to-wall, upstairs and down with the exceptions of the entryway, the kitchen and the two-point-five bathrooms we now had; those had an equally appalling faux-tile design linoleum. I cried over that, too.

When I asked if we could do something about the flooring, Tim was adamant. "Why would we spend good money ripping it out? It's brand new." I couldn't believe he didn't see what I saw. He had always been quite metro when it came to decorating his apartment. Tears started to well and I did my best to blink them away.

"I thought this was what you wanted," Tim rifled, throwing his arms out, and nearly hitting the living room walls.

"We talked about a house, Tim," I said softly. Not a bunk bed inspired condominium.

He put his arms around me. "This is our home now, El. You'll get used to it."

I had to sell or give away most of my furniture, since the Sliver didn't have room to house it. I was okay with that for the most part. My décor was comprised of post-collegiate Ikea. It was good for it to go. Tim's lasted a few months before his queer eye kicked in. We racked up quite a bill at Restoration Hardware furnishing the place, still paying that off. Don't even ask the interest rate.

"I was really hurt that you bought the place with your dad and not me," I stated.

"But, we couldn't have bought anything without my dad's help."

"Not at that second. But in the going-on-three years we've lived here, don't you think it would've been nice to be added to the deed?"

"When we got married it would've become yours," he offered.

"Pretty big *when*, Tim. Like pigs flying." I had to stop myself. I didn't want to get mean again. "I can't keep waiting on a when or a maybe or a someday. I have to move on to something I have a say in."

"You have a say here, Ellen. But do I? I mean, you didn't tell me about New York or producing with Karen or that guy. Don't I get a chance to say, hey, yeah, we have problems here, but we can work on them? We should work on them. Can you give me that? Give us that?"

The tête-à-tête continued for another two hours. He talked me out of moving to Jilli's, saying he would move into the bedroom that served as his office and sleep on the sleeper sofa we kept there for guests. His concern was that, if I moved away, we'd have less of a chance to work on us. He even offered to schedule couple's counseling.

"Stay. Please, Ellen. Say you'll stay," he pleaded.

When the man I once loved asked me to do something with tears in his eyes, how could I say no? I wanted to, but I couldn't figure out a kind way.

Chapter Ten

"I couldn't let him go. Not back to a hotel," Karen explained when I bumped into a near-nude Billy, clad only in a banana hammock, first thing on that Monday morning. I nearly dropped my latte at the sight.

It was my first day back to work since the funeral. Ruth had called the week before to let us know her mother had passed away. I booked Karen and I a flight that night to San Antonio to be with Ruth and help her make the arrangements.

We had gotten back from Texas that Saturday. Unbeknownst to me, Billy came in Sunday night after wrapping the film and packing up his Vancouver hotel room. Without a residence in L.A.—he had to sell it to pay his lawyers, ex-wife and the resort rehab tab—Karen invited Billy to stay with her. Without a maid and with me in the office. It was a recipe for catastrophe.

Ruth would return to Karen's after she took some time to mourn and settle her mother's affairs. In the meantime Rita, Ruth's cousin, would come in daily to tidy. Ruth didn't trust her, or anyone else, to do more. She wanted to be sure that, when she did return, "…the china's not chipped and the crystal's not cracked. Keep Rita away from the bleach, too."

Karen took the limited scope of Rita's work assignment as her opportunity to be domestic with Billy. Karen cooked and cleaned and ironed for Billy, and looked extremely content doing so. Billy returned the kindness by not venturing far from the sofa in the great room, containing his mess to that vicinity alone. What a guy.

I hid in my office, looking through newswires for potential show segments, trying not to call, text or email Wyatt. He didn't help the matter. I would get emails throughout the day. The messages were short and wonderfully sweet. In each one he would share something from his day or a memory that came to him. I was learning more about him and, with each discovery, my attraction deepened. Of course, I had to reply. Otherwise, that would be rude, right? I couldn't wait to see him again, but who knew when that would be.

Things at home with Tim were tense, but in the most polite way. Eggshells littered the floors, and we tread on them as lightly as we could. Tim wasn't handling the pseudo-separation that well. He seemed anxious, mostly. Maybe even a little scared. The pressure was compounded by the fact that he hadn't told anyone, not even Kent, that we had…well, what had we done, actually? Nothing definite, outside of separating our sleeping quarters.

Tim was careful when he spoke. His normally jovial spirit was dimmer. In spite of his promise, Tim had yet to set an appointment with a therapist. I didn't push. I didn't want to sit and pay lip service to a relationship at its end, but I thought it might help Tim come to terms with what was coming. We hadn't specifically called it quits but only something short of a miracle would turn our tide. Tim just needed to see that there wasn't much left to save. Or maybe that's what I needed from him. I was ahead of him on dealing with that, and I tried to keep that in mind, especially when my patience came up short. And it did in a big way when Tim asked me to come to a Crew dinner.

"They're expecting both of us," he said.

"Tell them I'm working or have another commitment."

"Please, El."

I looked into his eyes and saw how much it meant to him. If keeping up a pretense brought him less pain, I would suck up the tedium of being around those people and do it for him. It was a celebration for Roger, otherwise I wouldn't have relented. It would only be a couple of hours. Soon enough, I would never have to see any of them ever again.

"That's absurd, El," Emily stated.

We had just arrived at Vicki's residence, Llewellyn's palatial home in the hills above PCH and Sunset Boulevard. It was a concrete monolith atop a steep drive. Emily and I teetered in our tall, narrow heels, carrying our handbags and the hefty gift we all chipped in on. A large, Moroccan brass tray. It was ridiculous, but one of the few items left on the registry that we could all afford.

The week had been warm, clear and blue-skied, but today it was chilly and gray from the marine layer. A disappointing turn since the party was set to be outside. One of the downsides to living by the beach was the constant overcast from May Gray through Fogust. We were still a week away from Graypril. They had yet to come up with a rhyme for March.

"You didn't see the look on Tim's face when he asked, Em. It's just dinner. If I can suck it up for Vicki today, I can suck it up for Tim tonight."

"Well, if you think it's the right thing, but it sounds like it's going to blow," Emily stated.

"You may be right," I concurred.

We were greeted at the door by the housekeeper, who was in an actual maid's uniform. White tights and everything. She escorted us to the backyard. From the foyer through the great room, we saw the extent of Llewellyn's taste in décor: Modern museum. Clean and cold and missing anything resembling a female touch, which struck me as odd, both because of the rumors and that Vicki had lived there over a year.

The gathering seemed rather small in correlation to the space. Maybe twelve women scattered about on the massive deck. No one was down by the pool where tables were set for what seemed to be an ample number of attendees. The garden, too, remained empty. Perhaps it could be blamed on the weather. Not too many women were willing to risk frizzing an expensive blow-dry from the mist hovering overhead. Or maybe it was because this was the fourth shower/party/ celebration Vicki had tossed herself. More likely, and more sadly, it was that Vicki had never been all that popular. Her intensity and drive to befriend could be off-putting to say the least, and the consensus around town was the marriage wouldn't last. Not that many Hollywood marriages suffer longevity but, since the town believed Llewellyn was merely looking for a simplified surrogate for his offspring, it only added to the lack of enthusiasm for their impending nuptials. Of course, these naysayers would still go to the wedding. Not many are willing to pass up a free ride to a posh long weekend.

As soon as they saw us, Claudia and Remi were at our

sides. They left a noticeable gap in the crowd.

"We've been here for fifteen minutes and we can't wait to leave," Claudia whispered. "This is excruciating."

"At least the food is good," Remi said with her mouth full. "And they're pouring Veuve, El. Thank God, right?" Remi and I made our way to the bar, which was rude to do before saying hello to the hostess/guest of honor, but a girl has her priorities.

Claudia stayed with Emily to talk about "Plan P." With her awful luck in jobs and bosses, Claude was thinking about a career change, and leaning heavily toward following in Em's Pilates-instructing footsteps. It didn't seem as though any of my friends were in a state of contentment, as Remi was about to illustrate.

"Don't tell anyone, but there's trouble in paradise," Remi said in a hushed tone over the buffet table.

"Whose trouble? Which paradise?" I questioned.

"Tess.' She's not coming because she has to spend the weekend with her possible future stepchildren. Dane made 'family' plans without telling her. She's beyond not happy," Remi explained in between bites of crab cake. She was making good on her promise to eat her was through absconded cashmere. "Such a nightmare. I mean, ex-wives are bad enough, but their kids? Blech."

I nodded. Having been a stepchild, I had zero desire to be a stepparent. I could understand Tess' dismay to a point, but she was clear on what she was getting into when she started dating him. Dane did show her pictures of the kids on their first date. Back then, Tess had Julia Roberts-type fantasies of being the cool stepmom who would wind up being the kids' favorite and enable her to create a blissful mixed family. Of course, there is that annoying expanse between theory and application. Not to mention, the mother wasn't terminal. Tess couldn't really begrudge the kids at this point, now that she was almost two years into the relationship.

"Poor Tess," I said.

"Yeah. Relationships suck. We thought you had a good one, but then…you know," Remi shrugged.

"Gee, thanks." It's always nice to hear what your friends

really think.

Claude and Em made their way over to us as Remi filled up on what was left of the hors d'oeuvres. I took two glasses of bubbles from the bartender in time to hand one to Jilli who kept her promise to attend. Jilli said hello to the girls and excused us for a moment.

Pulling me to the side, Jilli asked, "Did you see it? That chain-smoking vegetarian is here."

I looked over Jilli's shoulder and, in the background, Dori passing a tray of caviar covered mini blinis. Surely, she had something to say about that.

"I guess Puck isn't catering," I muttered.

"Whatever. It's creepy," Jilli said as she threw back her champers. "Get this," she said, changing the subject. "Andy left her. He really did it. Moved everything out yesterday. Served her with divorce papers today. Can you believe it?" She went to take another gulp and saw her glass was empty. I handed her mine.

"No, I can't believe it. Can you? Are you okay with all this?"

Jilli hadn't been able to bring herself to end it with Andy. She tried for weeks and only succeeded in falling for him harder, and he for her.

"Ha! I have no fucking idea, El. I mean, this wasn't really part of the plan. I didn't mean for this to become a relationship. I didn't mean to…to…get attached." Jilli was almost Teflon when it came to love, and did her best to avoid it. She said it was like childbirth, something else she didn't see the point of. "It's messy and painful and leaves you marked up to the point that you don't recognize yourself when it's over." For her to fall in love was a big deal. For her to do it via revenge was utterly poetic. I smiled.

"What?" she demanded.

"Jilli's in love," I said in a singsong voice. "And I'm really happy for you."

"Well, don't book the minister just yet, Patterson. We've got a long, long way before any of that."

"Where's he staying?" I asked.

She looked around sheepishly and mumbled, "With me."

I stifled a laugh and put my arm around Jilli then led us over to the bar. We certainly deserved another glass. I caught eyes with Dori and gave her a wave hello. Somehow, she made even her serving blacks seem dingy.

Jilli and I rejoined our friends and saw Vicki make her way towards us. She was decked out in head-to-toe Tori Burch, holding court with a few familiar faces with names I couldn't place. Red carpet wives, I'm sure.

"Hello, darlings!" Vicki cooed as she approached our cluster. "Oh, so glad you made it," she said as she doled out air-kisses. "El, I love your skirt. Is that Posen?"

"Close," I smiled. "Vintage Gap."

"Oh, El," she laughed, "You are a wit."

The girls and I shared confused glances. Who was Vicki trying to be today? Zelda Fitzgerald?

"Ladies," Vicki said, "I'd like you to meet some of my friends and neighbors. Come, and then I'll give you a tour of the home."

We followed her over to a crowd of women like good little sheep. She rattled off the names like a machine gun. Two were the wives of entertainment chiefs, two more were married to real estate magnates, and one was the owner of a clothing shop on Montana that her husband, an actor, bought for her. They were seemingly young—faces frozen in time with Botox, any lines filled with Restalyne—wearing tasteful tea ensembles that easily cost a grand each, excluding the shoes and bags. They were emotionless; likely on antidepressants that robbed what little sex drive the endless juice cleanses left. Shaking their hands was like holding onto a Ziploc bag filled with bones. After making the introductions, Vicki stole us away.

"Now, for the tour," she said motioning to all of us to follow her again. Then she wrapped her elbow around mine. I gave Jilli a confused look.

We went through all of the sixteen rooms, each colder than the last, filled with art and the most expensive furnishings his percentage of clients' takings could procure.

"Isn't it just incredible?" she gleamed rhetorically. We nodded politely. "You know, it's like I've been preparing for this life my whole career. I mean, we all know what great training being an assistant can be, right? People misunderstand what we do and how far it can take us. I know every store, designer, landscaper, decorator, caterer, vendor, theme, fragrance and aspect of feng shui that will make this place even more incredible now that it's going to really be mine. I am ready to be a power wife."

The girls and I all looked at each other, wanting to be sure we hadn't imagined this.

Vicki continued with, "I have worked hard to get here, and I'm going to make the most of it. I start fertility treatments right after we get back from the honeymoon. And, when we get pregnant, I know the right trainers, chefs and nutritionists to ensure that I don't put on more than the required weight gain, and I'll be back to my normal size, or less, in a matter weeks after the birth. The surgeons will take care of the rest. I'm so happy. Isn't this exciting?"

Once again, all we could do was nod politely, especially Emily, whom I was certain was swallowing a fair amount of blood from biting her tongue. I made a special effort to not let Vicki see that I noticed how sad she looked behind that smile. This was no way to live.

Were we in the Palisades or Stepford? It was growing hard to tell. To have one's face and emotions stiffened with pharmacology wasn't living. To plan one's pregnancy by the pound wasn't living. To try to make oneself comfortable in a cold, hard-edged, concrete slab wasn't living. But, it was status in some circles. I was just happy I was outside that orb. It made me feel better about my messy little existence.

Out in the garden, we took our designated seats for tea, which would be eschewed for more champagne, salads that would be sent back to be undressed, and sandwiches that would mostly go untouched. I noticed there was tension around the table. I think it was the weight of obligation. It occurred to me that, unlike a typical wedding shower, the party wasn't filled with family and good friends but social acquisitions. There wasn't even a member of the bridal party in attendance, which was partially my fault since I turned down that request. Vicki's cousin, who lives in Sedona, was her maid of honor, but she couldn't make this party, after attending the other three. Out of guilt, I offered to do the traditional task of writing down the salacious statements she made while opening up her gifts and, after nudging her under the table, Claudia offered to make up the bow bouquet. The Palisades housewives looked down their nose jobs at this pedestrian tradition. That only made our side of the table giggle more, mainly because Remi and I were hitting the Veuve a little hard since we weren't driving.

The five of us got into the spirit of the afternoon, and that seemed to loosen up the rest of the ladies. It must have occurred to them we had no significant social ranking so, if they made themselves look silly, who would give a fuck? Suddenly, they were in the mix, sharing stories of their wedding disasters: mother-in-law getting drunk and passing out in her dinner plate and the paramedics being called.

"We thought it was a heart attack, but it was three too many gin and tonics," laughed one of the wives.

Another had her luggage lost on the honeymoon, which led to an impromptu Parisian shopping spree. "Not like I minded. I finally got the Vuitton luggage I wanted," she giggled.

Then there was the husband who forgot his Viagra and had to have a new Rx FedExed to Mykonos. "It took four days to get there. I finally finished *The Corrections*," another wife admitted with a modicum of pride.

The Palisades Mafia were turning out to be a fun group. One must never underestimate the power of champagne and a mood stabilizer. The table was in a fit of laughter when a commotion came from the house.

"I know that bitch is here! Where is she?" bellowed out from inside the concrete fortress and over the distressed-sounding Spanish of the housekeeper. The distinct clomping of expensive heels grew closer. Eyes around the table widened, but foreheads stayed immobile. Jilli remained blasé. She simply removed her napkin from her lap and placed it on the table.

"I'll be right back," she said to me as she rose from her chair. At that exact moment, Selma burst onto the deck. She looked at the women seated at the table, and then her eyes fell directly onto Jilli.

Jilli and Selma walked toward each other without saying a word. You could've heard a pin drop. Instead, we heard the cracking slap of Selma's hand meeting Jilli's face. It was a surreal sight. Something you never thought you would see in real life. But this wasn't real life. This was Los Angeles, the culmination of an ingenious plotting of revenge, and the natural end to it.

"You fucking whore!" Selma screamed and went to slap Jilli again, but Jilli caught her arm in mid-swing.

The two women struggled. Selma got a hand free and scratched Jilli's neck. Every woman at the table gasped. Remi let out a, "Holy shit!"

"Should we do something?" Claudia whispered.

"No," I asserted. "Jilli will handle it."

"How did Selma even know she was here?" Emily inquired.

"I invited her," Vicki blurted. "Selma and I go to the same spin class."

"Enough," Jilli snarled and grabbed Selma hard by the hair, yanking her head back and forcing Selma to arch into a C. "I'm not going to hit you back, Selma, because I don't want to get a letter from your lawyer or your plastic surgeon but, I swear to God, touch me again and you will walk out of here with a bald spot. Got me?"

Selma gave as much of a nod as she could with Jilli keeping a firm grip on her hair.

"You fucked my husband," Selma growled from her crooked position.

"Yes, I did," Jilli replied calmly.

The shower guests sat quietly, riveted by this show.

"He left me. Left me for you. You!" Selma screamed, sounding like a wounded animal. Jilli held the woman by her hair with an air of patience. "How could you?" Selma demanded. And that question seemed to be exactly what Jilli was waiting for.

Jilli pulled her former boss into her. She looked the now-frightened woman in the eye and said with a dagger's piercing chill, "Now you know what it feels like to be fucked over by someone you trusted." Jilli shoved her away, releasing her tresses and Selma stumbled back to find her balance.

Jilli stood there, steely-eyed, waiting for Selma's next move. Selma looked around to see that all eyes were on her, including those of the horrified maid, then she turned back to face Jilli. Slowly, the realization of the situation met her. Rage was replaced by pain and humiliation. Jilli faced her enemy without any readable emotion. She did not sneer or gloat, nor did she look away. She simply let Selma face the fact that she had crossed the wrong woman. Jilli might have fucked her husband, but Selma had fucked Jilli's career. You tell me what's worse.

Without saying another word, Selma walked back into the house. We heard the fast clicking of her running heels and the door slamming behind her.

"Sorry about that, Vicki," Jilli offered as she walked back to the table to retrieve her purse.

"Are you going, Jilli? Don't leave," Vicki pleaded. "Really. It's okay."

With serene dignity, Jilli smiled and said, "I don't think a homewrecker really belongs at a wedding shower, do you?" But the cracks in her armor were beginning to show. Jilli walked over and gave Vicki a kiss on the cheek. "I wish you all the best. I really do," she said and then walked to the house.

I looked over at Em and she nodded. I rose from the table. "I'm sorry, Vicki."

I chased after Jilli. I found her down the street, crying in her Rover. Ever so carefully, I drove us to the nearest Starbucks and brought caffeine back to the SUV where a puffy-eyed Jilli waited. The side of her face bore the handprint Selma left behind, almost in the shape of a scarlet A.

We sat in the massive vehicle for hours talking. The tears, she explained, were not of sadness, but release. After two years, from the time she watched her dream project be derailed, she had patiently plotted and gotten her retaliation. She didn't feel it was evil, but karmic. Selma had been the evil one, lying to Jilli's face, pretending to be a supportive mentor only to pull the film and rug out from under her.

Initially, she had only planned on flirting with Andy; perhaps have dinner or a few dates. Sex only if he wasn't too intolerable. Jilli's not the type to shag just anyone. She didn't mean to fall in love with him. But it happened. And, remarkably, Andy remained loyal to Jilli even after she admitted her scheme. He left Selma knowing how and why he and Jilli got together. Jilli wanted him to know the full truth, even the ugly bits. That would be the only way she knew what she had was real.

If falling in love and settling her score weren't enough, Jilli told me that, on Friday, Cassie offered her the president position at her production company, after firing her manager/producing partner the night before. Jilli was spinning.

"I'm so happy, I don't know what to do with myself," she said without a smile or glint of joy in her eyes.

Jillian Raines was spent. I had never seen her so overwhelmed. I watched my friend soften before my eyes. Jilli's hard edges were rounding; her thick shell had thinned. Her stiff posture relaxed and she melted into the leather seat. It was lovely to witness.

She let out a deep sigh. "Maybe our lives aren't all that off-track, El. Maybe we are on the scenic route rather than the express. And maybe that isn't such a bad thing."

I let out my own sigh. Maybe. I was growing sick of maybe, though. My life was nothing more than a great big futhermucking *maybe* lately. A little certainty would be greatly appreciated.

"I mean, look, we are both going to be running production companies," Jilli said and gave a tired smile. I had called her from San Antonio after the funeral and told her about KEEP. She was thrilled for me, like a best friend would be. "It may not be our own company, but this isn't a bad runner-up."

Now I saw how much it meant to her that we were seeing some success, no matter what turmoil had surrounded it. And this wasn't about money or status, it was about achievement; finally, we had attained our goal of being producers. It lacked the glamour we had fantasized about. No blazing headlines in the trades announcing our triumphs, though I was sure the slapfest Jilli and Selma shared would be all over *Page Six* in the morning. Or *Deadline* later today.

"God. What if Cassie hears about this and doesn't want to work with me? Oh, shit! Now *that* would be karma. I have to tell her. Fuck. What if she's already heard?" Jilli was starting to panic.

"Take a breath, Jilli. It will be okay," I hoped. I didn't want to see her lose another opportunity. I wasn't sure she would be able to cope with that.

Jilli's phone rang. It was Andy checking in on her after getting a call from a hysterical Selma. I saw my friend flush with love as she talked to her man. I smiled at the sweetness. She seemed reassured by the time she ended the call.

"He's going to go with me to tell Cassie," she smiled. "He said it would be better to tell her in person than on the phone." She started to well up again as she texted Cassie to request the get-together. "He's such a great guy."

The tension of the day had caught up with me inducing a yawn. I looked at my watch and saw how much time had passed. I needed to get back to go to a dinner I wanted to miss. I drove the Rover home, giving Jilli more time to relax. We didn't say much along the way.

"None of this changes the fact that we're best friends, right? You don't think less of me, do you?" Jilli asked quietly.

"You're my girl, Jillian."

The one thing I knew for certain was that relationships brought out the very best and the very worst in people. There was no point in judging. She and Andy were going to be facing enough strain. Selma would likely be repped by Laura Wasser.

Jilli and I said goodbye, promising to talk later. I wished her luck with Cassie. She wished me the same for Roger's dinner.

Tim looked as though he was going to have kittens when I walked in the door. "Where have you been? I've been trying to call you for hours. We're late," he said grabbing his keys and opening the door.

"Hold up," I said. "Can I at least pee?"

Roger's dinner was at El Cholo in Santa Monica. El Cholo is known for their lethal margaritas served in a pint glass. The first goes down so smoothly you make the mistake of ordering a second. As I took my seat, Tim ordered me a mango marg to fortify me for the night. I noticed many empty chairs around the large table, which meant the hens were roosting in the ladies. A moment of calm before the storm. I was grateful for it, and how quickly the waiter returned with my drink. It appeared that Roger was enjoying his celebration. He had a tequila-induced glow about him.

The guys were jovial and excited for their new gig. They bantered on, laughing and I noticed how odd it was to be sitting there next to Tim with his arm draped around me as he laughed. I put on a grin, so used to faking it in these situations. It was strange to have Tim faking it with me. It would only be a few more days of this. I had been keeping a keen eye on the calendar. He was leaving in a week and would be gone for almost a month. By the time he got back, I would be gone. Just not sure to where. I needed to get an answer from Wyatt.

The hens returned en masse to the table. Liza and Renee donning particularly wicked grins. I saw Dori coming up behind them.

"We heard," Liza couldn't wait to say. "I can't believe what your friend did."

"What a spectacle that must've been," Renee sneered.

"It was," Dori acknowledged, still looking shellshocked from the event.

"Is she all right?" Valerie asked.

"It must've been awful," Tab said with sympathy.

"What happened?" Tim asked.

"It's really not my place to talk about it. Besides, we are here for Roger," I said and raised my huge glass to him. The men followed. The hens, however, wouldn't let it drop.

"What a terrible thing to do. I mean, to sleep with a married man; it's just despicable," Liza taunted.

I swallowed my margarita, but my irritation didn't go down with it. My temper was lit. I could feel its force. I was going to lose control, and it wasn't going to be pretty. I took a deep breath.

"I don't know, Liza. Some women seem to repel their men into cheating," I volleyed back.

"More often than not, there's that type of woman who chases after it. So desperate to get what they don't have, they take it from someone else."

"We both know Jilli's not that type. And, since you don't know the whole story, it's not your place, or anyone else's for that matter, to judge. No one's perfect, Liza. Certainly no one at this table," I said, fighting the urge to hail an Uber.

"Especially at your end," Liza said in a low voice with just enough volume so I would be sure to hear it.

That was it. I got up and charged over to Liza. Her eyes widened, seeming to expect something similar to what Selma had dished out. Before Tim or Kent could get to me, I simply leaned in to her and whispered, "One day, Liza, you may find yourself in that wife's shoes. Because the one thing you and Selma have in common is that you are both miserable human beings. I can only imagine how miserable you've made your husbands."

Liza let out a little gasp, then recovered and said, "Of course you'd have to imagine, since you can't find a man willing to marry you."

I glared at Liza. Looks may not kill, but this one should've at least caused a few gray hairs. All the things I had wanted to say to her over the years went around in my brain like lottery balls. I was waiting for one of them to drop out of my mouth so I could deliver a winner, but then I realized how small she was. How empty and sad she had to be to be such a nasty little twat. She wasn't worth it. She wasn't worth any of the bother or headaches I had endured over the years. It was such a waste of my time, and I wasn't going to waste more of it.

"Sorry, Roger. I really am. Happy birthday. Sorry to spoil it." I walked back to my chair to take took my purse amid titters of "Don't go!" and "Please stay!"

Tim got up. "What are you doing?" he whispered coarsely.

"Pretty much what it looks like."

For the second time in my life, and that day, I was walking out of a party under a cloud of drama.

"I'm going with you." He started to follow.

"No. Stay here. These are your friends. They aren't mine. Some have made that absolutely clear from day one," I said clearly, and everyone at the table heard me.

I stormed out of the restaurant, ignoring the looks of the disturbed diners as I passed. I was confirming my Uber when

Tim caught up to me outside.

"What the fuck was all that about, Ellen?" he asked while trying to catch his breath. "And what does Jilli have to do with it?"

I went into a full-on ramble of what had happened with Jilli and Andy and Selma, everything at Vicki's shower and parts of my conversation with Jilli in her car. It wasn't exactly eloquent. It was more like word vomit, but at least I got it out.

"All of this made me realize, Tim, that what's meant to be is meant to be, no matter how it happens. But, as it happens, we just aren't meant to be together anymore. We are not a match. Try as I did to make me fit into your world, I don't. And you don't want to fit into mine. That's fine. But tonight was the perfect example. The last thing, Tim, the very last fucking thing I needed today was to have to put up with your friends. But I don't have to put up with them anymore. Because I'm done. Really fucking done."

"They are our friends, El. Don't put everyone else out because you and Liza don't get along. Everybody else adores you," he said, really believing it.

"Not really. We tolerate each other. Not just those people in there, Tim. *We* tolerate each other. How sad is that? I want more. Don't you? Don't you want something more than this?"

After I said that, I felt the stream of tears that had been running down my face. I wiped them away and started toward the street hoping to see my driver.

"Wait a goddamn minute," Tim shouted after me. "I'll take you home. There's no one in there, no one anywhere that's more important to me than you."

"Tim—" I started, but he cut me off.

"Let's go home, El." He held out my hand until I took it.

We weren't back at the Sliver an hour before a red-faced Kent and puffy-eyed Liza were at our door. I was on the sofa with Tim, who was again trying to talk me out of moving out when the phone rang announcing them at the gate.

"Sorry to disturb you," Kent said in a low voice, his perpetual smile missing. "We came to apologize."

I noticed he was holding Liza at the wrist rather than the

hand. She looked like a child contrite after being forced into a confession. He shot her a look and Liza began talking while fighting back tears, attempting to maintain a semblance of dignity.

"El," she said, then cleared her throat. "I want to... apologize for tonight. I didn't mean to upset you."

"Yes, you did."

I turned and looked at Tim, shocked that those words came out of his mouth.

"I've let a lot of things slide, Liza, because you are my best friend's wife, but you've never extended that courtesy to Ellen," he continued.

"But she's not your wife," she corrected.

"So fucking what, Liza? I've been with her for about as long as you've known me. We live together. You are standing in our home. How many times have we had you over here? Gone on vacations? Hung out?" Tim waited for a response. Liza didn't have one so he filled in the silence. "Who threw you a goddamn bridal shower when no one else here thought to do it for you? El did. And still you talk shit to her and about her, and I've absolutely had it. Sorry, Kent, but I have."

Kent just nodded in that kind of dude/no contest way.

"We will accept your apology when you start treating her with the respect she deserves. But, until then, Liza, we aren't friends," Tim finished.

Tim went to the door and opened it. He shook Kent's hand and they patted each other's shoulders confirming they were okay. I think I saw a smile pass over Kent's lips as he went. On her way out, Liza said again, "I am sorry." Tim did not respond.

He came back in to the living room and sat down next to me.

"Things have been fucked up, El. I get it now," he said with soulful eyes. "But I think we can work on it if you want to. I want to. Do you?"

I had a flash to earlier that afternoon. Vicki had approached me in the corner of the buffet while I was getting seconds, before Selma burst in and everything went pear-shaped.

"Can I tell you something, El? Do you promise you won't

repeat it?"

"Sure," I said, taking more of the mini lobster tostadas.

"I know what people say about Lew. I know the town thinks he's gay. They're wrong. And you know what, even if they are right, so what? Lew makes me happy. I feel safe with him. He takes care of me. He's a good man who makes me laugh. That should count for something, don't you think?"

I nodded at her, looking her in the eye. That should count for something.

And so, I nodded at Tim, looking him in the eye.

Chapter Eleven

Turning thirty-two meant I would be officially at the end of my early-thirties. It's not like I'm age paranoid, or have any plans to fudge my number. That's ridiculous. But thirty-two felt like an odd number. Peculiar. Like shoes a size off, it didn't fit. I didn't like it. But I had little choice in the matter. My birthday was coming, whether I was in the mood for it or not.

"It's that time of year, dear. Colonic and massage," Jilli reminded. "I made the appointments. You'll feel better once you get some of the crap out of your life."

I don't know how the unfortunate tradition began, but somehow my birthday marked our annual appointment for colon irrigation.

"Why do we always have to do this at my birthday?" I asked, more than insulted at having my DOB associated with a high-end enema.

"Because my birthday is the beginning of November, right before we go into feeding season," Jilli countered. "Yours comes after the holidays, including Easter this year. The perfect time for spring cleaning."

Perhaps no one outside of Los Angeles would understand paying good money to have the humiliation of lying in a room with a hose up your exit ramp while another woman monitored your output. I didn't really understand it either, but I did feel better after it was over. Although, not enough to do it more than once a year.

I was born on the second of April. "One day shy of being a fool," my mother would sign in every birthday card. It had been nearly six weeks since everything went ass over teakettle, and there was still too much up in the air. But, before I could think about removing the impurities from my system, I had to deal with the rest of my merde.

Tim had moved back into the bedroom for his last week home. After him defending me from Liza, we had emotional make-up sex. Yet, in the bright light of the morning, when I woke up in his arms, I knew it was a mistake. I didn't have the same feelings for him anymore. They were gone. He was ready to try, ready to work at our relationship, but I was done. My heart was hollow; I just didn't have the guts to tell him. And that somewhat dampened my birthday mood.

"I don't feel like celebrating this year," I groaned to Jilli as we left the colonic clinic and went out in search of an organic lunch.

"Get over it," she chided. "You are going to be spending it with the people you love and who love you."

"No, you are going to spend your birthday with us," Kitty barked over the phone. "We are your family, Ellen."

"Karen is taking me to dinner on my birthday. It's already been arranged, Kitty. I can't get out of it." Nor did I want to. And extending the invitation to my kin was not going to happen.

"Then come the night before, April Fool. We'll make your favorite dinner."

"Reservations?" I asked. I couldn't help but be sarcastic.

"Roast beef, smart mouth," Kitty retorted.

"You do realize that I haven't had red meat since my junior year in high school, right?"

"That's ridiculous. We had it last year," she asserted.

"No, the rest of you did. I had salad. Look, let's just go to one of the many chain restaurants out there and make it easy on everyone. Okay?"

"Well, it's your birthday."

No kidding. So why should I have to drive out there to have it acknowledged? Punishment for stretch marks, I'm sure.

"It will be a grand time," Karen said with delight. "All of your friends have been invited. We can celebrate your birthday and our new business venture."

She had planned a dinner for me at Mr. Chow with Jilli's help. I didn't have the heart to tell her that I'd rather skip it. Karen was beaming lately. She and Billy were having a wonderful time, especially now that Ruth was back.

Karen was never one for mess. Now she didn't have to ignore it or pretend to find his sloppiness another of Billy's charm. She was also quite excited to get the talk show going and to produce something of our own. Howie had started sending us scripts for small features and movies for cable. I was going cross-eyed from all the reading. That gave me a convenient excuse to avoid spending time with Tim before he left.

Tim took off for Phoenix on Sunday morning, driving out himself rather than carpool with Kent. It seemed that he, too, was keeping secrets. He and I had dinner the night before he went for an early birthday toast.

"I hate to miss it," he said, seeming to forget that he was also gone for my thirtieth, twenty-ninth and twenty-eighth.

"Thirty-two isn't a big deal, Tim."

"Your birthday is always a big deal to me," he said as he handed me my present. It was a bracelet from Celia. "Specially made for you. One of a kind," he smiled.

I took it out of the box to admire the three hammered, intertwined, square bangles in yellow, green and rose gold. The hammering allowed the metal to reflect the light and sparkle. I loved them.

He was making an effort, painful as it was to witness. I didn't want to mislead him, but I thought it better to accept his attempts than to rebuff them. By the time he returned from this gig, I would be packed up and ready to move. Each day was proving harder to be there and I kept wondering how long we could both hold our breath. Tim wasn't a dolt. Deep down, he must realize we're done. But, we continued the farce, perhaps out of habit, more likely it was to delay having to face the onslaught of questions and badgering from The Crew. For me, the townhouse was the only place to stay now. My two safe havens were currently crowded with new relationships.

Jilli and Andy were ass over teakettle in love. "When we told Cassie our story, she thought it was the most crazy, romantic thing she had ever heard and wants to make it into a romantic-comedy," Jilli blurted over the phone first thing on the Monday morning after Selma's slap. She and Andy took Cassie to dinner to explain the situation and be assured that Jilli still had the job. She did. The contracts were signed two days later.

"I can see it now," I told Jilli. "She was looking for revenge, but found love instead."

"Exactly what Cassie said," Jilli laughed. Then she told me that she and Andy were looking at new homes together. "Can you believe it?"

No. I couldn't. I couldn't believe the unlikely smitten couples around me. Karen and Billy were sweet enough to cause tooth decay. He was incredibly charming when the mood struck. I couldn't be sure if that was his true demeanor, or a character he created. Actors are hard to read and even harder to believe. As long as Karen was happy, I couldn't complain.

What I could bitch about was having to sit in traffic to see the diabolic duo for dinner. Just like everything else in my life, it was easier to go than to fight it. After seventy-five minutes in traffic, I met them at their local Outback Steakhouse. At least it was near the freeway. I was there on time, despite traffic. Kitty, Gwen and Daryl were ten minutes late.

"Well, you're never on time, dear," Kitty said.

I bit my tongue as I hugged them hello.

"Thirty-two. I can't believe it. I remember that day so well." Kitty would retell the day of our births every year. The water breaking. Excruciating labor. The epidural and episiotomy.

"God, your head was so big, Ellen," Kitty reminded.

I sucked down my glass of mineral water and pretended it was something stronger. The one occasion when I truly needed a drink was when I was with my family, but I didn't dare have a one in case I needed to flee the scene.

We made it through our dinner with surprisingly polite conversation. I opened my cards and presents over dessert. I received a terribly teal sweater, bath products that would likely cause a rash and a silver necklace with a block letter E hanging from it. I have always worn gold. Yellow gold. Always. I'm just not a sterling kind of gal. Or a teal wearer. Or a raspberry bath gel user. It is the thought that counts, and these gifts illustrated perfectly how little they knew me, or how little they cared.

It seemed impossible to share so much DNA with two people and still be virtual strangers. It wasn't them, though; it was me who was the odd Patterson out. Maybe Kitty was right and I was just like my father. Not just the annoying allergies that caused me to keep Kleenex at the ready; perhaps his tendency to abandon was passed on to me as well?

"Well, do you like your gifts?" Kitty eyed me as she took a spoonful of the chocolate cake now swimming in melted ice cream that could only be served after a humiliating birthday serenade.

I nodded convincingly with a pleased smile. "Thank you," I added. But I realized there was something missing. "Kitty, I hate to ask but where is the inheritance check I was supposed to get?" I inquired as tactfully as I could.

"Your birthday is not until tomorrow, Ellen. And since you couldn't see fit to spend it with us, you'll just have to wait."

"Seriously, when will I get it?"

"What's the rush? Are you in some sort of trouble?" She took my hands. "No ring, so we know it's not for a wedding."

Kitty and my sister burst into laughter. Daryl just sipped his beer.

"Don't tell me you're pregnant," my sinister insulted. For a second, she panicked. A pregnancy might not upstage her as a bride, but a baby bump on her unmarried, older sister would ruin her wedding photos.

"Oh, Gwen," I consoled. "I wouldn't do that to you."
Gwen relaxed.

"You'll get it soon enough," Kitty stated. "Right now I'm busy with your sister's wedding. It would be nice if her sister would lend a hand."

"Never mind, mother. My other bridesmaids are honoring their duties," Gwen sneered.

"Glad to hear it," I smiled. "So, Daryl, are you excited about your impending doom?"

"Don't be rude, Ellen. You can see how happy Daryl is," Kitty interrupted.

I watched Daryl shovel a forkful of cake into his face. Daryl was never a candidate for Mr. Personality. Quiet was an understatement. You might believe the poor man was mute. He could talk, though, sneaking in a word every once in a while when either Kitty or Gwen paused for breath, but that was a rare occurrence.

"Tell her how happy you are, sweetie," my sister nudged.

He also spoke on demand.

"Yeah, pretty excited. My brother is planning my groom's night," he reported after he half-swallowed his food.

I looked at him quizzically. "Groom's night?"

"Daryl is too refined for a bachelor party," my sister answered. "So, he's having a groom's night. Dinner at the country club. It will be nice." My sister looking lovingly, if not controllingly, at poor Daryl.

"Sounds like a rocking good time, Daryl. Have fun." I turned to my mother. "Kitty, I'll need the check sooner than later. I'm moving soon, so it will come in handy," I said, and immediately regretted sharing that information with my family.

"Are you and Tim buying a place *together*, finally? In this market? It doesn't seem wise. What do you think, Gwennie?" Kitty asked.

"It depends on how much Tim's place has appreciated, I suppose, and where they intend to buy. The beach cities offer so little for your dollar."

I rolled my eyes, landing them on my mother. "Just let me know when I can expect the check, okay?"

"Okay, greedy," Kitty mocked. And that was my signal to go.

I thanked them for dinner and explained I had to get back before it got too late. Big day tomorrow, blah blah blah. I gave the requisite hugs and bolted out the door. As I was buckling up, I saw my sister running toward my car, armed with the gifts I had forgotten. Almost a clean getaway.

The one upside to seeing my family was that they never asked about me, what I was up to at work, or how things were with Tim. They assumed status quo, which, to them, was this side of failure. As long as I didn't show up in tears, I must be okay. And I let them believe just that. They wouldn't understand, anyway. They didn't want to hear my concerns. To them, it just sounded like complaints, and I didn't want to hear their comments.

My mother's solution to everything was for me to move back home and go to school to be a dental hygienist. "They make good money and are always in demand," she asserted.

Scraping tartar out of random mouths was an easier job to explain to people than whatever it was I did. No matter how she explained it, she told me, I ended up sounding like I was a glorified gofer.

The next morning, I woke up and I waited to see if I'd feel any different at thirty-two. I checked everything. Toes. Knees. Fingers. Normal. I did find a new gray hair, though. It went well with the pimple on my chin.

Tim called to wish me happy birthday, but it went to voicemail. I was in the shower. When I got to my office, I was showered again. This time with flowers from Wyatt, from Karen, from the girls and a huge arrangement from Tim. I nearly fell over from shock. I had received three bouquets from him in the whole of our relationship. This made an even four. He really was going against type in his quest to salvage. Roses even. Deep red and fragrant. I called to thank him and got his voicemail.

"I told you not to come into work today. I swear, you are the most stubborn person I've ever known, Ellen Patterson," Karen chided.

"I have a lot to do," I defended.

"Not on your birthday, kiddo. There's nothing here that can't wait," she stated as she closed my laptop.

Karen liked to make a fuss about birthdays, and she had quite a day planned for me. Since I failed to stay at home as she had directed, Karen redirected the masseuse to the office/her home. A deep tissue rub was exactly what I needed. Sidney's expert hands found every knot and ache, and made them all go away. I felt high when I got off that table, and didn't want anything to take away from that blissful state. Karen was right. I turned off my iPhone and shut off the office phone. There was nothing that couldn't wait one day.

The massage would have been gift enough, but not for Karen. She took me to Barney's for a shopping spree, treating me to a new ensemble, much to my protest.

"Dammit, El, let me do this for you. Quit being difficult. This is fun for me," she admonished in the dressing room. "I want tonight to be your sort of coming out party. Ellen Patterson, Associate Producer of *The Karen Ellis Show* and Producing

Partner in KEEP." Her smile was broad and infectious. "You deserve this, kiddo."

"Thank you, Karen," was all I could manage with the lump in my throat.

It didn't stop there. Hair and makeup were waiting for us when we returned. We gabbed like schoolgirls as I got my coif on while she was made up, then we switched artists and gabbed some more. By the time we were through—two hours later—I was smoky-eyed, sexy-haired, Phillip Lim-ed and Louboutin-ed. I felt wonderful.

"You look amazing, El," Karen said hugging me. I hugged her back tightly. I couldn't be more grateful to Karen. When we broke from our embrace, we noticed that both our eyes were damp. We laughed at ourselves and vowed to get a grip so as to not need a touchup so soon.

A limo took Karen, Billy, Ruth and me to Mr. Chow. "You were supposed to stay home so the car could get you there, El. Now, I don't know what we'll do with yours," Karen sweetly complained.

"We'll figure it out," I assured.

Jilli and Andy, Emily and Ron, Tess and Dane, Claudia and Gabe, Remi and a really hot guy who looked barely old enough to drink were waiting when we arrived. We filled the table, but an empty chair remained. I thought Karen or the restaurant miscounted our guest list, but then I felt warm hands go on my bare shoulders, and soft lips brush my cheek. I knew from his scent it was Wyatt. He took the chair that remained between Jilli and Gabe, the hot seat. Karen and Jilli both wore huge grins, so I couldn't tell who was to blame or thank for his invitation.

The champagne cart arrived immediately. A bottle of Rosé Perrier Jouet was placed at one side of the table and a bottle of Dom at the other. We didn't bother with menus; the waiter ordered for us. You can't go wrong with anything offered at Mr. Chow. We ate, drank and toasted the night away. There was much to celebrate. Along with Jilli's new gig and new love, Emily also had big news.

"So, one of the wives at Vicki's party is best friends with a client of mine. She had heard about me—I guess her friend had raved—put two and two together and realized I was her friend's instructor. Anyway, she lives part-time in Palm Springs, she and her husband own a company that does infomercials and product development. She wants to branch out of that and develop a chain of training centers that would bring affordable Pilates to the people. She said she was looking for someone like me to partner with. Can you believe it? She wants to open a center in Palm Springs to start, and get me on all the network morning shows ASAP to get me known as an expert," Emily beamed.

"Well, my show, too," Karen said with a smile.

"Absolutely. We're going to start right away," Emily continued. "And Claudia is going to work on the project, too. She's going to run my studio here and help me with the new venture."

"I am so excited," Claude said looking ready to burst. "I'm going to give my notice at the end of the month. Ahh!"

"That's wonderful," Tess said. "And who will be doing your PR?"

"I'll have my people call your people," Emily laughed.

The mood was jovial. Even Ruth looked happy. That was nice to see. Karen had treated her to a new dress and hairdo, too. Ruth said she felt it was like her birthday, and was worried I might feel upstaged. I told her that my happiness was doubled by hers, and the best gift I could have was her smiling again.

"Shall we tell them, honey?" Dane asked Tess. She nodded.

"Dane and I are pregnant," Tess announced. It was then I noticed her glass of Pellegrino.

"That's incredible," I said, trying to hide my shock.

"I mean, we are like five minutes pregnant. Probably bad luck to talk about it, but we are so happy," Tess continued.

"And we're getting married," added a glowing Dane. "We picked out the rings earlier today.

"They'll be ready in a couple of days," Tess finished.

"Holy shit," Jilli smiled and raised her glass. "Here's to wedding bells and baby booties."

After the toast, I saw Remi lean in to kiss her beau, James, who was pretty enough to be an actor, but was a legal executive at Fox. They met by accident when he rear-ended her in front of the studio. They had only been dating a couple of weeks, but looked like they were falling madly for each other.

I had perma-grin from the champagne and all the good things happening to my friends. How much had changed in only a few weeks' time. I looked over at Wyatt and found him smiling at me. I felt myself go warm and blush. I loved that feeling of attraction and anticipation. It made my body buzz.

Wyatt cleared his throat. "I have an announcement that I hope Karen and El won't mind if I share here and now," he said.

Karen picked up her head from Billy's shoulder and said, "By all means, as long as it is good news."

"I hope it is." He cleared his throat again. "The show is going to New York. We got word this afternoon."

Wyatt gave a satisfied smile and raised his glass. No one followed. He looked around, and then at me. It took me a moment to recover. I let out a deep breath and lifted my glass.

"To New York. And new beginnings," I said with relief. It was an answer. I could now make a plan. Wyatt smiled back and the rest of the table came to life.

Karen and Billy followed. "New York," they said together and kissed.

Even Ruth was excited. "Oh my. I never thought I would live in New York City. Everyone delivers there, right?"

The rest of my friends tucked away their disappointment and bestowed their blessings.

"Congratulations," Gabe declared. "Remember to get a fold-out sofa, because I'm going to be crashing at your pad, sister."

"We'll rack up a lot of miles visiting you," Remi said wiping away a tear.

"Oh, Remi," I said, putting my hands over my heart. Leaving my friends would not be easy.

Jilli and Andy looked at each other and smiled. "We're thinking about moving to New York, too. Cassie wants to be based there. She just signed to do a play, and we're looking for a new start. What do you think, El?" Jilli asked.

"I can't think of anything better."

"Anyone else moving to New York?" Tess checked. Remi,

Emily and Claudia shook their heads. "Good. Two is too many."

Over cake, there was more laughter, more champagne and more joy than I had known in a long time. Looking around at my beautiful friends, laughing and smiling, content, in love and moving forward, I felt like everything had fallen into place in one night. I adored these people. I was going to miss having them a gridlocked drive away. And I knew for certain there would be a happy ending for me after all.

The paparazzi were waiting, as they were most every night at Mr. Chow, when we walked out. Karen graciously hugged each of my friends among the strobe of the camera flashes, remembering names and congratulating them on their bits of good news as they thanked her for a lovely night. Even Billy made a show of friendliness to my group, especially the ladies. Then my friends made their way to me to kiss me goodnight and gush over Wyatt.

"Yummy, yummy," Gabe whispered to me before shaking Wyatt's hand.

Karen offered the limo to take me home after it dropped off her, Billy and Ruth. Before I could respond, Wyatt, the gallant Knight, said he would take me, which pleased Karen nearly as much, if not more, than me.

"I like your friends," Wyatt said breaking the silence on our way to my home. He smiled at me before putting his eyes back on the road.

"I couldn't ask for better." Leaning back in the seat listening to the jazz playing on the car's stereo as we turned onto Beverly Glen, I felt completely at ease.

Wyatt smiled. "How do you feel about the New York thing?"

"Liberated," I answered, still floating on the champagne.

"That's a hell of an answer," he laughed.

It was true, though. For a girl who had lived in the same section of the globe for thirty-two years, as of that day, it was liberating to go into a new facet of my career in a new city. And not just any city, New York City. Life there would be completely different from what I had in L.A. And, with the chance of Jilli moving to Manhattan, too, it was more than I could hope for. I would have my best friend there to savor this new chapter with me. And maybe a new romance.

"Tim won't be coming with me," I said to Wyatt.

"Oh," was his simple response. "Is that why this is liberating?"

"Maybe. Mostly, though, it's like everything is lining up for me. It's just now all sinking in," I admitted with a smile stretched wide across my face. "How about you? Are you excited about moving to New York?"

"I just bought my place last year, so it kind of sucks to have to sell. But, yeah. This is a good move. I'll be closer to family. And who could turn down New York?"

We turned onto my street and I asked Wyatt if he wouldn't mind walking me to my door. He said he thought I'd never ask.

Wyatt wandered around looking at the framed pictures on the shelves while I put the kettle on for tea. He discovered the fireplace switch and turned it on and off, declaring it fantastic. I brought in cups full of chamomile and we sat on the sofa watching the gas-fueled flames flicker.

"We haven't officially broken up yet," I admitted. "Tim wanted to try to work things out, but it's too late. It didn't seem right to break up with him before he went off on a job."

Wyatt nodded. I explained that I would end things when Tim got back. Then, I'd stay with Gabe for a bit, since Karen and Jilli were both shacked up.

"Or you could stay with me," Wyatt offered. I looked at him with eyes wide. He put his hand on mine, reassuringly. "I have a second room. Guest bed. Own bath. Yours if you want it."

"That's a bold offer," I replied.

"I'm a bold man," he said as he went in and kissed me. It was a kiss that caused some of our clothes to fall off. Before it went any further, I had to stop.

"As much as I want to, I can't. I hope you understand."

"I do," he said then kissed my forehead.

"You're pretty amazing, Wyatt," I said, wanting him even more now, but the guilt I would inevitably feel would ruin it.

"So are you, Ellie. I don't want to mess this up, either.

There's no rush. Well…" He finished with a devilish smile.

He was almost too good to be true. But he was in fact human, and very much male. We both tried to politely ignore his erection. We went back to sipping tea and talking. He spotted Scrabble on the bookshelf and we started a game. Before we knew it, it was after two. Since it was late, I invited him to stay the night with the understanding it would be chaste. He agreed.

We went upstairs and crawled under the covers. I pulled on a nightgown, one I only use when staying with friends or at Tim's parents.' Wyatt kept on his t-shirt and boxers. Boxers, not boxer-briefs. I never would have guessed. We held hands all night, and I barely slept.

The next morning, I showered quickly and dressed for work in a haze. Wyatt drove us to his place so he could get ready for the day. Afterwards, he would drop me off at Karen's, which was not at all on the way to his office.

His condo was decorated in masculine blues and black. Tasteful to the point I suspected a hired hand. We'd stopped at the 'bucks on the way over, so I sipped my caffeine and took in his gorgeous view of the Pacific as I waited for him to reemerge. Stunned by another sight—a recently played Xbox. When he came out, he caught me perusing his bookshelves and the photos on them. I had grown antsy from the espresso and anticipation.

"My brothers and sister," he announced. "Parents, too."

"And her?" I asked, noticing the one couple photo in the back.

"Charlotte," he said.

I felt a twinge of jealousy. She was beautiful and smart. Her intelligence was evident by the confidence on her face. She was butter-blonde, blue-eyed, full-lipped, stylish and model-thin. She seemed both flawless and not fully out of his life. And they were going to be living in the same city again. That gave me a physical reaction. I started sneezing. A series of hard, violent explosions. I couldn't stop. My God. I was allergic to Charlotte.

"Are you okay?" Wyatt asked.

I nodded and reached into my bag for a tissue. "I'm allergic to something," I explained. The sneezes continued. Then I saw a black cat zip from the hallway and into the kitchen.

"That explains it," I said.

"Cats?" he asked.

I nodded.

"Sorry. She's only here a little while longer. Going back to her original owner."

"She's not yours?"

"No. She's Charlotte's."

The sneezes stopped and the urge to gag replaced them.

"So, you're still friends with your ex," I pressed as we drove to Bel Air.

Wyatt shrugged. "Kind of, I suppose. I mean, we don't hate each other. At least not anymore. We send the random email. Have the random phone call. You know, when you were together for that long there's still kind of a connection. But, we've both moved on and we wish each other the best."

"Sounds healthy," I smiled and tried to swallow down the remnants of jealousy. Constance had made a point of making me aware of Charlotte's presence in his life when I met her at the Spirit Awards, and that point stuck. Wyatt's explanation helped me to understand, though I wasn't completely content with their continued connection. "I mean, it must be something of a friendship if you kept her cat."

"When she moved to New York, her sublet wouldn't take the cat. She just bought a co-op, so I'll be bringing Sigourney out to her my next trip out."

"Sigourney?"

"The cat."

"It's nice that you would do that for her," I said, fighting to keep my eyebrows apart.

Perhaps Tim and I would eventually share that kind of connection; just wanting the best for each other since we couldn't give it ourselves. Send the random text and the odd Christmas card. Perhaps. Still, allergic or not, I'd make sure Tim would take his damned cat with him.

"It took time to get there, in a place where we could be friendly," he continued. "She did a good job of breaking my heart."

Ouch. I didn't like hearing that.

"But," he continued, "if two people don't want the same things, what can you do? The compromise required from one or the other was too big to make it work." He took a swig of his coffee.

For the first time, I saw him pained. I alternated feelings of sympathy and jealousy. I didn't like that he still felt for that relationship. Then again, it showed that he knew how to love and want and hope. That I found endearing.

"How long were you together?" I asked as we drove up the hill to Karen's.

When we had discussed this before, I avoided the details. I let him tell the story he wanted to share, not feeling I was in a position to inquire further. I also didn't want to open the door to my own inquisition. Now we were in a deeper in it. Time to open the worm cans.

"Just over two years," he answered. "I was ready to propose, settle down. She was offered a job in New York that was too good to pass up. My job here was too good to leave, and she didn't want to do the long-distance thing. So, we called it quits. Or she called it quits if you want to get technical." He looked at me and forced a smile.

"Now that you will both be in New York, do you think you'll try to work it out?"

"No. She's in a relationship, and I've moved on," he said smiling at me, and this one appeared more genuine. "You and Tim have been together how long?"

"It will be five years next month."

"You didn't want to get married?" he asked.

"Sure I do. But a girl needs to be asked first," I said as lightheartedly as I could.

"Oh," he replied.

"I don't want to get married just to get married, though. If Tim and I were to do it now, it would be because we had been together for so long, not because we couldn't live without each other. I don't want that. I want to get married because I can't picture life without that person, you know?"

Wyatt broke into a large grin. "Ellen Patterson, a true

romantic. I never would have guessed. But I like it."

When we stopped at the gate, he leaned over and kissed me. "What are you doing on Saturday night?" he asked. "I'd like you to meet my friends."

Chapter Twelve

There's a reason why jetsetters end up in rehab and I'm just beginning to understand it. I never thought Ambien would be my friend, but he's turning out to be. On the rare occasion I needed help getting to sleep, I would take a shot of Nyquil or pop a Benadryl, but serious drugs were required for me to sleep through the night in New York and get onto Eastern Time. Mornings were a bitch. And so was I.

Karen and I had taken an evening flight a week after my party. Once Wyatt gave the word on New York, Karen didn't want to waste a minute. She was on the phone booking tickets by the time Wyatt dropped me off. It was time to hunt for homes.

Karen's house was set to go on the market by the end of the month. Knowing it would sell in a hot second, she decided to purchase not only an apartment for herself, but one for me.

"I just want to show you my commitment to this move," Karen explained. "We are going to make it work here," she said in the back of the sedan. She sipped the green tea I picked up for her along with my latte as the car turned off Madison en route to our first appointment. "Though, if I have to go through the whole co-op board thing again, it will drive me batshit."

I nodded attentively, unable to use words first thing on a Manhattan morning. Seven in New York is a cruel four to my California body. I now ordered two ventis because who was I fooling? I hid my new addiction, though. The first latte was slammed on the way back to the hotel. The second, I handled with a little more class.

This was our third day in Manhattan. Karen thought it was important to slowly adapt to our new environment. Day One was spent shopping. Day Two was with the East Coast GFE team and a visit to the studio where Karen's show would be shot. We finally got to real estate on what ended up being a Saturday. Karen realized her error and stated rather contritely that we should get an early start. Painfully early.

Gramercy Park was the area Karen was most interested in and I immediately felt at home there. Wendy, her broker, was a magician. We only needed to look at two places: Karen's off Irving Place and mine on 29th between Lex and Third. We each fell in love at first sight with what Wendy showed us, and Karen put offers on both.

My discomfort must have been showing. After she signed the last of the papers on my place, she put her hands on my shoulders and said, "This is something I want to do. You need a nice place to call home here since I am stealing you from yours." I tried to imagine the piece of jewelry I would have to get from Celia to come close to showing Karen my gratitude.

The neighborhood seemed sedate by Manhattan standards. I liked that it was away from the too-hipness of the more southern territories on the island and lacked a snobby-ness I suspected places around "the Park" would have. Of course, these were assumptions based on nothing more than magazines and jetlag, and over-watched episodes of *Sex and the City*. Still, I was overjoyed to find a Starbucks two blocks away from what would be my home, and plenty of pubs within stumbling distance.

Karen was happy that we would live close enough to share a car in the morning. In the GFE building, we would have our own suites where we would run the production company that was now going to partner with GFE on the talk show. That move on her part made me a partner in the show. Karen did not have to do that. She could have kept the show to herself.

"I want any success to be shared within the company we are going to build together," she stated on our way out of the GFE meeting. That kind of consideration happens this side of never in Hollywood, just so you know.

I adored my oddly laid out yet spacious for New York two-bedroom-one-and-a-half-bath apartment that she let me decide on.

"You must have a two-bedroom, El, if you're going to have your friends visit you," she said, further commenting that couples like their privacy. The glint in her eye told me that she meant not only my friends and their mates, but me and Wyatt as well.

Not being naïve to the expense of Manhattan square footage, I knew this had to come with a shocking price tag. But money breeds confidence, and Karen didn't bat an eye when purchasing my place and hers, which was stunning three story townhouse near the gated park. After all, she was Karen Ellis—and, as it turned out, Karen Ellis was much more loaded than I realized. She had been blessed with good investments and even better divorce settlements. She treated these apartments like picking out Birkin bags.

"I'm already picturing the furniture in your home, El," Karen beamed. "Of course, that's up to you. But, if you get stuck, I'll happily lend you Kevin."

The apartment was only "mine" in theory. Karen would be my lovely landlady. She offered me free rent in lieu of a KEEP salary for the first year, which I thought was more than fair since I would be taking a salary on the talk show. No rent meant my budget now allowed for rental of a parking space for my car. Even though the thought of driving on New York City streets terrified me, I didn't want to be without my Jetta.

I stayed behind, lying that I wanted to get to know my neighborhood. Instead, I walked through "my" apartment one more time, appreciating the light that spilled in. The place was left empty. The current owners had just moved out and there hadn't been time to stage it. I enjoyed the blank canvas and let my imagination run wild.

The guest bedroom was near the front door. Gabe would love that and the cute doorman. I was going to live in an apartment with a doorman! Could there be anything more NYC?

What certainly screamed New York was the small kitchen. It was the size of a wide hallway, but equipped with Viking, both stove and fridge, and a Miele dishwasher. A stackable washer-dryer was also housed there. The deep sink looked like a baby's bathtub and there was a spigot over the stove for filling pasta pots. The fine amenities were fabulous but, unlike L.A., the kitchen would not be the heart of my New York parties. There seemed to be just enough room in there for me, and maybe one other. And that thought made me smile.

The floors were hardwood but for the kitchen and bathrooms. Those were tiled in lovely white, marble hexagons that balanced the chocolate dark wood. I took off my shoes and let my feet caress the floors. My gray carpet days were over. I danced around the wood. It was almost too exciting to take in.

The dining area took place in a long alcove off the wide walkway after the kitchen and the powder room that followed it. It ended as the living area began. The space was large and encompassed the width of the apartment with three banks of windows and a second floor view to the tree-lined street. It even had a fireplace that didn't come with a switch.

Within minutes of being there, I had already decided to divide the living into sections by putting two sofas back to back. One would face the fireplace; the other would face the TV I'd rest on a stylish credenza. The sofas could be faced together for a conversation area when entertaining occurred. And I planned on entertaining a lot. Dinner parties, brunches, cocktail hours and game nights with friends of diverse interests and backgrounds. It was no longer going to be "industry" and "civilians", but artists and professionals who read more than *Deadline* and TMZ.

Finally, through French doors, I made my way into the master bedroom with huge built-in closets. "Good" closets are important in New York, I discovered. A full tub and rain shower completed my bathroom.

The whole place was painted magnolia, but I intended to add color. I imagined every piece of furniture, every bit of fabric, every fleck of paint. Even my first bubble bath. It included champagne.

I would have been happy in a quaint studio. I would have, really. Thrilled with a one bedroom. But this was beyond incredible. And it truly felt like home. A grown-up home of a professional woman. I couldn't have dreamed up anything more wild than what was unfolding.

My daydream decorating was interrupted by the honking of horns. Rush hour had started. It was time to make my way across town to meet Karen. We were going to have a light dinner before the theatre. Not something I was really into. I'd rather see a movie. I found theatre too act-y, having suffered with the performances provided by the theatre students at film school. But, now that I was going to be living in New York, I supposed I'd have to embrace The Great White Way.

"I can't believe you," Celia said when we met for lunch the next day. "You are so fucking lucky, El."

"Does that make me flucky?" I joked.

"Seriously, a two-bedroom in Gramercy with a fireplace? Spoiled bitch," she said smiling, then added, "Spitch."

Celia McMahon was completely self-made. No one had ever given her anything. She started designing jewelry five years ago and now had offices on both coasts and employed nearly thirty people. Her jewelry was in all the big stores, and by *big* I mean Bergdorf's and Barney's, Neiman's and Saks, not to mention every chic boutique that catered to celebrities and celewannabes. She was about to open her first showroom, which was her biggest dream. I was so proud of her. Celia was the first of us to break out of being an assistant and find success. She was my hero.

Celia moved to New York two years ago and bought a loft in TriBeCa last year, but was already a seasoned Manhattanite. Within three months, she was president of her co-op board, befriended every host and manager (if not the owner) of every hot spot in her neighborhood. We met that day in Union Square and she properly bitched about having to go uptown—like a true New Yorker. I made the request so I could get to know my new neighboring neighborhood. After a chatty stroll, we settled in at L'Express for roasted chicken and glasses of wine. She was still tan from her trip to Cozumel, and pulled back her newly high-lighted curls into a knot. Her shoulders were broad and strong from her days on the swim team. She put her sunglasses on top of her head so she could look me in the eye.

"You are going to love New York, El. It's such a great city. It's so easy to meet people here because you are surrounded by millions everyday. I'll have a welcome party for you when you're settled so you can meet a bunch of people right off," she promised.

Her people were a mix of restaurateurs, designers, writers, artists and musicians, and her handsome new financier boyfriend and his buddies. Her last house party gotten a write-up in the *Post*. Rhiannon Shaw, in town for a premiere, is a fan of her jewelry. She heard about Celia's shindig, crashed the party and brought the paparazzi with her. "So annoyingly L.A.," Celia complained.

"We can make hanging out a regular thing, now that I won't be travelling as much. My fucking assistants can do the shows. Sorry, make that 'associates.'" Celia swallowed wine and continued with, "There's so much trouble to get into in this city, it's fantastic."

"I'm not looking for trouble," I said holding up my hands.

"It will find you. I've been here for half a minute and I've gotten into plenty," she said with a grin. "And we can fly to Paris or London for long weekends. How great is that? We should plan something for end of summer."

"How about Dublin?"

"Even better. I've always wanted to fly Aer Lingus, just because it sounds so pervy." She checked her watch. "Well, I've got to go. Jeremy should be done with his basketball game. He's so butch. Then we have to go to Long Island. Some family thing of his. Anyway, I'll see you soon." Celia said sweetly as we hugged goodbye, "I'm so glad you're going to be here."

Me, too.

I walked through the city rather than grab a cab and soaked in the brilliant spring day. I had utterly fallen in love with New York, already deciding I wouldn't mind the frigid winters or sweltering summers. I didn't even mind the blisters erupting on my feet from all the walking. Those were only temporary. I'd simply schedule a pedicure when I got back to the hotel. Hold on. I almost got one on the street.

"Jesus," I exclaimed as a glob of spit nearly hit my sandalled feet. I searched the crowd for the culprit, but everyone looked too sophisticated to be spitting. As I continued on my path, I noticed more gobbers. Men, boys, even an old lady who pulled over her walker to let loose a lugie. And no one seemed surprised by all this spit but me.

The cigarette-smoking, cell-phone-talking, overly-animated, hand-waver was one danger I had noticed early on walking around. Those offenders were easy to spot. If the smoke didn't get your attention, the volume of their conversation did. But these spitters were a more treacherous lot. You don't know who they might be, or when they might launch a glob of who-knows-what out into the public. Ugh. I lived in open-toed shoes in L.A. That was clearly going to change here. I should also consider getting immunized for Hepatitis.

"Shots tonight?" Wyatt joked. "I was thinking Jäger-meister."

"What's gotten in to you, Wyatt?" Constance chided. "The last time I saw you do shots was at your brother's wedding, and that did not end well."

"Well, then, should we be more refined and get a bottle of wine or two? I don't think we should bother lying to ourselves and go by the glass."

Wyatt came in two days before Karen and I were to leave New York. He and I met up at some restaurant-of-the-moment to have dinner with Constance and her boyfriend; a guy named Guy, but pronounced it in French fashion, *Ghee*.

Wyatt leaned into me and said, "Every time I say his name I think clarified butter."

I was getting used to his role as jester among those he was closest to. Before I left L.A., Wyatt introduced me to his friends. We met everyone at Bergamot Station for a party, a wild affair in one of the galleries. When our feet ached from dancing and we had lost the ability to hear from the music, the group of us went out for a late dinner.

We talked about art, politics, religion, the state of culture—or lack thereof—and laughed. There was no mention of camping, sailing, TV or movies. There was no real talk of work. No one was thumbing away on cell phones. We enjoyed real, live, stimulating conversation, none of which was considered crass or inappropriate, even when it got a little crass or inappropriate. I could easily picture my friends mingling with his friends and everyone becoming *our* friends. Too bad we were moving away from most of them.

Jeff, Wyatt's former roommate, was in real estate. He argued that buying in New York was insane. "Unless you're considering Queens. Or the Bronx. It's the new Brooklyn," Jeff teased.

Clay, Wyatt's best friend, was an agent. He lacked the standard arrogance that typically accompanied the vocation. Clay's girlfriend, Allison, was an artist who painted reproductions and antiquated styles for celebrity homes, and was preparing for her own gallery show. Her bohemian chic countered his Hugo Boss well. They were an open and funny couple. She leaned in to me at one point and whispered, "Wyatt seems so happy, El. It's nice to see. That ice queen made him miserable."

She didn't use her name, but I was happy that someone as nice as Allison didn't like Charlotte. Charlotte seemed so perfect. I hated to admit that I was shallow enough to take a little glee in the 'ice queen' comment. Pathetic, I know. But I was falling for Wyatt. I needed his ex to be just a little awful. Especially if we were all going to be residing on the same island.

That night, Constance and Guy/Ghee were in a world all their own, barely able to feed themselves as they spent the night gazing into each other's eyes and holding each other's hands. Wyatt and I carried the conversation on our own.

"TriBeCa for me," Wyatt shared. "That's the part of the city I prefer."

"A good friend of mine lives there," I said. "I think I'll be happy with Gramercy."

"I love living in Chelsea," Constance offered. She was now joining the conversation; Guy had excused himself to go to the lav, as he put it, and we finally had her attention. "So, what do you think of Ghee?" she asked excitedly. "Isn't he dreamy?"

"He's very nice. What does he do again?" I asked.

"You don't recognize him? He's in the new Polo campaign. So fabulous."

Wyatt rolled his eyes and poured more wine into our glasses.

"I noticed he doesn't have an accent. Where is he from?" I was curious. I'd hear him throw out Eurotrash terms, but without any traceable lilt or cadence.

"Maine. But he spent so much time in Paris that he just got used to being called Ghee, which is the correct pronunciation of the name, by the way. He lived there for four years. He's almost fluent," she said proudly.

Wyatt and I exchanged glances.

"Almost, huh?" Wyatt couldn't resist.

Guy returned and we finished our dinner. Or Wyatt and I did. Their plates were barely touched, and they refused the waiter's offer to have the remainder wrapped. Being that I was in the presence of a model and his date, I politely passed on dessert. Wyatt got the check.

As we waited for a taxi, Constance puffed away on a Marlboro Light. She asserted, after berating Wyatt for ordering a steak, "No, I don't eat meat anymore. Do you know what that stuff does to your insides? Being a vegetarian will put years on your life."

God, they exist on both coasts.

"But, didn't you have the salmon?" I asked remembering her order.

"Fish is different. Meat is disgusting." She crushed her cigarette with a Prada pump then lit up another. I'd never seen anyone smoke so quickly. It was like she was going for Olympic gold. No wonder Ghee/Guy seemed so smitten with her.

"Do you think that thing in your mouth is really good for you?" Wyatt taunted.

She gave him a *fuck you* grin and changed the subject. "Charlotte was really happy to see you, Wyatt. She said she had a nice time. Glad you didn't let my schedule stop you from meeting." She had wrapped herself around her date.

I was getting hints of Liza, and not just from the fish-eating-vegetarian thing. I wasn't sure if Constance was bringing up Charlotte to stir shit or give me a heads up. Constance was an odd bird. She gave me a tight squeeze when we gave our goodbyes and said she was looking forward to hanging out with me more when I got settled here, which seemed sincere. I couldn't get a real feel on her. I did feel Wyatt, though. His hand was at the small of my back, slowly wrapping around to my waist. He looked a little red in the face but then made things clear.

"Connie set up cocktails last night for the three of us to get together. Then, she cancelled at the last minute for some client in crisis. It was real. I checked. Charlotte was already there, and I thought it would be rude not to go. Or chickenshit. So, we had a drink. I had that business dinner after, so it was short. It wasn't a big deal, outside of the fact it was the first time we had seen each other in nearly a year." His delivery sounded like testimony or a police report.

"That's a big deal, Wyatt," I said.

He shrugged. "That's the funny thing. It wasn't. It was just something that needed to be done." He leaned in and kissed me. "That needed to be done, too. Let's have some dessert. My hotel has a great menu."

Wyatt was staying at The Sixty, located in the opposite direction from the St. Regis. The restaurant we were at was strategically placed somewhere between the two. I was still getting my directional bearings for New York, not that it mattered. There wasn't room for logic here, only desire. My room was across the hall from Karen's, which she now shared with Billy, in town for press on the film he did before going into rehab. Wyatt's direction seemed to have the stronger pull.

You can't imagine how delicious breakfast can be once you swallow your guilt. I owed Tim two phone calls and a text. I snuck in a reply while Wyatt was placing the breakfast order.

> Hi, Tim. Things in New York are going well. Karen
> found us both a wonderful apartment.

No, I couldn't write that…delete delete delete. It sounded like she found Tim and me a place, not to mention the grammatical crimes. Writing isn't something I normally do right when I wake up, especially when I wake up to morning sex. I can't do math first thing in the morning, either, which is why I set my alarm thirty minutes ahead. I've done that since high school and still wake up in a panic trying to figure out what time it really is. While I may not be able to add or subtract at the start of the day, I was able to count. Orgasms before breakfast: three.

Back to the text. Focus. Focus. I had to be kind but clear.

> Hi, Tim. Sorry I missed your calls. New York is beau-

tiful. Karen and I found apartments. I really like mine. I'll tell you about it when I get back. See you soon. xo

I had to put in the *xo*. I usually signed off with *Love you*. The *xo* was a demotion in emotion.

Tim had just returned from his shoot to an empty home, knowing that I was off looking for a new one. That couldn't have felt good. He didn't take it well when I told him New York was definite. News like that is hard to share over the phone. He seemed anxious to talk, and I kept delaying that inevitable. I sensed he would offer to move with me or do the bi-coastal thing. I had to be ready with the right words, the soft words, to let him down as gently as possible. Right now, I was being gently coaxed out of my robe and onto the bed.

"Room service apologized that it will take a little longer than normal for our breakfast to be brought up. So, I was wondering how we could fill that time," Wyatt said into my neck.

"Don't start something you can't finish," I laughed.

"I never do," he said, looking me in the eye before diving down to kiss my stomach, then my thighs, then…oh, God.

Wyatt seemed to know my body, what it wanted, what I craved. There was not a touch or a kiss that was off or awkward between us. The anticipation and expectation we had were exceeded by the actual event. And it was surprising that security had not been called on us. We weren't exactly quiet.

"I love your skin," he said kissing my back. "I must kiss every inch of your skin."

"You are making it hard to leave here, Mr. Knight," I said as I rolled over to kiss him again. Kissing him, I felt alive. Safe. Happy. I could forget the technicality of being unfaithful. This felt too good for it to be anything but that. After breakfast, I got dressed and prepared myself for the glide of shame back to the St. Regis.

"I'll see you back in L.A.," I said when my lips were free from his.

"I'll see if I can cut this trip short."

I didn't see him for two more weeks. He extended his stay

when he had trouble finding a place. It seemed Karen and I did get lucky. The offers had been accepted on both her place and mine, and we were in a forty-five-day escrow. It helps to have millions in the bank and Oscars on your shelf.

Wyatt changed his mind and opted to rent rather than buy.

"I'm going to keep my condo," he explained over our cell phones after his apartment hunting frustration.

"Hedging your bets?" I joked.

"Nah. Keeping my investment. I'll wait until I find the right place in New York. There's plenty of time for that. The first year, I think I'll hardly be home, anyway. Dinner when I get back?"

"Sounds good," I cooed.

Sounded great, actually. I was counting the days, the minutes, the seconds, and avoiding being in the Sliver as much as possible.

I spent time with the posse, hanging out and pretending like everything was normal and I wasn't leaving. We gathered at Emily's for a night of guilty pleasures: take-out and TiVo, set to binge on "Project Runway" and Indian food. We caught up with each other between commenting on fabric choices. Progress had been made swiftly on Em's deal for the studio in the Springs and Claude was over the moon about her new job.

After a particularly awful day, which was saying something for Claudia, she gave her notice. Donna would not let Claudia go unpunished and poor Claude had been given all the shit jobs Donna could come up with for her final two weeks. One of the crap tasks she had to accomplish before leaving was getting new linens for Donna's houses and having to deal with Dora Sharpella, a bedding designer who got or bought her way into *StyleNow* magazine, and was suddenly the go-to gal for custom sheets. Dora was also a raving bitch.

"She's a cunt, actually. I mean, bitches are tolerable. This woman is out of her fucking diva mind," Claudia sharply shared. Claude went on to describe the belaboring task of actually getting the linens made from Dora, which included three meetings just to get the style of embroidered lines right. "We are talking about two, straight, black lines separated by a quarter-inch. How fucking hard could that be? A quarter inch is a quarter inch. There's no question there. And how many shades of black can there be? One, if you ask me. Fucking black!"

We were all laughing at her hysteria, and the fact that we had all been there ourselves with one vendor or another who thinks they are a rock star and above talking to a mere peon; didn't we know they were much too fabulous for that? They should only have to deal directly with the celebrity/VIP, not an assistant. I mean, don't we know who they are?

Please.

"Seriously, when will these people learn that the worst person to piss off is an assistant," Claudia continued.

She had a point. We might be peons, but we are the peons who kept the gate. We can paint you in a good light or a bad one, protect you or hang you out to dry, talk our bosses in or out of doing business with you because we can always find someone more fabulous who will be better priced, can do it quicker and that we like more, and we will go to the ends of the earth to find that person. Assistants are fueled on Starbucks and spite.

"They don't get it," Remi stated. "They believe it when their overpriced publicists tell them they are it. No offense, Tess."

"None taken. We turned her down," Tess smiled. "We're too booked to deal with a high-maintenance flash-in-the-pan."

"I love you for that," Claudia said to Tess.

I took Tess' hand to examine again the huge stone that Dane had gotten her. It was tasteful, as only Tiffany would make it, but monstrous in size. She was luminous. I gave her hand a squeeze and she smiled at me.

"Doesn't she go through assistants like toilet paper?" Emily asked.

"Yes, she does," Tess added.

"That's a sign of a true twat," Jilli said.

"Well, we are just assistants, right? Dime a dozen. For another few weeks, anyway," I said, raising my glass to Claudia. We were almost done at those desks. Claudia wasn't finished with her rant, though.

"She's just an idiot, and she doesn't get that, guess what,

you have lost my referral. And, yeah, I will talk shit. Hello, I didn't sign a confidentiality agreement with you, bitch. I might be an assistant, but I'm an assistant with a big mouth and an even larger network. She's on the list." Claudia finished and poured herself another glass of wine.

Claudia has kept a long-running, lengthy list of anyone and everyone who has ever crossed her, done a crap job, mishandled business, or otherwise pissed her off. It's better than Yelp and she shares it liberally with other assistants, friends and a few bloggers. But don't tell her I told you that.

The rest of us offered our amens and vowed we would never buy bedding from that bitch Dora Sharpella, which meant a little more now that we were all on the verge of being minimoguls.

"Have you and Tim had the talk yet?" Tess asked me while we fast-forwarded through the commercials.

"Nope," I admitted.

"She's like a greased pig, this one," Jilli joked.

"Oi," I said with my mouth full. "Thanks a lot."

"I meant it in a good way, El," Jilli laughed. "You've been home a week and have avoided the subject like a Jedi master. Rock on."

Remi shook her head. "How can you live with him and not had the talk?"

It wasn't easy, let me tell you. It took some maneuvering. When I got back from NYC, I found that Tim had slept in what was our bed while I was away. Why wouldn't he? After all, I made the make-up-sex mistake. Now there was no way I could sleep next to him, even platonically, after sleeping with Wyatt. It just felt wrong. So, I conveniently fell asleep on the sofa the night I got back. Tim came down and found me there in the morning, and offered to move back into his office.

He was treading gently, like tending to a patient and, if he cared for the wound well enough, it would heal. If he was careful enough, everything would be okay. But this was terminal. I was merely biding my time until the plug could be pulled. It was a truly Kevorkian situation I created.

"Look, it's not like I have any place to go right now. Jilli's got a roommate, Karen's living with Billy, and the rest of you are semi-shacked-up or have pets," I complained in a demi-dramatic manner.

"Why do I suddenly feel guilty about having a dog?" Claudia asked with incredulity.

"You can stay here," Emily offered, being the one pet-less member of PETA. Her one-bedroom Brentwood abode was adorable and fit us all well on nights like these, but it was too small for two women to live in. "I can stay with Ron. I'm there most of the time anyway."

"Thanks, Em. If push comes to shove, I may take you up on it."

"You mean when push comes to shove," Jilli corrected.

"Well, Wyatt also offered his place." I said that for effect. The girls threw in their oohs and aahs. "But, that won't happen. He's got a cat. Actually, it's his ex's."

"He kept his ex-girlfriend's pussy?" Jilli asked.

"Did you have to put it that way?" I replied.

Jilli gave a shrug.

"I only have three weeks to go. I'll just stick it out at the Sliver."

The girls all looked at me.

"Three weeks?" Emily asked. I nodded.

"I thought it was longer," Claudia lamented.

"Shit," Remi said softly.

"The fuck?" Jilli blurted.

Karen's home, as expected, sold on the first day it was listed. No matter what the real estate climate, a home like Karen's would sell to the right member of the nouveau riche in a hot second. It went to a couple from London.

Karen hired a "mover" to oversee the packing and shipping of her home, which would leave me to my mess. Francine was militaristic in her approach to packing, and scared me just a little with her knowledge of the house after being there less than an hour.

Kevin, Karen's decorator, flew in from New York to assess what would go to Manhattan, what would be sold, and what would be left in Los Angeles storage. He had only eight weeks to prepare Karen's new place. She and Billy were going to take a vacation to give him time to get it done. They had decided to "summer" in the South of France. Flit about on the coast, borrowing a yacht of one of Billy's less than scrupulous friends. She would come back in mid-July, after her apartment had been decorated and pre-production on the show would start.

Karen kindly offered Francine to help me with my move, but I turned her down. I wasn't really going to pack as much as I was going to stuff my car with my clothes, computer and a few keepsakes. Everything else would be left behind. But, when I told Karen I planned to drive cross-country, she wouldn't hear of such a thing.

"Too dangerous, not to mention dull," she declared. "I can't think of a worse way to arrive in New York, El."

The car would be shipped over. Ruth and I would fly first class and stay at the Gramercy Park Hotel so we could get settled and acclimated to our new city. I would leave once Francine got packing after Karen left for Cannes. Ruth would come a little later, staying behind in case Francine had questions, which I had a hard time imagining.

The apartment would become "mine" on May thirty-first. If I got there in mid-May, I could shop for furniture, have it painted and schedule everything for delivery without rushing or scrambling or feeling any pressure. I couldn't wait. So, I accepted Karen's plan and moved my moving date up two weeks.

I started watching design programs on channels I never knew existed. I settled on a simple scheme for my new home. Clean and open. I considered color palates when I should have been researching show ideas or reading scripts, pulling pages out of *Dwell* and *Elle Décor* instead of articles from the *Times*. I designed my change of address announcement and planned my first cocktail party. I made a mental list of the clothes I would need to buy in order to deal with snow and the bitter cold of an East Coast winter, and how I would handle my first humid summer. I was already gone.

But here, with my best girlfriends, I was already homesick. There wouldn't be many more nights like this. I wouldn't be here to watch Tess' bump grow or Remi's relationship evolve. I wouldn't witness Emily and Claude's collaboration. I would hear about it, of course, see parts of it on FaceTime, but that's hardly the same.

I took some comfort in Jilli going to New York, though she wasn't sure when that would be. It was just a matter of timing. The reality was this might be the last night we were all together. And I started to cry.

I came home puffy-eyed to Tim lying on the sofa watching TV. He leapt up and ran over to me when he saw my swollen face.

"What's wrong?" he asked as he wrapped me in his arms. I started crying again, and I told him everything.

He took it in quietly, the fact that we would be over, that I would be gone. Despite my offer to go, Tim asked me to stay. He would stay sleeping in the office, there would be no need for me to move twice. He did have one request that I found quite odd, but also heartbreaking.

"Can I have these three weeks with you? Can we be friends and hang out? I'd like to still do things together. Simple shit. Go to dinner, see a movie, that kind of thing. Can we do that?"

When I saw how much he seemed to need it, all I could do was nod and say, "Yeah, sure."

I took a deep breath. I wasn't sure if I had done him a favor or a disservice. I was just grateful there wasn't a huge fight or, worse, tears. He took it with grace. I could relax now. All of this was going so well. Too well, maybe. And I was waiting for a shoe to drop somewhere.

Chapter Thirteen

I followed the trail of clothes strewn about the floor, hoping I would find my panties along the way. Dinner with Wyatt turned out to be dinner at Wyatt's, and dessert only involved whipped cream. It was after one in the morning. I had to get back to Venice.

"I still don't understand why you won't spend the night," Wyatt said, his annoyance showing.

"I'm just trying to be respectful. That's all," I said as I dressed. I left out the fact that I promised to have breakfast Tim, and possibly a movie after. It seemed that Tim was serious about this hanging-out-and-being-friends thing. We were actually able to keep it light and have a good time when we hung out. It was a nice way to leave things, I thought. Though, I doubted Wyatt would see it the same way. "Besides," I continued. "The remnants of the cat are getting to me." Wyatt had finally returned Charlotte's *chat* to her. "Don't be mad," I said to him softly.

"I'm not mad, I'm jealous," he said. "I don't get jealous, either. But, watching you get dressed to go back to him isn't making me happy."

"That's so adorable," I purred as I crawled over the bed to him to give him a kiss before I left. "Don't forget that he's in another room. We keep our distance. Only another two weeks and I'll be in New York."

"And I'll be here."

"Then, you'll have to find an excuse to come out and play before your move." I kissed him and he started to undress me.

An hour later, we both got re-dressed and he walked me down to my car.

"I know you have your hands full, but I want to see you soon, okay?" he asked. I nodded and kissed him one last time before I drove away.

Time was moving so quickly that I doubted I'd be able to do all that I needed to before getting on that plane. Like seeing Kitty, for example, and sorting out the inheritance thing. I was counting on that to help fund my decorating spree. Tim had offered to go with me to see her after the movie.

"Are you sure?" I asked.

"Yeah. Maybe she'll behave if you bring company," he joked.

He made that offer before I crept in well after two.

I snuck up the stairs, skipping the one that creaked, trying not to make noise or breathe. I went into my room, undressed in the dark and crawled into bed, not bothering to run water to wash my face or brush my teeth. Penance. When my head hit the pillow, I heard the door to Tim's room open and the bathroom door close hard. Shit. I barely slept that night, dreading the morning.

I wanted to be up before Tim and to look as fresh and happy as I could. It took a bit more makeup than usual to make that happen. I made a French press of strong coffee to help me shake off the night, but it probably would have served me better to eat the coffee beans whole. In the stillness of the morning, I sat and wondered how much of my life had been spent like this. Just waiting for something to happen. Pondering what was to come. I started the Sunday *Times* crossword puzzle to remind myself how little I knew, struggling with a six-letter word for "Dick" when Tim came down. He did not look happy.

"Good morning," I sang.

"You're up early," he grumbled. He came down straight from bed, his hair wild from sleep.

"I was looking forward to breakfast," I chirped. "Since it's such a gorgeous day, I thought we could walk over to the French Market Café. Coffee's in the pot." I thought I gave him enough information to distract him. Or at least I hoped I did.

He quietly poured himself a cup and I did what all guilty people do—I kept talking.

"If French Market isn't what you're craving, we can go to Maxwell's or the Rose. Then catch that movie after we deal with Kitty?"

"You still want to see a movie?" he asked, seeming to ease up.

"Of course I do," I lied. He looked at me sensing my dishonesty, but decided to overlook it.

"French Market sounds good. Let me hop in the shower," he said.

"Perfect," I chirped again.

This whole situation was anything but. I was going to do my best to make it through. I had a feeling it would come with a price, though. Just once, I'd like to be wrong.

At breakfast, Tim asked me—made me promise, actually—that I would go to Randall and Tabitha's anniversary party that Friday. He still hadn't told anyone we were "having trouble", as he put it, or that I was moving.

"I can't bring myself to do it," he explained over his eggs.

"You really think me going is a good idea, Tim?"

"You'll want to say goodbye to Val and Tab at least, won't you?"

"I wouldn't want to make a big production there. It wouldn't be right."

"I'll tell them later. After you leave, if you'd like. Just go with me. It would mean a lot."

"But why, Tim?" It seemed like the dumbest thing we could do, and we were in a situation that had long gone past idiotic.

"I want to ease into being without you, I guess. Going without you while you're still here would be hard. I know I sound like a pussy. I can't go by myself."

As much as it might pain me to attend, it hurt me more to see him like this, so I agreed to go. Had I known the kind of week I'd have leading up to that weekend, I would've had good reason to decline.

The network decided to get the promotion going on the show once they found out Karen and Billy were going to out of the country and scheduled a photo shoot for that Friday. The network also wanted Karen to be in New York when they announced the fall lineup.

"Don't worry, El. As much as I would love to have you there, I know you need to get yourself packed. You don't have to go unless you really want to," Karen assured.

"I do want to go, it's so important, but..." My head was

reeling trying to figure out how I could manage it.

Karen put her hand on my shoulder. "Kiddo, if you would've let me give you Francine, believe me, I would drag your ass there. Take care of your stuff. Besides, we'll only be there for a day. Billy and I will go on to France from there. We are crazy to go during the festival, but I need a break. Anyway, have the travel agent change the ticket and bill the network for the New York portion. I told them that would be easier at this point. Or, as my producer, why don't you ask them to fly me out on their private plane? It would be a kind courtesy."

Karen always had a way of sticking it to those who didn't take her schedule as seriously as she did. She was a team player, but one who saw her downtime as sacrosanct.

I had to agree that she was crazy to be going to the South of France during Cannes. It was Billy's idea. *Quelle surprise.* I think it was an attempt to impress her with who he knew—and who would give him use of their homes, cars and yachts. Sure, he was sober, but I'm fairly certain it was Karen they were trusting with their possessions.

I walked into my office and found it a wreck. Francine had started packing it up. I had pulled the things I'd need in the interim and set them aside in boxes. I'd be working out of those until the new offices were ready. The Jetta was set to be picked up the following Thursday and put on a truck destined for Newark where I would retrieve it and brave Manhattan traffic for the first time. A stomach churning thought. Wyatt offered to go with me. He would be in town for the announcement and would stay until I arrived. He was moving at the end of June and had Jeff set up to manage his place for future tenants.

There seemed to be only one wrinkle in what was turning out to be a smooth plan: I still had to deal with Kitty. She had called during my breakfast with Tim, claiming to have come down with a stomach bug and cancelled on me.

"Darling, I just don't want you to get this. It's awful. I'm so weak," she said, dripping with melodrama.

I could feel her stalling, but I didn't have the energy to fight about it. She never made anything easy and, deep down, I knew that I would have a better time getting a kidney from her than the money, even though it was rightfully mine.

In some ways, that was a relief. And it let Tim off the hero hook so he could join Kent at the Dodgers game. It seemed poor Liza had a headache.

"You don't mind that I'm flaking on the movie?" Tim asked, as he was halfway out the door.

"I'll live. Have fun." I gave him a friendly hug before he left.

"How soon can you be here?" Wyatt asked when I called to tell him my change of plans.

We walked along the strand, holding hands, taking in the beginning of California summer. We didn't say much. We didn't have to. It was all in the touch of our hands. As we watched the sun slowly dive into the sea, he wrapped his arms around me and I felt at peace.

"He can't be hogging all of your time, El," Jilli barked at me over the phone on my drive into work. "He's going to be New York with you. You have to figure out a date for us. The girls want to get this going."

The posse wanted to throw me a party, but the trouble was when? I had to make time for them and fast. If they found out about me going to Randall and Tab's with Tim and not putting them on my calendar, I would be disowned. Deservedly so. This was the cost of trying to keep things simple. What seemed to take forever to get here was now going a bit too quickly and spinning into a complicated mess.

Eleven more days. I can make it.

The pace of the week never lessened. We had a GFE meeting on Wednesday to go over some of the particulars; story ideas were solidified and slotted on the schedule. Thursday, I had a meeting with the writer of a script I had taken a liking to. I wanted to make an offer, but I needed Karen to see it first. That would likely happen sometime on the plane to France. I knew she would want it, so I thought it would be a good idea to meet the writer face-to-face while I was still in L.A. My first meeting as a producer, and I was a little too excited for it. Fortunately, the writer was also a first-timer. He didn't even have an agent. He's a friend of Gabe's, which is how the script got to me.

"I knew you would love it," Gabe gloated when I called him. "Just wait until you meet him. You are going to love him, too."

When I looked at my schedule, I realized there was another goodbye I had to schedule. Marco. We had been together for the last three years. There were times I saw him more than Tim, seeing each other at the gym six days a week, even though only one was really "ours." He had been an ego booster, a butt lifter and a good friend. When I saw that I'd have to cancel our Friday appointment, he wouldn't hear of me leaving without one last session, so he switched my appointment with his Wednesday client.

"Give me something to remember you by," I taunted.

"That ass of yours isn't enough?" he boasted, complimenting his own work more than my derriere.

Our final workout consisted of full body weights, deep stretching and cardio skipped in lieu of breakfast together at The Rose Café. We walked over after I quickly freshened up. Since I skipped the treadmill, I wasn't too gross. I tried to keep a polite distance anyway, but he pulled me into him and wrapped his arms around my waist, squeezing my obliques to verify their tone, tickling me in the process.

"I'm going to miss you, Ellen," he said sipping his non-fat cappuccino.

"I'm going to miss you, Marco," I said trying not to squirm. I had yet to find a comfortable position. I could already feel the ache in my muscles. He had worked me hard and given me something to remember him by, all right. I would think of him each time I moved or breathed too deeply over the next three days, causing me to wonder if I could find the time to fit in a massage.

I looked up from my scrambled egg whites to find him eyeing me.

"I have a bit of a crush on you, you know. I always wanted to ask you out, but you had that boyfriend. And now you are moving to New York City. You break my heart," he said.

"Um, Marco, aren't you getting married?" I mentioned if only to remind him.

He shrugged and tossed up his hands. "We'll see. I think she's more in love with the dress and the invitations."

I laughed and wondered who actually got married for the right reasons these days? Was it love, timing or the time invested that caused people to finally *settle* down? A short time ago, I was willing to make that kind of mistake. Now, I questioned it altogether. I still wanted marriage, but not if the cost was too high.

We changed the subject to our future plans. I told him of the talk show segments I was working on and the script I hoped to option for Karen and me to produce. He told me that he wanted to open his own gym, even though he knows the success rate of private gyms is near nil.

"But, everything in life is a gamble. If you don't take risks you aren't really living, are you? That's why I admire you going to New York. You are risking something. Good for you." He raised his cup to me, and I reciprocated. We promised to stay in touch.

"Any time you are in town, let me know and I will schedule you a workout, no charge for a dear friend," he said. He even gave me the number of a cousin of his who teaches Italian in Manhattan. "You never know when the language could come in handy," he smiled.

Marco gave me a long hug and a soft kiss on the cheek when we said goodbye. I wiped away a tear as I drove home. I had become a blubbering buffoon lately. Tears fell easily, but tearing up over my trainer caught me off guard. It was more than that, though. While I had prepared myself for saying goodbye to the bigger aspects of my life here, I had not considered the smaller ones: Marco; the baristas at my Starbucks who knew me by name, latte and demeanor, putting in a free add-shot when I was looking a little spent; Roland, my amazing-yet-overpriced hairstylist; Annie, my expert-and-underpriced bikini waxer. All of these people that I loved and trusted and spent years with I would no longer see. They wouldn't be a part of my life anymore. How would I find people as wonderful as them in New York? More tears fell. Jilli's call caught me in the midst of it.

"Well, you should be crying over the fact you never tapped

that rock-hard trainer's ass," she laughed.

She had called to tell me the posse had come up with a plan. "Clear your weekend. We have a house in the Springs. Emily's business partner came through with a loaner. All the girls are going. We'll shop, eat, drink, get massages, and have a good, old-fashioned, girly slumber party," she said with excitement. Jilli's not a girly kind of broad. For this to appeal to her, it must mean a lot. I mean, we were talking about fitting six women into one house, something that would normally bring a tear to Jilli's eyes. But it was me who started crying again.

"What is wrong with you, El?" she said mockingly.

"I'm starting to miss everyone already. Leave me alone," I said, wiping away my mascara. This was so not the day to be weeping off my makeup. I was seeing Wyatt and the GFE-ers at eleven. Not only that, I felt a boil-zit brewing on my chin. The kind that was connected to every nerve on my face. I caught a glimpse of the offender in the rearview mirror. It was red and my chin swelling more by the minute.

I explained to Jilli that I had a commitment on Friday night, avoiding telling her what it was, but that I would drive out after. "I'm sure I will be there before midnight," I said

"We'll be there waiting, and a few cocktails ahead of you. Except poor Tess," Jilli laughed.

Poor Tess was right. Six weeks pregnant and already experiencing morning sickness morning, noon and night. She had to work from home last week and this.

"Tossing my groceries in front of everyone in the office is not really professional," she explained before throwing up over the phone. I was surprised that she was going to attempt the drive out to Palm Springs.

When I got to Karen's, I found Francine at work again in my office. It was nearly cleared. She greeted me with a cheery hello as her workers finished the deconstruction. I managed something like a "Good morning," and promptly walked out of the room. The house was full of boxes and wrapping papers, bubble wrap, foam pads, moving blankets and gaping holes where furniture, books and lamps had once been. It was a pathetic sight. And, yes, I cried again.

I did my best to pull it together. Reapplication of makeup was needed. The pimple had grown more. I could only imagine what I'd look like by the time we got to GFE.

I dragged Karen away from Billy for our final meeting in L.A. We got into her Mercedes, which I'd turn into the dealer on Monday, and headed down the hill.

"Billy and I are almost packed. We want to leave Friday right after the photo shoot, spend a few days in New York before we head to France." She must have seen the panic in my eyes. "Don't worry," she continued. "I already called Madeline. She's changed the ticket and will email the new itinerary in a bit."

I let out a sigh of relief and kept my eyes on the road. The last thing I needed to do was deal with a travel clusterfuck. Trust me when I tell you the best friend a girl can make is a good travel agent, one with the patience of a saint and the savvy of a criminal. Madeline was the perfect embodiment of both.

"Ellen, I'm beginning to worry about you. You seem a little stressed out," she said.

"A little?" I retorted.

"Ellen, dear El. Take the rest of the week off. As a matter of fact, take the rest of the month off. Pack up your things and go to New York. Charge everything you need to the hotel. Manicures, pedicures, massages, facials." The zit must have been caught her attention. "Charge it all. I want you rested, relaxed and pampered by the time I get back. I can't have you there like this, kiddo."

"What about the photo shoot?" I asked.

"Well, take tomorrow off, do the shoot with me Friday, then no more work, got it?"

I nodded and said, "Thank you."

Sitting at the GFE conference table, I did my best not to make too much eye contact with Wyatt. Then tried not to smile too broadly when I did. Instead, I tried to keep my eyes on the speakerphone as Arlene gave her rundown.

"We have Julia confirmed for the first show," Arlene's disembodied voice informed. "She's a huge fan of yours, Karen, and feels so bad about dropping out of *Jonah*. She was going through some personal stuff."

In the background, Henry William Freeman-Harris was crying. She shouted for the nanny to do something; she was paying her to keep him quiet. I tried not to laugh, but thought it might make a great story for the show: *Power Moms and the Nannies Who Cover for Them.* Then see how other kids raised that way actually turned out. I jotted the idea down in my notepad.

"That's wonderful, Arlene," Karen said. She turned to me and mentioned, "I always thought she pulled out of the film because she didn't like me. We'd dated the same director."

Arlene overheard. "Don't forget to mention that when you interview her," the speakerphone bellowed. "Get her into the personal shit."

"And we have other major artists to fill out the first week," Wyatt interjected as little Henry continued to wail. "George and Benicio for their film, Cameron and Drew for theirs, Timberlake can't wait to do the show, and DeNiro and DiCaprio, too. We'll start in with the more poignant stories the second week and continue with current topics, rescue heroes, tragedy-to-triumph in the weeks that follow."

I could feel Wyatt's eyes on me, but kept mine averted. Tried to keep the sides of my lips from rising up. I couldn't stop my toes from curling, though.

"And we are developing stories for sweeps now. El, we like your ideas for that. Overcoming-the-odds stories are winners. We need to narrow those down," Arlene said. Baby Henry whimpered in accord.

"I can't remember when I've been so happy," Karen said as I drove us back. "I have the show, a great guy, a wonderful place in New York, and a fabulous producing partner in you, El. I have to say, this just might be the best time of my life."

I looked over at Karen and she was positively beaming.

We got into the house and she gave me a hug. "This is one of the last times we'll see each other before New York. Take care, kiddo. That's an order," she said smiling.

"I'll see you Friday at the shoot," I said. Then I gathered my two file boxes and the laptop, gave Ruth a hug goodbye, and headed home. So not the right word for it, but that's where I was going. Then my phone rang.

"Meet me for dinner," Wyatt asked without adding a question mark.

"I'm nearly to Venice," I said. As much as I wanted to see him, I was so tired that crawling into a hot bath then bed was more what I needed.

"I'll meet you at James' Beach. I'm on my way now."

"Guess I can't say no," I said, slightly annoyed that I wasn't asked.

"You can if you want to, but I'm hoping you won't."

My growling stomach answered for me.

"I could tell you needed some cheering up," Wyatt said as he poured from a bottle of Veuve. "The kind of cheering only chocolate soufflé could provide. Missing your friends already, huh?"

I nodded and put my head down, biting my lip to stop more tears. He took my hand and kissed it.

"It will only hurt for a little while. Then, you'll be busy with work, meeting new people and, next thing you know, your friends will be coming out to see you and you'll fly back to see them. You'll be fine. I promise," he said.

I finally looked up and into his blue eyes. I couldn't help myself. I leaned in and kissed him. And we kissed until the server brought over our scallops.

When I came into the townhouse, I found a dozen roses, a four-piece luggage set, and Tim sitting in the leather chair waiting for me.

"Hey. What's all this?" I asked.

"Happy anniversary," he said.

Oh, shit. It was. I had gone the whole day not even realizing that today marked five years since our first date. Me, the one who remembered our half anniversary, the day of the week we met and what we wore. The one who would make plans for our anni weeks in advance. That day had once meant more to me than any other, and I didn't even see it coming this time.

"Tim, I'm sorry. I don't know what to say," was all I could offer.

"I had reservations at James' Beach and Casa del Mar. I wanted to take you wherever you wanted to go, but…where were you?"

I had no choice but to lie. "Packing up. Karen's house is a wreck. My office is in boxes. They're in the car now. I just couldn't bear to bring them up."

"Want me to?" he asked.

I shook my head. "I'll deal with it tomorrow. The roses are beautiful, Tim. And the luggage. You shouldn't have." The Tumi set was lipstick red. I would soon fit my whole life in those bags. "I love them," I smiled. "Thank you."

"It's not like I want you to go. But if you're going, it should be in style," he said and made his way over to me. I gave him a hug when he reached me, and avoided a kiss by giving him my cheek instead of my lips.

"Can I get you a glass of champagne? It's chilling in the fridge."

"I don't know, Tim. I'm really tired. I should get to bed."

"Come on. We should have a toast after five years," he said. I smiled in agreement. He went into the kitchen and then the pop of the cork sounded. I sat on the sofa, drained from the day when he handed me the full glass.

"Jesus. You really are leaving, aren't you?" Tim asked rhetorically. I nodded. "I can't believe it. The last five years, I've had you in my life everyday. Even if we weren't together, you were there. We'd talk or text, or at least you were on my mind." He forced a laugh. "It's going to be weird without you."

"Sure it wasn't weird with me?" I offered, trying to keep things light.

"Just weird that it's ending."

"Changing," I corrected. "We'll have a friendship. At least I hope we will."

"Can I visit you?" he asked. "When I go back to see my parents, I mean. I'd like to see you in the city. I think it will suit you."

"Sure," I said, believing that, as time passed, he would find someone new and would not see the point in seeing me.

Tim reached over and took my hand. "I'll always love you, El. You'll always be in my heart."

"You'll be in mine, too."

He leaned in for a hug and held me tight for a long while. It didn't feel right to break from it. These were the last moments of our relationship. They should end on a sweet note. Tim seemed to feel the same. He kissed my neck and cheek and moved toward my lips. I pulled back and saw his tears.

"I don't want to lose you, El," he said softly. He came toward my mouth and I let him. Softly and sweetly he kissed me. Before it could move beyond tenderness and into passion, I pulled back, cupping his face in my hands, and put my lips to his forehead. He let out a sigh. I pulled his head to my chest and held him as he quietly cried. We stayed there on the sofa until the sun rose. I pulled myself out from under him, took the biggest suitcase upstairs and began packing.

Over the past few weeks, I had started to shed what I didn't need, what I wouldn't take or what I would leave for Tim. I had narrowed my wardrobe to what I loved and wore most. A few books, my photos, shoes and toiletries rounded out the rest of what I would come to New York and they would all have to fit into the luggage and two boxes that I would ship to the hotel next week. Everything else I would buy new once I was in Manhattan. New bedding, new plates, new glasses, new life. As I packed, I became even more ruthless. The value of items started to diminish and I found what I truly needed wasn't as much as I had accumulated. I was happy to be without it.

Tim made his way up the stairs and into his room, giving me a wounded smile as he passed. I glanced at the clock and saw I was running short on time. I had my writer meeting at eleven-thirty. Enough time for a quick shower and a trafficky drive over to West Hollywood.

I stood outside the Urth Caffé on Melrose waiting for my writer. There's nothing more awkward than meeting someone you've never seen before. You could never be sure which stranger walking toward you was yours. To be easy to spot, I wore a white dress—a casual, cotton, 50s-inspired, sleeveless shirt-dress that I wore with red, flat sandals. My hair was in a high ponytail since I didn't have time to fully style it. My Chanel shades covered the dark circles formed under my eyes from my night on the sofa.

The wait was made incredibly painful with a gaggle of loud ladies behind me. They had just left the Urth to suck down cigarettes as they recanted their escapades from the night before. Something about The Nice Guy and Bar Marmont.

"He just asked me to blow him right there. And I was like, 'Excuse me? It's not like you have a production deal or anything,'" said Her 1.

"And he wasn't even hot," said Her 2. Hers 3-5 giggled.

One smoker is a headache. Five and I've got an immediate migraine, exacerbated by the fact that I desperately needed a latte. They seemed to be growing roots where they stood, and my migraine was spinning into nausea.

"Hey, girls, do you mind? The smoke is coming right at me," I said as kindly as I could.

"Then move," Her 3 said to me.

"Without citing West Hollywood smoking ordinances, I'm simply asking, kind of nicely, to maybe mind where your smoke is going, which is all over me," I smiled.

"Deal with it," said Her 4, blowing smoke in my direction.

There was a time when I would've engaged in a verbal assault and taken them out one by one. But I'm older now. Wiser. I reached into my bag for my mini can of hairspray, turned my back toward them and fired, missing my mane, but nailing them in a cloud of Kenra.

"Hey!" they shouted.

"I'm sorry. Did that get you?" I asked with eyes batting. After a few *bitch*es were uttered, they decided to head to Maxfield and burn through their trust funds.

"Have a nice day," I shouted after them with a *fuck you* smile.

I checked the time on my iPhone. I hated standing outside the café. While uncomfortable, I learned it was harder to miss someone outside than waiting for each other inside. I had that happen to me on a first date with a hot, young, Irish director, pre-Tim. I waited in the entry of the restaurant. He waited for me inside the bar at a corner table. I didn't see him. He didn't see me. He didn't have cell phone reception, and we both thought we were stood up. Since then, I meet everyone new outside.

In the midst of a full yawn I heard, "Ellen?"

"Yes," I said and I turned to find a tall, handsome, smiling guy in a white t-shirt, jeans and man-sandals. Mandals. Oh my.

"Hi, Vince Channing. Good to meet you," he said shaking my hand.

We took a seat on the patio and ordered food and caffeine. Vince had a tan, a fresh face and an easy laugh. I went into how much I liked his writing, the talent I thought he had, but he stopped me.

"Look," he said. "I'm not really a writer. I'm an architect. But I had this story brewing in me and who doesn't take a screenwriting class at some point living in L.A., right?"

That's where Gabe met Vince. That sneaky bastard never told me he was taking a writing class, or that he was in a writer's group, which is where his friendship with Vince continued.

"I dropped out of the group a few weeks ago since everyone said the script was as good as it was going to get. If it gets to the screen, that's cool. If not, no biggie. It was a one-off. Not a career aspiration or anything." He went on to tell me he was studying for his contractor's license, taking the test next month.

"Architect and contractor?" I asked, noticing his broad shoulders, strong arms and how the sun has worked into his hair.

"I realized I'm a hands-on type," he said.

The espresso was kicking in. I felt brave enough to lift my sunglasses and rest them on my head so I could get a better view. He wasn't Gabe's normal type. He usually went for the quiet, brooding, frustrated artists. Vince was more outdoorsy, but way hot, which Gabe always attracted. Good for him.

"I love to watch something go from plans and empty ground to a space where people will live or work or eat," he told me, and explained that he's designed two restaurants and would be partnering in a third.

"Impressive. Any time for a social life?" I was wondering if he was in any other partnerships. It was the least I could do for Gabe. He'd do the same for me.

"My ex and I broke up a few months ago. It was hard juggling everything. The relationship ended up on the losing end," he said.

I nodded sympathetically. He had lovely green eyes. His full lips parted into a wide smile.

"So, you really are interested in the script?" he asked.

"Yes. I think it's a sweet story. I love the interaction of the young boy and grandfather. The way they make everything such and adventure. And, I have to say, I held my breath when the boat capsized and the boy had to swim out for help," I said, noticing my intensity.

"I did, too," Vince said.

"The boy was you?" I asked, finally cluing in. He nodded and told me of his summers in South Carolina with his mother's parents. It was his grandfather who taught him to build.

"And fish, and swim," he continued.

I told him that he would have an answer on the script in the next two weeks. "I'm anxious to make this my first project," I admitted. "Probably not the right thing for a producer to say to a writer." My lack of experience was showing. I was just happy he didn't have much himself.

"Like I said, this is a one-off for me. If I could put it in the right hands and see that it gets done, it would be awesome. And I'd like you to be the one to do it. Probably not the right thing for a writer to say to a producer," he smiled.

We walked out of the Urth and shook hands.

"I kind of feel like I should give you a hug," he said.

"Okay." I was excited to have my first meeting completed and with such a nice guy. His embrace was warm and welcoming.

I called Gabe from the car. "Why didn't you tell me he was so cute? Did you two hook up? If not, you should."

"You think Vince is gay?" Gabe laughed.

"He's not?"

"No, you hag. Why would you think that? Did he show up in drag? No, wait, he seems like more of a leather type," he mocked, serving up another cackling laugh.

"I just thought that, you know, you two being friends—"

"I do have straight friends, you know. You being one of

them. Then again, I always thought you and Jilli would make a cute couple."

"So my gaydar is off," I said laughing with embarrassment. "It's really your loss. But, I like him. He's nice, and his script is so good. I can't wait for Karen to read it so I can get it going."

"Good for you. By the way, when are we going to get together for a sloppy goodbye? The clock is ticking and I'm missing you already," he said.

"How about tonight? As a matter of fact, I'm free now," I said.

He made a quick call to a friend who works at the downtown Standard. His friend comped us a room and dinner, which was perfect. The photo shoot the next morning was a few blocks away. This would save me a hellish commute, and give me quality time with Gabe. I ran home and grabbed something for the overnighter. I had left a week's worth of clothes hanging in the closet and managed to get the rest packed. I packed for Palm Springs in a separate bag I'd keep hidden in my trunk. If Gabe saw double luggage, I'd never hear the end of me over-packing for a one-night stay. He still brings up my three bags for a long weekend we took after graduation.

"What the hell is all this?" he blurted when he saw my array of baggage.

"Options," I told him. "I like to have options."

"This is another reason I'm happy I date men," he scoffed and tossed his backpack in the trunk.

I scribbled Tim a note and made my way downtown with the mistake of taking the 10. Sometimes you get lucky and traffic moves. Other times, you are just effing stuck sitting there. Today, it was the reality version of Pole Position, zigzagging through the lanes to hit the open pockets left by those not paying attention. If everyone just took driving seriously—and, oh, I don't know, actually paid attention—half the traffic cock-ups would not occur. By the time I made it there, only having to honk and flip the bird a half-dozen times, I was ready for a cock-tail. I went up to the room and it was suite.

"This is massive," I exclaimed, dropping my bag.

"Throw on your bathing suit and grab your hotel robe,

lady. Let's get fabulous," Gabe ordered.

We lounged on the rooftop next to the pool sipping martinis. We knew we looked silly wrapped in our robes to combat the breeze, but we didn't care. You have to take advantage of opportunities as they come.

"You know, Karen couldn't imagine you sleeping on the couch so she got you your own room. You'll even have your own key," I smiled.

"I can finally tell my mother I'm bi. Coastal," he laughed, then went quiet for a second. "I'm really going to miss having you here, though."

"I know. But we can't talk about it or I'll start crying. The swelling's finally gone down from my last jag and I don't want to get puffy again," I said with a forced smile.

After our sunbath, we had dinner in the room and watched *Shaun of the Dead*, shouting "Shooon" every time his girlfriend did. Serious damage was done to the minibar. We laughed and laughed until I laughed myself into an asthma attack when he ordered porn and ran commentary over it.

"Gay porn is so much better than straight porn," he commented.

"Do you watch a lot of straight porn?" I asked.

He shook his head. "Look at these blowjobs. They are terrible and I can't get past the sad boob jobs. They're so distracting."

I nodded in agreement, growing dizzy from watching the askew nipples bouncing up and down.

"Promise me we'll stay close," he asked with a seriousness that didn't go with the bowm-chicka-bowm-bowm music playing under the fake orgasms.

"Of course we will," I said taking his hand.

"That's easy to say and harder to do. I just don't want us to get busy and let our schedules and the distance come between us," he said. "Even with a key and a place to stay, which will come to a quick end once Mr. Hot Stuff moves in, I just don't want us to grow apart."

"I won't let that happen, Gabe. We'll always stay close. And I'm not going to be living with anyone any time soon. I've learned my lesson there."

"Good," he said and kissed my hand.

"Hey, tell me why you took a writing course and never bothered to say anything about it," I chided, hoping to lighten the mood.

"Thought it would help me envision the doc. Tallulah Bankhead lived a life, honey. I've got to map it out somehow."

The clock caught my attention. It was well after midnight and the shoot was an early call.

"I have to get to sleep, Gabe. I don't want to look like shit at the shoot."

"I promise to be a gentleman," Gabe said batting his eyes.

I curled up in his arms and fell into a deep slumber. We were in the same position when the wake-up call rang. Gabe rolled over and cursed me a little and I readied myself as quietly as I could. I kissed him softly on the cheek before I left.

"Goodbye, beauty. Let me know when you're ready for me to knock on your New York door," he said groggily.

"I will. I love you, Gabe," I said.

"Love you, babe," he returned, replete with the finger-gun point.

I took a deep breath and made my way to the studio. It would be my last day in L.A. with Karen. I hoped it would be picture perfect.

Chapter Fourteen

These situations are very delicate. If you don't give a show of strength, you'll get nowhere. Too much? Disaster. This really isn't much different than approaching life itself. You have to find that balance between too much and not enough. Gently. Gently. Find the balance. Fuck.

Peanut M&M's everywhere. Bouncing, making a clatter as they met the concrete floor again and again and again. I wondered if they'd ever stop.

Heads turned in my direction. Even with the music blaring, the candy cacophony caught everyone's attention. I stood holding the bag. The bright, yellow, plastic bag of my embarrassment. Once I recovered from the shock of the explosion, I scrambled to pick up the multihued, lopsided balls. At least Karen was still in with hair and makeup and didn't witness this gaffe. Surely this would cause her to question my professional ability since I couldn't produce an open bag without catastrophe.

"You're next," I was told by the overly veneered hair guy. His teeth were the size of Chiclets. I kept pursing my lips together in hopes he would do the same. But it seemed to make he smile more.

Karen thought it would be a good idea for me to get headshots and for us to get photos together for KEEP. "Might as well since we are here. It will be fun," she assured.

I haven't posed for a portrait since my high school graduation photo, unless you count the DMV or a quick shot for my passport. The thought of a professional photographer snapping me was distressing enough, but that I'd have my photo taken with Karen in something more than a personal setting drove me right to the craft service table for comfort candy. Far from model behavior, but my thumb was not enough to chew on and I wouldn't be able to twist my hair once it was styled.

In this arena, it's not socially acceptable for anyone over a size two to eat high-calorie foods in public. I'm a four on a good day, six on the three hundred and sixty-four others. And M&M's

before lunchtime? Eyebrows of the photographer's assistants rose at this curious site. *Morte.* On the upside, about half the candies were still left in the one-pound bag so it wasn't a total loss. That would be just about enough to get me through the morning.

In order to fully pick up my colorful mess, I had to humiliate myself further by getting down on hands and knees to crawl under the table. Fucking little oval orbs. I tried not to picture the sight of my ass sticking out from under the table. I hoped that everyone was busy finishing the set, or simply bored of my presence. I heard the photographer bark something like that through his thick accent.

I finally collected the rest of what spilled and backed out from under the table. Halfway out, I bumped into something. Or someone. Double *morte.*

"Nice to see you, El. You're looking lovely this morning."

Wyatt stood there with a wide smile. I can't say that I was flattered that he recognized me from my backside.

"Thanks," I said as I pulled myself up with all the dignity that I could find—which wasn't much, by the way—and dumped the floor-kissed candies into the trash. Just so you know, they do melt in your hands, especially when said hands are moist from a not too fabulous start of the day.

Tim had called right when I arrived at the studio, which was the majestic downtown loft of the photographer, Daniel Laurent. As soon as I answered, I regretted it.

"You are still coming tonight, right? The barbecue starts at six," he said with an unattractive dash of desperation.

Barbecue? Six o'clock? On a Friday night?

"Jesus, Tim," I blurted. Tact is not something I possess when the morning is still in single digits.

"What time will you be home?" he asked.

"I have no idea how long this is going to be. Magazine shoots can take all day," I explained.

Because no plan is ever set in stone in the entertainment industry, the photo shoot for the network was bumped for a photo shoot for a six-page feature spread in *Vanguard* magazine.

"You don't have to stay the whole day, do you? I mean, it's

not like you're in the shot. Karen will let you leave." He could still get a dig in.

"Tim, it's not a matter of me being in the shot or not. This is the last time she and I will be together until New York. We have a lot to go over. I won't see her for months."

"El, you promised."

"Tim, the best I can do is meet you there. I'll let you know when it looks like things are wrapping up, but that's the best I can do. Karen's here. I gotta go. Call you later."

This is why normal people move out when they end a relationship. It's Breakup 101.

Karen arrived chipper, giving me a big hug, exclaiming how much fun we were going to have. Music was thumping as the set was being put together, and my headache's throbbing kept time with the beat. She chatted merrily with the hairstylist and make-up artist. Even in curlers and pale face, Karen was radiant. When she was deep in conversation with the beauty team, talking about which actor was inching out of the closet, which married actress was banging her married agent, who quietly snuck into rehab after quietly overdosing…again, I stepped out to get those M&M's.

Wyatt walked back with me to the room where Hair and Makeup was making their magic, then hovered in the doorway chatting to Karen while the stylist finished curling my hair onto large rollers. When the makeup maestro took over my face, I would catch Wyatt looking at me in the mirror's reflection. I wanted him to leave. I'd had enough mortification that morning, and I'm a woman who believes that one should keep some mystery from her man. Sure, he's seen me without makeup, but he didn't need to see it being applied. Having the makeup artist comment on my poor eyebrow plucking ("Have you not heard of Anastasia?"), my need to use a primer ("To minimize your large pores and keep that shine down, though you'd come in handy if we got lost in a desert and needed to signal a plane."), how I should invest in a good moisturizer ("Because you are about six months away from needing Botox, honey."), and asking when was my last facial ("It looks like you did surgery on that chin zit, and it's gonna leave a scar.), was not exactly what I wanted my new lover to hear. Especially because he might have missed a few of those flaws on his own. But he stayed. The whole time. He finally stepped away to take a call right when we were told the photographer was ready.

"Karen, do I really have to do this?" I whined before walking to the set.

"Yes, of course. Daniel is doing this as a favor to me. But, don't mention it to the journalist. The magazine doesn't need to know," she reminded.

The photo shoot was a rush switch that must have been blessed by the gods. When Meaghan, Karen's publicist, told *Vanguard* that Karen wouldn't be available until July, the magazine moved heaven and earth to find a photographer available in L.A. to do the work on Friday, and jetted a journalist out here on Thursday's red-eye to start what they would finish over the phone. The network was happy to rearrange their shoot to Saturday and to have it on her new set when Karen was in New York. It was important to them to get this story into *Vanguard*.

You have to be flexible when you work in Hollywood. Anything could happen at any time. Like me being interviewed for the article. I never saw that coming. Karen was giddy over it, and Meaghan actually thought it was a good idea.

"It shows the full evolution Karen's going through, from actress, to show host, to producer. Her moving you into a producer position highlights her commitment to this change. It's good storyline. Just keep your answers short and to the point. Don't elaborate. Don't think the writer is your friend. Don't forget this is going into print. Once it's there, you can't take it back. Ever." Then Meaghan finished with, "Good luck. Don't fuck it up."

Her vote of confidence was moving. I couldn't blame her. I didn't think sitting down with a journalist for my first time on the same day of my first photo shoot was the best idea. I felt like a virgin on prom night.

"Quit shitting yourself," Jilli chided. I snuck out to call her and grab more M&M's, this time with greater stealth. "You'll be fine. I just emailed Tess to text you her advice. You aren't a moron. You'll do great. What time do you think you'll get to the

Springs?"

"I'm not sure. Depends how long this goes and then the Tim thing. But, believe me, I will be on my way as soon as I can. I'll call when I'm in the car."

Jilli let out a huge sigh before she said goodbye. Tess' text arrived shortly after.

> Stay calm and focused. Answer the question by including the question in your answer. Do not say anything negative, even in jest. Short, sweet and to the point. See you tonight. Got to

And that was all she wrote. We were getting used to the unfinished-yet-sent emails and texts from Tess. Her morning sickness was unrelenting. She carried airsick bags with her and used them regularly. We had gotten her a case of them as a gag gift. Literally. Remi would be driving Tess to the Springs. She has the strongest stomach in the group.

"Back at the scene of the crime," Wyatt said as he came up-on me again at the craft service table. He was there to be interviewed for the article, too, but since the writer had yet to arrive, all Wyatt was doing was making me more nervous.

"You cannot be here when I take my shots," I begged. "I won't be able to focus if you do."

"Not sure how my ego should take that," he replied.

"Take it the right way. I can't pose and act the fool with you in the room."

"If you say so," he said and gave me a kiss on the cheek.

Were it not for the forty-five minutes I spent in the make-up chair, I would have grabbed him by the belt, dragged him out onto the balcony and kissed my lipstick off. Let him tangle my overly coiffed hair. Wrinkle my freshly steamed shirt. Instead, I accepted the friendly bisou and chewed the candies. Then, I had to go to the bathroom and floss the peanut remnants away. They called out my five-minute warning.

The least natural thing in the world to do is sit in front of a camera holding a forced smile, attempting to "smolder", and try not to laugh at the ridiculousness of the photographer's direction.

"Zair. Wotevahr ewe wuhr sinking abow, keyp et. Zat's za luk I vant fer ewe," Daniel said in Frenglish.

Perfect. I was thinking that I had to poo. After forty ounces of coconut milk and espresso, you would, too. I was trying to figure a polite time for a bathroom break, but I didn't see that on the horizon. Once Karen was done changing into something more casual, she and I would do our sitting.

The journalist had finally arrived and was on the balcony talking to Wyatt. Meaghan told me in between shots that I would be interviewed next. Ugh. My stomach rumbled again.

"Pairfekt. Weef gah tit, Elluh," Daniel said.

I was so not looking forward to seeing the contact sheet. I thanked the photographer and gave him a kiss on each cheek, then hastily skipped to the loo. I passed Karen as I ran down the hall. "Be right back," I blurted.

The least natural thing to do next to a photo session is talking to a journalist and trying to carefully phrase each reply so that it sounds natural and not carefully phrased. In three months, I'll know if I pulled it off. Meaghan walked by several times to eavesdrop and said, "It sounded good. We'll just wait and see."

Even though Wyatt's interview was done before mine, he had stayed to say a proper goodbye to me when my makeup could get smudged. He was leaving on an evening flight that night for the network's fall lineup announcement.

"I really wish you were going," he said as we made out at his car. "It's kind of a big deal."

"I know, but I'll be there soon. I'll move my flight to Thursday. We'll have the weekend, right?"

"All of it. I'm going to hog all of your time. You don't mind, do you?"

"Wouldn't have it any other way," I said before kissing him again.

When I waltzed back into the studio, Karen noticed. "That must've been some goodbye," she laughed.

It was.

I picked up my iPhone, after neglecting it for hours, to send Madeline my flight change request. So many messages.

Most of them seemed to be from Tim:

It's 4:00. Have you left yet? We need to be in the car by 5.

Did he really think I would drive from downtown to Venice then from Venice to the Valley? I thought I had made it clear I'd meet him there.

Still working. I'll meet you there. Call when I'm in the car.

"You can leave if you'd like, El. We're almost done," Karen kindly offered in between costume changes. "It's Friday. I'm sure you have big plans." She gave me a hug and said, "You looked so beautiful today. Have a wonderful time in New York. I'll miss you." She gave me a harder squeeze before we broke from the embrace.

I told Karen that I would miss her, too, to have fun in France and that I would see her in a few weeks. It wasn't like we were just saying goodbye to each other, but farewell to what was. We hugged each other once more for good measure, then I said my goodbyes to Meaghan, the photographer, his team and the hair and makeup duo, who kindly touched me up after Wyatt felt me up. I made my way out to the parking lot. It was like leaving school for summer vacation—suddenly, I missed everyone; even the people I had just met.

Summer doesn't wait for June around here. It must've hit a hundred today. Wyatt had parked under the building. I missed the turn for that and opted for a lot rather than backtrack on one-way streets. Mistake. Leather seats are fabulous until the temperature rises. Days like this, I was happy I selected beige interior. Still, there was no oxygen in my car; the heat had burned it away and what was left singed my lungs. Even with the AC on, I felt myself beginning to stick. A bead of sweat ran down the expanse of my cleavage of my barely-B cups. The expertly applied makeup would soon be sliding away. It was five-thirty and I was a good hour away from Randall and Tabitha's. This wasn't going to be pretty.

About the only time I feel claustrophobic is in traffic. The moment I pulled onto the freeway, I regretted it. I believe I saw a snail whizzing by me. I should've taken side streets. I knew better than to get on the road in traffic without consulting Waze. I typed my destination into the app and waited for the next exit to escape. Then, I noticed my gas gauge. Fuck. One more thing to do tonight.

People around me were honking, fighting to get into another lane, get ahead of someone else. Fruitless efforts. I don't know why we all seem surprised by L.A. traffic. It's part of the price of living here. But on this Friday evening, you could reach out and touch the frustration. I understood. I wanted to smile, let them know, *I feel you, friends. I feel you.* But when I did smile over to my lane neighbor, she merely looked at me and mouthed, *Fuck off.* I nodded back. Yes, my friend, I feel you. I feel you.

"You are going to feel like you are melting," Jilli told me on the phone while I crawled to the Valley.

Jilli had left early on the last day of her job to meet up with Emily to help her set up the house for the rest of us, but it was her next move that was on Jilli's mind.

It was official—Jilli and Andy would be in New York in two months' time. Andy had taken off for Manhattan the night before to take a meeting with an art house production company he was interested in merging with. He was also planning to look at apartments for the two of them.

"That scares the shit out of me, El. I've never lived with a guy. My last roommate was junior year in college and I couldn't stand her. I don't know if I can do it," she said with a hint of panic. Never in her in most warped dreams did she think her plot for revenge would end up with her in love and living in the Big Apple. "I'm worried this is all a big mistake and karma's going to yank the rug any minute now."

"Stop it," I told her. "You're just really happy, for the first time ever. Let it happen."

"What if he gets sick of me? What if I get sick of him?" she asked. "What if you get sick of me?"

Cassie was taking office space in the studio's Midtown high-rise, blocks away from the GFE building where the KEEP offices would be. We planned on meeting for lunch or drinks as often as our schedules allowed.

"We'll probably see each other more there than here," she laughed. "God, El, how much fun is this going to be!"

Jilli had the excited anticipation of a five-year-old. But, as she flipped on the blender, I had to slam on my brakes to avoid having my picture taken at a red light. The contents of my purse sprayed all over the floor. It was deserved, though. I was being the driver I hated. On the phone, lost in thought, and distracted while driving a lethal weapon of steel and combustible fuel. And, were it not for the camera, I probably wouldn't have run the way-too-yellow light. There's an odd sort of need-for-speed after sitting in traffic. I just wanted to go go go. Get to Randall and Tab's, get through the barbecue, get on the road to the desert and get to my friends. I just wanted to get all of this over with so I can finally get to New York and get on with my new life.

I said goodbye to Jilli as I turned onto Randall and Tab's street, passing familiar vehicles along the way. Everyone was there. I got lucky and found a spot across the street, flipped a U-y and grabbed it. It pays to have a car with a good steering radius in L.A.

After reassembling my bag, I checked myself in the vanity mirror. It was laughable that I would even have a shred of vanity left at this point. Sitting in that stop-start, bumper-to-bumper, summer-hot traffic, I was not the fresh daisy that left downtown. I blotted away some of the shine from my forehead, reapplied lip gloss and pulled my hair back into a ponytail to get it off my neck. My jeans were stuck to me like a thick skin. My white button down clung to my back. I did the eco-unfriendly act of running my AC full-blast while I was parked, and stuck my face in front of the vents. It dried out my contacts more than it cooled me off.

I let myself in the open front door. Eerily, the house was empty. Everyone was outside. I snuck in and perused the crowd. But a familiar voice rang out.

"Jesus Christ! Randy, you cannot touch my dog with that!" shrieked Dori, her voice scratching the air like nails on a chalkboard. Déjà vu all over again. "Ugh. Did you even clean the grill before you put my veggie dogs down? You have to clean the grill and use separate utensil. You have no respect. No respect at all," Dori accused as she took a deep inhale. She blew out the smoke with, "Like, really, Randy. I can't eat those now. And I only brought the two." Dori took another long drag off her cigarette, crossed her arms and flicked her ashes as she waited for his reply.

"Sorry, Dori," Randall said as his glasses slide down his nose slick with perspiration brought on by the fire. He uselessly pushed them up with the back of his tong-clenching hand. He offered her a weak smile and said, "But, you know, fire sterilizes everything."

Dori started in on Randall with, "You cannot be serious. You have animal fat and flesh stuck to those tongs. Just look at them Randy. Just look!"

Tabitha came over to referee, offering a frozen soy patty to replace her tainted dogs, then she saw me.

"El! You're here!" squealed Tabitha as she ran toward me. "We were wondering if you were ever going to make it."

"Happy Anniversary, Tab," I said. I pulled a card out of my purse and handed it to her. "The gift will come in the mail," I fibbed. At least it would once I ordered it.

"Thanks so much," she said a little misty-eyed. She got that way after a couple of drinks. "I'm so glad you made it." She smiled and squeezed me again.

"So am I," said Tim, sneaking up behind me. "I was beginning to doubt you'd come." He handed me a glass of white wine then put his hand on my waist and softly kissed my forehead.

Tim walked me into the heart of the party. He smiled at me and kissed my cheek. We looked like our happy-couple selves. How looks do deceive, especially in L.A.

The hens were gathered in their typical pockets throughout the backyard. They went silent as I passed. Whispers fluttered behind me. They loved to dissect me like a pickled frog in middle school biology, their verbal scalpels at the ready. I no longer cared who's saying what about me, what the *rumeur du jour* happened to be. Tonight, I walked through the crowd with Tim's arm firmly around my waist and I could feel his ease. Perhaps this was a good thing. Perhaps.

"Good to see you, El," Kent smiled and gave me a warm hug. "Tim was like a cat on a tin roof waiting for you. You should have seen him pacing."

I looked over to Tim, his eyes averted to the ground. He recovered and put his arm around my shoulders, pulling me into him. "I was just worried about your long drive."

I played along and put my arm around his waist.

I looked around and everyone was wearing smiles, giving me waves. A bit too friendly. Must be the booze. I usually got there at the beginning of the night. They were all a good hour ahead of me. It seemed to make them nicer people. Even Renee was charming. My knees nearly buckled when she came in for a hug and an air kiss.

"You look very pretty tonight, El," she offered.

"Thank you," I said wide-eyed, unable to hide my shock.

Kent gave a nod to Liza, and she slowly walked over to me with what appeared to be a smile. I tapped the earth with my foot to feel for any ice; it appeared Hell had frozen over.

"Ellen, hi. It's good to see you," she said. I could see her trying to decide if she should attempt a hug or a handshake. She couldn't muster either. "Did you have a good day?" was all she could awkwardly come up with. This was so delicious it should have been served up in pastry and chocolate.

"My day was spectacular. Thank you for asking," I said, doing my very best to hold in a burst of laughter.

Had I known coming to the party late would make it more enjoyable, I could've saved myself a lot of grief over the years and been tardy. I wondered if Tim might have mentioned my leaving, or if everyone was doing him a favor by playing nice after the El Cholo debacle. Who cared? It was my last Crew barbecue. I looked at my watch. The goal was to be on the road no later than eight-thirty. T minus fifty and counting.

Randall rang the dinner bell. Literally. He installed a triangle last summer for this purpose. One more quirk of the Crew I couldn't say I'd miss.

I made my way over to say hello to Roger and Valerie, and took a seat next to Gordon and Mavis at the long table assembled for the occasion. My luck ran out when Liza and Kent took the seats next to me.

My iPhone blurted out Blondie. I still hadn't changed it. Everything else took priority. Folks around the table shot me looks. Even Tim's eyebrow rose. Phone calls during Crew gatherings were frowned upon. I gave an apologetic shrug. Tim knew I had to take business calls as they came in. Normally, that was a rare occurrence. Karen wasn't needy and was pretty good about not calling after hours unless it was truly important, and my friends were no more interested in phone conversations after six than I was. The "Unknown Caller" could have been anyone. I excused myself from the table and walked to the other end of the yard for privacy.

"Hi, El. Sorry to bother you, but I couldn't wait." It was Karen, and by the bad connection, I could tell she was on the plane. I had gotten her the network's private jet after a bit of begging.

"Is everything okay?" I asked, trying to sound calm.

"Great. Absolutely fantastic. We are about to take off and I had to call you to say I loved the script you gave me. *Grandfather's Lake* is just marvelous. I read it while I waited for Billy to get here and couldn't put it down. I cried and laughed and we have to do it. Call Howie. Let's start on this on Monday. Have a great weekend, El," she said before the phone cut out.

I stood there for a moment and took a deep, joyful breath. We were going to make a movie. Or at least make a move toward purchasing the screenplay. There wasn't a shoe about to drop. Things were only getting better. Better by the minute. I noticed it was quiet. I turned and saw the whole group staring at me, waiting to eat. Why, I had no idea.

"Sorry," I said walking back to the table. "Business."

I wanted to scream out my good news. Call Gabe, Jilli, Wyatt, or Vince to let him know he'd better get an agent ASAP. But, I had to eat that for now along with badly barbecued chicken.

I took my seat on the timber plank and exaggerated how good the food looked. I placed the napkin in my lap and took a long drink from the only glass of wine I'd have. I swallowed the wine hard, choking down my delight.

"Do you have a date set yet?" Tabitha asked Valerie and Roger as we finished with dinner. The conversation had gone from congratulatory remarks to Randall and Tabitha and their upcoming vacation to Hawaii to Valerie and Roger's future vow exchange.

"Not yet. We're still trying to figure out where as well as when," Val said.

"God, that was the worst part for us," Renee said. "Al and I fought about that for months. But, we finally worked it all out. Obviously." She leaned in and kissed his cheek.

"Kent and I didn't have any problems," Liza beamed. "Once he proposed, I looked at the calendar, picked a weekend, called the church and the country club, and that was it." I'm sure Kent didn't realize that when he gave Liza her ring, his balls went with it. He plastered on a grin to show his accord.

"Gordon and I just went down to the registry with some of our mates, then we all went down to the pub and got legless," Mavis said. "We just kept it simple. And that's worked well for us going on thirty years."

"Right it has," Gordon concurred.

"I can't even fathom that," I said without thinking.

"That's the secret, dear. Don't overthink it," Mavis said with a wink. I smiled back.

"Roger and I are talking about not having a wedding, or just having a few friends and family come along. Those who want to," Val explained.

"We might elope to someplace we've always wanted to go. Greece or India," Roger said. "Roll the wedding and honeymoon into one."

"Oh, surely you would miss having the dress and the church and everyone there," Liza admonished.

"I wouldn't," I said, smiling to Val. She smiled back.

"What's the big deal, anyway?" Dori asked rhetorically, with a full mouth. While she wouldn't touch the soy dogs, she was on her third grilled cob of corn. "Isn't the institute of marriage officially dead? At least it should be. I mean, you pay a huge amount to get into it. Rings and weddings aren't cheap. Then there's the toll you pay emotionally while you're in it. That seems never-ending. Marriage counseling; what's that, about two, three hundred bucks a pop? And, finally, there's the divorce, where everyone pays through the nose. I don't see why anybody bothers anymore."

The whole table went silent. The couples were surely adding up their financial and emotional tabs. I burst out into laughter.

"You may be on to something there, Dori," I giggled.

Liza and Renee vehemently disagreed.

"Marriage is so important," Liza asserted.

"It gives you a deeper sense of who you are," Renee added.

"How?" I asked. "Seriously, how can a dress and a ring and a cake do that for you? I think that if you don't know who you are before you get married—or worse, if you think marriage will make you who you should be—you are screwed."

"One day, El, you'll see," Liza offered. "When you are married, you'll see."

"Well, that day may never come, Liza," I countered with a smile. "So, I think I'm better off knowing who I am now."

That brought the conversation to a halt.

"Okay," I said. "On that note, I'll be off. I have a long drive to Palm Springs. I should get on the road." I walked over to the hosts and gave them each a cheek kiss. "Happy anniversary, Randall and Tab. I mean that. I wish you many more years of happiness."

I gave a wave to Tim and the rest of The Crew and made my way to the door.

"Wait," Tim said.

I turned to find him jogging toward me. He took my hand.

"Ellen, don't go," he said.

"Tim, you know I've got some place to be."

"No, I mean don't go," he said. He dropped to one knee.

Oh, shit.

"I love you, El. I love you more than you know, more than I have shown you. You are my best friend, my life and, I hope, my future. And, wherever that future takes us, I want it to be together. Forever."

The Crew had made their way over and stood behind Tim,

smiling at us like Body Snatchers.

Double shit.

I kept pleading with my eyes for Tim to stop. Stop now. Please. Just don't say it.

"Ellen Louise Patterson, will you marry me?"

Chapter Fifteen

If a Guinness World Record existed for dragging luggage into a compact sedan as a solo effort, I would have held it. All that stair running Marco forced me to do was paying off. What didn't fit into the suitcases I threw into bin bags to be sorted out later. What I didn't absolutely have to have was left behind. It was a beat-the-clock situation, because I wasn't sure that Tim wasn't right behind me. For all he knew, I was on the 10 headed toward the desert. Just in case he was coming home to deal with the blow I dealt, I wanted to be long gone. It was cowardly of me, maybe. But, perhaps it was really kind.

Once everything was in, I hit the road and made it to Palm Springs in record time.

"You are kidding me," Jilli said pouring me a margarita.

"Unbelievable," Remi uttered.

"And you said no?" Tess confirmed before biting down on a saltine.

"Actually, I think I said, 'What the fuck were you thinking?' I believe the *no* was implied." I took a swig of the drink. It was potent.

"Wow," Claudia uttered.

"At a barbecue, in front of The Crew? Geez. Talk about a bad way to ask you. I would think Tim would've done better," Emily said shaking her head.

My friends were scattered about the living room. Some on the furniture, others on the floor. They were a few blenders a-head of me. Except for Tess. She was sipping ginger ale and nib-bling crackers.

"Did you at least like the ring?" Remi asked.

"From what I could see, it was pear cut," I answered.

In unison my friends winced.

"No wonder you said no," Jilli joked.

Everyone laughing shook the last of the shock from me and the tension lifted. I sat down on the ottoman next to Jilli's chair and the six of us dove into girl talk. We were no longer women in our early-thirties dealing with adulthood but the younger versions of ourselves, before we were jaded by our jobs and disillusioned by life's disappointments. Laughter came easily and lasted until water rolled from our eyes. We were up until three, which made for long days for all of us. The laughter slowed and the conversation regularly stalled by a series of yawns. It was time for bed.

The three bedrooms meant we all had a roommate. Emily bunked with Tess in the room with two single beds, since Emily can sleep through anything and Tess would be up several times in the night. Claudia and Remi took the middle room and granted Jilli and I the master. Jilli and I were up talking and giggling until after four when Remi shouted out, "Will you two shut up already?"

We spent the morning at the pool quiet. Dark glasses hid our bleary eyes. When the heat became intolerable, we made our way to lunch, all of us squeezing into Emily's SUV.

"Boo," the girls all chided when Blondie sang from my purse.

"You still haven't changed that?" Jilli asked incredulously.

"I've been focused on other problems."

"I thought the deal was to turn those things off," Emily reminded.

"Sorry. I need to keep it on for Karen until she's in Europe, you know, in case," I explained, which they all understood. But it was Wyatt calling, and I couldn't resist answering.

"Hi," I whispered into the phone.

"Are you with the girls?" he asked.

"Yes," I said, trying to act casually.

"Is that Wyatt?" Jilli asked.

I blushed.

"It is," Remi surmised.

Then, in unison, they sang, "Hi, Wyatt," and burst into laughter.

"Tell them I said hello," he chuckled. He told me that the network shoot went well, New York was beautiful and he missed me. "Will you be in on Thursday or Friday?"

"Thursday. I land at five, " I answered and the heads of my

friends turned to me.

"In time for dinner. Will you be up for that? I know it will be a long day of travel."

"I'll be up for it. Can I call you tomorrow, though?" I asked, not wanting to be rude to my friends.

"Please do. Give my best to the girls. Can't wait to see you, Ellie. Bye."

"Bye." I hung up the phone and faced my inquisition.

"You're leaving on Thursday?" Jilli asked, none too pleased.

I nodded. "My car goes on the truck on Wednesday, and I just really want to get there. Not that I want to leave you guys, but I just want to get there, you know?"

My friends were silent.

"Don't be upset. It's just one day early."

"We understand, El," Emily offered. "It's just not fun to think about."

The rest of the drive to lunch was quiet. I made the mistake of checking my email. I'd had the device on phone-only mode since I left Tim in the Valley, but turned email back on when Jilli was in the shower. I heard the flood of messages from the endless chimes but didn't have the guts to see whom they were from. It was easy to assume at least one was from Tim. I also had voice messages from him that I would need at least two cocktails to face.

I started from the top of the email list. Howie got my message and would get on the phone with me first thing Monday about the script. Gabe sent his best wishes. And then there was Tim's.

> I guess your phone will be off, at least to me, until you are in New York. I left you three messages. Don't bother returning them.
>
> I can't believe you ran out like that, Ellen. I can't believe you went back to the house and grabbed your shit like you were escaping. Is that how you see this? Do you need to run away? I can't help but think that guy is part of the reason, if not the entire reason things have fallen apart between us. I know

I have my share of the blame, but you aren't innocent here. Maybe last night wasn't the right time or way for me to propose. I should've asked you years ago. I wasn't ready then. Maybe I'm not ready now. I just don't want to lose you. Now I see I already have.

Let me know what you want me to do with the rest of your things.

"Crap," I said flatly.

"Tim?" Jilli asked.

"He's equating me with someone on the lam. That I took my stuff like I was escaping," I told them.

"Well…" Jilli started.

"You're not agreeing with him, are you?" I asked, slightly pissed.

"Not exactly. Look, what you two have gone through makes Andy and Selma's divorce look normal," Jilli said matter-of-factly.

"I don't think that's fair," I complained.

"It wasn't what you would call a clean breakup," Emily continued.

"Jesus. Are we on our way to a cross so you can nail me to it?" I retorted.

"Don't take this personally, El," Remi consoled.

"Is there another way to take it?" I spit back.

"Maybe we should change the subject," Claudia offered.

"I'm going to throw up," Tess said. Change of subject. Change of lanes, and a hurling of crackers.

It took a while for the atmosphere to thaw. Maybe a little spat was what we needed to make the separation easier. Perhaps it was helping to keep us from remembering this would be the last weekend we would have together like this before we all moved on and became wives or mothers or executives or just too busy with where life was taking us. There's enough history between us to find forgiveness. We can always pull a story from our past to get us laughing at how silly we were then, how silly we are now, and remind us how far we had come. Luckily, we were still doing it together.

"I have a surprise to show you," Emily said after lunch. She drove us over to where her new Pilates studio would be. I thought things were moving fast for me, but Emily had made a land speed record. The lease was signed and the remodel was under way on the studio, then she drove us out to a house with a 'Sold' sign on it.

"I signed the papers yesterday. This is my new home. Or, it will be once escrow closes," Emily smiled.

We went into a group hug and congratulated our first homeowning friend. It was a boxy, mid-century, typical of the desert. She assured us it had been remodeled inside, with a quaint kidney-shaped pool out back.

"It's so retro," she laughed.

"What about Ron?" I asked.

"He can commute. Spend the weekends here. Or not. But I needed this for me," she said smiling. "I'll still be in L.A. a few days each week with the studio there. Placate a few of my clients until they get used to a new trainer. I know everything will go smoothly with Claudia running the studio and managing me."

"She's making me train as an instructor, too. Classes every night and on the weekends. My ass and abs are going to be so tight," Claudia added.

Without the key, we turned into Peeping Toms, peering in through windows and over the fence. Neighbors took notice and Emily introduced herself. We decided to take off in case one had called the cops.

We were all yawning on the drive back to our rental home. Everyone tucked in for a disco nap, but Tess and I couldn't sleep. We snuck out to the pool to soak our toes and share some time.

"We thought of a destination wedding. Someplace great like Paris or even Hawaii. But, if this morning sickness keeps up, there's no way I can travel. The backup plan would be to have it at a hotel in L.A., or my bathroom," Tess explained.

"You are going to do it before the baby?"

"I want to do it before I get too huge," she laughed.

"Do you feel rushed?"

She shook her head. "No. This is a done deal. Dane and I are going to be joined for life now no matter what," she said rubbing her near-flat belly. "This is a permanent thing. Marriage or a divorce won't change it. But, we might as well try to make it right and make it work." She splashed water with her toes.

"You are going to make a wonderful mom, Tess."

"Thanks, El. I hope so. Motherhood isn't something I want to fuck up."

"Tell me about it," I said with a grin.

I pointed over to a group of hummingbirds buzzing around the feeder. We sat there mesmerized by their lightness and speed, and how happy they seemed. And then they all flew away.

As the rest of the girls got ready for our hot Saturday night out—and by hot, I mean over a hundred degrees—I decided it was as good a time as any to take the heat from Tim and gave him a call. He deserved more than an email.

"I didn't think I'd hear from you," was how he answered the phone.

"I suppose I called to say I'm sorry. I didn't handle this well, and I'm sorry for hurting you." I paused to give him a chance to speak, but there was only silence. "I hope one day you can forgive me and maybe we can—"

"Don't say 'be friends'," he said softly.

"Then be fond of each other and remember what we had sweetly. I always will."

"What do you want me to do with your stuff?" was his only response.

"I can come by on Tuesday and clear it out. You don't need to deal with my mess anymore than you already have."

"I owe you for your half of the furniture," he said plainly. "How much do you want for it?"

"Nothing. It's yours."

There was a space of silence. I heard him clear his throat.

"I'll be gone on Tuesday. Let yourself in and leave the key. Good luck in New York, El. I hope you'll be happy there," he said and hung up.

"How did it go?" Jilli asked when I came into our room.

"Relatively painless," I admitted. "He's angry, but didn't

lash out."

"He was never really showy with his emotions anyway," Jilli said flatly.

I nodded.

"God, nothing's the same, is it?" she asked.

"Weird, huh?"

"It's like you started this domino effect. Knocked everything out of order."

"Sure, blame it on me," I moaned sarcastically and plopped on the bed.

"It's usually down to you anyway," she smirked. "I'm not sure I'm ready for all this, though."

"Me, either. But, fortunately, all we need to do is be ready for dinner right now. We'll just take life one meal at a time."

"Perfect. I'm starving."

We ate up the rest of the weekend with more laughter and Monday morning came too quickly. Especially at the hour we all rose.

I made everyone coffee and cinnamon rolls from a cardboard tube. In spite of the carbs and calories, the girls ate them up, if only as a gesture. Tess and Remi had to leave early to get back to L.A. for work, so we all got up with them to say goodbye.

"Maybe we can get together Wednesday night?" Remi inquired.

"I have a red carpet to do," Tess said. "I really hope I don't barf on it."

"I'll still be here. I thought we'd have Thursday," Em admitted. I saw them all do the panicked schedule scramble in their heads.

"Look, don't worry. I'll be back for my sister's wedding at the end of June," I said calmly. "I'll make it a long stay and we'll see each other then. And you'll come out and see me, too. It's only New York, not New Guinea. The flight's the same as driving to San Fran. Unless Jilli's behind the wheel."

That, at least, made them smile. We said goodbye to Tess and Remi, then an hour later to Claudia and Emily, who had a meeting with their development team. Jilli was in between jobs so we stayed watched the network announcement online. Karen was the big news for the fall daytime lineup. I left a message on her cell phone congratulating her and wishing her and Billy a great vacation one more time.

Howie called as we were packing up. He had read the script over the weekend.

"This is really good, El. Nice job," he said matter-of-factly.

"Thanks. That sounded like it hurt to say," I joked.

He laughed back. "You and Karen are going to do really well, El."

"That means a lot, Howie."

I placed my call to Vince and was happy to get his voice-mail. It was a heads-up to let him know Howie would be calling and we were interested.

"More than interested. Get an agent on board, Vince, or at least a lawyer. We look forward to making this deal with you. And I'm sure that's something a producer shouldn't say to a writer. Congratulations."

"Your first script. You popped your producer cherry," Jilli said coming in for a hug. She has such a way with words.

Jilli and I headed out for lunch in town before making our drive back to L.A. We had grown accustomed to the scorch of the desert, or maybe we simply grew bored of saying, "It's so fucking hot," every time we walked outside. We'd certainly made the most of our weekend together and, over lunch, Jilli and I kept laughing at our antics.

Saturday night, after dinner, we went dancing at a gay bar. Palm Spring is West Hollywood East. So many beautiful men to sweat next to without any guilt or end-of-the-night grope. Emily actually left with phone numbers, though. New clients.

Sunday, we drove to Rancho Mirage for our spa day. Massages, facials, manis and pedis. We were pudding by the time we left. Unanimously, we ditched our plans for dinner and more dancing for ordering in and Sunday night cable.

"Does this mean we're old?" I asked, somewhat concerned by my contentment for a night in on my last weekend in Southern California.

Shaking her head, Remi said, "We're too young to be old. If

sixty is the new forty, we are still pubescent."

"Maybe that's why men expect us to go bald down there," Claude philosophized.

"God," Tess uttered through a cracker.

"I prefer 'sophisticated'," Emily stated. "We are wiser and a tad complex."

"Face it, we're old," said Jilli. "Remember when we would go out no matter what? No matter what. Broke, we would go cheap. Tired, we would do espresso shots. Pimple on forehead, we would cut bangs. It's nine-thirty and we are in our jammies ready for night-night. We have crossed the threshold into old."

A few pillows were tossed at her head, which were quickly chucked back.

I couldn't sleep that night. Quietly, I got out of bed and poured myself the last of the wine. I sat out on the patio and listened to the crickets chirp. Gazed at the stars, which were so rarely seen in the skies of L.A. The night was moonless black and soothingly warm. The cold wine went down easy.

I thought of nothing and everything. Four more days and I would be on a plane. Four more days and everything would be different. Would I? The next time I saw my friends, these women who knew me better than anyone—sometimes, even myself—would they see a change in me? I could only hope it would be from growth. That they would see me as happier and content. I hoped that when I came back, the only change I would see in them was from joy, love and success. We all deserved some good now. We had all worked hard and long enough for that.

As I walked back into the house, it occurred to me that, for the first time in my life, I didn't have a home in L.A., except for that of my mother, which had long been foreign land to me. I would have to make a final stop there on Tuesday night for a quick goodbye to Kitty and Gwen until I was forced back for my sinister's nuptials. If I thought I could get away with it, I would find an excuse not to attend. I suppose that makes me sound awful. I did wish her happiness, but we really weren't part of each other's lives. She had played her hand smartly. She never wanted what Kitty doled out to me, so she parroted our mother.

It saved her, but ruined our relationship. We've made a few attempts to bond, but none of them stuck. Sadly, we have nothing in common but a womb.

Without a place to go, I figured I would check myself into a hotel. Perhaps the Ritz-Carlton in the Marina. Or the Marriott. Maybe the Jolly Roger Motel. It really didn't matter to me where I stayed; I just needed a bed and a shower until my time in L.A. was up.

"I guess it doesn't make sense to hit the outlets on the way out. Especially since your car looks like your closet puked in it," Jilli said as we walked into the restaurant.

"Yeah. I wonder if I can check the plastic bags. I'm kind of over packing right now."

"Look. You should stay with me, El. Checking into a hotel is silly. And I can help you finish packing."

I was just beginning to warm to the Jolly Roger idea when Jilli made her offer. "Are you sure?" I asked.

"Positive, you dork. Andy's still in New York until next week. The place is kind of a train wreck, but then who are you to judge," she said with nudge.

Taking Glendale over Marina del Rey was difficult, but choosing my best friend's company over being alone in a room infested with strangers' DNA was easy.

We were fortunate to hit a pocket in traffic that was without congestion and made it to her door before my bladder burst, Jilli running ahead to open the it for me. Accepting multiple iced tea refills before a long drive was just idiotic. And I repeat that mistake a little too often.

Once we dragged my luggage in, Jilli helped me re-pack my clothes.

"I am happy with Andy," Jilli said as she folded. "The thing is, El, I really can picture my life with him. Old age and everything."

"Isn't that a good thing, Jillian?" I asked, folding up a skirt. The clothes were now wrinkled and looking a wreck. If I had the gumption, I would have ironed them. But, that's what the hotel valet is for, no?

"It scares the ever-loving shit out of me. What if I really let go and it doesn't work?"

"What if you don't and that kills it?" I countered. She rolled her eyes at me. "Jilli, you are thirty-two. If you don't go for it now, then when?"

"Don't play the biological clock card with me, El. You know that doesn't apply."

"It's not the clock, Jilli. I think it's more like fate. Maybe Andy is your fate. Maybe not. But you can't hold back just because you're afraid. That's almost all the more reason to go for it."

"Since when did you become the philosopher?" she smiled.

"Since I woke up to the fact that I was too chicken shit to ask for something more out of life. Maybe you should stop hitting the snooze button and wake up, too."

"If this producer thing doesn't work out for you, maybe you could make slogans for Hallmark or tea companies," she quipped. "C'mon. Let's make up a bed for you. If you're half as tired as I am, you are bushed."

Tuesday morning came with a jolt. A small earthquake rumbled our side of town.

"They still freak me out," Jilli said over breakfast at Jinky's. Both of us had been in the big '94 quake. That one actually roared, not rumbled. This one was just a little shaker.

"I think I'll kind of miss them," I told her. "I'd still take a quake over a tornado or hurricane."

"What do you think New York's natural disasters are?" Jilli wondered.

"Aside from Hurricane Sandy, I'd say muggers."

After breakfast, it only took me twenty minutes to clear out the rest of my property from Tim's. Three bin bags, a stop at the dumpster, another to Goodwill and one more to FedEx to ship my boxes to the hotel. I left the key behind as he requested with a short note:

Dear Tim,

I don't know what to say but thank you. Thank you for the love and all that you gave me. I wish you *only the best.*

Always,
Ellen

I wasn't sure if this was better or worse than leaving only the key. I hoped it offered him some closure. For me, that was as simple as shutting the door.

"Is that all you came for Ellen? That damn check? What are you in such a rush for? Did you lose your job or something?" Kitty asked, deflecting the fact that she had yet to honor her word and cough up my inheritance.

"I'm leaving day after tomorrow for New York. I wanted it before I left. Why haven't you gone to the bank? My birthday was six weeks ago. I think you've had plenty of time to run that errand," I asserted.

"The world does not revolve around you, missy. I've had a lot to do getting your sister's wedding planned since you're too good to lend a hand. I can't believe you didn't offer to throw her a shower."

"What, the five she planned for herself aren't enough?"

"You are such a disappointment to me, Ellen."

"I know, Kitty," I deadpanned. What I wanted to say was, *You aren't exactly a dream come true to me either.* But I'm a nice enough daughter to keep that to myself.

"Why in the hell are you going to New York, anyway?" she barked.

"I'm Karen's producer now and we are relocating to Manhattan."

"What, Hollywood doesn't want her anymore so you have to hit the road?"

"You know, you are a good antidote for homesickness. I'll tell you what, I'll see you next month for Gwen's wedding. Have the check ready for me then. Cashier's check, nothing personal," I said as I got up to leave.

"Aren't you staying for dinner?" she asked.

"Um, no," I said then closed the door behind me.

"Do you think she's embezzled it?" Jilli asked over our

shrimp tacos. We went out for Mexican food at the mom-and-pop a few blocks from her place. Gorging on chips and guacamole sounded like the thing to do. We had both gotten our periods. "Imagine if your dad was loaded and left you and your sister a bundle. How sweet would that be?"

"I really don't care if it's a million bucks or five pesos, it's the fucking principle. She is such a control freak. I pray to God that it's not genetic. My greatest fear is to turn into her. If I do, please put me down like a rabid dog."

"You won't be anything like her, El. But, if by some freak occurrence that happens, I'll do the right thing and have you institutionalized. That way we can still visit."

In spite of her typically spiky demeanor, Jilli had a distinct way of finding the bright side to a nightmare. And she was in fine form that night. Andy had found a place he liked for them and asked if she wanted to see it before he put an offer down.

"I said, 'Andy, if you love it, I'll love it. I trust your judgment. I don't need to see it.' And the truly odd thing is, I don't. And you know how picky I am," she said with atypical glee.

"It has a Park view, doesn't it?" I asked rhetorically.

"Yeah, but, for the first time in my life, I completely trust a man. That's bigger to me than any view."

Nothing was the same anymore.

I cancelled the pickup for my car and drove it downtown where they would load it on a truck and drive it cross-country. In ten-to-fourteen days, it would make it to New Jersey. I was going to take up Wyatt on his offer to drive it in to the city. I still needed to sort out a parking garage. I suppose I could do that next week.

Without a car in L.A., you feel naked. Totally vulnerable, like someone took your legs. Since I had to be downtown at seven, I left before Jilli woke and took a Lyft back.

"What are you going to do on your last day in L.A.?" Wyatt asked as we FaceTime'd during my ride back to Glendale.

"I don't know. I think I've done it all. Now I just want to get there," I replied.

"I can't wait to see you. In person, that is. I miss you. All of you. Especially that spot where—"

"Okay, reign it in, mister." I had to take a deep breath. The thought of Wyatt touching me anywhere made me go warm.

"Come on, you'd make the driver's day," Wyatt laughed.

"I'll see you tomorrow, you perv." I noticed that caught the driver's attention.

"Bye, baby. Have a safe flight."

Baby. That's the first time he's called me that with his clothes on. I liked being his 'baby', all feminism aside. I wish I could've gotten on the red-eye that night. Who would have thought that would be fully booked? Just one more day. I've waited this long, a few more hours wouldn't kill me.

Chapter Sixteen

Rarely is it good news when your phone rings before your alarm does. I even have my phone set to sleep until then. You have to be a favorite to get through. Or call repeatedly. No, this could not be good news.

"Ellen, did you hear?" Wyatt's voice said softly.

"Hear what?" I asked, still groggy. My phone beeped. Call waiting. Two calls before my alarm, which was set to go off at five-forty-five. This was bad. "Wyatt, can you hold? That's Howie on the other line. I'll be right back," I said without waiting for his answer.

"Ellen," Howie said in a voice deeper than I had heard before.

"What's wrong with Karen?" I asked. She was the only thing we all had in common.

What was wrong was a boat accident. Billy had her in a friend's racing boat. He took it up to high speed when he shouldn't have. Not knowing how to navigate the current at that speed, he hit a wake the wrong way and flipped it. Friends in a boat behind them found Billy first, busted up but alive. A second boat found Karen twenty minutes later, floating face down. They believed she died instantly.

I had forgotten Wyatt was on the other line. I had forgotten to scream or cry or call out for Jilli. I sat there in the dark in disbelief. The buzzing of my iPhone shocked me into awareness.

"El, are you okay? Baby, are you okay? I'm here, Ellen. Talk to me," Wyatt said.

His emotion came through in his voice. I didn't know what to say or what I felt, but the pain was coming. I could feel it heading my way.

"El, say something. Please," he begged.

"Howie's going to call Ruth, but I think I should have done it. It should have come from me," I said.

"It's okay, El. It's okay for Howie to tell her. Are you okay?" Wyatt asked.

"Probably not," I answered, devoid of any emotion. I suppose I was in shock. Terrible shock. How was this possible? How could someone so kind and vibrantly alive be taken like that? An accident. It didn't make any sense. So, I just waited for someone to call and make a correction. Say it was an awful mistake. Or, maybe I would wake up from this horrific dream. Perhaps I had a fever and it had yet to break. My mind sorted through every possibility to avoid accepting that Karen was gone. I could not fathom that as fact. I needed proof. I went into Jilli's room, crawled into her bed and turned on the TV. *The Today Show* went live in L.A., trumping the local morning news.

Matt Lauer broke it to me. "We are shocked and saddened to report the death of Karen Ellis. The two-time Oscar-winning actress was vacationing with actor Billy Harding in the South of France. The couple went out for a day on the water when the speedboat Harding was driving veered out of control, flipping several times, killing Karen Ellis instantly. Billy Harding is in a local hospital in critical condition. Karen Ellis was fifty-three."

Jilli reached over to me and I was finally able to cry.

The media frenzy that ensued was somewhere between that of Whitney Houston and Princess Diana. Every channel interrupted their broadcast to break the news. CNN, E!, and MSNBC had quickly assembled retrospective montages.

My friends flocked around me, protective and supportive. Tess got the news shortly after I did from the press wires. She called the rest. By the time I should have been at the airport, they had convened at Jilli's, bringing me lattes and pastries and long embraces.

My phone rang incessantly with comment requests and appearance invitations. Tess stepped in for me, working with Meaghan who was on overload and in mourning. Ruth had to leave the house escorted by security, and guards were posted at all four corners to keep the paparazzi in line and ghouls from trespassing.

Tim called Jilli to see if she knew where and how I was. He told her that photographers were staked out in front of his place.

"How would they even get your address?" Remi asked.

"Nothing is private anymore," Claudia reminded.

"Well, no one will come looking for you in Glendale," Jilli said in an attempt to soothe me.

Death is surreal enough. Death mixed with media makes it even more bizarre. No one even took a moment of silence. A moment to breathe or grab a tissue. It was immediate chaos. All I wanted to do was shut the door and try to wrap my head around the fact that Karen was gone.

"Is Wyatt flying out?" Emily asked. She had left Palm Springs at dawn that morning to avoid traffic, and came right to Jilli's when she heard.

"I don't know," I answered numbly. "Howie wants to know if I'll go with him to get Karen. Should I go?"

"Do you want to?" Jilli asked.

"I don't know," I answered. If I went, then it would be real. There would be no more denying it, which I believe is the first phase of grief. I wasn't ready to make it real.

Tess was answering my phone like the pro she was. "I think you need to take this. It's Meaghan."

Meaghan asked me if I wanted to be on Anderson Cooper that night. "No. Why would I want to do that?" I asked.

"You know he and Karen were friends. He's doing the show on her tonight and I thought…Never mind. I agree with you. You shouldn't. We'll issue a statement. I'll draft something and send it over," she said. Her voice was wobbly, but I admired that she could still function. Karen was her first big client. They had been together for twelve years.

Why anyone would want to talk to me or hear a comment from me seemed absurd. I was just her assistant. But, since she didn't have family, her colleagues were solicited. Targeted. It made me feel dirty.

Howie would do the show. "Only to honor her," he told me. He had been her manager for more than twenty years. "Warners offered the jet to fly us to France and back. They'll take us right after the taping. El, if I send a car, would you come with me?" He sounded like he needed support. With four kids, his wife couldn't really drop everything and go. I decided to suck it up and take the flight. It was the least I could do for him, and for Karen.

It was my first time on a private jet. That should be an exciting thing, but it couldn't be a worse occasion. I dulled myself further with Xanax borrowed from Claudia. I woke when the plane stopped in London to refuel. From there we went on to Nice. Flashbulbs blinded us as we made our way to the waiting car and police escort. We were told that Cannes went dark for two minutes that night in honor of Karen.

We were taken to the hospital where Howie had the unfortunate task of identifying her. He came out of the room pale and quietly cried on our way to the Hotel du Cap where, in spite of the film festival and the summer weather, they found two rooms for us.

"Isn't it stupid for us to go there?" I asked Howie. "The press is there en masse for the festival. I don't think I can deal with that."

"We should accept the courtesy they extended for Karen," he said. "It's just for the night."

By this time, the Xanax had worn off, and I was unable to stop crying. I no longer sobbed, I merely trembled at the reality and leaked from my eyes. While it was painful to lose my grandparents, that was to be expected. They were quite old when each of them passed. While it was sad to think of my father being dead, he was barely a part of my life, so it was the concept of him that was mournful. To lose a friend, a massive part of your life, so suddenly without a hint of warning, devastated me to a low that I had not known before. I had to function, though. For her. If it were only about me, I would have crawled into Jilli's bed and not left it for weeks. Or months.

In the four years we had worked together, Karen had become family to me. How could she not? We spent nearly every day together, sometimes literally every day together when we were on location or travelling. She was a sister/auntie/friend who taught me about life, made me laugh and let me see myself in a new way. There was no one like her. And now she was gone. The next morning, Karen would be cremated, and then we would take her home.

"You made the tabs," Jilli said softly when I got back. There, on the cover of the *New York Post* was a photo of me carrying the box that held Karen's urn. I never saw a photographer, which made it even more creepy. The photo ran in every weekly, tabloid and pseudo-news program.

"Some fifteen minutes, huh," I bemoaned.

"I should have gone with you," Jilli said as she stroked my hair.

"I wouldn't have been any fun."

The following weeks were a blur. And, were it not for my friends, I wouldn't have gotten through it. They gave me strength and support, helping me to rise to the occasion and organize Karen's memorial in the midst of scandal.

Billy was arrested and would be charged in her death. They found cocaine in his system. Broken pelvis, broken leg, broken ribs and punctured lung, he remained hospitalized in France. My sorrow was replaced by anger.

"I never liked him," I told my friends. "I knew he would be trouble for her, but I couldn't tell her that. He made her so happy." I was experiencing something like survivor's guilt, believing my silence contributed to her demise.

"The important thing is that she was happy, El," Emily consoled.

"It's good that she was happy," Gabe echoed.

There was nothing good about any of this. No matter how my friends tried to see the upside, I couldn't see any good. What good comes with planning a memorial?

We agreed Karen wouldn't want anything ostentatious. The offer to have a service at the Shrine Auditorium taped and televised was quickly dismissed.

"How ghoulish can people be?" Tess asked as she read the request to me. "This is beyond wrong."

To avoid the media circus that had pitched its tents around this, we held a private service at dawn in Malibu. It would have been more fitting to scatter her ashes off into the sea at sunset, but that would allow the helicopters to hover. Her closest friends and colleagues, including the GFE team, came. Actors, directors, producers and personalities all showed up at the ungodly hour.

"You can't smoke here," I snapped at one Oscar winner.

"Karen wouldn't appreciate that." He nodded politely and crushed his butt.

We waited for the rosy glow of sunrise to say our final goodbyes. It was a nearly mistless morning and a cloudless sky. I could feel her with us, smiling. Comforting each one of us there. I missed her so much.

I didn't want to hear compliments that day. "It was a lovely ceremony," meant nothing to me. Of course it was. It was for her. We wouldn't have allowed for anything less. "She was so fond of you," fell on deaf ears. I didn't need our relationship validated. I knew its worth. The anger phase of my grief was strong. Since there wasn't any bargaining to be done, that only left depression and acceptance. I wasn't looking forward to either one of those. I had a feeling I would linger in the anger. I felt a hand wrap around mine and leaned into Wyatt.

The day before the service was the first time I had seen him. It took Wyatt two weeks to get to L.A. Karen's death had to be dealt with swiftly on a network level. I tried to hide my resentment at that, pretending to understand. I didn't. But it's not something I wanted to talk about. I didn't want to talk at all.

He came to Jilli's to collect me. I spent the night with him at Shutters. It was out of convenience to save on the morning drive. The irony of the venue was not lost on me, but buried by the drugs. We slept together but sleep was all that occurred. He held me until the Xanax took its hold. I knew I was inconsolable, but I needed something more than his presence to make me feel better. After the memorial service, I realized what had been absent. Never once did Wyatt say that everything would be all right.

Now that Karen's ashes were scattered, the time had come to pick up the pieces. We went back to Wyatt's house to stay the night and I was going to attempt to be human.

He poured some bourbon over ice and handed me the glass. It tasted like high school.

"Celia said I could stay with her until I found an apartment," I stated flatly. Karen's death put an end to the purchase of the New York properties. "When should I be at work?" I asked innocently enough.

"El, I have to tell you something." Wyatt warbled on about Karen's replacement, then he hit me with the reality.

"What do you mean I don't have a job on the show?" I demanded.

"I'm sorry, El. You were Karen's producer. Part of her deal. Now that we have a new host, she wants her assistant in your role," he explained a little too matter-of-factly for my liking.

"So much for me being a valuable asset to the team," I growled. My blood pressure rose to stroke level. He took a step toward me. "Don't!"

I stepped back and nearly fell. Boxes were all over the floor in various stages of packing for his move to New York. He was moving forward. I was left behind. I no longer had a job or a home in Manhattan, but I did have a car in Newark. The company was kind enough to hold it for me for there to the tune of eighty dollars a day.

"Did you even fight for me, Wyatt? Or was all that talk about how good I was just talk?"

"El, I know you are upset," he started.

"Of course I'm fucking upset, Wyatt. What else am I supposed to be? Over the moon? My boss was killed by her addict boyfriend, I've lost my job, I have no place to live, I'm still mourning the loss of my friend and my fucking car is on the East Coast sitting there waiting for me, but I don't have a reason to go there now, do I?" I waited for him to respond.

"Look, El," he started again, but I didn't need him to finish.

"No job, no us. I get it," I stated curtly.

"I'm sorry. Charlotte and I..."

"Charlotte? What about her boyfriend?" Not like that mattered, I was only trying to fathom what had happened to my life.

"They broke up. They'd been having trouble for a while. And she was there for me when Karen..."

"She was there for you?! You were supposed to be here for me. You fucking asshole. You said you were trying to get out of New York as soon as you could but really you were there sticking it in your ex. Unfuckingbelievable."

Like I said, the anger stage and I was in it deep.

"I'm sorry, El. I didn't want to tell you like this."

"It doesn't fucking matter, Wyatt. It's better to know now what a dickhead you are than to waste another second thinking you were a good guy." I grabbed my bags and started for the door.

"Where are you going, El?"

"Do you care? Enjoy New York, Wyatt. I hope the fucking show tanks."

I dragged my suitcase out of Wyatt's building. He chased after me. I didn't want to have a fight on the street, but I wasn't really getting what I wanted lately.

"Ellen, don't go like this," Wyatt said as he blocked my path.

"Wyatt, move."

"El, I really do care about you," he said, as if that was going to make me feel good. "How can I make this better?"

I felt my right knee rise until it hit his testicles. He doubled over and fell to the pavement groaning.

"There," I said. "I feel better." I left him writhing on the sidewalk, a living illustration of how I felt. I made my way over to the nearest bar and called Gabe to come get me.

"I can't believe you, El," Gabe laughed. "That's so wrong and so right. I love it. What if he sues, though? Or charges you with battery?"

"He won't. Wyatt's too much of a mangina for that. I should have known."

"Known what?" Gabe asked.

"That if it's too good to be true, it's probably a lie," I said and started crying again. But, I decided that was the last time I was going to break down.

I went back into organized assistant mode. I called the transpo company and had them put my car back on the truck to bring it back to me. I called the hotel to ship back my boxes. I called Howie to find out what was going to happen to Ruth and me. He asked me over to his office. I borrowed Jilli's Rover and went over to Century City.

"El, there's kind of a hiccup. Let's get Larry on the phone so he can explain." Howie looked at me dolefully. Larry was

Karen's business manager, in charge of her finances. Another pit grew in my stomach. It was now a pit within a pit within a pit.

Larry and Howie explained that Karen was in the process of revising her will. She was planning on leaving me a fair share of her estate, including the apartments in New York. Since she didn't have any family left to inherit it, she saw Ruth and me in that category. Because we were business partners, she wanted me to be taken care of so that the company could survive without her.

"Unfortunately," Larry explained through speakerphone, "since that will wasn't finalized, her previous and fully executed will stands."

What that meant for me was twelve weeks of pay, which she had written in years ago for any assistant to benefit from. Ruth, who had been with her for ages, would be getting more. It comforted me to know that Ruth would be taken care of. It helped me to know that Karen was thinking of me, but the reality was I had to figure out my life quick. Three months' pay was nice, but it wasn't going to last me that long, even with adding two more weeks for my vacation pay. I had to find a place to live, and that meant first and security, and furniture. And I was in no state to be looking for work. Kitty needed to get me that check.

"We can also keep you on the payroll for a few more weeks if you'd like to help close Karen's affairs. I know that won't be easy, but it would help us out if you could manage it," Howie said as he forced a sad smile.

"Of course, I'll help," I assured him. I thanked Howie and Larry for their kindness and made my way out. Howie gave me a long hug. I could feel him holding back emotion.

"Kid, whenever you are ready to look, I'll help you get a job. Just let me know. Anyone would be lucky to have you," he assured me.

I couldn't comprehend working for anyone else. Karen was a once in a lifetime opportunity. Sane and nice didn't come along every day in L.A. I couldn't picture myself working for a drama queen, diva or dickhead. Besides, I had put my assistant mindset away. I was supposed to be a producer.

"I don't think I can go back to assisting," I explained to Jilli. "And it's not like there are producer positions open and a headhunter to place me."

"We'll come up with something," Jilli said, attempting to console me. "What about the script you were getting?"

"Shit. I've got to call Vince about that. He left me the nicest message."

"Maybe you can still shop that and attach yourself?" she suggested.

Maybe. But first, I needed to find a place to live and figure out how to afford life. Andy had come back for Karen's funeral and took off again for New York. He acquired the art house film company and he and Jilli were moving there at the end of June. I had another week before Andy came back, and I wanted to have a place to call my own by then. With that timeframe in mind, I descended upon Kitty without warning.

"I need the inheritance now," I explained.

"Fine," was all she said and walked quietly into her bedroom. She was gone for a short time, and walked contritely over to me with a personal check for ten thousand dollars.

"That's it?" I asked. Now, granted, that's a nice chunk of money. However, that was the amount of my half of his policy. One would think that ten grand accruing interest over twenty years would be a tad fatter than what Kitty handed me. "What happened to the rest of it?"

"That's what your father left you, and that's what you are getting," Kitty said plainly.

"You hold that money hostage from me, then steal the interest and tell me that's what I'm getting? Kitty, I should have you arrested," I said and started to laugh. It was beyond absurd.

"How dare you suggest I stole from you," she said, crawling up on her cross.

"Uh, you did. You pocketed the interest. That's textbook theft," I retorted.

"I did not steal it. I used it for your sister's wedding. It's what your father would have wanted," she said stoically.

"You gave it to Gwen? Jesus!"

"Do not use the Lord's name in vain," Kitty shouted.

"Don't get all bible-ly on me, lady. Thou shalt not steal. Remember that one? You'll need to get me that money back, Kitty. I'm serious. This one is even too much for you," I said to her directly.

"I can't," she said meekly.

"You will. One way or another. This isn't about the money. It's about doing right by me for once. You are my mother. You are supposed to look out for me. I'm not supposed to be keeping an eye on you."

Later that day, I got a hysterical call from Gwen. "How could you threaten our mother like that?! She said you were going to send her to jail. How could you?!"

"I didn't say I'd send her to jail, Gwen. You ought to know how your mother exaggerates by now," I said trying not to chuckle.

"She's cancelled half the florist order and cut the menu, Ellen. Now we can't have a sit down dinner. We have to have a buffet and she wants the guests to pay for their mixed drinks," she said as she burst into heaving sobs.

"You'll live, Gwennie."

"This is just you being jealous of me, Ellen. You always have been. I just can't believe you would try to ruin my wedding over it."

"Did Kitty loan you her *How To Be A Martyr* handbook? Because you are sounding exactly like your mother," I stated curtly. "I want you to have a wonderful, happy wedding, Gwen. I just don't want to foot the bill for it, especially since no one bothered to ask me if that was okay."

"You are no longer my maid of honor, Ellen. I don't want you at my wedding," snarked my sister.

"Really? Do you mean that?"

"Yes," she hissed.

"Thank you, Gwen. You have no idea how much that means to me."

Finally, some good news after a month of merde. I hung up and let out a relieved sigh.

"I can't believe you found a place already," Jilli said.

"Well, you haven't seen it yet," I stated sheepishly.

"It has carpet, doesn't it?" she asked with a wince.

I nodded. "It's a studio. And, at only $900 a month, it's a steal."

"I know you are a zip code snob, but taking a studio in Venice…El, aren't you rushing things a bit?"

"I had to act fast. I need a place that I can afford, since I don't know when I will find the right job. I just want to get on with my life." Or what was left of it.

Few things are more depressing than the loss of a loved one, but beige carpeting does come close. Add beige paint and a smattering of beige linoleum, and you have my new home. It wasn't so bad, I tried to believe. A studio was all I needed, and all I could afford to furnish.

I stood in the apartment and ached for what almost was. There would be no dinner parties, no cocktail parties, no game nights. Not here. There wasn't enough room. I was now in the depression stage, though anger did come about every now and again. This was a far cry from where I was going or even where I had been. But, it was mine. The neighborhood was relatively safe, and I would be living in the part of town I wanted to remain. I couldn't face having to go further inland. I had been through enough; I needed one perk. I took the tiny, affordable apartment so I could still breathe beach air. And, I could move in right away.

After I signed the rental lease, I went straight to Ikea. It was my last day with Jilli's Rover, and I wanted to make the most of it. At thirty-two, I would be sleeping on a futon, dining at a bistro table, working from a small console that I would utilize as a desk.

I dragged my purchases up the stairs and into my shoebox. The sofa bed/futon fusion I selected was set to be delivered next week. My Jetta was due back in three days. Gabe offered to help me in the interim. I still needed go to Target for incidentals. Linens would be fetched at Bed, Bath and Beyond, and discounted with coupons. It was all about watching my budget and getting by.

Before I headed back to Glendale, I had to pick up the boxes that were sent back from the hotel. They were stuck at the

FedEx depot and that meant I needed to get the delivery tags. I was lazy in my grief and had the hotel send the boxes back to the return address. I had absentmindedly wrote in my old address, the one that Tim owns.

"How are you doing?" he asked softly when he opened the door.

"It's hard, but I'm hanging in there."

I didn't invite Tim to the memorial. It would have been awkward since Wyatt was accompanying me. If only I had known then how wrong I was about him. That's not to say I regretted ending things with Tim. That needed to be done, even if it took a jerk like Wyatt for me to see that clearly. To see myself clearly.

Tim had been kind enough to call or text each day to see how I was, see if he could help, let me know he was thinking of me.

"I'm really sorry, El. It's got to be tough," he said taking my hand.

"Thanks," I said gently releasing myself from his hold. "Can I get the door tags?"

"Sure." He went into the kitchen to retrieve them. When he returned, he said, "I was surprised…You're not moving now?"

"I really don't want to talk about it, if that's okay," I said, knowing the anger phase wasn't completely put to rest.

I was trying to embrace the depression, but for that I would have to spend money on a TV and TiVo. No matter how I needed to watch my pennies, a girl had to have a few perks. Cable and a digital recording device were necessities. When you are melancholy, HBO helps.

"Do you want to take my Cherokee?" Tim asked.

"Thanks. I've got Jilli's beast."

"Well, let me go with you. Help you get the boxes in it."

"You don't have to. I carried them in; I can carry them out. Lugging them up the stairs is going to be interesting, though" I thought aloud.

"Upstairs? Did Jilli move?"

After explaining my new living situation, Tim insisted on

meeting me at my apartment to help me with the boxes. I had to tip my hat to him. I deserved nothing but his contempt. Even in my time of grief, I wouldn't have blamed him for handing me the door tags and kicking me off his doorstep. Instead, he ended up on mine. With the television we'd had in our bedroom and all our pots and pans. The Calphalon stainless steel set I had bought us when we moved in. He also had a set of wine glasses and a bottle of Chardonnay.

"I thought we'd order in so I could help you set things up," he said with a smile.

"I can't take all this, Tim. It's yours."

"It was ours, El. Some of it should go to you. This was all I could grab fast. I couldn't count on there being a line at FedEx."

We sat on the floor eating delivered Thai, as we had done so many times before, looking at the success of the built bookshelf and dresser, and the failure of our relationship. It was a kind conversation, one that we were able to take the lesson from. How easy it was to take something for granted, or assume your expectations would be met by another on your timeline.

"You've taken this well, Tim," I said putting my hand on his shoulder. It was the first time I could recall reaching out to someone else since Karen's death. That is unless you count the contact I made with Wyatt's junk.

"I didn't have much of a choice. By the way, our breakup brought Liza a lot of joy," he said with a smirk.

"Well, it's not like I got her anything for her birthday," I shrugged.

"Kent's forcing her in to couple's therapy, if you can believe that."

"Poor guy," I said then took another sip of wine.

"No relationship is perfect, huh?"

We sat there silently in my beige abode. The tension in the room was palpable. All the things still left unsaid were better left unsaid at this point. Our first face-to-face meeting since I ditched him and his ring had gone rather well, but we didn't need to push that luck.

"I should get back before Jilli reports the Rover stolen," I said getting up from the floor. I gathered my glass and the half-full wine bottle. Tim followed, like he'd always done, getting his glass and the leftovers. We could still function as a team, if only from habit.

"Do you want the rest?" he asked, holding the bag of take-out.

I shook my head. "You take it. And thanks for dinner and bringing over all this stuff. It helps, Tim."

He came in for a hug. I worried that he would try to make it more, but he pulled away before it became uncomfortable.

I locked up my new home and walked with Tim to the street where we parked.

"Let me know if you need any help, El. I still want to be there for you."

I smiled at his kindness.

"I still care, El," he said softly and kissed my cheek.

I'm glad somebody did because, in my depressive state, I really couldn't care less. I was not one for the doldrums but I was pissed at the world, hurt by Wyatt, disappointed that I came so close to success but was now back again at the bottom rung. I listened repeatedly to Nine Inch Nails and watched sappy British rom-coms on a loop. Incongruous, but it seemed to be helping. Almost.

"*Love, Actually* again?" Jilli asked rather loudly when she caught me sprawled out on her sofa with my computer on my lap and headphones in. "Do we need to start talking medication here, Patterson? This can't be healthy for you," she said as she shut my laptop.

"I just need to know that there is hope out there," I whinged.

"And Bridget Jones, Muriel and Hugh Grant are going to help you see that? I don't really think that *Four Weddings and a Funeral* is what you should be watching now," she added as she looked through the pile of DVDs I dragged out of her closet.

"It's one funeral against four, well, three happy occasions. See? That's hopeful."

"I can't leave you like this, Ellen. I can't in good conscience go to New York with you living in a beige nightmare watching these types of films. I need to know that you are going to be okay."

"Am I going to top myself? Is that what you're asking? The answer is no." Although, the thought had occurred to me once or twice. Depressive and suicidal were definitely not states of mind I'd been in before. I quickly shook it off as part of the grieving process.

"Top yourself? Okay, enough with the Brit flicks. I need to know that you are going to get back on your feet, Ellen. I need to know that you aren't going to stop with your dreams just because—"

"They're dead?" I interjected.

Jilli went quiet.

"Well, they kind of are, Jillian. We tossed most of them into the Pacific along with Karen. I kicked the rest of them away when I kneed Wyatt's balls."

Jilli burst into laughter. "I love that you did that and just left him lying on the sidewalk," she cackled. "You can't write shit like that and get away with it."

I felt a tickle in my throat. I tried to swallow it down, but it wouldn't relent. And then I recognized it. Laughter. As much as I didn't want to, I laughed. I laughed hard and long with my best friend.

"Thank God," Jilli smiled and pulled me into a hug. "I just needed to see you again."

I hugged her back, knowing just what she meant.

Chapter Seventeen

Jilli was gone. Tess was showing. Emily had moved to Palm Springs, and Claudia flourished in her element as Em's partner. Remi was in love with James, and casting a huge studio film on her own—actually, she had just gotten her first assistant. And I was still in the process of piecing life back together. Each one of us was in a different place, rediscovering ourselves. The difference was, they had moved forward. I was floundering back at Square One.

My headhunter would call regularly with dreary jobs to consider. The options were bleak, but so were my financial prospects. I had finished closing up Karen's affairs, collected my severance and was on unemployment. I couldn't fathom how anyone could survive on that alone. It just covered my rent. Thank God my car was paid off. That helped.

It had gotten to the point where I had to take a job. Any job. But, as much as I needed to find work, I wasn't confident I could handle a full-pressure day yet. And how absolutely mortifying it would be to be the girl who got teary when things got intense. Especially since I was a far cry from a girl anymore. I didn't want my reputation to go from capable assistant to emotional ass.

"El, is that you?"

I was meandering around Abbot Kinney after a stroll on the beach when I passed Marco on the street. He walked me over to The Brig and we started happy hour early. He was a strong shoulder to weep on. The crying had started again.

A snore woke me the next morning. I lifted my head from the pillow and dropped it immediately. It must have weighed eighty pounds. I rolled over and found Marco next to me; his bare, perfect ass on display.

Reality slowly washed over me, along with a wave of nausea. Oh, my God. What have I done? And then it all came flashing back.

From The Brig, we somehow made our way to Hama for

sushi, and loads of sake. I recalled feeding each other the fish, and then, if memory served, we started making out. We quickly left before anyone from the gym or around town would have seen us and went back to my place where we had sex. Lots of sex.

"Shit," I whispered when the full flood of memory engulfed me. Marco stirred.

"Buona mattina, bella," he smiled and pulled me in for a kiss, his hands roaming over my body. I felt myself surrendering, then thought better.

"Stop. We can't, Marco."

"But, we already did, El. Many, many times."

"You are getting married." Oh my God. Oh my God! How did I let that happen? "This is terrible, Marco. We shouldn't have done this."

"But we did it. We both wanted to for a long time. And you needed comfort. I wanted to give it to you."

"I'm sure you did." My grief had buried my morals. Now, I had to dig them up. "You have to leave, Marco. Jesus. What are you going to tell your fiancée?"

"El, calm down. She is at her parents' in Chicago. She won't be home until later tonight. She'll never know."

"Promise me that," I demanded. I didn't want to be the cause of someone else's pain just because I was trying to ease my own.

"I promise," he said. "*Madonna*. I thought this would make you feel better, El."

Nothing was making me feel better. Especially sleeping with my affianced former trainer.

Gabe attempted to cheer me up by coming over and cooking me dinner.

"The place really looks good," Gabe said as he served up penne arribiatta with shrimp that would surely stink up the place for days. "You did a good job with it."

"If you say so," I blandly replied.

"El, you have to get over this. So what if you shagged Marco? You were drunk and depressed. He was hot and available. He's the one who should feel bad about taking advantage of you. Just let it go."

"I don't think I have anything else to let go of. Gabe, if you haven't noticed, my life has kind of spiraled into the shitter. I'm unemployed, single, and quite possibly a homewrecker. I think I can be a little distressed about that."

"Will you stop? It's been two months. You need to put this into perspective. Karen is gone, and that is terrible. But you have the rest of your life to live."

"You sound like a Lifetime movie, Gabe."

"Don't be mean. You know, Vince was asking about you. He wanted to know how you were doing. I told him you were fine, but now I see that I lied. And you know I hate to lie."

"God, I feel terrible for him. To be that close to having the script sold and then have it all go away."

"Yes, I'm sure you know exactly how he feels," Gabe returned. "You should call him. He said you are the one, the only one he wants to have his script. So, it sounds like you still have it."

"That's foolish. If he got an agent, he'd have that snapped up in a weekend read."

"That's not what he wants. He's kind of an interesting guy. Dripping with integrity. You almost don't know how to take it," Gabe chuckled.

"Integrity? Hollywood will beat that out of him in a heartbeat."

"Bitter much?" Gabe mocked. "Look, work some magic with Jilli and get it done. I know you can do it, El. We all do."

Despite Gabe's enthusiasm, I couldn't deal with another uphill battle. The smart thing for me to do would be to get a job. Any job at this point.

"I just need to find work," I told him. "But, the positions I've been offered are ghastly. I could be Miss Deva Jones' assistant, if I wanted to work 25/8/366, and be on both London and L.A. time all the time."

"Ellen, you aren't an assistant anymore. Face it," Gabe said as he handed me a plate.

"I'm not a producer anymore, either," I stated plainly. We made our way over to the red futon/sofa/bed/scene-of-the-crime, which took about four steps to reach, and sat down to our meal. "Maybe I could be an office manager at a production company. That almost sounds almost promising," I lied.

Gabe rolled his eyes. "It sounds soul-draining. Take the creative director position Andy offered you in the L.A. office."

"I don't want a charity job, Gabe."

"Knock it off, Ellen. When have you known anyone in this town to be that charitable? It's an opportunity for you to get back on track. What are you waiting for?" he asked with impatience.

Perhaps it was pride. I didn't want a handout, especially from my best friend's boyfriend. I didn't want pity, especially from my friends. I wanted to stand on my own, and if that meant a crap assistant job, then that's what I would take. But, when I've tried to stand up by myself lately, I've fallen.

"Um, I'm waiting," Gabe said, pulling me from my trance. "This is really tasty, by the way, if I do say so myself. Eat up, El."

"I'm still a bit fragile, if you haven't noticed," I said before biting into my dinner.

"Hate to break it to you, but we've all noticed. I think it's time for some tough love." Gabe took another bite of food and with a full mouth said, "Vince's restaurant is opening on Thursday. Private party. Come with me. I need a date. And this way we can both flirt with the pretty boys."

I shook my head. "I'm not ready to be social."

"El, you need to get out. You are going if I have to drag you there. Free food and drink. How can you pass that up?" Gabe could be as bossy and persistent as Jilli.

I missed her now that she and Andy lived in their Central Park-view apartment. She was in madly in love with him and the city. Cassette Films, Cassie's company, had purchased two more screenplays since Jilli started, and she was shining. The first film was set to start as soon as Cassie ended her Broadway run at the end of autumn. The other two were in development.

"I miss you, too," she said, her mouth moving before the words came over our poor FaceTime connection. I couldn't afford the good internet. We made time to see each other a couple times a week. It helped to see her, but I couldn't hide behind a faceless voice like I could over the phone. "Will you come out and visit? You still have that first class ticket. Use it. It would be so good to have you here."

"I'll try," I lied. "I do want to see you. I just need to get things sorted here first." The truth was, I couldn't bear the thought of being in Manhattan now. One more ghost to haunt me.

"Well, I'll keep nagging until you do. Maybe fly back with me after Tess' wedding?"

"Maybe," I answered vaguely.

"You have to get out of this rut, Ellen. And I thought you were going to paint your place. That couch looks like a period stain on some very big, beige granny panties. Brighten it up. That goes for your demeanor, too."

My friends were sympathetic to what I was going through, but also concerned. I was the upbeat optimist in our cynical little circle. They were beginning to grow uneasy with the lingering gloom that covered me.

Tess was making regular calls and offers for me to go out with her. When she asked me to come look at dresses, she reminded that she had done me that same favor not too long ago. Now, it was payback.

"It's a bitch, ain't it," she teased.

Tess and Dane were getting married at the end of August, and that was only five weeks away. It would be a small ceremony on a Wednesday evening that marked the second anniversary of their first date.

"It's beyond hokey," she said as she flipped through maternity wedding dresses. "But, it's so much cheaper to have something midweek. Not that renting out parts of Casa Del Mar is cheap. Should be nice, though. Hope it's not too fucking hot. I don't want my ankles swelling."

"It will be beautiful. You will be beautiful," I assured. "This, not so much." I held up a garish white dress, spangled in gold and silver beading.

"Good thing I'm over the morning sickness or I would toss my cookies," she laughed. "You really didn't go to your sister's wedding?"

I shook my head and sipped the complimentary mimosa Tess couldn't have. "I was 'disinvited', as she put it. Thankfully. I've had it with her and Kitty."

Neither my mother nor sister bothered to express any kind of condolences over Karen. Kitty even muttered something about, "That's what happens when you run with the wrong crowd." Between that, the thievery and utter disdain we had for each other, I thought it best to cut ties and leave it at that. My uncles understood. They didn't go to the wedding either. Kitty had said rather awful things to them at their mother's wake, which were neither apologized for nor forgiven. We had one incredible family dynamic, and I wanted nothing more of it.

"It's a shame it came to that, though. I'm sorry, El," Tess offered.

"Don't be. It's for the best." I could only handle so much at the moment. My family issues exceeded that limit. "You don't think I'm a terrible person for that, do you?"

"What? For breaking up with your family? El, that's the sanest thing I can think of. They are crazy. No offense."

I gave her a blasé shrug.

"Speaking of crazy, Vicki is driving me nuts giving me all sorts of wedding advice. And she said she might have a job for you, but I think you should take the Andy thing. How does this dress look?"

"Lovely," I answered.

I was having trouble taking some of the kind gestures my peripheral friends had made. Grief is not a social experience. It's isolating, and the only people allowed to breach it are those in your inner circle. I appreciated the expressions of sympathy from those I had known and worked with over the years. They tracked me down through one of the posse or kept my ancient cell number. While I'm sure they didn't mean to be shallow, I think more than a few of them had trouble figuring out what they were more sorry for: the loss of Karen or my career.

"I'm really sorry," they would stutter, trying to find the right words to follow that. "I feel awful for you."

Even worse were those trying to play pimp. Anise called a

few weeks after the service to say, "El, Bev wanted me to call you. She just fired the second assistant and would love to hire you."

Being the underling to both Bev and Anise would be on par with moving in with my mother. "Thanks, Anise. I'm still not ready to work. Please let Bev know I appreciate the offer, though."

"Come on, El. Please? I was up for a promotion, and that twit blew it for me. Think about it, but I have to hire someone by the end of the week."

Vicki's suggestion was only slightly more interesting. "The daughter of the man I used to work for is looking for someone, El. It's out of the business, but you would be assisting her with raising funds for their foundation. It would be like a party planner position. Would you like to meet with her?"

"Is that the daughter who just got out of rehab or the one hangs out with Lindsay Lohan?"

"It's the one who is going through the divorce and custody battle."

"I don't know, Vicki," I answered.

"Don't say no yet. Think about it. Get back to me next week and I'll set the meeting," Vicki offered.

I sent her an email later that night saying thanks but no thanks. My headhunter was running out of patience with me, too.

"I'm going to need a decision from you by Friday on both jobs," Colleen explained. "I can't keep holding them off. If you aren't ready for work, I understand, but you need to let me know."

By the time Thursday had rolled around, I had turned everyone down. Everyone but Gabe. As much as I didn't want to go, he wouldn't hear of it.

"Jesus, Ellen, you have got to get out of that shoebox. Three hours is all I want. Not too much to ask since it's so early," he chided. "I swear, I'll have you home by ten."

He drove us over to Abbot Kinney and the north end of the street to Trio, the restaurant Vince was partnered in. The valet took Gabe's antique Beemer and we made our way into the crowded, buzzing venue. I was already tense from the size of the party and energy from the crowd. Something that used to make me excited now made me want to run and hide in my apartment with a Netflix binge.

The Venice evening was lovely and warm. The sun was still providing daylight even though it was nearing eight. We were in the throes of summer and the atmosphere was perfect for a celebration.

This was the first time I had dressed up for a social occasion since donning black for Karen. I didn't go overboard. I wore a decent pair of jeans, a fitted tank top and bone-crushingly high heels. I had lost a fair share of weight in the past weeks and I kept yanking up my pants. For once, I found a situation where comforting eating brought no comfort. I also lost muscle tone from skipping the gym and avoiding Marco. That had to end. Being unemployed was no reason to be out of shape.

The place was crawling with beautiful people and tech hipsters. Since becoming Silicon Beach, Venice felt more like Silver Lake than the wacky, hippy beach town it used to be. Nothing stays the same. Everything good gets ruined.

"Come on, we'll have fun." Gabe put his hand around mine and led me in.

He was a great date. I had a cocktail in my hand about a nanosecond after we entered. Something about a Limoncello martini. I had no idea what was in it, but the sunshine yellow liquid went down rather smoothly, and there were an abundance of them within reaching distance when my glass ran dry. I lost count after three and realized that I needed food.

The restaurant was amazing. It had been two other restaurants and a clothing shop before. I didn't really see any architect-influence other than the converted house seemed to have expanded, adding a patio deck to the front and a large "backyard" that was beautifully landscaped. The interior was warm and welcoming with natural wood and candles flickering. The bar would be a perfect loitering area for singles. Which I was now one of. God, I couldn't bear to think of when I would actually have to date again.

Gabe read from the menu that the fare was "light" Italian.

"Low in fat, 'appropriate' portion sizes, and sensible prices. And, they'll have a happy hour. Sounds like a winner," he read from the menu/press release.

"Let's hope it lasts," I said. "Cheap is my new favorite word."

I was shoving a bruschetta-covered crostini into my mouth when Vince approached us. He seemed taller and tanner than I had remembered. He was again in mandals, dark washed jeans and an ivory linen shirt, the sleeves rolled up in a casual manner. His smile was broad, his eyes bright and warm.

"Gabe, buddy. So good to see you," he said shaking Gabe's hand and putting his left on Gabe's shoulder. "And El, I'm really happy you came tonight." Vince came in and gave me a hug. "I'm really sorry for your loss," he said as he held me.

"Thank you," I muttered with my mouth full.

He gave a nod toward one of the waiters and shortly thereafter a bottle of beer was in his hand.

"Not really into the mixed drinks," he explained. "Hope you like the specialty. One of my partners' girlfriend came up with it. Seems to be going over well."

"They go down even better," I said with swagger. Gabe's eyebrows bolted to his hairline. Vince chuckled.

Vince escorted us out back to his table, introducing us to his two partners along the way. One was called Adam, and he was a shorter, thicker man. The other was Tony, a tall, lanky guy who looked like he was raised in Malibu. Tony was in commercial real estate, and had flirted with being a "flipper", which is how he met Vince. They hit it off and while Tony was looking for property to turn around in Venice, he stumbled upon this place.

"Tony always wanted to own a restaurant. Somehow, he talked me and Adam into it and, well, here we are. Trio," Vince said with an affable shrug.

"It's great. And yummy," Gabe said, shoveling in another bite of mini pizza appetizers they made for the party. We were standing by the booth he had reserved on the patio. I wasn't ready to sit yet. The sugar in my drink was making me jumpy.

"I'll let Adam know. He's our chef," Vince said.

"Ah," I said now remembering the full introduction. "He's a good one."

Vince smiled at me. "You are enjoying those cocktails, aren't you?" he inquired rhetorically.

"Yep," I smiled.

For the first time in weeks and weeks, I didn't ache. I wasn't swirling in self-pity or flailing with frustration. I felt good. Really, really good. I was beyond drunk.

"This place is great by the way." I made the mistake a making a grand gesture with my martini hand, splashing some of my drink out of my glass and onto Gabe's shoe.

"You might want to have some of that chicken, El. Or, how about more bread?" Gabe offered, likely having a premonition via flashback of our college days.

"I'm good," I lied.

How did I know how I was? I was feeling nothing except the smile that wouldn't drop. Perma-grin. A sure sign I was shit-faced. At this point, I was not slurring. I appeared steady. The ugliness would come later. Or sooner, in this case.

"Come into the kitchen with me, El. We have some extra special grub in there we set aside for the partners. A little lobster done just right. And a chocolate bread pudding from my grand-mother's recipe. Not Italian, but it's really good," Vince tempted.

"I've never said no to chocolate," I smiled.

He reached his hand out, and I took it.

"Don't worry about me," Gabe said with sarcasm. "I'll be fine." He took a seat alone at the table.

Vince started us toward the kitchen, but was soon mobbed by well-wishers. I stood beside him, feeling the world tilt every now and again. One such shift caused me to grab onto his arm to steady myself. He looked at me and smiled and pulled me into him. I smiled back. I took a gander around the crowd as he talked to his friends and spotted some unfortunately familiar faces. Liza, Kent and Tim. And Tim looked like he had a date. And his date was walking toward Vince, which made Liza, Kent and Tim follow. Before I could bolt to the back, they all saw me.

"Shit," I said under my breath. Vince heard and looked at me.

"Hello, Vincent," chirped the pretty brunette.

"Hey," he said as he leaned in to kiss her cheek. "Good to see you."

"Is my brother here?" she asked.

"Out back. We have some seats there," he said as the charming host. "This is—"

Before Vince could finish his introduction of me, Tim said, "Hi, El."

"Hello, Tim," I returned.

"Good to see you, El," Kent said, then leaned in to kiss my cheek.

"You know each other?" the brunette asked.

"That's Tim's ex," Liza blurted. "Funny to find you here. What happened to New York?"

"Karen's death kind of killed it," I said. "If you'll excuse me, Vince." I turned to leave, but Vince gently took my arm.

"Wait. I haven't given you the tour yet. Jessica, good to see you. Hope you all enjoy yourselves tonight," he said to the brunette, Tim, Kent and that bitch.

I grabbed another Limoncello thing and sucked down a rather large portion of it. This one was a great deal stronger than the previous versions.

"Are you all right, El? Gabe said this was the first time you'd gone out since…I just want to be sure you're okay." I noted the kindness, not pity or awkwardness, in his Vince's voice.

"I don't know if I'm ever really going to be okay again?" I said laughing, hoping that would stop the tears. It didn't.

"Come here," he said, pulling me into a hug. "I lost my brother a few years ago. Car accident. I can guess how you must be feeling."

I pulled myself together. "Sorry for your loss. And thank you. I must be a sight. Forgive me. It's bad manners to sob on the host when he is celebrating his new restaurant."

He shrugged his shoulders and gave me a grin. "I'm just in it for the money." I laughed at his sweet humor. "Do you want me to get Gabe? Or I could take you home."

"Don't be silly," I said wiping my eyes with the napkin

Vince handed me. "I promised Gabe I would last at least until ten." It wasn't even nine. I would've been lying if I said I wasn't counting the minutes.

"Come on then," he said. He took a bowl and scooped up some warm, molten, chocolate something and plopped it in the china. "You can't leave without experiencing this."

He escorted me back to the table where we found a shocked looking Gabe sitting next to the brunette who sat next to Tim who was placed next to Liza with Kent on the end. He mouthed, *What the fuck?!* I just rolled my eyes and shook my head.

I didn't want to be the difficult bitch and say, "I'm not sitting there with those people." Instead, I sipped my drink, sat next to Gabe and I patted the seat next to mine, smiling at Vince. He gave me an *Are you sure you want to sit here?* eyebrow raise. I gave a quick nod that suggested confidence. That high school acting class was really paying off. In an attempt to take away from the bitterness I was feeling, I took a bite of the dessert.

"This is incredible," I whispered to Vince.

"Told you so," he smiled.

"Well," Gabe said. "It is a small world after all."

"Jessica is Tony's sister," Vince explained.

"I work with Liza," Jessica said, almost apologetically.

"Nice to meet you," I smiled. I felt bad for her. Not only for having to work with Liza, and seeming to befriend her, but for being a part of what looked to be her first date with Tim. Even if it was their second or fourteenth, I felt bad for making it awkward. Tim deserved to be with a nice woman. He deserved to be happy. And he didn't need me intruding on that.

Instead, it was Liza infringing. Hogging the conversation, as usual. Trying to make an impression on Gabe and Vince, especially after she found out he was one-third of Trio. Gabe already knew Liza via my diatribes and Vince didn't seem to be taking much interest in her, which made her try even harder.

Having reached his limit, Gabe excused himself to go to the loo. Vince directed him to the very back of the backyard where a converted garage served as their office. Vince and I both had to stand to let Gabe out. Before I took my seat, Vince asked, "Would you like to dance?"

"Sure," I said.

As we walked away from Liza's drone, I could hear the music playing overhead. It sounded like Nina Simone or some similar chanteuse singing along with a saxophone, making your body sway. And, now that I looked around, there were many other couples making an impromptu dance floor in that space of the yard. Vince and I joined them.

"We weren't going to get a chance to talk there, were we?" Vince stated diplomatically as we moved together.

"Nope," I said feigning a smile.

"Hanging in there? I think you've nearly met your time allotment." When he spoke, I could feel it in my chest. It was a calming vibration. "Not that I want you to go," he continued. "I just want to make sure you are doing okay."

As he spoke, I felt the oxygen leave the area. I grew hot and it was hard to breathe in. I felt dizzy and a cold sweat started to cover me. My once-dry mouth was watering. I knew I had to act fast.

"I'm not feeling well, Vince," I said hoping my stomach would stop churning.

"Come with me," he said with concerned eyes. He grabbed my clammy hand and guided me through the crowd to his office, which I prayed we got to soon. We didn't have much time. I kind of remember seeing Gabe and his eyes widen as we whizzed by him. Vince opened the door and I rushed past him to the first open container I could find: a wastebasket.

With my face in the container, and the contents of my stomach at the bottom of it, I became aware of my hands. They were grasping on to mesh. Wire mesh. I was vomitting into a wire mesh wastebasket. Oh no. Under the horrific sounds I was making, I heard the rustling of plastic. I reached up to the top of the receptacle and, gratefully, I felt the bin liner. I became aware of my auditory sense. I could recognize voices and heard Gabe saying, "I can't deal with vomit, Vince. If I hear any more of this, I'm going to join her."

Vince replied, "Go to the bar and bring back some napkins

and two bottles of cold water. Tell whoever's behind the bar it's for me. Get yourself a ginger ale."

I heard footsteps and then felt Vince kneel down next to me. He put his hand on my back and gathered my hair to hold it. If ever I should've worn it in a ponytail, it was tonight.

I wanted to crawl into that bin and disappear. I had a few additional dry heaves before I was sure it was done. Were it not for the aroma, I would've kept my face there to avoid looking up at Vince.

"It's okay, El. I did the same thing after my brother. It's part of the process. Stage six of grief: the purge."

I pushed the wastebasket away, but not too far. Just in case. I heard someone rushing toward the door.

"Is it safe to come in?" Gabe asked.

Vince got up and went to meet Gabe. He took what Gabe had brought him and said, "Go mingle or whatever. I'll get you when she's ready. If my partners or anyone asks, just tell them I'm talking to a friend in the office and not to disturb me."

"Okay. I love you, El," Gabe shouted.

Vince came over and handed me a bottle of water. "Sip it slowly. You'll probably yak that up, too, but that's good. It will help you get the rest out."

"Vince, I am so sorry. I am absolutely horrified."

"Don't worry about it. Sip your water," he said with comfort and command. I did as he said. He went into the bathroom and ran water. While he was gone, I did a quick swish and spit, and almost hurled again when I put my face over the barf bucket.

Vince returned and kneeled down with me. He handed me a cold, damp napkin. I pressed it to my face.

"That feels good. Thank you," I said softly. "I haven't been sick like that since film school."

"It's just another way of getting it all out. For me, there were weeks when I was face in the toilet letting it out. I did that until I learned to cry," he said directly. There wasn't a hint of embarrassment or self-pity about him.

"I thought I'd cried enough already."

"It's still really early days, El. Gabe told me how close you and Karen were."

"You and Gabe talk a lot?"

"I asked about you when I heard about Karen," he admitted, and I believe I saw him blush just slightly.

"She loved your script. She called me from the plane to tell me. She really loved it. I do, too," I said, and then felt my water rise. I couldn't make it to the bathroom, so it was head in wastebasket again. And Vince was by my side, again, one hand holding my hair, the other stroking my back.

"This is so humiliating," I said. "Where can I dump this?"

"I'll take care of it," he said sweetly.

"No! It's bad enough you had to witness this. You certainly don't need to clean up after me."

He smiled and said, "You seem to have gotten it all into the trashcan. I appreciate that. The carpet is new."

I had to laugh. "Seriously, I'd like to take care of it."

"Seriously, no. You clean yourself up in the bathroom. I've got this. Go on. You'll soon learn I won't take no for an answer."

Not wanting to drag it out a moment longer—the room was small and the odor strong—I let him tend to my waste removal while I tried to sort myself out. Then it occurred to me. My purse! Where was it? I started to panic. iPhone, house key, car key, lipstick and mints. I needed that bag. Now!

"Vince," I shouted when he walked back in the door. "I lost my purse!"

"What did it look like?" he asked as he stroked my arms to comfort me.

"It was red. A red clutch," I said, trying to hold back the panic.

"A clutch?" Gabe was right. He's not gay.

"It has no straps. I carry it in my hand or under my arm," I explained while miming and trying to remain calm.

"Gotcha." He dashed out the door.

I tried to stay calm. The tension further churned my stomach. This time I made it to the toilet. I rinsed my mouth and did my best to fix my face. Cleared away the fallen mascara. Splashed cold water on my cheeks. This was far from the acceptance phase.

Vince finally came back with Gabe and my clutch in tow. My stomach was uneasy even after I saw it was intact.

"It was at the table. Tim kept and eye on it," Gabe explained.

A handsome young man poked his head in the door. "Um, Gabe, don't leave without taking my number," said the guy.

Gabe grew a big smile.

"I'll Uber home, Gabe," I smiled. "Stay and have fun."

"No way," Gabe protested.

"Yes way. My place isn't that far from here. I'll be fine. Please. It will make me feel better," I insisted. "And I would feel awful if I puked in your car."

Gabe cringed. I had played my trump card.

"You sure?" he asked.

I nodded. "I'd give you a kiss, but…" I teased.

"Let me get you into the car at least," he persisted.

"Nope. I want to freshen up a bit more. I can manage. Remember, I was almost a New Yorker." Why did I say that? My stomach cramped.

Gabe gave me a hug before he and the cute guy went back to the party. I turned to Vince to thank him yet again.

"You do realize that I'm not about to let you Uber," Vince said with his arms folded and a slight air of stubbornness.

"And you're not one to take no for an answer," I replied.

Vince walked me to my door as well. Just in time for me to burst through it and barf one last time.

"I feel bad for ruining your night, Vince."

"You didn't ruin anything, El. I spent the evening with a very interesting and very lovely lady. I hope to do it again. Maybe we could skip the Technicolor yawns next time, though."

I laughed at his humor. "That sounds like a plan."

Vince pulled me into a hug. "You are going to be fine, El. It just takes time. Call me if you need to talk. I'm a good listener," he said before leaving.

It wasn't yet eleven. I hoped he would go back to the party and finish up his night with some actual fun. I pulled my couch into a bed and laid on it. Not bothering to take off my clothes or my makeup, I pulled the throw over me, but it was barely needed on such a warm night. I closed my eyes and let the tears fall again. The purge. He was right. I decided to stop counting all the things I'd been wrong about.

Chapter Eighteen

I woke up the next morning surprisingly not hungover. I stayed in bed for a bit just to be sure it wasn't going to sneak up on me, but no. I was fine. Not only did I feel good, I felt a new sense of determination. Without noting the time, I grabbed my phone and rang Gabe.

"Wha?" Gabe mumbled into the phone instead of *Hello* or *Why the fuck are you calling me this early?* Generally speaking, after a night purging such as mine, one wouldn't expect to see the light of day until about dusk. It wasn't even seven. The clock on the cable box caught my eye and I realized I had slept with my contacts in. Unfortunately, they aren't the kind meant for slumber and, after a moment of visual clarity, I felt the dry burn and pulled out the lenses.

"Gabe, tell me again why you joined that writing group."

"What are you talking about?" he said with a deep morning voice. It sounded like his face was still in the pillow. In the background I heard another man asking, "Who's calling you so early? Tell them to go to Hell."

"I think I've come up with a way to get you completion funds for the documentary. More importantly, I think we can make it into a feature. A feature based on the documentary," I rattled.

"They do that?" He sounded much more awake.

I went on to ask if he could work his Tallulah Bankhead doc into a screenplay. If he was willing and able, we could take it to Andy. "But, I want it to be really polished before we take it in, and I want to attach myself as a producer to both projects, work with you on both. Would you be okay with that, Gabe?" I held my breath as I waited for his answer.

"Ellen Patterson, I thought you'd never ask."

My next call would be to Vince. But I decided to wait a few more hours first. I had been rude enough the night before; I didn't need to press my luck or the measure of his kindness. I made coffee and drafted notes before I finally got the nerve to call.

"I was going to call you and see how you were," Vince told me. "Doing okay?"

"I guess that was just what I needed because I really feel great and I'd like to talk to you about *Grandfather's Lake*," I stated rather directly. I didn't mean to sound so abrupt. I should have made more than a Pop-Tart for breakfast.

"Cool. Wanna meet for lunch?"

That caught me off guard so I said, "Okay."

We met at Maxwell's because what I wanted more than lunch was a breakfast of turkey bacon and pancakes. At this rate, I would be putting back on the grief weight I'd lost by dinnertime.

Vince came in shorts and a t-shirt, wearing those damn mandals again. He had a big grin and gave me a warm embrace when he reached me.

As soon as our grub was served, I started right in. On the conversation, that is. Though, I did shove some turkey bacon in my mouth before I began.

"If you are still willing to work with me, I'd like to try to package your screenplay with me as a producer. We could attach the actors and get the funding to make it, or find a studio to do it. That will take some time and, if you'd rather just sell it, I'd understand." I tried to present myself as poised and professional. A nice little change from my Linda Blair episode.

I had done my hair up in a twist and wore a casual dress. A bit fancy for Maxwell's but it felt good to doll up a little, make an effort, reach a little more for what I wanted out of life. Still, that didn't stop me from dribbling syrup down the front of myself. Dammit. I grabbed a Wet Ones wipe from my purse, where I always keep a solid stash. I learned of their stain-removing magic from Wardrobe.

Pretending not to notice my sloppiness, Vince stayed on topic. "El, I meant it when I said I only want to do it with you. Go for it. I know you can do it."

Vince was the most certain person I had ever met. Not simply positive or optimistic, just sure. Not only of himself but of situations and circumstances. It was a little unnerving. I questioned questioning myself when I was around him. If he was so sure, who was I to doubt?

I called Howie on my way from lunch and asked to meet with him on Monday.

"I'll move my breakfast and see you then," Howie said.

"You don't have to do that, Howie."

"This sounds important. Farmshop at eight. I'll see you then. Have a good weekend, El," he said and hung up.

Finally, I called my headhunter. "I'll let you know in the next couple weeks if I'm ready to look again." But I was hoping I would never have to make that call.

Over the weekend, Gabe and I went over the treatment and the footage he already assembled. I had to get to know Tallulah and Gabe was truly an expert. The woman lived one helluva life. After having her uterus removed because of an advanced case of gonorrhea, she said to her doctor, "Don't think that's taught me a lesson."

"And that's just the tip of her witty iceberg," Gabe said as we cut together a trailer of sorts for the documentary.

"This is really good stuff, Gabe. She's an incredible character."

"I know. Did you think I'd waste my time on a bore?"

This was going to sell. I could feel it in my gut. Not that my gut hasn't steered me wrong before. Wyatt was the poster boy for that. From time to time, that still stung. I'm only human and remained a little tender, especially around my heart.

By the time I met with Howie, I was Bankhead-able. I told him my plans for packaging both Gabe's and Vince's projects. He listened intently and didn't say much, which was so very unlike Howie. He's a chronic interrupter, especially when he's excited about something. In spite of his apparent lack of enthusiasm, I continued.

"I'd like to keep KEEP and make that my production banner. Can you put me in touch with the right lawyers for that? I don't have much money, but I want to continue with the company and do the kind of projects Karen and I talked about. I know Vince and Gabe's projects will hit, and I know I can develop them in the right way. But I might need to turn to you for advice every now and then. I'm hoping I can count on your support."

I waited for Howie to say something. He was focused on his eggs and chicken sausage. Finally, he nodded and looked up at me.

"You should do it. I'll help however I can. I'm proud of you, El. Karen would be, too," he said. He even offered me an office in his. Howie couldn't help but mention his guilt over what had gone on with Karen's will; that he should've had her finish it before the trip.

"I don't care about that," I consoled. "It's enough she even thought to do something like that. But I need to move on, Howie. And this is the way I want to do it."

I felt strong again. I knew this was it. Time to call in favors, use my contacts and be bold. This was my shot, and I wasn't going to blow it.

I called Madeline and booked a flight to New York. I waffled on whether or not to cash in the first class seat and fly coach, but first class was the way Karen wanted me to travel. I wasn't going to argue. Two weeks later, I was off to prove myself as a producer and sell three projects in one week.

Manhattan was hot and muggy. Everything stuck to me, but my makeup. I kept my face and body as bare as I could. While a red, full-skirted sundress may not make for proper business attire, it was better than a sweat-soaked blouse and clinging skirt. I tied a white cardigan around my shoulders to add a touch of polish, and be prepared for over-chilled offices. My hair was up, and Celia's jewelry added the finishing touches.

Laughably, the meeting with Andy was at his office instead of the living room. I was staying with him and Jilli in their incredible Upper East Side apartment. The view was staggering and the interior was comfortable and welcoming. Watching the two of them together was an animation of domestic bliss. Even with Selma contesting the pre-nup and dragging out the divorce, their relationship was steady and tight.

Jilli was radiant. She had found love, success and, dare I say, contentment. I remembered how good that felt when I had a momentary glimpse of it. She had a lightness about her that I envied. Her smile was easy and her stride confident.

"Now, don't put the screws to my man," she jested. "Go easy with your negotiations. I'd like him to have his balls when he gets home."

She stuffed her new black Birkin (a gift from Andy he gave her on her first day with Cassie) with scripts and her laptop and adjusted her skirt. She looked every bit the part of President of Production in her heels and tailored top. Her hair was long enough now to be collected into a clip at the nape of her neck. She kept her fringe, which drew your full attention to her piercing eyes. She was the epitome of Manhattan chic, and she admitted she was accused of being a native New Yorker regularly.

"I don't think you need to worry about his balls, Jilli. I left my rubber bands at home," I teased. "Are those earrings Celia's?"

"And the necklace. Love them, and her. Andy and I had fun at her dinner party last week. Sorry you missed it. Tell her I said hello." She checked her lipstick in the mirror before grabbing her keys. "Good luck, El. I know you'll do great," she said and hugged me hard before leaving. "Call me and let me know how it goes."

I took a taxi from their apartment to Midtown. I overestimated drive time and found I had extra to spare. Spotting a Starbucks on the corner, I popped in to get cool and down something that would quell my jetlag. I took a seat by the window and relaxed knowing that I wouldn't be yawning in front of Andy and his execs. I took my time sipping my iced coffee as I mentally prepared my pitch.

I stared out at the bustling street and ached a little for what I had missed. What Karen missed. Strangely, I felt her presence rooting for me. This is what she had nudged me toward and now I was taking the leap. But I nearly jumped out of my skin when I saw Wyatt standing on the corner, talking on his cell phone.

My blood ran cold at the sight of him. He was waiting for the light to change so he could cross the street. I held my breath, praying that he would not look through the window and see me. Fortunately, the conversation he had kept his focus. When the light finally signaled he could walk, I exhaled.

I could have gone my whole life without seeing him again. I rolled my eyes and looked at the ceiling. I whispered to the heavens, "Karen, next time, do me a favor and block my view."

I checked my phone for the time and noticed a new email. The volume of New York seemed to drown out the chimes I would normally hear in L.A. Vince sent a message wishing me luck. I took a deep breath and I walked to the building, still early, but not embarrassingly so, and rode the elevator up to the fifty-fifth floor.

I met with Andy and two of his veeps: Sherry, who ran the documentary division Andy brought in when he acquired Veritas Features; and William, the head of development at Picture Motion. I had made it clear to Andy and Jilli that I didn't want a handout or a courtesy option. "It's bad enough I'm imposing on our friendship by requesting the meeting."

"It's only an imposition if the projects suck, El," Andy replied.

I did like him. He was perfect for Jilli, no matter how they met. Or even because of that. In his mid-forties, he was boyishly handsome, and still had a decent hairline.

After the introductions, I showed them what Gabe had cut. I was impressed that they actually read Vince's script rather than the coverage for it and absorbed the treatments I sent.

"We are concerned about the feature and documentary cannibalizing each other," Andy said about Gabe's projects.

"I know it breaks convention, but there have been several circumstances where two films on the same subject come out close together and are still able to stand on their own. In this case," I explained, "we'll corner our own market. The documentary would play the festivals and premiere on cable. I would almost be so bold as to have it come out right after the release of the feature to get the cable-viewing couch potatoes into the theatres. If not that, then it's a great double DVD to offer with the feature to incentivize sales."

They gave a *We'll think about that* nod and went on to talk about Vince's script.

"We like it," William said. "It will come down to casting. We don't really do family films."

"I think it's more coming-of-age film than family. *Little Miss Sunshine* was far from family. This isn't a comedy, but it is more adult-oriented if we keep it true to the script. The story is really how that summer affected him as a man than what occurred as a boy."

Again, they nodded.

"I also want to be clear that I want to be an active producer. Co-producer is fine, but nothing like 'associate', either in title or positioning," I asserted.

"We understand," Andy said holding back a smile.

"And Gabe Parks will be attached as a consulting producer on the feature. He's ready to write the script, too, but that isn't a deal breaker," I continued.

"Does this Vince Channing want to be a producer, as well?" William asked with a smidgeon of disdain.

"No," I said plainly, keeping eye contact with William until he looked away. "I realize that I am coming in here with no films under my belt, but this isn't folly for me. This is what I was going to be doing with Karen Ellis. These projects were set to be bought by our company before her death. I'm picking up where we left off. I'm bringing them here because of the level of integrity you have. That's what I want for these projects. But, while I'm starting here, this won't be my last stop," I said, mainly for William's benefit.

"El, we are interested in the projects, and we appreciate you bringing them to us first. We'll call you tomorrow to give you an answer. Time is money for all of us," Andy clarified.

I stood and did the thank-you-for-your-time handshake shuffle and met Celia for a drink in TriBeCa. We went to Landmarc and ordered champagne to go with our array of midday desserts.

"I felt like a fool," I told her. "Like a little girl playing dress up. That William was a dick and a half."

"Welcome to doing business in New York," she deadpanned.

"It's equally a Hollywood thing. I'm sure they knew I was there because I'm Andy's girlfriend's best friend. But, the projects are strong. They should feel fortunate that I brought them there," I said with a bit of faux-bravado.

Blondie sang out from my purse. I really have to change that.

"Shit, sorry," I apologized to Celia.

"Go ahead and take it," she said. "I have to pee anyway."

Celia headed to the loo and I grabbed the Unknown Caller call.

"Is it true you're shopping scripts?" Anise questioned rather accusingly.

"It is. How did you know?" I was completely perplexed by her knowledge and the rapid rate she got it.

"Our New York office heard about it. Picture Motion is preparing an offer for all three projects. Why didn't you come to us, El? Bev is really hurt, and it makes me look like an inept ass. I'm waiting for that promotion, remember? I thought we were friends. Bev wants to see the projects. You know how competitive she is. How quickly can you get them to me?" Anise was practically panting when she finished.

"Let me see what I can do."

This was going to be a fucking pickle. I wanted Andy to have first dibs, but I knew better than to put all of my eggs into anyone's basket. With only my iPhone on me, I retrieved the email Gabe sent me of the treatment and trailer for the Bankhead projects, cleaned it up like new and forwarded it to Anise. I did the same with Vince's script, then emailed them both separately to let them know their projects were also going out to Bev's company.

Celia had returned to the table midway through this exercise and watched me with her mouth hanging open.

"Fuck me. I'm with a mogul," she grinned. "You are equal parts scary and amazing right now."

My phone rang. Gabe. I shrugged to Celia and answered the phone. She shoved a forkful of cake in her mouth, riveted at the activity.

"What does this mean, El?" Gabe asked. "Did the meeting go that badly with Andy?"

"No. It means the meeting went well. Really, really well." I could smell a bidding war.

Vince texted back: This is awesome, El. Way to go!

"You are good," Celia uttered.

"Thanks," I said with a broad smile.

I called Jilli next. "Look, I've got kind of a situation."

"I heard," she said flatly.

"I didn't do it," I said in my defense.

"I know. Andy does, too. Did you know he and Bev hate each other?"

"No. Shit. How much?" I asked, suddenly feeling surrounded by eggshell covered landmines.

"A lot. A whole fucking lot. She lost a major project to him. This isn't going to be fun for Andy. But it's going to be great for you," she laughed. "Congratulations and good luck!"

My next call was to Howie. "What the hell do I do?"

"Ride it. Go with whom you trust," he advised. "And get on the phone with your lawyer."

"I don't have one for this. My guy was an employment attorney," I said feeling my knickers starting to twist.

"I'll put a call into Frank Elliot. I don't think he reps either Bev or Andy. He'll keep them both in line."

I took deep breaths. Calm. Stay calm. Celia ordered us another round. Once my glass was full and drained, I steadied myself to call Tess.

"Do you want me to leak it?" she asked.

"I don't know. Should I?"

"If Andy wasn't involved I would say yes. But, let's keep this clean," she advised. "Besides, if Bev's office knows, everyone else soon will, so there's no need for us to spin it."

"Thanks, Tess."

"As soon as it sells, I'll work on the release. I'm really happy for you, El," Tess said before hanging up.

"Shit," I muttered.

"What?" Celia asked.

"It's going to be really awkward at dinner tonight."

Celia laughed.

The back and forth lasted three days. Each side upped the ante and more production companies made inquiries. I had a conference call with Gabe and Vince, which wasn't exactly kosher, but it did help expedite everything. It helps to be friends with those you're in business with…sometimes.

While Bev was offering more money, she didn't want the documentary and saw Vince's script as a kid flick. It's not what I wanted, but I felt it only fair for Gabe and Vince to have a say in their fates.

"I think we should go with Picture Motion, but it comes down to what is right for each of you," I proffered. "If you would rather go with Bev, either of you, I could split the projects and go where you want."

Simultaneously they said, "Picture Motion."

Frank Elliot took me on as a client and had the contracts the next day, and then I was on a plane back to L.A. In less than a week, I sold three projects and made us all a tidy sum. I was a producer, officially. I walked in with my luggage and stood in my small, very beige, studio apartment, and laughed. I did it. I had made it. And I did it all on my own. Well, almost.

I walked over to my sofa and sat down to let the happy tears roll. "Thank you, Karen," I whispered.

Knock knock knock.

I jumped and wondered, if only for a second, if it was Karen reaching out from the hereafter. Then, another *knock knock knock* was at my door again.

"Who is it?" I said, my words a little shaky.

"Delivery," said the voice.

I opened the door to find a huge bouquet of flowers in front of a rather small man. I brought them in. The fragrance was lovely. It was a sculptural design of roses and lilacs, my two favorite flowers. It took up nearly all of my bistro table. I opened the card and saw it was from Vince.

Congratulations and thank you, El. My grandfather would get a kick out of this.
x~ Vince

The card was handwritten, apparently by him. I picked up the phone to thank him.

"They are incredibly beautiful. You really didn't have to, but it's lovely that you did, Vince."

"You deserve it," he stated simply.

I paused for a second and asked, "Would you like to go to a movie this weekend? Check out some of the competition?"

"Sure. Pick you up for dinner first? Say about seven on Saturday?" he replied.

It wasn't a date. I just needed some company, and my posse were all preoccupied.

Tess was busy with the wedding, moving in with Dane and getting practice parenting by being an active stepmother. "I'd go on Prozac if the doctors would let me," she moaned. "But love him, love all of him, including his kids." She complained so much about their eating habits and addiction to video games she sparked Emily into developing a Pilates program for kids.

"What do you think of Chillates? You know, short for Child Pilates, but with a cool twist with 'chill'? Or Kidlates? But that reads 'kid lates'," Emily inquired.

"She is driving me nuts," Claudia told me over the phone. "She needs to chill herself. Between commuting back and forth to here from the Springs for clients, developing new workouts and lording over the other trainers, she's doing us all in. And this is Emily we are talking about. You know, the Zen Goddess. She's making Donna look like a walk in the park."

"She just needs to get laid," Remi said about Claudia when I stopped by her office for lunch. "I keep trying to set her up with a friend of James' for a double date and she keeps flaking out. Maybe you would like him. He's an agent."

"No thanks. I'm done with industry boys. I want someone normal. One day. I'm still not ready," I admitted.

"Not too many 'normal' guys are going to dig you being away on film sets with hot actors and intense directors to distract you," she corrected.

"Then it should make you wonder why industry boys are okay with it," I returned.

Remi was absolutely besotted with James. She said she felt ready to settle down now, too. "Freaky, huh?" she smiled. "It's like we all came down with commitment at the same time."

Even Gabe was involved. After I left the Trio party, he met a doctor. "Well, a chiropractor, anyway," he clarified.

"That boy I saw when I pulled my head out of the bucket?"

"No. Please, El. This guy looks like you took Russell Crowe and Eric Bana and tossed them together with a little fat-free dressing…and don't think I wouldn't…then add completely ripped muscles, you have Doctor Dave. He adjusted me that night and it was wonderful," Gabe swooned.

"If you're in love with a chiropractor, does that make you a crack whore?" I teased.

"You bet it does."

I could make light of the situations, but my friends were filling up their own lives and leaving little room for me. I couldn't begrudge them. There was a time when I was too engrossed with my relationship to fit them in. Karma can be bitchy. Soon enough, work would be taking over and I wouldn't feel so lonely.

Development meetings were happening for *Grandfather's Lake*, which I attended over Skype at seven-thirty each Monday morning. Screenwriters were being considered for the *Untitled Tallulah Bankhead Project*, which I hoped to title *A Lady Tarnished*. In the meantime, I had a stack of screenplays to read, and more were emailed each day. I had to take Howie up on his offer to set up shop in his office. My tiny place couldn't handle big business. I had outgrown it already. But I wasn't planning on getting a bigger place. I wanted a second "home" in New York.

"You really want to move there?" Vince asked over our dinner. We didn't go to Trio; he said it felt too much like work. I was happy to avoid it. If I saw or smelled a Limoncello martini, I was afraid I'd hurl. We went to Chaya Venice instead for scene and sushi before catching the latest Amy Schumer flick. Not really market research, just a guaranteed laugh.

"Not move, but stay from time to time. L.A. is my home, but I really like the energy and pace of New York. Have you been?"

"Not since college. It was interesting," he said.

"When you go again, I think you'll like it more."

"When, not if?" he inquired with a grin.

"When you meet with the other producers and take their notes. Bring your thick skin, my friend. The VP is quite a character," I warned.

"You'll be there to protect me, though, right?" he laughed.

"Yes, I will."

Forgetting that it was Saturday night, the lines to the theatre were rounding the block of the Promenade. We looked at each other and telepathically agreed to skip the flick.

"There's a great pub a few blocks over. Want to go for a Guinness?" I asked.

"You drink Guinness?" he asked

"Yeah. Why?"

He gave a light chuckle. "After the other night, I thought you were strictly a sweet martini girl."

"After the other night, I may never have a sweet martini again."

After a civilized two-pint chat we took a stroll down the Santa Monica Pier. When we paused to watch the waves, he kissed me.

"Vince, I don't think this would be a good idea," I said, not able to look him in the eye when our lips parted.

"Why?" He was a man of few words, getting right to the point.

"The last time I got involved with someone I worked with, it started out fine but ended in disaster. I wouldn't want that to happen to us, or the film. We're going to be working together for a long time."

"Okay," he said.

"So, you understand?" I asked hopefully.

"No. It seems I'm paying the price for what some idiot did before," he said, and the right corner of his lips crept up in a half-grin. "Do you think that's fair?"

I had to think about it for a moment. "I suppose not. But I've been through a lot, a metric shit-ton in the last six months. I don't know if I'm in the right place for this right now."

"El, don't get me wrong here, but I think all we had was a date and a kiss. It's not like I proposed marriage or asked to move in."

I started laughing. "Touché."

"So, why don't we take it a step at a time. Sound okay to you?"

I nodded.

"Good," he said and kissed me again. On my forehead.

Chapter Nineteen

A step at a time. That's good advice. Not always as easy as it sounds, though. One misstep is all it takes to fuck shit up royally.

Now I understood why someone gives the bride away. She needs assistance. Someone to keep her steady. Tess decided to walk it alone. The five of us stood at the altar waiting for her, wearing the expression of concern and encouragement; the same look parents have when they watch a toddler make her way toward them all by herself. Her bouquet was shaking as she made her way to the minister and Dane's extended hand. She had a frozen grin that caused us to wonder if it was nerves or the morning sickness had returned.

Vince and I had done a good job of taking it a step at a time. We had been seeing each other for three weeks and still hadn't seen each other naked. Instead, we got to know each other from the neck up (instead of waist down) and between the ears (not the legs). Our pace was calm and steady and I felt in no rush.

Bit by bit, he revealed himself to me. One afternoon, he drove me around town and showed me the work he had done. He gave me one major clue to who he was when he stated, "My work doesn't stand out," which wasn't an invitation for assurances. "I don't want it to. Each structure should compliment its surroundings, not offend it." Still, his work stood out to me as elegant.

Vince was busy working with clients on various projects, some as small as a room addition. His big project—"The Killer," as he called it—was an apartment building renovation owned by bickering partners that kept going through change after change.

"It'll never get done," he said without a hint of bother.

His home was the top apartment of a Spanish style triplex below La Cienega in an area with stunning architecture from the 1920s, but no quaint neighborhood name. It was too far from the ocean for me, but the building was glorious. He had the entire top floor with two units beneath it that he rented out. "They pay the mortgage and taxes," he said with a grin. He decorated it with dark wood and soft leather, respecting the era that it was constructed. "Next, I'm building myself a home from the ground up."

"Where?" I asked.

"Not sure yet."

That was the first time I heard anything short of certainty from him. I liked it. He was only thirty-four and I couldn't get over how grown up he was. Men remain boys here a little too long. Too many toys to provide distraction. Vince knew himself, what he wanted and how he planned to get it. That was incredibly sexy. Minus the sex part.

"You have got to sleep with him tonight," Jilli said under her breath as we posed for photos. She said it like she was the one aching for it. "He's so hot. I can't believe you haven't done anything yet. What's wrong with you?"

Vince was waiting patiently for this bridesmaid's duty to end so we could eat and dance. He watched us as we posed. Him smiling at me made me smile broader, which caused the photographer to yell out, "You, there. Bring it down a notch. You look happier than the bride."

"Thanks, El," Tess laughed.

For a small wedding, we made a huge wedding party. Each of us served as a maid of honor. I got to use the dress I bought for Gwen's wedding. The rest wore a similar style in a complimentary color; the bride kindly spared us from looking like clones. We made an attractive portrait. Tess hid her bump behind the ornate bouquet, which had finally stopped moving.

Claudia waved to her date, Sonya, in between shots. She was Claudia's certification instructor. They started dating two weeks ago.

"It's true. The heart wants what the heart wants," Claudia said with a smile and shrug.

What was also true was that none of us were in any rush to catch the bouquet. Vicki literally pulled us onto the floor. I think she missed playing this game of catch. Jilli, Remi, Claude and I looked at each other, devising a plan as to how to avoid the flowers as Tess looked in our direction, calculating the velocity it would take to reach one of us. Fortunately, a girl from Tess' office leaped up to nab it.

My purse was vibrating when I returned to our table. It was Gabe ringing from New York. His was the only call I would take.

"Talk about a pompous ass," Gabe harped into the phone. I could hear him pacing the carpet bare in his room at the Algonquin. He was there to meet with the writer/director signed to do the Tallulah feature. It wasn't going smoothly. "El, he is driving me nuts. I don't know how to deal with this guy. Help me."

"Sounds like you have a crush on him," I joked.

"Do you hear my middle finger? It has something to say to you."

Gabe was beyond grumpy. He wasn't used to collaborating with someone who challenged his authority. I'm sure it wasn't easy for him to take after working on his documentary for the last two years.

"I'll see if I can fly out this weekend. Be nice, though. I'm sure it's only overenthusiasm."

"And a need to get fucked," Gabe growled.

"Well, you could always rise to that occasion," I said with a sarcastic lilt.

Gabe hung up.

Yep. I was a producer.

I flew out to New York to help Gabe deal with his dilemma. While we were there, he and I found a small apartment to split the rent on. A tiny one bedroom in the Flatiron. We set up the living room to serve as a second bedroom for when we were in town at the same time, spending too much money on a high-end sofa bed to do so.

"I have my standards," he quipped. "I know it's me who'll be sleeping out here."

I met the director Gabe was at odds with at the Picture Motion office along with the execs. After a three-hour meeting, we fired him. He was more of an auteur than a collaborator, who wanted to make a dark biopic. Tallulah Bankhead was a tragic figure on some levels, but was too much of a pistol to lose the humor she brought to her life. We called up the next director on the list, Natalie Wilson, who happened to be my first choice. Luckily, she was available. Gabe met with her the following week.

"I love her. She totally gets TB," he said of Natalie. They wrote the script together in less than six weeks. It was approved on the first pass, the budget was agreed on, and we actually had A-List actresses doing battle to play our Tallulah.

"I smell Oscars," Jilli sang while we were curled up on her couch with glasses of wine.

"I know!" I shrieked. But, now that I learned to take things a step at a time, I didn't want to get ahead of myself. I simply enjoyed the process and the journey. No more ass over teakettle for me. That leads to nothing but mess.

"While you were in the shower, some lawyer called for you," Vince said. We had stayed the night at my place for a change after I got back to L.A.

"On my home phone or iPhone?"

"Home," he said.

Vince had permission to answer that line. Come on, he was my boyfriend. Believe me, I answered his. I had permission for that, too.

"Was it Frank?" I checked my iPhone to see if anything important was in.

"No. Some guy named Angelo."

"That can't be good," I mumbled.

And it wasn't. Fucking Billy Harding wanted me to be a character witness for him at his trial.

The *Vanguard* article had hit the newsstands earlier that week. It was difficult to see those pictures we shot on her last day in L.A. Karen looked so content. I had received a package from the photographer of the photos she and I took, but never opened the box. I couldn't bring myself to look at them, but couldn't miss them when I read the article. A photo of the two of us was included in the spread, which was turned into more of a memorial. In the article, Karen talked about how it was the best time of her life. I echoed that with how excited she was to take this next step. Billy and his lawyer were trying to turn that into how happy she was with Billy and they were ready to take the next step, meaning marriage.

"Let me put it to you this way," I told Angelo Noya, Billy's U.S. attorney. "You can call me to the stand, but all I will say is that I never liked Billy, never thought he was good for Karen and that I completely blame him for her death. It's your call. I won't mind a free trip to France, so let me know."

I wasn't called. Billy pled to involuntary manslaughter and was to serve twelve years. During the time given to settle his affairs, he O.D.'d, whether by accident or intent was not clear. That left justice un-served as far as I was concerned. All he did by dying was bring more scandal to Karen's death, and more media coverage of it. Just when I was finding my footing, I was hit with grief again.

"That mutherfucker," I cried to Jilli on FaceTime. "I was just starting to feel good about things, and now the scab has been ripped right off. It's fucking horrid."

"Do you want me to come out, El? I'll book a flight right now," she said and I could see her reaching for her iPhone as we talked through our laptops.

"No. You're busy. I'm busy. I just don't like her name and memory dragged through his mud."

"I know," she consoled. "Is Vince helping you deal?"

"This isn't his to deal with," I cried.

"If you love him, it is."

That she didn't say, 'If he loves you,' hit me. She was right. If I loved him, I would have to let him in. And I did love him. So, instead of holing myself up in my apartment and ignoring the world, I let Vince know my anger, my utter rage and my pain.

"I'm almost embarrassed by mourning over Karen this long," I admitted

"Why?" he asked in his standard direct manner.

"Because, she isn't blood, she wasn't family," I said through heaving sobs.

"Don't feel bad about that," Vince stated bluntly. "Friends can hurt as much as family. Sometimes more."

Vince told me that he lost a good friend in college. A freak accident. His friend was drunk, dove into a pool and drown. It was the first loss Vince had in his life.

"It shook me hard," he admitted. "I was nineteen. You can't believe you're mortal at nineteen. He wasn't family, but I didn't get over his death until after I dealt with my brother's."

I let the tears fall freely for the first time in months. I curled up into a vulnerable ball and put my head on his lap. He stroked my hair.

"This," I told him, "is why I love you." I knew I could lie there and cry, that Vince would take care of everything else, and keep the world at bay.

It took me another month to work through all the emotions I had accumulated, both good and bad. Success isn't the ultimate salve, let me tell you. It's an amplifier. And thank God for that. It's better to deal with it all and move on then to have that ache lugging behind you ages after. Karen wouldn't want me weeping over her. She would actually be pissed that I wasn't focused on the plan at hand. Every once in a while I would hear, "Kiddo, get on with it," ringing in my ear. It was a comfort.

I wanted *Grandfather's Lake* to shoot in the early summer, which meant castings for the boy had to happen first of the year. Remi was hired for that task. Nepotism, in all forms, is the grease that keeps Hollywood running. I was happy to apply it here. I could trust her to bring the best. She delivered Vince's juvenile doppelganger, and we would start shooting in Georgia that May.

Everything was going quite well, and I wasn't waiting for another shoe to drop. I accepted that I was in control of my life. No matter what would come at me, I wouldn't treat it as a punishment for bad karma, but as a simple part of life. I came to realize that, if it were always sunny, we'd all burn to death. Now, no matter what was going on, I took it in stride and, as corny as it sounds, I saw each day as a rebirth.

"I want it natural."

"Why?" I asked Tess. We were in her room at Cedars and she was catching her breath between contractions. I was the first to arrive, doing my best to calm her and mimicking breathing scenes from movies. "If it were a natural act, God would have made your vagina much bigger. Get the drugs and don't feel bad about it."

"Really?" Tess asked through her hoo-hoo-hee-hee-hoo-hoo breaths.

"If you were really serious about 'natural birth', you'd be at home with a midwife in the bathtub."

"You're right," she panted. "Get 'em in here."

Garret Riley Thompson was born at eight twenty-three at Cedar-Sinai on New Year's Day.

"Shit. The whole world will be hungover on his birthday," the proud mother cried.

"Especially his aunties," I concurred.

The posse had had its first baby and, ironically, it was a boy.

"Damn," Jilli said as she viewed him through the protective glass, "I'd be arrested for any insight I could give him."

"Yes," I consoled, "you would."

"With six women doting on him, it will be a miracle if this kid grows up straight," Gabe mocked.

At the christening, Vince asked, "Do you want kids?"

"I don't know," I answered. "Do you?"

"Sometimes."

Dating a man of few words can leave your mind reeling. I learned not to fixate and just enjoyed the mystery. There was no uncertainty in Vince's kiss, however. I was sure in his lips, his hands, his caress. You know you are a compatible couple when neither winces at the other's morning breath.

We did indeed consummate our relationship the night of Tess' wedding. Everything about Vince was different than any man I had ever known. And I do mean everything. I didn't notice until the morning after the wedding just how different until we were in the shower.

"You don't look the same," I stated cautiously.

"What do you mean? I look happier?" he asked and kissed me as he lathered his hair.

Actually, I was referring to his penis. It didn't look like any I had ever seen before. Not that I had seen so many, but the handful I had did not look like that. Not only was Vince a Magnum man, he came fully intact.

"He's not circumcised," I whispered to Jilli on the phone.

"So?"

"So, I'd never seen one like that before."

"Really?" Jilli asked with surprise. "Is it bad? Does he have a lot?"

"I don't think so."

"What does it look like?" Jilli inquired.

"I'm not going to describe my boyfriend's penis to you."

"Well you brought it up. Literally," Jilli laughed. "I wasn't talking about his pee pee, just the additional skin. What does that look like?"

"Like sort of a turtle neck, I guess." I felt stupid having this highly personal conversation with Jilli, but I couldn't bring myself to discuss it with Vince until I had more information.

"Then consider yourself lucky. That's not bad, and they make much better lovers. More sensitivity," she explained.

That's for sure.

"My dad's off the boat English. He came over from Islington when he was eighteen. He didn't see the point of it," Vince was kind enough to explain when it became apparent I was fascinated with his stuff. "Does it bother you?"

"Not at all. It's just new to me." And he laughed.

"Just to be clear, you are the only woman to ever ask me for paperwork," he joked as we snuggled in bed.

"I believe in safe sex," I stated. "No one knows for sure until they are tested. I'll go with you if you are embarrassed."

"I'm not embarrassed," he said plainly. "But, I wouldn't mind the company."

From my days at film school, when we were encouraged to get tested for HIV and other STDs on a regular basis, whether you were getting any or not, I believed in a full check-up before going condom-free. The near miss with Tim/Angie reminded me that while I might be faithful, my partner might not be. Vince, however, had never been tested.

"Do you think I was super slutty or something?" he jested.

"No. Do you think I was?" I asked.

"Not if you've never seen foreskin before," he said through a laugh.

"It's not about being *slutty* or *dirty*, just being certain. And certainty is something I know you enjoy." I leaned in to kiss him. We were taking the big leap into monogamy. The swab up the urethra was an eye opener for him. Having gone through regular pap smears, I had little sympathy.

"I must love you," he said flatly after his appointment.

Oh, romance with the exchange of lab work. We each received a clean bill of health, and a large bill from the labs.

Manhattan was my second home now. I rarely suffered from jetlag anymore and dove right into my East Coast life, spending time with Jilli and Andy, and Celia and her man. Vince fit right into that. He and Andy quickly bonded over boating.

"Does he know you get seasick?" Jilli asked.

"He knows, but as least I know he's the kind of guy who will hold my hair back."

Vince also held my hand while we attended premieres and went to art galleries and my friends' gatherings. He didn't mind letting me beat him at Scrabble, although he did kick my ass at Backgammon, much to my competitive chagrin. He couldn't always leave work to travel with me, but there were no guilt trips over my trips, or complaints when I had to leave again. He got it. He got me. And I got him.

Another script had fallen into my lap. This one came from Anise of all people.

"Bev turned it down, but I think it has something," she said over lunch. She slid the script across the table like it was a packet of top secrets. She didn't want to email it, figuring that would leave more of a paper trail than an actual copy. She had gotten her promotion, but Bev had yet to take seriously anything she brought in. "I thought you could do something with it. It's flying under the radar now. Move fast."

"Thanks, Anise."

It was a romantic comedy/farce with two strong female leads. It could go either studio or independent, but I was ready to take on a studio. I met with the writer, attached myself, called Frank and sent it out for weekend read.

"You are part barracuda," Claudia complimented. Her romance with Sonya soured after she finally passed her certification. She was now dating Erik, the agent Remi wanted her to meet months before. "I just have to take the rougher path," she explained when she cleared up the myth that women weren't easier to date than men.

She was again enjoying her partnership with Emily, who had finally relaxed and trusted Claude and the rest of her staff. While Em's relationship with Ron didn't survive her move to Palm Springs, let alone the focus of her career, Em did meet a nice guy—a partner in one of the thriving boutique hotels in the desert—and was enjoying dating him.

"It's nothing serious. Just some fun. I'm too busy for any bullshit these days," Em said, sounding less like the Zen Goddess and more like an entrepreneur.

"You know," Claudia started, "I was thinking the other day that if you stayed with Tim, none of this would have ever happened."

"How do you mean?" We were sitting at a high-top table at, ironically, The Detour, on our third Irish Mule when she made that statement.

"You kind of unravelled the ball. Made us all realize that playing it safe wasn't the better move."

"You really think that?" I asked more than perplexed by her take.

"Kind of. Maybe it all would have happened like this anyway, but you rattled the cages. You got promoted and ended it with Tim and we all changed our lives. That kind of rocks, don't you think?"

I was flattered, but asked for some bread for my friend anyway. Maybe it was like Jilli said and I was the first domino to fall, but we were all lined up for bigger and better things anyway. I was just glad that no one was left standing alone. We had all gone through this together. And for that to happen in L.A., where competition is vicious and friendships are fleeting, it was almost miraculous.

A year from the day in Karen's kitchen when my life went ass over teakettle, I was lying in a business class seat-bed, flying to London for the filming of *A Lady Tarnished*. Vince was beside me, breathing in his sleep rhythmically, just this side of a snore.

Gabe was in the seat behind me, annoyingly leaning over to see if I was asleep. He had forgotten his Ambien and was in desperate need of comforting.

"What if the film isn't good? What if this bombs?" he asked.

"It won't. And I don't think you can say the B-word on the plane. Have another drink. I'll wake you when we hit Heathrow."

As someone who always wanted everything fast, I highly recommend the slow lane. It took a while for me to get where I wanted to go but, when I got there, I was ready for it. I had two films in development, one in production, and one in post. I had negotiated a three-picture deal with Picture Motion from the script Anise brought me, with budgets up to twenty million. It was groundbreaking for Andy's company, and put us in the headlines.

Not only was I doing what I loved, I was with a man I loved. And what I loved most was that I didn't have to build my life around Vince. I didn't have to give up things to be with him. He even understood when I turned down his offer to live together. We simply took things a step at a time, and that worked for us. There wasn't any pressure. I'd had enough of that. There were no expectations. I was finished with those, too. It was just living day-by-day, and what came out of that was most surprising: Happiness.

The flight to London and the snoring man next to me illustrated how much my life had changed. The drama queen behind me showed how much had stayed constant. We made our way to the hotel from the airport and settled in. Shooting would begin in two days. Vince and I made an effort to see as much of the city as we could the day after we arrived. Gabe found a crewmember who lent him an Ambien and was catching up on his sleep.

"Kind of damp," Vince mentioned as we walked in the rain.

"It's London in February, what would you expect?" I asked smiling.

"I don't know. Global warming to have some sort of effect

maybe."

"Not funny. Leo's playing a role in the film, so don't make that kind of comment on set," I gently admonished.

We came upon Big Ben and he announced it was two o'clock. We stood there and took in the view.

"This is really lovely, isn't it?" I asked. He simply smiled.

"I'd like it if you'd marry me, El," Vince said out of the blue. He didn't drop to one knee, nor did he have a ring, pear-shaped or otherwise. There was no big monologue on how much he loved me or that he couldn't picture life without me. There was only his certainty.

"You would?" I asked fighting my smile.

"Yes. Very much. What do you think?"

"I think yes," I said.

He pulled me into a kiss, one so potent I floated.

"Excuse me," he said to a passerby. "Will you take a picture of me and my fiancée here?"

The older gentleman obliged. And, in front of Big Ben, we had our moment captured.

We sent out that photo with our engagement announcement. It was titled *About Time*.

By then, I had learned that it really was about timing. If I just let things take their course, everything would fall into place. It only took me shy of thirty-three years to figure that out. Next stop, rocket science.

The next stop was actually Rockefeller Center. I met Celia there for her first appearance on *The Today Show*. It was a segment on successful women and how they've made their businesses thrive. I watched from the green room.

"Aren't you Ellen Patterson?" a young P.A. asked me. She was in her early-twenties and had that hungry look of curiosity I remembered having.

"I am," I replied.

"I'm Gina. I was going to be a page on Karen's talk show. I wanted to say I'm sorry. I was really looking forward to working with her, and you."

"Thanks, Gina. That's really kind of you to say."

"Did you know they're cancelling the show? I got laid off a

few weeks ago and landed here. Much better. The woman they hired to replace Karen was a real bitch, if you don't mind me saying."

"I don't mind at all. Good luck. I'm sure you have a bright future."

"Thanks. I want to get out of television, though. Film is really my thing," she said. I gave her my card and told her to email me her resume. I passed it on to Jilli who was looking to hire her first assistant.

"When you are ready for a ring, let me know," Celia said as we wandered around New York. "You know I will be both hurt and offended if I'm not asked."

"You're not the one responsible for what Tim showed me, are you?" I teased.

"Christ, no!" she said with a laugh and gave me a playful shove.

"Vince said he already has ideas for the rings. Will you work with him on that?"

"Do you want me to report back to you?" Celia asked.

"No. I trust him. I think you'll be surprised."

"Believe me," she said, "I'm surprised already."

That's the way life is supposed to come at you. As a surprise. It's a gift. And when you unwrap it slowly and patiently, rather than tearing through it like sugar-high child, you get to savor it. Surprises once annoyed me. I took them as a disruption instead of seeing them as opportunity. Now, I wanted to be surprised everyday. I didn't want to lose myself to routine, to what was predictable. I didn't want to plot out my life on a calendar map anymore, or look for signposts to prove I was on the right road. I wanted to let things happen and be curious again at what the world had to offer. And what I might offer the world.

I snuggled into bed with Vince when we finally made it back to L.A. It felt good to be home, especially because it was his we were sleeping in. I had given notice on the beige box.

"I think it's time you met my family," he said as we were falling asleep.

"I think so, too," I said and nuzzled his chest.

"And I think it's time I met yours."

Damn. So much for the fairytale ending.

Acknowledgements

A huge thanks goes to Joe Marich, the first to read this book (twice)…and he actually liked it (twice). Love you infinity.

To my wonderful friend, MJM, who was the first true supporter of my writing: You have been an endless source of inspiration. Cheers, my dear.

Thank you, Lynne D., for helping me remember that I already had a finished novel. You are wonderful.

To Sue Black, for always being there to take what I hope for and make it better than I could imagine: I am endlessly grateful for your generosity and artistry. CAKE!

And to my Captain, who's been the best surprise ever: MTMTLYVVM. You do make me swoon.

Dear Reader

I probably shouldn't tell you that I finished this book back in 2007. But, that's the truth. This was my first book —*A Sassy Little Guide to Getting Over Him* was written in the middle of creating this tome. But, by the time I was done with both books, I had lost interest in publishing and went back to screenwriting.

Over time, more stories that were longer form than those for the screen were coming to me and, slowly, I've moved back to writing novels. It turns out that I can never just write one story at a time. While in the middle of writing what will now be my next book, a conversation with a friend caused me to recall *Chain-Smoking Vegetarians and Other Annoyances in L.A.* Yes, I had actually forgotten I had a completed novel. So, I took another look at it and realized that I liked these people, and thought that you should get a chance to meet them. I hope you find them as wonderfully quirky as I do. I also hope that if you've set something aside, you'll pick it up again. You never know where it might take you. It's too easy to set aside a goal or step away from a dream. Especially if you're a writer.

If you are a writer, there's a wonderful thing about being an independent publisher. Whether it is a book or a blog, there's a beauty in controlling what you're creating, without having to get permission to do it. Without waiting for someone else to say *yes*. I say, create your own *yes*, and then keep creating.

Finally, dear reader—the wonderful one who took a chance on this book: Thank you! I truly appreciate your bravery in putting faith into an unfamiliar writer. You've earned some serious karmic brownie points in doing so. So, I hope you get a raise and find money in the street. Buy a lottery ticket, too. I'm rooting for you to win.

xoxoxo ~ SAM

About the Author

Sandra Ann Miller is a writer of wrongs. Her first book was *A Sassy Little Guide to Getting Over Him—10 Steps to Heal Your Heart After an Unhappy Ending* (2006). *The Young Adult edition* was released in 2017. *Chain-Smoking Vegetarians and Other Annoyances in L.A.* (2016) was her first novel. The follow-up, *Temporary*, was released in 2018. All books were released on her independent imprint, SAME Ink. Sandra is a graduate of CalArts with a BFA in Live Action Film. She is also a sometime screenwriter and intermittent blogger who lives in Venice, California.

9 780999 762530